Series Info

Hell for Hire
Hell of a Witch
Hell to Pay
Hell Hath No Fury
Tear Down Heaven

Publishing and Copyright Info

Hell Hath No Fury

Aaron Bach LLC
"Writing to Entertain and Inform."
Copyright © 2025 Rachel Aaron

ISBN Paperback: 978-1-952367-49-6

Cover Illustration by *Luisa Preissler*
Cover Design by *Rachel Aaron*
Editing provided by *Red Adept Editing*

Tear Down Heaven : Book 4

Rachel Aaron

Chapter 1

In THE MIDDLE OF nowhere in western Massachusetts, on a sunny autumn day so clear and bright that the turning leaves looked like red and yellow jewels, Bex was standing in a dusty field, picking out a pumpkin.

"I think this one's the best," she said, pointing at a gorgeously orange gourd. "It's got a nice shape and great color."

"It's too small," insisted the human male who'd driven all the way out from Boston for this. Something Bex knew for a fact because he'd told her fifteen times. "I want a *real* pumpkin, not one of those little table ornaments."

The pumpkin at Bex's feet was twenty pounds if it weighed an ounce, but she just shrugged and walked a few rows over to the biggest pumpkin in the field: an asymmetrical monster of a squash with blotchy skin and a wonky stem that stuck out sideways.

"How about this one?"

The human screwed up his face and turned to yell at his wife, who'd been talking to the witch running the jam table for the last thirty minutes. They had a short discussion loud enough for the whole pumpkin patch to overhear, and then he nodded.

"We'll take it. Hand it over."

Bex dutifully leaned down to pick up the pumpkin—which was the size of a malformed beach ball. She was working on getting her arms around all its various lumps when the human suddenly squawked.

"What's the matter with you?" he cried, rushing to Bex's side. "You can't be picking up a pumpkin like that with only one hand!"

"I can manage."

The man was still trying to grab the pumpkin from her when Bex slid her one remaining hand under the enormous gourd's flat end and hoisted it easily into the air. It was more strength than she was wise to show in public, but the risk was worth it for the dumbfounded look in the human's scaled eyes. If she'd been her old self, that stunt would've gotten her kicked into Limbo for sure, but it was a lot easier to get away with stuff like this now that she had no horns and her eyes didn't glow. A very, *very* small consolation, but Bex had learned to take her wins where she found them these days.

"Pumpkins are priced by the pound," she informed the slack-jawed human as she carried his pumpkin toward the rack of old-fashioned metal scales at the edge of the field. "Once you get your ticket, you pay over there."

She pointed across the dirt road at the beautifully carved wooden table shaded from the sun by a hand-quilted black-and-orange banner with words skillfully embroidered across it in looping cursive.

Blackwood Family Farms, it read, *Est. 1754, Hemlock Bend, Massachusetts.*

"Are you one of the Blackwoods?" the customer asked as Bex set his giant pumpkin on the cast-iron farm scale, which was big enough to fit a full-sized hog.

Bex could see why he'd think that. She hadn't realized back when the only Blackwood she'd known was Adrian, but her paper-pale skin and long, jet-black hair fit right in with the hordes of black-dressed women working the handmade festival tables. It would've been simpler to just tell him yes, but Bex was done pretending to be someone she wasn't, even if she didn't have the most important parts of herself anymore.

"I'm not a member of the family," she said as she noted the pumpkin's prize-winning weight and wrote it down on a scrap of paper. "Just helping out for the festival. Do you want help carrying your purchase to your car?"

As always, the man said no. They *never* wanted help after watching a five-foot-two girl carry their pumpkin one-handed, but Bex saw the moment the human changed his mind when she set the giant squash—which had weighed in at an impressive one hundred and seven pounds—in his arms.

"Are you *sure* you don't want help?"

"Maybe a little," the man gasped, breathing through his teeth as he struggled to keep from falling over.

Bex nodded and waved at Iggs, who'd just gotten back from loading a hundred and fifty wholesale pumpkins into a Rotary Club bus for a fundraiser.

"Can you help this customer check out and get the pumpkin to his car?" she asked when the towering demon jogged over.

"Righto, boss," Iggs said, taking the pumpkin from the struggling human before it crushed him. "Also, Lys is looking for you. They said to meet them in town when you've got a minute."

"I have one right now," Bex replied, looking over her shoulder at the other Seattle Anchor refugees on pumpkin duty: a pair of young wrath demons with the same wide, bull-like black horns as Iggs, who were blatantly showing off their strength to a gaggle of awestruck human teenagers. "When you're done helping this guy, would you mind keeping an eye on the kids? I don't want anyone getting kicked."

"Will do," Iggs promised, putting on a good show of having normal-human levels of lift capacity as he carried the giant pumpkin toward the checkout line while the still-wheezing customer trailed behind.

When Bex was certain everything had been taken care of, she took off her green Blackwood Farms apron, smacked the pumpkin-field dirt off her one hand using the leg of her black jeans, and set off down the road toward town.

Not that there was much town to go to. The city of Hemlock Bend, Massachusetts, consisted of eight historical wooden structures and a post office. A stop sign had been installed at the city's one intersection a few decades ago, but otherwise it looked like it hadn't changed since the seventeen hundreds. All the buildings still had their old colonial style with steep roofs, long eaves, a single short central door, and small windows filled with tiny panes of wobbly glass so beautifully maintained they looked like they could've been installed yesterday.

The town was a dozen miles off any major roads, so one stop sign was normally more than enough. Today, though, the place was packed with Fall-crazed tourists who'd driven in from all over New England for the Blackwood's annual pumpkin festival. All the historic buildings were open and doing brisk business, selling every sort of autumnal food, drink, and decoration. On the main street outside, traffic was completely shut off by a wall of craft tents selling handmade candles, handmade cutting boards, handmade soap, handmade sweaters, handmade whatever you wanted. It was the perfect picture of a small-town American craft fair with two major exceptions. One, every tent and shop was worked by a woman wearing a black dress and a pointy witch hat, and two, there were nearly as many cats as people.

There were so many familiars darting around that it was hard to walk in places. If Bex hadn't still had most of her speed, she would've tripped straight into someone's display of artisanal local honey. Iggs had been nearly incapacitated by the sheer number of pettable cats before Bex had ordered him out to the pumpkin patch. She still felt the move had been necessary to save her demon's sanity, but it was coming back to bite her since, with Iggs in cat-based exile, there was no one around who could tell her where Lys was.

Bex had never realized how much she'd relied on Drox to locate her demons until he was gone. It'd been a week since they'd been forced to flee the destroyed Seattle Anchor for the Blackwood, but she was still discovering all the things she'd lost. For example, she used to be able to recognize Lys no matter what form they took. Now, though, Bex couldn't say which of the hundreds of disguised lust demons working the crowd was hers. To add insult to injury, she was too short for Lys to spot now that she no longer had a foot-tall pair of horns serving as a flagpole.

It was so *frustrating*. She'd thought she was in the clear after Nemini had helped her climb out of the void left by the loss of her name, but every day brought challenges Bex felt completely unequipped to deal with. She couldn't even get one of the random demons' attention to ask for help since, with no horns and no name to give her magical presence, they all assumed she was human and steered clear. She was digging for her cellphone to just call Lys and ask when someone tapped her on the shoulder.

Bex nearly jumped out of her skin. The fact that people could sneak up on her so easily now was another new vulnerability she hated. If she'd still had her sword, she would've pulled it on instinct and probably killed someone. Fortunately for everybody in a ten-foot radius, Bex couldn't do stuff like that anymore. A fact the person who'd tapped her definitely knew and was taking advantage of, because when Bex whirled around to face her attacker, Adrian's youngest aunt was smiling right behind her.

"Hello, no-longer-Queen of Wrath," said the fresh-faced Witch of the Future. "I brought you the apple fritter you're going to want in five seconds."

The words were barely out of her mouth when the delicious smell of fried sugary dough hit Bex's nose. This was followed by a loud growl from her stomach, and the black-haired witch's smile turned into a grin.

"Here," she said, pressing an absolutely beautiful slab of golden-fried, apple-stuffed pastry into Bex's sole remaining hand. "You eat while I talk."

"Okay, but what are we talking about?" Bex asked nervously as she took a bite of the piping hot fritter, which tasted even better than it smelled.

"That depends," Muriel replied as she nibbled the corner off her own fritter, which was even prettier than Bex's. "My sisters are always telling me to be more mindful of others, so why don't we start with how you're doing."

"Better than we should be," Bex reported at once, taking a step back so she could bow her head without hitting the wide brim of the witch's enormous pointed hat. "Thank you again for taking us in, and for letting us help with your festival. Large concentrations of human emotion are hard to come by out here in the countryside. A big, chaotic event like this is a feast for my demons."

"I'm happy to hear it," the Old Wife of the Future replied as she licked the sticky cinnamon off her fingers. "But that second one wasn't actually my doing. We hold the festival at the same time every year. Sometimes a coincidence is just a coincidence."

"Well, I'm still grateful," Bex said stubbornly. "My people would be dead right now without your coven's help."

"That is true," Muriel agreed around a mouth full of fritter. "But I didn't ask how your demons were doing. I asked about *you*."

She looked pointedly down at the stump on the end of Bex's right wrist, and the former Queen of Wrath sighed.

"There's nothing new to report," she muttered, trying hard not to sound as bitter as she felt. "My hand's not coming back. Nemini and Lys both tell me I've regenerated limbs in the past, but this time..." She shook her hornless head. "I don't know if it was losing my crown or my name or what, but I haven't recovered any more of my power than I had when you rescued us from the collapsed Seattle Anchor."

"I see," Muriel said as she led Bex around the long line for the cider tent. "But you're still leaving tonight."

Bex jumped. She hadn't told anyone about that yet. She'd barely made the decision herself, though she really shouldn't have been surprised. What was the point of being the Witch of the Future if you didn't know what was going to happen before everyone else?

"Will I be successful?" she asked instead.

Adrian's aunt didn't reply. She just stared off into the distance, her blue eyes locked on the wall of trees that loomed over the village's eastern edge like a cliff.

Bex stared at it, too. When the witches had first brought them in, she couldn't believe that the Great Blackwood was just *there*. Even way out here in the boonies where trees were expected to be big, how could the scalies not notice oaks the size of skyscrapers? *Especially* right now, when the giant forest was decked out in its autumn splendor. Most of the crowd clogging the festival tents were leaf watchers who'd driven out here specifically to stare at the scenery. How was it possible that shutterbugs with gigs of leaf photos on their cameras could walk right by the giant forest rising like an ancient city not three feet beyond Hemlock Bend's final building and not freak out?

"The same way the good people of Bainbridge never noticed Adrian's lovely witchwood," Muriel said, answering Bex's question before she could even consider asking it out loud. "Gilgamesh's scales steal from all of us, including those who have no idea they're being robbed."

"All the more reason to bring him down," Bex growled, turning away from the glorious red-and-gold forest to glare at the witch. "You never answered my question. Will my mission tonight succeed?"

The Witch of the Future sighed and ate the rest of her fritter.

"Parts of it will and parts of it won't," she said when she'd finally finished chewing. "Sadly, I can't tell you which parts because the future isn't actually mine to control. It's more like pruning a sapling. You do your best to coax the branches into the shape you want, but only the tree itself knows what its final form will be."

She flashed Bex a cryptic smile. "You're one of my sharpest pruning cuts yet. The reason I voted to allow Adrian to go to Seattle was to make sure that he met you. I have great faith in both of your potential, but when it comes to the specific twists and turns of what is yet to come..." She shrugged. "Part of mastering soul magic is learning to live with uncertainty."

Bex was starting to see why soul magic was Adrian's least favorite school of witchcraft. "So you can't give me any hints? Nothing at all?"

"I can tell you that Lys is at the Brew Ha Ha," Muriel said, pointing down the busy street at the largest of Hemlock Bend's perfectly maintained colonial buildings. "The other thing you were waiting for is there as well."

"Really?" Bex whistled. "That was fast."

"You're not the only one in a hurry," the witch replied, reaching into the pocket of her simple but beautifully sewn black linen dress. "I suspect this will be the last time we talk for a while, so I'm going to give you this now. If you see my nephew before I do, would you do me the favor of passing it on?"

The mention of Adrian made Bex's stomach clench. She'd been trying her best not to think about what was happening to him in Heaven, but she knew it had to be horrible. What flavor of horrible was still up for debate since she still didn't know why Gilgamesh had kidnapped him in the first place, but his family was being no help at all. They refused to even discuss Adrian in her presence, but Bex hadn't forgotten that the first princess who'd come to Bainbridge had also tried to take Adrian away. She didn't know if that was because of the Spider or if Adrian Blackwood had always been part of Gilgamesh's long game, but Bex was determined to get him back.

That was a big part of why she'd decided to leave tonight. Lys kept begging her to take more time to heal, but Adrian had been in the enemy's hands for an entire week. Bex was so upset at the idea of him being tortured in some sterile white prison cell filled with creepy golden eyes, she didn't even notice Muriel holding something out to her until the witch gave up and slipped the object into the front pocket of Bex's oversized black T-shirt.

"What was that?" Bex demanded, patting her chest in alarm. "A curse?"

Muriel shook her head. "Just an acorn."

Bex arched a dark eyebrow. "You want me to give Adrian an acorn?"

"He'll know what to do with it," the witch promised. "My nephew isn't *that* bad at soul witchcraft, and seeds are the essence of the future."

Those were some pretty cryptic instructions, but Bex didn't get a chance to ask for clarification. The Old Wife of the Future had already wandered away, vanishing like a shadow into the rowdy crowd surrounding the apple strudel booth.

Bex stared blankly at the wall of humans for a few more seconds, and then she turned on the heel of her stiff new combat boots—a replacement for the pair she'd burned to ash during her first fight with Havok—and started walking toward where the Witch of the Future had told her Lys was waiting.

As the only permanent restaurant in Hemlock Bend, the Brew Ha Ha wore a lot of hats. During the day, it was a coffee shop. After sunset, it was a pub. On crowded weekends like this one, it served as a shady retreat from the blazing autumn sun. Every table in its massive common room was packed with tired-looking festival-goers while the witch at the bar served drinks that smelled suspiciously like the potions Adrian used to brew.

Whatever they were, they were definitely filling people with energy. The moment exhausted customers drank their orders, they went right back outside to spend more money at the craft tents, creating a convenient wall of chaos that kept the scalies from looking too hard up the rickety steps to the shop's second floor, where Lys was waiting with an unexpected—and extremely *early*—tall, green guest.

"Can't be," Bex said as she climbed the ladderlike stairs to see Felix, the Goblin Prince of Seattle, struggling to balance his lanky, seven-foot-tall body on one of the coffee shop's antique wooden chairs. "How did you get here so fast? I only called you last night."

"It's called hustle, sweetheart," the goblin replied, his voice sharp and curt with none of the usual flirtation. "I flew into Albany on the red-eye to pick up the cargo from my freight guy. Had a hell of a drive getting out here, though. You could've warned me the witches would be clogging every road into this boondock with their bake sale traffic."

"I didn't realize you'd be coming in person," Bex said, plopping the remaining half of her pastry on the table before taking a seat next to Lys's current go-to body: a lanky young man with a photographer's vest and perfectly trimmed hipster beard who was practically bouncing up and down in his chair.

"Enough about your traffic problems," Lys snapped, leaning over the antique sawhorse that had been retrofitted into a tiny café table. "Did you bring what we talked about?"

Felix curled his long arm down to pick something off the floor. It looked like an old-fashioned soldier's knapsack that had been taken on one too many campaigns. Every inch of it was stained with something, but the heavy brown canvas beneath was finely woven, and the straps that held its top flap closed were stitched with magic symbols Bex didn't recognize.

"What in the Hells is that?" Lys demanded, their amber eyes flashing dangerously in their disguise's friendly face. "We asked for weapons."

"And I delivered," Felix insisted with a sharp-toothed grin. "That, my impatient chameleon, is the Armory of Solomon."

Lys's scowl deepened, and the goblin heaved an enormous sigh.

"Are you Luddites familiar with the concept of a Bag of Holding?" he asked, leaning as far back in his chair as his ridiculously long limbs would allow. "The Armory of Solomon follows the same principle, but for weapons."

"Is it sorcery?" Bex asked suspiciously.

"Nope," Felix replied, reaching out to pat the unassuming bag's lumpy top. "This gorgeous baby was made in the fifteen hundreds by a renegade alchemist turned smuggler. He got purged by Gilgamesh shortly after completing his masterpiece, which is how my grandfather was able to acquire it on the cheap, but it still works like a charm. Despite its small size and unassuming appearance, this little knapsack can hold a functionally infinite number of weapons. Since it was made during the Renaissance, that used to mean only swords, bows, and black powder cannons, but I've spent a pretty penny updating it to accept modern firearms as well, including automatic weapons, grenades, explosives, towable artillery, and so on."

He unbuckled the knapsack and reached his arm in up to the elbow before pulling out a brand-new, shiny AK-47.

"I've got your whole order in here," he explained as he dropped the gun back into the apparently bottomless knapsack. "Only way I could do it. You asked for enough weapons to outfit an army, but while I've always got the goods on hand, even I can't drive twenty big rigs stuffed with illegal munitions across America without drawing suspicion. With this little beauty, though, all that destruction fits in one conveniently portable package."

"*Too* convenient," Bex observed tersely, keeping her hands firmly away from the knapsack. "You're telling me there's an entire army's worth of weapons packed inside one small backpack?"

Felix grinned. "Now you see why it's a treasure of my clan."

"And now *you* see why I'm suspicious," Bex snapped. "You're the one who's always telling me not to be a mark, but blindly accepting a treasure like this is absolutely mark behavior. We're out of money and cornered hard right now. I know you know that, so why are you showing up with too-good-to-be-true treasures? Is this some kind of trick?"

Given their past interactions, Bex felt that was an extremely valid question, but Felix's beady eyes narrowed like she'd just challenged him to a duel.

"Not everything goblins do is about money," he said, uncrossing his legs and straightening his shoulders until he was back to his full looming height. "There's pride to be answered as well, and mine will be paid in full."

"Pride?" Bex repeated, more confused than ever. "What does that have to do with—"

"You think I got on a plane at midnight and flew across the entire damn country just to cheat you?" Felix snapped. "I'd make more cash ripping off tourists back home! I'm not here for profit. I'm here because Gilgamesh played me for a chump."

"Played you how?" Lys asked. "I thought you never worked with Heaven directly."

"I don't," he snarled. "But I buy from warlocks all the time. Gilgamesh knew that, so when he wanted to set up the Havok situation, he had one of his damn minions sell me a famous demon who wasn't a demon knowing full well I'd take the bait and end up calling you."

Felix waved his green hand in Bex's direction before slamming it back down with a *thump* that almost cracked the table.

"He played me for a fool, and what's worse is he made me spend *my own money* to do it! I don't care how many gods he's slain. No one makes a chump out of Felix the Fixer and gets away with it! That's why I'm here. I don't care about your damn crusade, but if you're taking the fight to Heaven, I'm your goblin."

He shoved Solomon's Amory across the table into Bex's lap.

"That's all yours on two conditions. First, you gotta bring the bag back, and second, I want you to burn Gilgamesh's precious Heaven to the ground. Just make sure you tell him Felix sends his regards before you rip his head off. I want that gold-plated ass to know *exactly* who pulled the trigger on his downfall."

That was giving himself a lot of credit, but Bex wasn't about to argue.

"I'll be happy to tell Gilgamesh anything you want while I'm ripping Anu's crown off his head," she promised, grinning down at the battered knapsack. "So how does this thing work?"

"Just picture whatever weapon you want and stick your hand in," Felix explained impatiently. "It can only cough up what it's stocked with, but I told my warehouse team to make me proud. There aren't any vehicles because my staff couldn't figure out how to drive a tank into a backpack, but anything else you can think of should be in there."

"Thanks, Felix," Bex said, holding the bag open for Lys, who was already digging through it like a mad mole. "This is way more than I expected and exactly what we need for tonight."

Lys stopped pulling out random weapons and snapped their head toward Bex. "*Tonight*? I thought you said we were waiting until next week!"

"I did," Bex said, picking the remains of her apple fritter up off the table. "But then I realized there's no point. I'm no more recovered now than I was when we arrived. If I keep waiting, all I'm doing is making everyone suffer longer for no reason."

"But we're not ready," Lys insisted, their amber eyes terrified behind the mild face of their disguise. "If you face the Queen of War again like you are now, you'll—"

"Be no more screwed than I was the first time she beat me," Bex finished. "I know what we're up against. That's why we're doing things differently this time." She crammed the last of the apple fritter into her mouth before adding, "You're the one who came up with most of this plan, don't forget."

"I haven't," Lys grumbled, scrubbing their hands through their hipster human's perfectly styled hair. "It's just... I thought we'd have more time.

"Well, I'm glad we don't," Bex said, brushing the crumbs from her hand as she rose from her chair. "I'm tired of waiting around. Having an on-demand arsenal is nice for everyone else, but all the things *I* need to win this—my hand, my horns, my sword, our witch—is up in Heaven, and every day we waste down here just gives Gilgamesh longer to prepare."

"Prepare for what?" Felix asked.

"We don't know," Bex snapped. "That's part of the problem. We have no idea what Gilgamesh is up to, but he didn't kidnap Adrian and put the whole Blackwood on the warpath for no reason. Whatever he's doing up there behind his locked Anchors, it *can't* be good."

"I dunno about that," Felix said, scratching his sharp chin. "My current burning need for revenge notwithstanding, Gilgamesh's war has been great for profits."

Bex and Lys shot him matching murderous looks, which the goblin gleefully ignored.

"If we're done here, I'm going back to Seattle," he informed them as he rose to his feet. "I stepped on a lot of greedy toes getting that armory stocked so fast, so I've got to go back and do some management." He pointed a long finger at Bex. "You'd better live up to your violent reputation. I put a lot more than a magic bag on the line to come help you today. If you can't make all that murder talk into murder reality, the

Armory of Solomon isn't the only thing I'm going to lose."

"Don't worry," Bex promised. "I'll smash Heaven or die trying."

"That I believe," Felix said, patting Bex on the head where her horns used to be. "Good luck, little underdog. Make me proud."

He moved his hand before Bex could smack it away and strolled down the stairs, walking out the coffee shop's front door without drawing so much as a sideways glance from the scale-eyed tourists he pushed out of his way.

"I will never understand how he does that without getting kicked," Bex muttered.

"Wouldn't matter if he did," Lys said, taking a scribble-covered piece of paper out of their pocket and sliding it across the table.

"Is this for real?" Bex asked when she'd read all the way to the bottom.

"Afraid so," her lust demon replied grimly. "That's what I wanted to talk to you about before Felix showed up and gave me better news to share. We've had fifteen kicks reported since we arrived in Massachusetts, mostly from demons who went into the surrounding towns to feed. The weird thing is that all those incidents were self-reported. That doesn't normally happen since getting kicked into Limbo is a death sentence for anyone other than you, but now..."

Lys's voice trailed off as they pointed at the paper in Bex's hands. The one that was covered in a list of times and dates all with the same cryptic description.

No kick demons observed.

"How can there be no kick demons in Limbo?"
Bex demanded. "It was literally created to hold them."

"I don't know," Lys said. "But I do know that all
those demons were telling the truth. I took advantage
of the festival crowds to get myself kicked this
morning, and—"

"You got *kicked*?" Bex cried. "Without *me*?"

"I didn't want to upset you," Lys said quickly.
"And I wanted to make sure this wasn't another trap."

"By walking into it?!"

Lys crossed their flannel-clad arms over their
human disguise's narrow chest. "Are you going to let
me finish?"

Bex sighed and motioned for them to go ahead.

"As I was saying," Lys continued, "I was worried
the missing kick demon rumors might be a trap to lure
you into a place Gilgamesh controlled. When I arrived
in Limbo, though, I saw the same thing everyone else
reported. The whole place is empty. I ran as far as I
could before my five minutes ended, but there was
nothing to find. It's just a big gray room."

Bex bit her lip as she sank back into her chair.
"If they're not in Limbo, where did they go?"

"I don't know," Lys said, reaching out to squeeze
her shoulder. "But this is why I think we should wait.
It's never a good idea to rush into a situation we don't
understand."

"We're never going to understand it if we stay
here," Bex argued. "All the Anchors are still locked
tight. You're the one who infiltrated the local warlock
cabal and discovered they don't know any more than
we do."

"That doesn't mean there's nothing to find out," Lys said. "We haven't even tried the sorcerers yet. They could know—"

"If my people aren't in Limbo, that just means Gilgamesh moved them somewhere even worse!" Bex yelled, drawing nervous looks from the scalies downstairs. "He has my horns, Lys! That means he can give orders in my name. He could be doing horrible things to my demons, and I'm just *sitting around!*"

Lys opened their mouth to keep arguing, but Bex stopped them with a look. "Am I still queen or not?"

"Of course you are."

"Then we're going," Bex snapped. "How long will it take you to get ready?"

Lys glared at her for a moment before their shoulders slumped in defeat.

"Give me four hours."

"Four hours it is," Bex said as she got back to her feet. "I'll tell the others."

Lys dutifully bowed their small, hidden horns, but Bex had already grabbed Felix's magic bag full of weapons and stomped down the stairs to start the long, dusty walk back to their camp.

The demons' new home was two miles down the road in a big hayfield that separated the towering wall of the Blackwood from the little-used country road that ran along its border. The coven owned all the land around their forest, and they'd graciously allowed the demons to stay on a portion of it. They'd even provided tents, though Bex was pretty sure that was less about the demons' comfort and more about avoiding trouble with the locals over thousands of strangers sleeping uncovered in a field. The tents also let them pretend the demon camp was part of their fall festivities. They'd even piled pumpkins at the fence gate and put up a big cooking pavilion to add to ruse, which would've been awesome if any demons other than Bex actually ate human food.

Since everyone was currently at the festival helping their hosts and sucking emotions out of the tourists—the only source of substantial food they'd gotten since they'd arrived a week ago—the campsite was deserted when Bex walked in. Even the wrath demons had gone into town. Only Zargrexa, ever dutiful, was still there, sitting in a rocking chair with a sword she'd gotten from Ishtar-knew-where, guarding what was left of her queen's RV.

No matter how many times Bex saw it, the sight still made her wince. Their brave little Winnebago had made it through Heaven's bombardment and the sudden appearance of the Blackwood, but only just. It'd never taken a direct hit, but being thrown around by all those cannon blasts had snapped both axles and torn off the entire front end.

It was going to take months of repairs before it was drivable again, if it ever happened, but Iggs had absolutely refused to leave the RV behind. Even after the witches' sudden arrival had left it stranded in one of the towering treetops, he'd set up a pulley system to get it down and carried it through the root tunnel with the help of several other wrath demons. The whole thing had been ridiculous and made the evacuation take twice as long as it should've, but Bex hadn't said a word because she couldn't bear to leave it behind either.

Even when it looked like a dented pile of scrap, the Winnebago was the closest thing any of them had to a home. They were all still sleeping in it despite the holes and the busted plumbing because Bex didn't feel safe sleeping anywhere else, and her crew slept where she did. If they'd had a sorcerer, they might've been able to get the power back on, but none of the demons or the witches Iggs had talked into looking it over could make heads or tails of the cuneiform carved behind the RV's plastic panels. They had been able to save Norma, though.

Bex had feared the worst when she'd seen the cab. One of the lion's blasts had gone straight through the RV's windshield. If Norma had been an actual old lady, she'd be in Heaven with Gilgamesh right now, but fortunately for Bex and the others, she was a construct. The moment they pulled the bent steering wheel out of the wreckage, she'd popped right back into existence. She was a little glitchy—constantly asking for a destination, aggressively talking about the weather, and throwing handfuls of grandma candy at anyone who came within five feet—but just seeing her sitting in the replacement driver's seat Iggs had rigged up for her using salvaged parts from an old tractor made Bex feel like everything wasn't lost.

It was good to be reminded of that. She thought their plan was pretty solid, but there was no changing the fact that they were going into the lion's den. No amount of clever strategies could fill the gaping hole where her name used to be, or stop the sad numbness that spread through her hands whenever she tried to call her fire. She'd honestly never felt less ready for a fight in her life, which was the only reason she'd agreed to take her demons with her.

Bex normally preferred to do the really dangerous stuff alone. Even now that she was on her last life, she was still the toughest demon on her team, and not having to worry about anyone but herself made things less scary. She would've already left if she'd thought she could survive on her own, but with no horns, no fire, no sword, no hand, and no witch in her corner, Bex's demons were all she had left. Fortunately, her crew was the best there was. She was more worried that she'd be the one holding them back as she marched across the grass toward what was left of the RV's side entrance.

Lys had already discussed their plan with Zargrexa this morning, so all Bex had to do was tell the old village chief that it was happening today. That would've sparked a whole barrage of questions from anyone else, but despite the loss of her horns, the wrath demons she'd freed from Limbo had never stopped treating Bex as their queen. The moment Bex told her the schedule, Zargrexa bowed her horns and promised to keep Ishtar's Children safe until the queen's return.

With that, Bex's final duty in the Blackwood was absolved. Zargrexa and the other leaders who'd come over from the Anchor would make sure the camp kept ticking over, which meant Bex was free to make the most of the four hours Lys had given her.

She did so by climbing into the RV. The whole front end was toast, including their sitting area with the built-in table, but the back half of the kitchen was still mostly intact. She took one more minute to send a few final texts, and then Bex put her phone on silent, set Felix's magical weapon bag on the counter for Iggs, and went upstairs to take a nap.

It felt anticlimactic, but Bex had already learned the hard way this week that she couldn't go nearly as long without sleep as she had before she'd lost her horns. Rest on the battlefield was also iffy, so she was determined to get as much as she could now, forcing herself to stay in bed until there were only thirty minutes left before Lys's deadline.

Bex used twenty of those to shower and dress for combat in her new boots, a loose-fitting set of black fatigues with plenty of cargo pockets she could stuff full of survival essentials, and a black long-sleeved shirt made from a heavy synthetic material that was supposed to be stab-proof. She also took the med kit from her bathroom, a hundred feet of rope, a metal-handled flashlight, the black plastic box containing all their comm equipment, and her heavy combat knife.

There was no way all of that was fitting in her cargo pockets, so Bex also grabbed a backpack from her only-slightly-crushed closet. When her combat supplies were accounted for, she filled the space she had left with bottles of water and leftover coffee-shop sandwiches from the minifridge Lys had found for her bedroom. When the backpack was stuffed as full as she could get it, Bex topped the look off with a high ponytail and her favorite black leather bomber jacket.

That last one was a controversial choice. Bex's leather jacket was her longest-surviving piece of clothing. Taking it with her now was practically guaranteeing its demise, but if this was going to be

Bex's last mission, she wanted to do it wearing something comfortable. If nothing else, the familiar weight of the leather made her feel more at ease as she hoisted the bulging backpack onto her shoulder and tromped down the stairs to find Iggs waiting for her in what was left of the RV's kitchen.

"Bex!" he cried excitedly, holding up the canvas knapsack she'd left for him on the counter. "Is this the thing you messaged me about earlier?"

"That's Solomon's Armory," she told him with a grin. "I'm not sure how much use it'll actually be, but Felix said—"

"Not sure how much use it'll be?" her wrath demon repeated in horror. "What are you talking about? This thing is *incredible*! Just look at this."

He shoved his hand into the battered knapsack bag and pulled out a gun the size of a leg. Iggs's leg, not Bex's.

"You see?" he demanded, holding the weapon out for her to admire. "There's like twenty of these in here! Isn't that amazing?"

"Very," Bex said, making appreciative noises at the costly-looking weapon. "What gun is that?"

"Heavy machine gun," Iggs replied with a smile so giddy he looked like he was about to burst into song. "They're usually mounted on tanks or the decks of battleships, but Felix's goblins must've taken demonic strength into account, because all the ones I've pulled out of the bag have shoulder straps." He heaved a dreamy sigh. "It's *so* beautiful. They even packed us ammunition!"

"It'd hardly be useful if they didn't," Bex said as Iggs started pulling out belts of the biggest bullets she'd ever seen. "But can those sorts of mundane weapons even hurt Gilgamesh's constructs? I thought we needed sorcerous weapons for that."

"Enough kinetic force hurts anything," Iggs insisted. "These are actual military weapons, not the low-powered civilian and militia stuff we were stuck with before. Each of these bullets can punch a hole through a fifty-millimeter armor plate, and the heavy machine gun fires *fifteen hundred* of them per minute." He gazed at the giant gun lovingly. "I bet I could Swiss-cheese a prince with this baby."

"I'll leave it to you, then," Bex said, hefting her own backpack higher on her shoulder. "Use that bag well, and if anything happens to me, make sure all the guns inside get into demon hands before you give it back to Felix."

"I swear I will," Iggs said as he carefully replaced the ammo and the giant gun into the sack. "But you don't need to make plans like that. We're going with you this time, so nothing's going to happen."

"Survival is never guaranteed," Bex reminded him, then she smiled. "But it'd have to go pretty horrible to end up worse than my last mission, so at least the bar's on the floor."

That was supposed to be a joke, but Iggs wasn't laughing. "We won't let that happen," he promised, his red eyes determined as he stared at her. "We're going to get through this alive, all of us, and we *will* win."

His sudden seriousness caught Bex by surprise, though it really shouldn't have. Lys's reluctance this afternoon had thrown her, but Iggs had been ready to charge all Nine Hells at once from the moment she pulled him out of Limbo. That was pretty much the plan tonight, so of course he'd be pumped. Bex just wished she could steal some of his confidence as she set her backpack down for a final check. Iggs was the most tactically-minded of their group thanks to his obsession with war games, so she always liked to get his opinion. She must've done a good job this time, though, because the only addition he suggested was the exploding short sword he normally used as part of his backup-roll-everything loadout.

"So," Iggs said as he helped Bex adjust the short sword's sheath at the small of her back so its handle wouldn't knock against her backpack. "Now that we're doing this for real, have you made a final decision about who you're bringing? I'm going, obviously, but who else?"

"I was planning on just our normal crew," Bex said with a frown. "Why do you ask? Did you have someone in mind?"

"There's a few extra candidates," Iggs said when he was finished strapping her in. "You'll see when we get outside."

"What's that supposed to mean?" she asked as Iggs maneuvered Solomon's Armory—which, as a knapsack sized for the average human, now looked comically small on his giant frame—over his shoulders.

"You'll see," he promised, waving for her to lead the way out of the RV.

Bex did so with a scowl. One of the big reasons she'd decided to go ahead and do this tonight—other than all the obvious ones—was because she'd hoped to avoid making a scene. Her demons were jumpy enough after having their safe haven bombarded and seeing their queen crawl back defeated. She'd hoped to sneak out and score a victory before anyone outside her inner circle even knew that she was gone, but she should've known better. There was nothing demons paid more attention to than a queen, even a hornless, handless, swordless one, so Bex wasn't actually surprised when she stepped through the RV's busted door to find a crowd waiting for her.

Nemini was there, of course, and actually looking combat-ready for once. She normally went into battle in the same sweaters and running shoes that she wore to read books in the RV all day. This evening, however, she was wearing a sleek, dark-gray turtleneck and the same practical black military fatigues as Bex. She still had her usual comfy sneakers, but her snakes were all up and looking around above her head, which Bex took as a good sign.

Lys looked similarly battle-ready standing beside Nemini in a no-nonsense older female form. They also had what appeared to be a tied-up body with a black bag over its head squirming on their shoulder, but that was fairly normal for Lys, so Bex didn't think much of it. What she hadn't anticipated was the crowd of witches standing in front of the forest to the lust demon's left.

There were over a dozen of them, all ladies of various ages dressed in the same all-black clothing and pointed hat that Adrian always wore. His mother, Agatha, was at the head of the pack, along with a shirtless, fully transformed General Kirok. That would have been strange enough all by itself, but the witch wasn't just standing close to the four-armed demon. She was *painting* him, using a brush made from nightshade flowers to trace spiraling black patterns all over the towering war demon's bronze chest, neck, and shoulders.

"What is going on?" Bex demanded as she stomped down the RV's bent metal steps. "Kirok! You're supposed to be guarding the eastern road with the other war demons."

That wasn't entirely true. The war demons weren't actually "guarding" anything. They'd been sent to the other side of the Blackwood to keep them away from the rest of the refugees because (a) no one wanted to be around them after the betrayal that had gotten half their army shot in the back, and (b) no war demon could be trusted so long as their queen was still alive to give them orders. Bex knew Kirok understood these points because he was the one who'd volunteered to separate the war demons in the first place. He wasn't even supposed to know she was leaving since Bex didn't want to risk Heaven getting a heads-up, but here he was.

"What are you doing here?" she demanded, looking him up and down. "And what are you doing *to* him?"

That last question was directed at Agatha, but the old witch just flashed Bex a smile that looked so much like Adrian's it made her heart skip a beat.

"Helping," Agatha said as she returned her attention to the intricate patterns she was painting into the hollow of Kirok's bronze clavicle. "We'd hardly be good hosts if we let you go into battle without backup. Of course, a good *guest* would have warned us sooner that she was planning to leave, but we

Blackwoods are an adaptable lot, and as you see, we've made do."

"Made do with what?" Bex asked, more confused than angry now. "What kind of backup are you sending? And you still haven't explained what you're doing to Kirok."

"She is doing what I asked," the war demon replied, tilting his head to look at Bex around the tall point of the witch's black hat. "The Old Wife of the Future informed me that you were beginning your assault tonight, so I am here because I'm going with you."

"The Hells you are," Lys snapped, tossing the tied-up body they'd been carrying onto the ground, where it landed with a startled grunt. "You're a war demon whose queen is still alive and proudly on Gilgamesh's side. Saying 'we can't trust you' is a *fact*, not an insult."

"I'm well aware," Kirok replied curtly, pointing one of his four hands at the black spirals that now covered most of his upper body. "That is why I asked the witches of the Blackwood to curse me."

He said that last part as if it were the ultimate argument in his favor, but Bex immediately shook her head. "A curse can't make you ignore orders from your queen."

"But it can render me incapable of following them," Kirok insisted, turning his head so that Bex could see how the black markings curled all the way up his neck and past his ear to the underside of his flat horns. She was still trying to figure out why that was important when Agatha explained.

"I'm cursing him against disobedience," the witch said, keeping her eyes on her work as she deftly added more spirals to the dip between Kirok's pectorals. "If he disobeys any order, even a minor one, the paint covering his body will release a poison that even demonic regeneration can't keep up with. I've warned him it will be a slow and painful death, but he said he's willing, so I'm making sure to be thorough."

"The curse part I get," Bex said. "By why would you rig it to trigger on *dis*obedience?"

"Because I still intend to obey your orders," Kirok explained gravely. "The poison is only there to ensure that, if I am given a command I do not wish to follow, the mere thought of refusal will activate the curse and kill me."

"Again," Bex said, "why would you do that?"

"Because death is the only force strong enough to allow me to ignore my queen's commands," the war demon replied, lowering his horns as far as he could without getting in the Witch of the Present's way.

"I am prepared to endure any suffering," he said before Bex could get a word in. "Even a slow, agonizing death is acceptable if it means my queen can never make me a traitor again. I beg you, Queen of Wrath, allow me this opportunity to make amends for the evil my demons and I were forced to commit. I used to be a slave trainer in the Hells. I can guide you to whatever goal you seek in that terrible place. Just give me a chance to redeem myself and the soldiers under my command, and I swear on my life and my name that I will never betray you again."

"He won't be able to," Agatha added, putting the final touch on her painting before stepping back to admire her work. "If he even thinks about disobeying your orders, the curse will kill him. Likewise, if his queen tells him to slay you, all you have to do is say 'don't,' and the poison will cripple his body before he can react. It's a custom mix of all my best toxins, and now that it's on, they won't even be able to see it's there. Watch."

Bex squinted in the fading sunlight, but the witch was right. The black lines that had looked so vivid just a few seconds ago were already fading into Kirok's metal skin, seeping beneath his armored exterior until she could no longer tell which parts of him had been painted and which hadn't.

"The poison will stay until the next new moon," Agatha said as she wrapped her toxic paintbrush in a square of stained leather and handed it to one of the witches behind her. "I suggest you don't give him any controversial orders until then. That curse has a hair trigger."

"All the more reason not to risk it," Bex argued, crossing her arms over her chest. "I'm doing this to *save* demons, not kill them by accident."

"And that is why I must go with you," Kirok insisted, squeezing his giant fists. "War demons are the guardians of all of Gilgamesh's domains. If you wish to infiltrate them successfully, you'll need an inside man. One who *isn't* a transformed lust demon."

He finished with a glare at Lys, who glared right back, but as much as Bex hated to admit it, Kirok had a point. One of their plan's biggest weak points was the fact that Lys was the only one of them who'd actually been to the Hells, and they hadn't been back in centuries. An updated guide who knew both the jailer and the jailed's side of things would be extremely useful, but Bex still shook her head.

"It's too much of a risk," she said. "Once we start, we can't afford to make any mistakes. If that curse screws up, you could betray us to the enemy."

"My curse won't 'screw up'," Agatha huffed, glaring at Bex. "Who do you think taught Adrian how to do these things?"

"That wasn't what I meant," Bex said quickly. "It's just—"

"You're much more likely to kill him by accident than he is to kill you," the witch spoke over her. "This curse will punish him for disobeying *any* order, no matter how insignificant. If you tell him to go left and he goes right, he'll be dead within five minutes."

That sounded like the biggest reason yet not to bring Kirok along, but the war demon's bronze face was resolute.

"I don't care," he said, dropping to one knee in front of Bex. "When I was trapped in the Anchor doing those horrible things under my queen's command, I swore a thousand oaths that I would make it right. If I do not go with you, and you die while attempting this attack, I'll never get a chance to keep my word. I don't care if my life is lost. I'd rather die by accident tonight than live another thousand years with this betrayal and no way to make amends."

He looked her straight in the eyes as he spoke, and Bex's whole body slumped with the force of her sigh.

"Can't argue with that," she said, holding out her hand. "Welcome to the team."

She'd meant to help him back to his feet, but Kirok took her hand and bent his horns over it instead. It was the same position Iggs came out in whenever she used his name to calm his raging demon, the one that had made Adrian so angry after their first trip into Limbo. Bex secretly hated it too. It looked so subservient, but she knew better than to say so in front of old demons. To them, it was still the greatest show of respect, and it was a queen's duty to accept that, even if she didn't have a crown anymore.

"Does the paint come off?" she asked instead, turning back to Agatha as Kirok rose to his feet. "Like, do we have to be careful about getting him near water or anything?"

The Old Wife of the Flesh laughed. "What's the good of an obedience-enforcing curse if it could just be washed off? No, no, no. I'm afraid the only way that poison's coming off before the new moon is if I lick it off him."

Bex blinked. "I'm sorry, but did you say 'lick it off him'?"

"It's a very specific sort of paint," the witch replied, looking at Kirok's towering, muscular, four-armed body with a wicked gleam in her blue eyes. "Please make sure he survives to come back for his cleaning. I'm *quite* looking forward to it."

By the time she finished, all the demons except Lys and Nemini were blushing to the roots of their hair. If Adrian had been here, Bex was certain he'd be dragging his hands over his face. She was smiling at that mental image when something heavy and warm slammed into her arm like a furry cannonball.

"*Oof*," she grunted, looking up just in time to see a pair of green eyes staring back. "Boston?" she said, leaning away from the extremely large cat that was suddenly sitting on her shoulder. "You're here too?"

"Of course I'm here," the familiar replied in an insulted voice. "You're sortieing into the afterlife, correct? That's where my witch is, so, naturally, I'm coming with you. I'm just borrowing your shoulder for a moment to give Bran something to aim at."

"Aim at?" Bex repeated in alarm. "Why is he aiming—"

Everything else she'd been about to say was lost in a loud *whoosh* as Adrian's raven-carved broom swooped out of the evening sky like a diving falcon. It missed Bex by a fraction of an inch, shooting past her shoulder before pulling up at the last second to finish in a hover position over the ground right in front of her feet.

"*Bran!*" Boston cried, ignoring Bex's startled gasping as he leaped off her shoulder as hard as he'd just landed to go bump noses with the broom. "So good to see you again! How was the flight from Seattle?"

The broom hovered silently while Boston nodded.

"That does sound dreadful," the cat said after several seconds of this. "I'm glad you made it here in one piece, *and* you brought what I asked for! Thank you."

He trotted down the broom's length to pull a large, oblong object out of the cone of bristles at the end with his teeth. Bex's first thought was that Bran had brought him one of those giant dock rats that were always scuttling around Seattle's piers. Then Boston began wiggling his paws through the loops on the front, and she realized it was a backpack.

A tiny backpack. For cats.

"Boston," Iggs said, desperately trying, and utterly failing, to hold in his laughter. "Is that a *cat pack*?"

"It's a *work* pack that my witch sewed specifically for *me*," Boston told him angrily. "And before you say another word, it's filled with things that are going to save our lives." He turned his head around to nudge the top of the pack open with his nose. "It's got all sorts of useful reagents collected from Adrian's Blackwood before Gilgamesh corrupted it, which I'm certain my witch will appreciate. Spell components for witchcraft are probably impossible to find in Heaven, and no one would be stupid enough to imprison a Blackwood without emptying his pockets." He smiled smugly. "Adrian will be overjoyed when he sees this!"

"I'm sure he will be," Bex said with a smile, crouching down beside the cat to get a better look in his bag. "I don't suppose you've got anything in there that could help us find Adrian's location."

Boston huffed. "What kind of slacker familiar do you think I am? Of *course* I've got finding spells tuned to my witch, though once I get close enough, I should be able to find him using only my nose. Bran also has his own means of locating Adrian, which is a good Plan B, though he's mostly coming along because he also wants his witch back."

The carved broomstick rattled furiously, and Boston gave it a sharp nod. "Well said, my friend, well said. We'll show Gilgamesh the vengeance of the Blackwood!"

"No one deserves it more," Agatha agreed, her previously flirtatious voice now as sharp as a knife. "No one escapes their karma forever, and Gilgamesh's wheel is heavy indeed." She nodded at Bex. "I think throwing the Queen of Wrath at him is quite fitting, considering the great anger his actions have built up over the years."

Bex dropped her eyes at once. As always, the urge to insist she wasn't the Queen of Wrath anymore was burning on her tongue, but she'd learned the hard way not to say such things in front of her demons, *especially* not Lys and Iggs. Horns or no horns, they needed her to be their queen, and Bex had always done what her people needed. Right now, that meant keeping her mouth shut, so she stood by with her lips dutifully sealed while the witches moved out of the way to allow Boston and the demons to form a circle around her.

"Okay," Bex said when everyone was in position. "We've got me, Nemini, Lys, Iggs, Kirok, Boston, and Bran. Is that everybody? No more last-minute additions?"

"Better not be," Lys grumbled. "This boat's full enough as it is."

"Let's do it, then," Bex said, putting her hand on the lust demon's shoulder. "When you're ready."

Just like in the café earlier, Lys gave her a pleading look. But while they didn't hold their opinions back in private, Lys never contradicted their queen in public. When Bex didn't back down, Lys's transformed face pulled into a determined mask as they reached down to grab the bound human with the bag over his head, who'd been wiggling in the grass at their feet this whole time.

The man yelped when Lys pulled the bag off, raising his tied hands as high as he could in a last-ditch effort to protect his face. Bex already knew what to expect, but she still glowered when she saw his tattooed fingers. The look of utter terror on his face, however, was quite enjoyable.

"Hello, little warlock," Lys said in a deadly voice. "Ready to do the job we discussed?"

"Hells no!" the man yelled, undulating his bound body like a worm in a desperate attempt to get away from them. "You said you were the wife of a sorcerer who needed a demon banished! Then, when I said I'd do it, you clubbed me over the head, tied me up, and dragged me out to…"

His voice trailed off as his eyes finally moved away from Lys to all the other figures standing around them.

"Great Gilgamesh," he muttered, his goateed face going pale. "Are you *all* demons?"

"Not the cat," Bex said, crouching in the grass beside him. When they were face-to-face, she pulled a small velvet bag out of one of her many cargo pockets and shoved it at the warlock's chest harder than was strictly necessary.

"Oof," he grunted when the bag hit his sternum. "What's that?"

"Fuel," Bex replied, pulling the string to open the bag so the warlock could see the quintessence glittering inside.

"I know the cabals are short on magic right now," she said. "So I'm giving you what you need to banish all of us to the Hells."

"You *want* to be sent to the Hells?" the warlock asked, flabbergasted. "Why?"

"If I told you that, I'd have to kill you," Bex replied with a smile. "We're not fans of your profession here, so I suggest you get to work before Lys decides it'd be more fun to gut you."

Lys punctuated that with a crack of their knuckles, making the warlock jump.

"I can certainly perform a banishment, if that's really what you want," he told Bex with a swallow. "But you'll have to untie my hands, and I'll need to know all of your true names."

"Ah, ah, ah," Lys said, waggling their finger at him. "You only need to know *one* of our true names. Banished demons can take anyone they want to the Hells with them if the passenger doesn't fight, though it's much more fun when they do."

The warlock scoffed. "That's not true."

"Of course it's true," Lys said. "I've done it. Where do you think the phrase 'drag me to Hell' came from? It's for demons who fight, and I've always loved a fight."

"That's ridiculous," the warlock insisted, though he sounded slightly less certain this time. "How can a common lust demon know more about the mechanics of banishment than a cabal-trained warlock?"

"Easy," Lys replied. "I'm older than you are, and, unlike all you 'trained' warlocks, I've actually been banished. Now, are you going to do this, or should I take the easy kill and go find someone who asks fewer stupid questions?"

The warlock looked over his shoulder for help only to cringe back to the grass when he saw the witches standing next to their forest, which was looking very foreboding in the evening light. That must have been enough to convince him there was no way out of this, because he lowered his head a second later, holding out his tattooed hands for Lys to untie before meekly opening the bag of quintessence.

"Which one of you will I be banishing?" he asked politely.

Lys dropped their human guise, shifting back into their true, towering form as they wrapped their dusky pink, leathery wings around the entire group. When at least one inch of their body was touching everyone, they answered.

"Lysanae."

The warlock's hooded eyes went huge. "Lysanae?" he repeated in a fear-choked voice. "Right hand of the Queen of Wrath?"

"That's my title," Lys said proudly, leaning forward until they were towering over the much shorter human. "Now put it to use, or I'll show you how I got it."

The warlock got to work in a panic, grabbing the quintessence out of the bag and shoving the only four coins Bex had managed to scrape together into his mouth all at once. He cracked them with one bite and began speaking the words of sorcery. He was going too fast for Bex to translate, but she heard the world *Lysanae* right before the ground split open under her feet, and a coil of chains shot out to drag Lys—and everyone Lys was holding—straight down into Hell.

Chapter 2

IN A LAVISHLY DECORATED, beautifully sunny, pure-white bedroom located in one of the most important, most coveted sections of the fourth tower of Gilgamesh's palace in the Highest Heaven, Adrian Blackwood awoke to a crushing weight on his chest.

Not a figurative weight. This was a literal twenty-five-pound lump of smooth-carved bone and hammered gold courtesy of the princess who'd slipped into his bed and curled up against him with her extremely heavy head resting on his chest. *Again*.

"I thought I told you not to do that."

"And I thought I could make you change your mind," she replied in the voice he was learning to hate. Bex's soft, warm, happy voice whispering intimately from the smiling lips of a creature that was not her.

Adrian clenched his jaw and wiggled out from under her, grateful once again that he'd gone to bed fully clothed. It'd been seven days since he'd stupidly fallen for his father's lies and gotten trapped here, and every night, there'd been an incident. He would have avoided going to bed all together if he could've, but there was no way to make bottled sleep in Heaven, and Adrian hadn't figured out enough sorcery yet to curse his body into wakefulness. He *had* figured out how to magically clean the muddy clothes he'd been wearing when he'd crawled out from under his quintessence-soaked heart tree to find Gilgamesh waiting like a smug tiger, so at least he hadn't been forced to strip yet, but that felt like small consolation when he had to pry the princess's white arms off his body like he was escaping a bear trap just to get out of bed.

"I don't understand why you're being so cold," the princess said when he finally got free, sitting up in the rumpled bed to look at him with the golden version of Bex's hurt eyes. "You loved it when I rested my head on you back at the Anchor."

"That wasn't you."

"Yes, it was," she insisted, her voice heating with that familiar Bex anger Adrian refused to acknowledge, because she wasn't Bex. "I proved it the day you arrived when you asked me all those questions. I got everything right, so why are you still acting like this? Why don't you believe I'm me?"

Adrian didn't dignify that with a response. He just picked up his black boots off the carpet and walked over to the white fur-covered ottoman in front of the white marble wardrobe full of elegant white-silk clothes he refused to wear. He sat down with a huff and stomped his boots onto his feet before turning to grab his black pointed witch hat off the white dresser. The hat had been a gift from his aunt Muriel for passing his coven tests. It had no magic of its own that he knew of, but just putting it on his head made Adrian feel more like himself. A feeling that instantly vanished again when he grabbed his enchanted coat off the wall sconce he'd been using as a coatrack.

It felt like picking up nothing at all. Adrian couldn't remember the last time his beloved black coat had been so light. It should've been brimming with useful curses, charms, and magical materials, but the very first thing the Crown Princess had done when she'd locked him in here was force Adrian to empty his pockets down to the seams. He'd tried his best to hide things from her, but the disguised queen who'd ripped the real Bex's horns off was thorough. Probably because Gilgamesh had told her the same thing Malik had told Adrian back when he was pretending to be a loving father: that a witch outside his forest was only as good as the spells in his pockets.

There were no spells in his pockets anymore. Adrian would've gladly sacrificed all nine of his remaining fingers to the Morrigan for even one of his trusty curses, but the goddess either couldn't hear him in Heaven or didn't want his new white blood, because no matter how much of it he offered, she never replied. He couldn't reach his forest either, thanks to the sharp-toothed seal Gilgamesh had placed over the hollow where his heart had been. He could still feel his actual heart beating far, far away, but he couldn't touch the roots that bound it or the magic of the Blackwood that flowed through them, which meant he was dead in the water. He was patting down his coat one more time in the vain hope that maybe he'd find a sap trap stuck to the lining, when the princess darted out of the huge white bed to wrap her arms around him.

Adrian jumped so hard he almost bashed his chin open on the crown of her carved, hornless head. Great Forest, he *hated* when she did that. Gilgamesh's princess was every bit as fast as the real Bex, but much less conscientious about her movements, or her strength. She was squeezing Adrian hard enough to bruise, and she didn't stop when he gasped in pain. If anything, the sound made her clench her arms even tighter, wrapping herself around his chest like a vise as she buried her cold, hard face in his wrinkled black shirtfront.

"Why are you ignoring me?" she whispered in Bex's hurt, shaking voice. "This was supposed to be our reward. We're supposed to be *happy*." Her head snapped up, the interlocking, cuneiform-marked gold rings of her eyes spinning as they focused on Adrian's face like camera lenses. *"Why aren't you happy with me?"*

"Because you're. Not. Bex," Adrian snarled, shoving her as hard as he could even though he already knew he wasn't strong enough to move her. "Having her memories doesn't make you her, because the real Bex wouldn't hurt me with her strength. She wouldn't hang on me or sneak into my bed after I explicitly told her not to, because the *real* Bex actually gives a damn what I think."

"But I do!" she cried, squeezing even harder. "I *do* care! You're the only one I care about anymore! You're supposed to be my *prince*!"

She was screaming by the end, but Adrian didn't reply. He already knew she wouldn't listen, so he kept his mouth stubbornly shut, letting his silence do what his arms couldn't until, finally, the princess pushed herself away.

"Why are you being so mean?" she sobbed, wiping her eyes pathetically even though she was a carved doll incapable of shedding tears. "I finally got what I wanted. Gilgamesh set me free of my endless burden. He let me put down my sword so I could live the life *I* dreamed of for once. This was supposed to be our happily-ever-after, but you aren't even trying. You've already made up your mind to hate me because you're not a noble prince at all. You're just a cruel, heartless *witch*!"

She started crying in earnest then, the biggest sign yet that she was nothing but a carved fake. The Bex Adrian knew hated for anyone to see her cry, and she'd *never* use tears to get what she wanted. He didn't know why Gilgamesh had bothered trying to pass this bad copy off as real if he was going to do such a terrible job on her personality, but who knew? Considering how unstable every princess seemed to be, maybe this was the best his father could manage.

It gave Adrian great pleasure to imagine the haughty Gilgamesh failing at something, but while he was never going to accept the princess as anything but an enemy, he still didn't like listening to her cry. He had work to do in any case, so Adrian turned his back on the sobbing parody of Bex and strode across his bedroom prison toward the golden door that led to the only other place in Heaven he was allowed to access: his workshop.

True to his word, Gilgamesh had provided his son with a lavish space to study the Queen of Pride's horns. The room on the other side of the golden door was bigger than Adrian's entire cabin, with towering, arched white ceilings, a polished white marble floor, and an entire wall of perfectly clear glass windows (unbreakable—he'd tried) overlooking the White City. The walls that didn't have windows were lined with white stone shelves containing solid-gold versions of every tool a witch or sorcerer might need, but no reagents, potion ingredients, cauldrons, brooms, or anything else that could be used to escape.

There was also a parchment scroll posted on the locked door to the hallway outside listing all the sorcery that had been temporarily banned for Prince Adrian's "safety," starting with teleportation. These limitations would be lifted when the prince finished repairing the Queen of Pride's horns, the pieces of which were spread all over the worktable at the center of the room like a giant unfinished jigsaw puzzle.

Adrian didn't even spare them a glance. He strode right past, walking straight through the giant workroom to the only thing in the whole place that wasn't white or gold: a little heap of bright-green needles carefully positioned in the workshop's sunniest corner under the windows.

Seeing them made Adrian smile for the first time since he woke up. It didn't look like much at the moment, but that little pile of green was a tree. A white pine sapling, to be precise, and it was Adrian's most prized possession. He'd gone through hell to get that tree. Not literally, but he had written a five-page petition to the Crown Prince's office explaining in triplicate why a tree was necessary to complete his work. His first petition had asked for three trees, the lowest number that could possibly be considered a grove, but that request had been denied. After a long back-and-forth where he'd been forced to make a point-by-point justification for why a witch of the *Blackwood* needed a *forest*, he'd finally been permitted one seed, a gold basin containing five cubic feet of sterilized soil, and a watering jug with ten gallons of nutrient-enriched liquid.

Not a bad starter kit for a houseplant, but it had still taken Adrian all of yesterday and no small amount of his quintessence blood to grow the seedling to its current three-foot height. That was pathetic compared to the monster trees he'd grown in twenty minutes using the same technique back in his forest, but growing anything up here was an enormous challenge. All those letters just to get one seed and a pile of dirt hadn't been the Crown Prince stonewalling him out of spite. They were real restrictions set eons ago by Gilgamesh himself for the preservation of the Eternal Kingdom.

It might be called Heaven now, but this place had originally been Paradise, the land of the gods. It had been Ishtar's land in particular, goddess of life, death, war, love, beauty, and—most relevant to Adrian's current situation—fertility. Anything that sprouted, germinated, or pollinated was a potential lever the goddess could use to pry herself out of her grave. Because of this, every type of plant, from ornamental gardens to sidewalk weeds to the slime that grew on the inside of wastewater tanks, was considered dangerous contraband. Procreative activities were also forbidden within the city for the same reason, as were all living creatures except Gilgamesh's chosen humans and their demon slaves, bodies of water larger than one liter, and all nonmagical fires.

Adrian didn't see how any place you weren't allowed to have sex, grow flowers, take a bath, or pet a cat could be possibly called Heaven, but such were the sacrifices required by an empire whose entire existence revolved around keeping the undying gods dead. They took it damn seriously up here too. There were so many anti-growth spells on the palace that just getting the pine tree to sprout had taken every bit of Adrian's magic, experience, and skill. He had it going now, though. The sap collectors he'd put in last night were full as well, which meant he was in business.

Peeking over his shoulder, Adrian reached down like a thief and began detaching the small gold finger bowls he was using as collectors from the cuts he'd made in the young tree's bark. There was no obvious reason to be so cautious. He could still hear the princess sobbing in the bedroom, and despite promising they'd work together, Gilgamesh hadn't set foot in the workshop since the night he'd locked Adrian in. That was fine with Adrian, of course, but the king's absence made him almost as nervous as his presence would have. Back in the Blackwood, Gilgamesh had made it sound like Adrian's work was the single most important thing in his entire empire. Now he was being an absentee boss, and while Adrian was sure his father was still keeping tabs on him through the princess's golden eyes, the whole situation felt very strange. What was the point of forcing Adrian into such a hard corner if his father was just going to leave him to his own devices? He hadn't even set a deadline. Adrian was just stuck in here with nothing to do until he finished. It almost felt like his father expected him to complete the horns out of boredom.

If that was the expectation, then Gilgamesh had made a grave mistake, because Adrian could always think of something else to do. He'd spent the first three days trying every spell he could think of to get a message out to Boston and his family. Those had all failed, of course, but that didn't mean he was done. He just had to get more creative. His plan for today was his most out-of-the-box solution yet. Also the riskiest, but prisoners who played it safe were prisoners who stayed caught.

Adrian was certainly ready to roll the dice. If he had to spend another night in that silent, bright-white box of a bedroom with an unstable doll-woman who wouldn't stop touching him, he'd go insane. Put it like that and the risk felt much more acceptable, allowing Adrian to keep his hands steady as he painstakingly scraped all the sticky, naturally antibiotic pine sap into the golden bowl his soup had arrived in yesterday. He'd just carried it over to the worktable where the Queen of Pride's broken horns were scattered when a teary voice called his name.

"Adrian?"

Adrian looked up with an irritated scowl to see the princess standing in the bedroom doorway with a covered golden tray in her white hands.

"The servants brought your breakfast," she said. "Do you want to come eat?"

Her voice was soft and apologetic, which meant he was getting the contrite princess today. That was better than the furious one who kicked over tables and screamed at him to love her, but he still didn't want to deal with it.

"Leave it," he said, ignoring the delicious smell of fresh coffee that wafted from under the tray's cover because he wasn't a dog who could be conditioned into obedience with food. "I'm busy right now."

"Are you finally getting to work on the horns?" she asked excitedly, her distraught tone completely flipping around as she dropped his tray on one of the workshop's empty tables and ran over. "That's fantastic! Your father will be so pleased."

Adrian shrugged and put his back to her, focusing all his attention on stirring the sticky sap with a metal file he'd found in one of the tool sets on the wall. He'd almost gotten it to the right consistency when the princess leaned her white head into his field of view.

"What's that yellow stuff?" she asked, wrinkling her perfect copy of Bex's nose. "It smells like air freshener."

"It's glue," he lied.

The princess tilted her head sideways to give him a golden-eyed look of shock. "You're *gluing* the Queen of Pride's horns?!"

"Do you know a better way of sticking broken things back together?" he asked, putting the bowl of sap down with a clatter before walking away from her to inspect the shelves that lined the workshop's far wall.

He'd already spotted what he was looking for yesterday, but there were so many golden tools and cuneiform-covered gewgaws that it took him a while to find it again. After a few minutes of shuffling, Adrian spotted it behind an enchanted set of jeweler's magnifying glasses: a gold-inlaid mahogany box containing a delicate set of woodcarving knives, awls, and chisels.

Those were all going to be useful, but what Adrian was really after was the box. He broke the lid off by whacking it across his knee, ripping all three tiny golden hinges out in one clean hit. He removed the rest of the metal ornamentation with the sharp

point of the wood awl until he was left with just the
mahogany. The ancient wood was so covered in
lacquer that Adrian could hardly make out the original
grain anymore, but despite all that, it was still the
product of a tree. Not a tree that grew anywhere he
was familiar with, but all forests were part of the Great
Forest, and that made it good enough.

"Why are you breaking things?" the princess
asked as Adrian carried his prize along with the
woodworking tools back to the worktable where he'd
left the sap. "If you needed a piece of wood, you
could've just asked me to get you one. Your father put
me here to help you, remember?"

Adrian *did* remember, which was why he hadn't
asked. He still hadn't figured out how much Gilgamesh
was able to see through her golden eyes, but there was
no way that white spybot wasn't reporting in. The less
she knew the better, in Adrian's opinion, which was
why he kept his mouth shut tight as he sat himself
down on an elegant white-and-gold-covered stool in
front of the windows, braced the wooden box lid
between his knees, and began to carve.

Approximately one hour later—it was impossible
to say for sure since Heaven's blinding light shone
from the sky, not from an actual sun that moved—he'd
whittled the thick cover down to a palm-sized carving
of a fluffy, long-haired cat. The ancient mahogany was
dustier and more prone to tear-out than the oak, pine,
and poplar he was used to working with, so it wasn't
his best carving. He must've done a good enough job,
though, because the princess's golden eyes widened
with a soft whir when he held the final product up to
the windows to inspect the grain.

"Is that Boston?"

Adrian nodded, too overcome with emotion to bother lying. Even when it was just a rough image, seeing his loyal familiar hurt more than he'd expected. Boston must be so disappointed in him right now. He'd warned Adrian over and over not to put so much trust in Malik, but Adrian had been flying high on his father's praise and hadn't listened. He was determined to get back home and apologize, and for that, Adrian only needed one more ingredient.

Placing the little, dark-brown carving carefully on its wooden paws, Adrian reached into his empty coat pockets and started scraping his fingernails against the lining. The Crown Princess's search had been very thorough, but no amount of pocket-emptying could ever entirely remove cat hair. He had to scrape every inch of the big pocket Boston liked to hide in plus three other pockets that had simply accumulated hair over time from being an everyday part of Adrian's wardrobe, but eventually he managed to collect a nice, fat, fist-sized cloud of Boston's long, black fur. He rolled it into a ball between his palms, and then he picked up the carving he'd just made and dunked it by the tail into the bowl of sap. When the whole cat was coated in sticky, piney glue, Adrian pressed it into the wad of fur he'd made, crushing the two together in his fist to make sure every inch of the little Boston was covered.

"*Ew!*" the still-watching princess cried, recoiling in horror. "What'd you do that for? Now your carving's ruined! All that sticky hair is never coming off."

Adrian certainly hoped not. The reason he'd requested a seed from the white pine in particular, aside from their very sticky sap, was because white pines were the most common tree in Massachusetts. There were over a million of them growing in the Blackwood's main forest, which made their sap a powerful connector to his home just as the fur he'd collected was a powerful connector to his cat.

By chaining those connections together, Adrian hoped to reconnect himself back to the roots of his witchcraft, because while he was currently cut off from his grove thanks to Gilgamesh's seal, Boston wasn't. *He* was still an active member of the Blackwood coven with a deep connection to the forest's web, and since Boston was connected to Adrian through oaths even older than the ones he'd sworn to become a witch, that meant Adrian was still connected to the Great Blackwood as well. He just had to use a different path.

It already seemed to be working. He could feel the sticky mash of sap, fur, and wood heating up inside his hand. The warmth was tiny compared to what he felt when he plunged his fingers into the loamy soil of his own grove, but it was still the closest to home he'd felt since he'd arrived. Even the sticky film the pine sap made on his skin was beautifully nostalgic, and Adrian clung to it as hard as he could, pressing the flat of his thumb against the cat's sharp-carved nose until the wooden point broke the skin.

The moment his new white blood touched the sap-and-fur-covered effigy, the tiny connection Adrian had felt exploded into something he could actually use. It still wasn't enough to cross the enormous gap between the lands of the living and the dead, but this was a bone-witch charm that was designed to be used on dead things anyway, so that didn't matter. All he needed was a link to the Great Forest that connected all things (provided by his fur-and-sap-covered wooden cat), magic (supplied by quintessence), and bones.

That last one required no substitutions. The worktable in front of him was covered with the shiny black fragments of the Queen of Pride's broken crown. Horns didn't technically count as part of the skeletal system, but the nice part about bone witchcraft was that its spells weren't picky. Any body part would work in a pinch, so Adrian reached hard through his connection to Boston's connection to the Blackwood and gave the spell a push of quintessence.

The whole worktable rattled in response. The princess rattled as well, her bone feet clacking against the marble floor as she jumped away in surprise. She jumped back a second later, her carved face lighting up as she stared at the broken pieces of horn, clearly expecting them to lift themselves off the table and start snapping back together, but that wasn't what this spell did. Adrian had no interest in repairing a stolen crown so his tyrant father could solidify his power. This spell only used the horns as a jumping-off point to look for Adrian's *real* objective.

Bex.

Once again, it was a link to a link to a link. Since the Crown Princess had emptied all of Adrian's pockets and he hadn't seen Bex in person in over a month, he didn't have anything of hers to use as the focus for a finding spell. These horns, however, belonged to her sister, and since Ishtar's daughters had all famously come from the same goddess, Adrian was hoping he could kludge it.

The bone-witch spell helped with that as well. Typical Witch of the Flesh finding charms like the one he'd used to locate Bex on the ferry had narrow focuses because they were meant to pinpoint the specific location of a living person. Bone-witch finding spells, on the other hand, were designed to locate corpses, which could be scattered all over the place.

Because they had to find so many parts, corpse-finding spells used much broader specifications. It wasn't uncommon for them to turn up items that were only vaguely connected to the deceased, such as the bones of relatives. Weeding out the false positives was usually the most tedious part of using the spell. This time, though, the errors were what Adrian was counting on, because the Queen of Pride had famously died during Gilgamesh's conquest of the Riverlands. That meant her bones were likely still scattered outside the White City, so any blips Adrian found *within* the walls had to be Bex. The *real* Bex, not the unhinged doll Gilgamesh had assigned to be his jailer.

Just thinking about it made his heart pound beneath his distant forest. Adrian hadn't seen what happened to Bex after his father dragged him away, but he was certain Heaven hadn't let her escape. He was also certain she wasn't dead because he hadn't fixed the Queen of Pride's horns yet. He'd only promised to do it to save Bex's life, which made her Gilgamesh's best leverage, and even when Adrian had only known him as Malik, his father had never been the sort to throw away leverage. Bex *had* to be alive, and since Gilgamesh wouldn't be dumb enough to send her home, she *had* to be imprisoned somewhere in Heaven or the Hells. So long as he knew those two facts, Adrian had everything he needed to find her.

His options after that were less certain, but Adrian was determined to figure it out because this whole mess was his fault. He was the one who'd stupidly fallen for his father's tricks and left Bex to fend for herself while he chased shortcuts. If he'd been less impatient, if he'd listened to Boston, if he'd made even one better choice, everything would be different. This whole disaster was his doing, but Adrian was going to make it right if it killed him. He'd find Bex's location, figure out how to get to her, and then the two of them would come up with an escape after he told her how sorry he was. He was already imagining what he'd say when the sap-and-fur-covered cat he'd been clutching suddenly leaped out of his hands.

Adrian jumped. That was a bigger reaction than he'd expected. Corpse-finding spells were usually lethargic, but his little wooden cat was rattling across the marble worktable like a haunted chess piece.

"What's it doing?" asked the princess, who was much closer than he'd realized.

Adrian didn't know. He'd never seen a reaction like this before, but his hopes were now sky-high. When he grabbed the cat to feel the results for himself, though, the sensation that came back wasn't the distant connection of a sister or even the powerful bones of a queen. The corpse-finding spell was excited because the body he'd commanded it to locate was *alive*. Now that he was clutching the sticky charm, Adrian could actually feel the target moving like a fish at the end of a line somewhere below his current location. Not "down on Earth" below. *Physically* below, as in under the ground beneath the palace.

Adrian went perfectly still, his new mirrored eyes going wider and wider as the full implications of what he was feeling hit him. The Queen of Pride *wasn't* dead. She was alive. Alive and *moving around* somewhere below him.

She had to be in the Hells, his scrambling brain realized. It was the only location that made sense. Now that he thought about it, Adrian had never seen a daughter of Ishtar that actually stayed dead, so her still being alive actually made sense as well. He'd just never considered the possibility before because the Queen of Pride was always depicted as being super-crushed-under-Gilgamesh's-foot dead, which was just plain gullible in hindsight. Gilgamesh lied about everything. Why wouldn't he lie about this? Especially since the story of him destroying the Queen of Pride was so much better for his image than a hornless queen still kicking around five thousand years after her supposed demise?

No, it made *total* sense that she was alive. It also changed everything, because that signal wasn't just for a hand. The tug Adrian was feeling through his charm was for an entire living, moving body. The only thing it felt like she was missing was her horns, which were right here in front of him. Adrian had literally been ordered to fix them, which meant that unlike Bex's horns, which were Gilgamesh-only-knew-where, he could actually give these back to her. He could repair the horns just like he'd been ordered, but instead of handing them to Gilgamesh, he could find the Queen of Pride and *put them back on her head*. If he could manage that, they'd have a new queen in the fight, one who *hadn't* been ground down over five thousand years of constant fighting. He'd be putting a new weapon back on the field! One who could help him rescue Bex and get them all out of here!

"You look happy," the princess said as Adrian's face split into his biggest smile since arriving here. "Did you figure out what you're going to do?"

"I figured out everything," Adrian said, clutching the dancing cat in his fist as he ran over to the workroom's writing table to grab a piece of parchment. He scribbled out a long list using the table's golden fountain pen, then turned and shoved the paper at the princess, who'd never stopped hovering behind him.

"I need you to get me these materials."

"Of course," the fake Bex said. "Helping you is why I'm here. When do you need all this by?"

"As soon as possible," Adrian said, looking into her golden eyes as he flashed his most charming smile. "I think it's time I took your advice and started acting like a prince. If you can gather all of that for me within the hour, I'll have the Queen of Pride's horns fixed before you know it, and then the two of us can take them to Gilgamesh together."

He was choking on his own shamelessness by the time he finished, but it worked like a charm. In the space of those two sentences, his princess went from sullen and suspicious to smiling so wide he was worried that her face would crack.

"I'll gather it all, my prince!" she cried, her golden eyes flicking back and forth as she read the list he'd given her. "Some of these are pretty restricted, but

I'll make the quartermasters hand them over. Wait for me while I find a servant!"

"I'll be right here," Adrian promised, tucking the still-dancing cat statue into his coat's front pocket. "This is the start of a new leaf for us. I hope you'll give it your all."

It didn't seem physically possible, but the princess's smile got even bigger. She leaped forward next, crushing Adrian in a brutal hug before dashing out the door like a shot. The joy of finally getting the affection she craved must've addled her magically-programmed mind, because the princess actually left the door hanging open behind her.

It was the first time Adrian had seen her make a mistake like that, but he didn't take advantage of it. Getting caught doing something suspicious now would undermine the act he'd just gagged himself to put on. He'd already made his move. Now he just had to play it through, so instead of bolting for the door she'd just left open, Adrian walked over to his breakfast tray and poured himself a cup of coffee from the gold carafe, fortifying his brain with caffeine for the massive puzzle of the queen's shattered horns waiting on the table behind him.

And at the bottom of his pocket, the finding spell kept buzzing like a trapped hornet, its sharp-carved cat nose pointing like an arrow at a spot way, way down and far to the west, beyond the walls of the palace.

Chapter 3

BEX HAD NEVER BEEN to the Hells in this lifetime. She was pretty sure she'd never been in *any* lifetime because Gilgamesh had made them after he'd used Anu's crown to banish her from Paradise. Drox would've been able to tell her for certain, but for once, Bex was glad to be alone in her head. She didn't want anyone to know that she was actually kind of excited to finally see the place she'd fought against all her lives.

She didn't want to insult Lys by looking eager, either, so Bex kept her face locked in a furious scowl throughout the entire banishment, which did feel uncomfortably like being dragged. It reminded her of the force that had pulled her out of Heaven after Enki's death, except this time, instead of falling with a weight tied to her feet, Bex felt like she was being sucked down a drain.

They all were. She could feel her demons trembling around her as an inescapable force pulled them faster and faster through a yawning emptiness Bex recognized as the gap between worlds. Gilgamesh must have put his city back in its original position, because the journey was much longer than when she and Adrian had crossed it on his tree. She was starting to worry about oxygen when the sucking pressure suddenly spat them out.

The first thing Bex checked when they landed was her feet. They'd been planning this assault since the first day they'd arrived in the Blackwood, but while everyone else seemed confident that Anu's banishment was tied to the name she'd lost when War tore off her horns, Bex had had her doubts. She definitely didn't feel like Rebexa anymore with no fire, no sword, and no ability to even touch her empty forehead without brushing the void that still lurked like a pit trap deep inside her. Still, thinking something probably wouldn't happen wasn't the same as actually being safe. She'd helped plan every step of this assault, but Bex hadn't known for certain that she wasn't going to arrive in the Hells and fall straight back down to Earth until her new boots hit the ground and it didn't crumble.

It took three solid breaths before the relief that she wasn't falling subsided enough for Bex to actually raise her head and look around. When she finally managed it, what she saw was not what she'd imagined.

Humans always described Hell as a flaming pit that reeked of sulfur, but the place they'd landed on looked more like a mountain cliff. The ground that hadn't broken beneath her combat boots was actually a wide stone ledge that looked over—not the terrifying void she'd ridden Adrian's tree through or the infinitely dark riverbanks where Nemini had caught her after she'd fallen off the walls—but a very high-up version of the sight she'd seen when she'd first stepped onto the golden chain that used to tie the Seattle Anchor to Heaven.

It was beautiful. Thinking that made her feel like a traitor, but there was no denying it. Over the edge of the cliff where they'd landed was a deep blue sea dotted with hundreds of tiny green islands, each with a glittering golden chain that ran up into the air like a wire. But while those were obviously the Anchors, Bex couldn't see where they attached. All the golden chains went past their position to vanish over the slope above them, which curved outward from where they were standing like a giant overhang.

The longer she stared at it, the more Bex felt that wasn't right. The sweep of rock above their heads that blocked the sky wasn't an overhang or a cliff or some kind of rock formation. The entire mountain they were standing on was *upside down,* with the broad base above their heads and peak way down below. The flat top—or bottom—must be the plain that Heaven sat on, which explained why all the chains went up there. But while she could see all the bridges to Heaven hanging above her like glittering golden contrails against the pale-blue sky, the Rivers of Death that usually flowed below them were nowhere to be seen. She was still looking for them when her ears picked up the distant sound of roaring water.

Following the sound took Bex closer to the cliff edge. Much closer than Iggs was comfortable with, given how he was hovering, but it worked. The moment her boots touched the lip of the stone ledge they were standing on, Bex saw the Rivers of Death glittering in the distance below.

Like everything else up here, they looked dazzling beautiful through the rosy lens of Gilgamesh's Paradise. All that bright-blue water shining with souls was nothing at all like the terrifying freezing reality she'd fallen into, but they did still follow the chains. Or, rather, the chains followed them, rising together from the glittering ocean dotted with the circular islands of the Anchors far below. They climbed most of the distance as a pair but split apart just before they reached the downward-pointing peak of the upside-down mountain. As Bex had already noticed, the golden chains kept going up toward Heaven, but the rivers veered off just before they reached Heaven to pour into a dark hole near the top of the upside-down mountain like a waterfall in reverse.

It hurt her brain to watch. Water was *not* supposed to move that way. No one must've told the rivers that, though, because they were gushing like floodwater in a thunderstorm. She was leaning farther out to see if she could get a look inside the cave all that magical water was vanishing into when Lys grabbed her shoulder.

"Could you *please* step away from the cliff edge?" they whispered, using their wings as a counterbalance to pull Bex back. "You're going to make Iggs hyperventilate."

Bex nodded and stepped away from the ledge at once.

"How real is all of this?" she asked, waving her hand at the dazzling archipelago of Anchors sparkling in the blinding white light that came from no sun she could see. "It feels like there's actual rock under my feet, but I know the Rivers of Death don't look like that, so is this all just an illusion?"

"No idea," Lys said as they let go of Bex's shoulder. "It's looked like this for as long as I've been alive, but I know the mountain we're standing on isn't actually wide enough to hold all Nine Hells, and the flat area up top *definitely* isn't big enough to hold the entire White City plus the remains of the Riverlands."

"So it's fake," Bex concluded.

Lys shrugged. "I don't know if that matters when it comes to Gilgamesh. Limbo also makes no sense, but it was still real enough to imprison an entire race of demons."

"I prefer to think of what we're seeing as an interpretation," Kirok offered from where he was standing next to Iggs far away from the cliff edge. "Gilgamesh rules it now, but this realm was originally created by and for the gods. It was never meant to make sense to mortal minds. That said, while the scale might not be accurate, most of the physical landmarks are as they appear. The Rivers of Death really do flow in through the bottom of the Hells, and Heaven truly is above us, which is why the chains keep going up."

Bex lifted her eyes hopefully to the glittering chains passing over their heads, which looked no thicker than power lines even though she knew they were actually big enough to drive a truck down. "Do you think we could jump up there and grab one for a straight line into Heaven?"

"I tried that once, actually," Lys said with a laugh. "But either the chains are a lot farther away than they look or they're not actually here at all, because the one time I said 'screw it' after a banishment and tried to fly up to them, my wings got so exhausted that I almost fell out of the sky before I even got close."

Bex scowled. She'd really been hoping for a shortcut, but Lys was the only one of them who could fly aside from Adrian's broom. If they couldn't reach the chains, then operation "Stairway to Heaven" was out. That was probably a good thing since walking up a golden bridge into the heart of Gilgamesh's city while the Anchors were still on lockdown sounded even more dangerous than their actual plan of sneaking into the Hells. And speaking of plans, since they were currently standing on the barren side of a dark stone mountain with no threat in sight, Bex decided it was a good time to make sure all their new additions were up to speed on exactly what it was they were about to attempt.

"Okay, everyone, listen up," she said, holding her hands over her head. "We got ourselves banished to the Hells for three objectives. One, retrieve my hand with my ring so that Drox and I can get back to cutting slave bands and freeing demons. Two, rescue Adrian and return him to his coven. And three, find my horns so I can get my powers back."

"Four, kick butt and take names!" Iggs added, reaching back to pat the knapsack of endless weapons that Felix had given them. "It's time Heaven remembered we're the rightful people of Paradise."

"I'm sure you'll get plenty of chances for that," Bex promised, pulling the box of comms out of her backpack and handing it to Lys so they could start passing out the sleek black earbuds. "Just don't forget that this is an intrusion and retrieval mission. I want to smash the Hells as much as the rest of you, but if we draw too much heat and get ourselves killed, it's over. I need you all to keep a cool head and stay on target. Got it?"

"Yes, my queen," replied everyone except Boston, who was busy digging through his cat pack.

"Good," Bex said, taking her own comm from Lys and fitting it into her ear. When the bud was safely locked in place and communications were established, she repacked the empty container into her backpack and turned to Lys.

"You're the only one of us who's been banished before. How do we get inside?"

"You'll see in a second," Lys promised, tilting their head to the side so they could wiggle the comm's black bud into their delicate pointed ear. "Banishments always land on the outside. I'm not sure if there's a legitimate magical reason for that or if warlocks are just assholes who like putting people's backs to literal cliffs, but the wardens have definitely noticed our arrival, which means we should be seeing a retrieval team soon."

"I'm astonished we haven't seen one already," Kirok said, scowling gravely at the stone wall of the mountain in front of them. "What's happened to discipline in the Hells that they leave a banished demon unattended for so long?"

Lys snorted. "I thought you weren't on their side anymore."

"I'm not," the general insisted, folding his top two bronze arms with a sniff. "It's the principle of the thing."

"Well, I'm glad they're late," Bex said, reaching down to make sure the explosive short sword Iggs had loaned her was still ready in its sheath at the small of her back. "Gives us time to sort ourselves out before—"

Her voice cut off as the cliff they were standing on began to shake. Bex's first thought was that the reason the guards were late was because she'd been recognized, and now some warlock in a command room was hitting a button to drop the cliff and kill them all from a distance. Fortunately, reality wasn't nearly so coordinated. The cliff was shaking because the side of the mountain directly in front of them was changing, the hard, featureless stone pulling back like a curtain to reveal an enormous pair of jet-black stone doors.

Bex took an involuntary step backward. So far, nothing about this trip had matched her expectations, but this? *This* was hellish.

The black doors were cut deep into the mountain's side like a wound. Their fronts were covered in carvings of terrified demons trying desperately to escape while chains pulled them back into the dark. The art was so realistic, Bex swore she could hear them screaming in the silence that suddenly covered the cliff.

"Well," Boston said nervously from his perch on Bran's broomstick, "that certainly drives home the point."

"Gilgamesh never was one for subtlety," Iggs agreed, gripping the worn strap of Solomon's Armory with both hands. "But at least now we know we're in the right place."

"There was never any doubt of that," muttered Lys as they switched out of their elegant, pink-winged true form into a lanky, dangerous-looking male body that reminded Bex of Desh. "Get ready. Retrieval teams always come out swinging."

Bex was about to ask how many they should expect when the air was split by the horrible sound of stone scraping against stone. The noise went on forever as the doors slowly opened outward to reveal a middle-aged man wearing the elegant white clothing of a Heavenly denizen accompanied by a squad of four war demons dressed in the same golden armor the Anchor Guards wore.

It was clearly intended to be a dazzling show of force, but Bex had already noticed that these war demons were not prime specimens. All four of them were in their bronze-skinned true forms, but only one was old enough to have grown all four of his arms. The other three had only two each, proof that they were barely more than teenagers.

That must be why they were wearing armor, she realized. Young war demons hadn't had enough time to develop their famously thick bronze skin. Even their flat, protective horns looked narrow and small beneath the visors of their golden helmets. Iggs could probably take all of them by himself, a thought that was definitely already crossing his mind from the smirk on his face. Bex was about to give the order to go ahead and roll 'em when Lys suddenly shot forward.

They moved so fast, Bex almost didn't turn her head in time to see the lust demon shoot past the first two guards to plant their knife—the same black sin-iron dagger that Desh had brought to kill Bex—in the warlock's chest. The human didn't even seem to realize what had happened. He just stood there, dumbfounded, watching his white shirtfront turn red with eyes that were already black from sin-iron exposure. When his body went limp a second later, Bex couldn't say if it was from the knife in his heart or the poison in his blood. Whatever it was, he was dead within five seconds of walking out the door. His guards were still gaping in shock when Iggs slammed into them like a truck.

He wasn't the only one. Kirok was also in there throwing punches with all four of his fists, which were *way* bigger than any of the baby war demons'. By the time the guards realized what was happening, all four of them were face down under Iggs's boot and Kirok's dinner-plate-sized hoof.

"Great job," Bex said, sliding the short sword she hadn't even had time to swing back into its sheath. "That was so fast I almost blinked and missed it."

"I'm sorry it had to be this way at all," Kirok said, easing up on the hoof he was using to crush the only actually mature war demon into the stone. "Despite what our queen's betrayal has forced us to do, war demons are slaves the same as any other demon. The vast majority of us do not fight willingly. Just look at these children's necks."

He leaned down to hook a finger under the biggest war demon's metal collar, pulling back his golden armor to reveal a thick black ring of sin iron wrapped tight around the young demon's throat.

"You see?" Kirok growled as he let the boy go. "This place is a Hell for all of us. These children didn't have a choice. Please don't judge them too harshly, great queen."

"I'm not judging them at all," Bex said, giving the terrified-looking demons a smile. "They could've yelled the alarm the moment their warlock went down, but they held their tongues. That's as good as helping in my book."

"We'd help more if we could," said the smallest war demon from his position under Iggs's left boot. "You're the rebel queen, right? The one Gilgamesh spared because Prince Adrian begged him?"

Bex winced at the mention of Adrian's name after the hated title *Prince* then winced again when she saw how the young demon was looking at her. It felt every kind of wrong to meet that hopeful look when she had no horns or royal name or divine sword to cut him free. Still, Bex had been doing this queen thing for a long time now, and she knew exactly what reply was needed.

"I am Rebexa," she lied. "Queen of Wrath and Ishtar's Sword."

The young demon's dark eyes were huge by the time she finished. "I knew it!" he cried, thrashing against Iggs's weight as he tried to get closer. "The old folks always said you'd come for us! So is it true? Have you finally come to free the Hells?"

Bex dropped her eyes at once. Hoo boy, how to answer that? She was still struggling for the right thing to say when Kirok reached down and snatched the boy's helmet off to cuff him behind the horns.

"You do not ask questions of a queen," the old general snapped. "Now get up and get out of that armor. Quick now!"

The war demons looked disappointed, but they did as they were ordered, taking off their golden armor and piling it on the ground at Kirok's feet as fast as they could. They stole glances at Bex the entire time, and eventually she couldn't take it any longer.

"Let me get those collars off you, at least," she said, walking over.

She wanted to give them totally clean necks, but she couldn't burn their slave bands without Drox. She should still be able to cut the collars off their necks with the sin-iron dagger, though. When she looked over to ask Lys if she could borrow their knife, however, the lust demon was still crouched on top of the fallen warlock.

The human was long dead, but Lys still hadn't stopped stabbing their black knife into his chest. They were raising their arms to stab him again when Bex stepped forward to grab their elbow.

"It's okay," she whispered when they jerked. "It's okay, Lys. He's dead."

"He can't be dead," Lys growled in a voice Bex had never heard from them before. "He hasn't paid enough yet. Do you know how many times I was banished back to this place? What warlocks like this one did to me? To *all* of us?" Their still-raised arms quivered in Bex's grip as Lys bared their small fangs. "I shouldn't have killed him so fast. I should've made him *hurt.*"

"We will," Bex promised, using her still-superior strength to pull Lys toward her until the lust demon lost their balance and toppled into her arms. They landed against her chest with a sob, dropping the black dagger at last so they could wrap their arms around her.

"It's okay," Bex said, doing her best to copy Adrian's soothing tone as she petted the soft hair between Lys's short horns. "You're safe, Lys. I've got you. They can't hurt you anymore."

It felt so odd, comforting the person who'd been her parent multiple times over. It must have been the right move, though, because Lys clung to her like a child. Their body shifted as they bawled, becoming smaller and younger as they clung to their queen. The outburst lasted less than a minute before Lys pulled it back together, but Bex didn't let them go. She held on as tight as she could, squeezing Lys into her body until they finally went limp in her arms.

"Sorry," they whispered after a long silence. "I didn't realize it would hit me that hard."

"There's nothing to apologize for," Bex insisted. "You have every right to be angry, but I swear we're going to fix this. I'm going to get back my sword and my fire, and then we'll rip this place open like a rotten log. We'll tear down Heaven and smash the Hells, and none of Gilgamesh's lackeys will ever have the power to hurt you again. I swear it, Lysanae."

That was a reckless oath to make when they were only supposed to be here for a limited mission. It must've been the right one, though, because Lys let out a long, relieved breath.

"I believe you," they said, pulling back just enough to lower their horns. "I've always believed, my queen."

Bex knew they did. Lys had always been her most steadfast supporter, but Bex herself was having second thoughts. She'd *just* ordered everyone to stay on mission. It was the only sensible strategy, because no matter how much they all hated this place, they couldn't defeat the Hells with five people, a cat, and a sentient broom. This was supposed to be a stealth intrusion, dammit, but when Bex felt Lys start shaking against her again, all she could think about was how she was going to tear this whole place down with her teeth.

That was not a good mindset for what was supposed to be a precise, disciplined mission, but Bex wasn't the only one feeling it. Iggs was already showing off his bag of weapons to the young war demons and bragging about how much damage he was about to do. The kids were eating it up, and honestly, Bex couldn't blame them. If she'd still had her fire, she'd already be blazing with fury. That sort of power was beyond her reach now, though. She'd gone from her demons' champion to their weakest link. If she was going to lose her head and plunge in with no sword, no fire, no plan, and no reincarnations to pick her back up when she inevitably failed, she might as well jump off the cliff now and save everyone the trouble.

That angry thought was enough to kick some sense back into her. But while Bex was determined to be nothing but mature, strategic, and responsible from this moment forward, there was no reason not to help the demons right in front of her. She kept holding Lys until they stopped shaking, and then she scooped the sin-iron knife off the ground, cleaned the warlock's blood off it, and walked back over to the four war demons Kirok and Iggs were keeping an eye on.

"Hey," she said, striking a deliberately casual tone in the hope that the new demons would forget they were talking to someone who was supposed to be an all-powerful daughter of Ishtar. "You guys ready to get your collars off?"

All four of them bowed their horns at once. "Great queen," said the biggest. "Thank you for your generous offer, but we couldn't possibly—"

"*Yes!*" cried one of the younger ones, snapping his head up to give Bex a desperate look. "Get this horrid thing off me!"

"Brother, no!" the four-armed demon snapped. "If the warlocks see—"

"They're going to punish us anyway," the young one argued. "We let our warlock get killed. They're going to shove us into the smelters no matter what, so I'm not going to miss getting this stupid poison ring off my neck for once in my life."

The other two were nodding furiously by the time he finished, but the one who looked the most moved was Iggs.

"No one's getting shoved into anything," the wrath demon said fiercely. "My queen is the Wrath of Ishtar! As soon as she gets her hand back, she's going to—"

"Iggs," Bex said quietly.

Iggs snapped his mouth shut, but the fiery light didn't go out of his red eyes as he came over to hold the war demon's sin-iron collar while Bex cut.

It was *hard* work. Drox cut sin iron like paper, but he was a divine blade forged by Enki himself. Lys's four-inch sin-iron knife looked like it'd been beaten into shape with a rock. It was technically capable of cutting the collars, but Bex had to push with all of her—and all of Iggs's—strength to actually drive it through.

While they were working, Kirok interviewed the boys one by one. He mostly asked about patrol patterns and security, but also how things were in the Hell of War and who was in charge. Bex was focusing too hard on not letting the knife slip and accidentally cutting someone's head off to listen, but she was certain Kirok would tell her. He might not officially be her general anymore, but it was impossible to keep that man from giving reports. Sure enough, when all four war demons were finally out of their collars and rolling around on the ground for the sheer joy of being free, Kirok walked over with a salute.

"At ease," Bex said, sitting down on the stone to catch her breath after all that brute-force metal cutting. "What's the situation?"

"Better than expected," Kirok replied, folding his huge bronze body into a crouch so he wouldn't have to talk down to her too much. "I mostly asked them why they were here. Guarding the Hells is usually done by constructs who don't need shift changes and feel no empathy toward the slaves."

Iggs made a disgusted sound, but Bex was smiling.

"I bet I know why there's no constructs," she said. "I must've slagged them all during my fight last week."

Her fellow wrath demon leaned down and gave Bex a high five for that one, but Kirok's bronze face was still grim.

"You destroyed many," he acknowledged. "But even if you'd melted Gilgamesh's entire army, the Hell of War's forges are designed for instant troop replenishment. They should've produced enough new constructs to at least bring the Hells back up to operational standards by now, but the boys told me that all the young demons are still on emergency Hells duty *and* they're running on a skeleton staff."

"That's good news for us," Iggs pointed out.

"Yeah, but why is it happening?" Bex asked. "Why aren't they making more constructs?"

"I asked that exact question," Kirok replied, glancing at the four young war demons, who'd moved to the far side of the cliff where they were now sitting with their legs dangling off the edge, staring out into the sky. "Unfortunately, they didn't know. All they could tell me was that Gilgamesh has had the forges in the Upper Hells running nonstop. They don't know what he's making since they're not on forge duty, but it's not constructs."

Bex frowned. No constructs and skeleton crews of baby war demons working guard duty was great news for them, but she did *not* like the idea that Gilgamesh was cranking out thousands of unknown somethings.

"What's that bastard king up to?"

"No way to know that except to go and see for ourselves," Kirok said as he straightened back up. "We should proceed with the mission and see what we find. The Hell of War is the last Hell before the gate to Heaven. If your crown is in Gilgamesh's palace as assumed, we'll have to pass by the forges no matter what. Maybe we can learn something."

"So long as we don't get too far off target," Bex said, pushing back to her feet as well. "My horns are the biggest throw of this whole mission. We need to stay focused if we're going to get up there without raising the alarm. Speaking of, how're we doing?"

That last question was directed at Iggs, who sighed. "Not as great as I'd hoped," he confessed, pointing at the pile of golden armor the captured guards had stripped off. "The original plan was for us to crush a construct, put me inside the clockwork body, and then I'd march the rest of you into the Hells as slaves while Lys played our warlock, but..."

"But what?" Bex asked. "Still sounds like a good plan to me, especially since we've got four suits of armor now."

"Except for the part where they're all tiny," Iggs said, holding up one of the golden chest plates in despair. "This thing barely fits over my horns! War constructs are big enough to fit my entire body inside, but if I put on one of these suits, I'm going to look like a dad in his kid's Halloween costume. Also, my skin's not bronze." He shook his head. "Unless all the warlocks in the Hells are blind, there's no way we're fooling anyone."

"I can wear the four-armed set," Kirok volunteered.

"No way," Iggs snapped. "That thing's half your size! Where're you going to put it? On your arm?"

"They might not be big enough, but we have got four of them," Bex reminded him. "I'm sure we can cobble something usable out of all those pieces."

Iggs winced. "We're going to look stupid."

"So make it look better," Bex told him with a smile. "You brought your art kit, right?"

"Yeah, but this is a lot more complicated than painting fake slave bands." Iggs looked at her pleadingly, but Bex just kept smiling, and eventually he sighed.

"I'll see what I can do."

"I'll help," Bex offered, grabbing the armor off the ground. "Let's do this quick before someone notices that warlock didn't come back."

Iggs nodded and bent down to grab a huge handful of the golden armor pieces, bringing them over to Bex so they could get to work.

It took a lot of bending and some pretty creative placement, but eventually they managed to spread four suits of too-small armor over two demons. It would've been easier to just do Kirok, but Iggs's wrath-demon horns were a dead giveaway. If they just made him the guard, though, then Kirok would have to play the prisoner, which would make them stand out even more since he was gigantic, gleaming bronze, and apparently pretty famous. He'd claimed to have been just a normal trainer, but all the young war demons were staring at him like he was a rock star.

Under any other circumstances, Bex would've been impressed. On a stealth mission, though, Kirok's surprise star power was a serious liability. She and Iggs covered him up as best they could, tilting the helmet to cover his face and patching the gaps in his too-short armor with gold paint from Iggs's kit. The result looked decent from a distance, but up close it was another story. It was still better than Iggs's though.

They'd used up most of the best pieces on Kirok, which turned out to be a mistake since Iggs was just as big and had *much* taller horns. He also had only two arms, which was a serious problem for someone pretending to be a war demon. By the time they'd used up all the armor, Bex was seriously starting to worry about their ability to pull this off, but she should've had more faith in Iggs's resourcefulness. After a lot of digging, he found a bunch of brass artillery shells in the bag of endless weapons Felix had given them and pried the casings off to get extra metal.

The result was actually pretty awesome. It would never survive close inspection, but the gleaming shell casings really did look like golden armor on a passing glance, and since passing glances were the only attention most warlocks gave their demons, that was good enough. It was definitely less eye-catching than wrath-demon horns. The only downside was how long it had taken to make.

By the time Kirok and Iggs were both ready to go, their team had been on the exposed banishment platform for forty-five minutes. Lys had been standing guard at the doors from minute five, ready to jump any investigation teams that showed their faces, but no one did. The dark hall on the other side of the horrifying doors was still completely silent, which was almost scarier than being swarmed.

"I don't understand," Lys said at last, turning to look at Bex with the scowling face of the dead, white-robed warlock whose identity they'd stolen for the intrusion. "We killed a banishment retrieval team. We should be up to our necks in trouble by now. Where in the Hells is everyone?"

"It's probably the staffing problems Kirok was talking about," Bex said as she banged her elbow against the top of Iggs's golden helmet to wedge it down over his tall horns.

"I think you mean rank incompetence," Lys growled, crossing the warlock's arms with a scowl. "If I'd known security had gotten this slack, I would've suggested invading the Hells years ago."

"I believe we have been blessed with a unique set of circumstances," Kirok said, holding himself with such confident military precision that Bex was hard-pressed to notice how badly his armor fit. "Clearly, Ishtar favors our mission."

"I wouldn't say no to some divine intervention," Bex agreed, grabbing one of the collars she'd cut off the war demons and handing it to Iggs so he could bend it around her neck.

"Okay," she said when the awful-feeling metal was wrapped around her neck tight enough to look real but not so tight that she couldn't get it off again. "Everyone remember your roles. Iggs and Kirok, you're our guards. You also have the worst costumes, so I want both of you to stay in the back. Lys, you're our warlock and the only one who can actually take scrutiny, so you're on point. Do you have everything you need for that, by the way?"

"I should," Lys said, pulling a piece of elegant and only slightly bloody paper out of the pocket of their new white robes. "I grabbed this off the warlock before I shoved his body off the ledge. It was the only thing in his pockets, so I'm pretty sure it's his warden pass."

"Pretty sure?" Iggs asked in alarm. "Why only 'pretty sure'? Don't you read cuneiform?"

"That doesn't mean I can make heads or tails of Gilgamesh's stupid poetry," they snapped, holding up the paper, which was covered from edge to edge in gleaming gold markings. "This whole thing's nothing but Ancient Sumerian 'thees' and 'thous,' *and* it's written in calligraphy." They shook their head as they returned the paper to their pocket. "It'll probably be fine. No one actually reads this stuff. I'll just flash the badge and bully my way through any problems."

That wasn't what Bex wanted to hear, but "flash the badge and bully through" was how Lys got them into most places, so she wasn't too worried. It was the combined effect of all their hack jobs that had her really scared. Even her role playing the prisoner was compromised by the fact that she had no horns. She'd brought a headband from an online costume store with some fake devil points that looked a lot like lust-demon horns after a little paint, but nothing could cover up the fact that they had no magic. Any demon who looked too hard at her head would know her horns were fake, but it was the best Bex could do on a week's notice.

They were *all* doing their best. If they'd had months to prepare, Bex was sure they could've done better, but that would've meant leaving Adrian alone up here for months as well. It also would've meant giving Gilgamesh more time to prepare and her own people more time to starve in the wilderness outside the Blackwood. None of that was acceptable, so here they were, doing their best with the time they'd had. Bex just hoped it was enough.

"Let's do this," she said, sliding the fake horns into her hair. She'd just gotten them straightened and was about to step through the door when Bex realized she'd forgotten something.

"Wait, where's Nemini?"

"I brought her in with us," Lys said, looking around the cliff with the warlock's concerned scowl before pointing over Bex's shoulder. "There she is."

Bex turned around to see Nemini standing at the farthest side of the cliff. She hadn't said a word since they'd arrived, but that was pretty normal for her. The weird part was *how* she was standing.

Nemini was perched so close to the edge that Bex was shocked she hadn't already fallen off. She leaned even farther out as Bex watched, curving her body away from the doors to the Hells like she was trying to avoid an oncoming train. It was strange behavior even for her, and Bex walked over with a scowl.

"Nemini? You okay?"

"That depends on what form of 'okay' you're asking about," the void demon replied, staring down at the glittering sea full of Anchors like she was seriously considering jumping. "I'm not in any physical discomfort, but this place is worse than I'd anticipated."

Bex actually thought the Hells had been shockingly easy so far, but she didn't want to tell Nemini her feelings were wrong.

"Do you want to stay out here and watch the kids?" she offered, tilting her head at the four war-demon guards who were still sitting on the cliff talking and laughing like a bunch of teenagers skipping school.

Nemini's shoulders rose in a long, shaky breath. "No," she said, stepping back from the edge at last. "I agreed to come here with you, so I will see it through."

"Glad to hear it," Bex said with a relieved breath of her own. "You're on scout duty, then. Can you do your shadow thing down that tunnel and make sure there's not a giant ambush waiting for us?"

She pointed at the deep black hole beyond the terrible doors, but Nemini was already gone, vanishing between one blink and the next.

"Guess that's a yes," Bex said, looking around for the last of their loose ends. only to spot his furry tail lashing in the same spot where Lys's banishment had dropped them out originally.

"Boston!" Bex called, jogging over. "Come on, it's time to go."

"Almost done," the cat replied, his black, whisker-covered face set in a deep scowl as he nudged what appeared to be a pile of yard trash artfully arranged inside a circle of twine.

"What's that?"

"A finding charm of my own creation," Boston explained as he nudged one of the seemingly random leaves slightly to the left with his paw. "Since Adrian and I are so closely connected, I was able to combine the strongest elements of all seven finding charm variations into one super spell that should cover every possible parameter. Observe."

He grabbed the end of the twine circle in his teeth and pulled it, closing the noose around the pile of plant parts until they were tied together. It looked like a leaf-and-stick corsage at first, but as he kept pulling, the bundle changed shape until suddenly Bex was staring at a leaf-art miniature of Adrian.

"That's incredible," she said, getting down on her knees for a better view. "It looks just like him. You even got his hat."

"It's the best effigy I've ever made," Boston informed her. "I crammed it with every personal element I could think of—Adrian's hair, feathers from his pillow, samples of his handwriting, five drops of his blood from before it turned white, crumbs from the last piece of food he ate, the *works*." He thumped his tail proudly. "Not bad for someone with no opposable thumbs, eh?"

"You're amazing," Bex agreed, leaning even closer. "Can we talk to him through it?"

"No," the cat said sadly. "A speaking spell requires an actual witch, not a moonlighting familiar. I still think I did a good job, though. He might not be able to talk, but my little Adrian knows exactly where his big brother is. See?"

He nudged the doll with his nose, and sure enough, the little effigy rose to its feet and pointed its fir-needle finger at the mountain above them.

"Wow," Bex said, legitimately impressed. "Can he feel if we touch him?"

"It's not a voodoo doll," Boston snapped. "That's a completely different spell. Mine is much more useful. All we have to do is follow where the effigy points, and he should lead us straight to the real thing."

The little Adrian nodded and pointed even more vigorously at the base of the upside-down mountain above them, and Bex's giddy heart began to sink.

"I guess that means he's up in Heaven, huh?"

"More than likely," Boston agreed, squinting his green eyes at his spell. "It looks like he's moving, though, which is a good sign. If he's got that much room to walk around, he's probably not locked up in some Heavenly prison."

Bex prayed to Ishtar that that was true. If Gilgamesh had been foolish enough to let his youngest son wander freely around the palace, then Bex was certain that Adrian was already up to his witch hat in escape plans. That was going to make rescuing him *much* easier, but they had to get to Heaven first, which meant it was time to get this plan on the road.

"All right," Bex said, rising to her feet. "Let's do this. Boston, can you keep yourself hidden?"

"Of course," Boston replied with a huff as he tied the little leaf Adrian to Bran's carved handle using the loop of twine that held him together. "What sort of cat do you think I am?"

"The best sort," Bex assured him as she checked to make sure her fake horns were straight and the cut in the slave collar was still hidden behind her hair. When everything was exactly where she wanted it, Bex ordered the four war-demon kids to keep slacking out here in the sunlight and signaled her team to move out, hanging back to let Lys's warlock take point as they marched through the terrifying gates into Hell.

Chapter 4

It'd been impossible to see from out on the bright cliffside, but the tunnel that led into the Hells was just as horrible as the doors outside. Also absurdly enormous. The arched ceiling was twice the height of even the tallest transformed wrath demon, and the walls were so far apart that the five of them could've walked side by side with room to spare.

The proportions were absolutely ridiculous for what was essentially a connector tunnel, but the longer Bex thought about it, the more convinced she became that that was the point. This tunnel hadn't been made to efficiently transport banished demons back to the Hells. It'd been designed to dominate and oppress, and by those measurements, it succeeded spectacularly.

Just like the doors leading in, every inch of the gigantic, black-stone walls was covered in carved reliefs of demons being punished. Some were being whipped by warlocks while others burned in giant fires. Sometimes they were shown being tied to posts and carved open while they were still alive; other times they were simply cut into pieces that the sobbing survivors were forced to sort into piles.

Each torture was uniquely horrible and rendered in stomach-churningly lifelike detail. Bex was just glad they were carvings and not paintings. If she'd had to see all that torture in color, she would've lost her lunch.

She was already losing her cool. Even if it was just art, the sight of all those demons being abused while Gilgamesh's warlocks watched and laughed sent her fury into overdrive. If she'd still had her horns, her bonfire would be filling the tunnel right now. Thankfully for their stealth mission, Bex's smoldering was purely emotional. She hadn't produced so much as a candle flame since she'd lost her horns, and no matter how angry she felt, that didn't change as they made their way to the doors at the awful tunnel's end, which were carved in a giant depiction of Gilgamesh.

The symbolism was as subtle as a kick to the face. The Eternal King's image was twenty times the size of the largest tortured demon. He had Anu's crown on his head and Ishtar's sword in his hands, and there were nine grotesque female figures with huge horns kneeling at his carved feet. That was blatantly false since Pride was broken and Wrath had *never* kneeled, but propaganda didn't need to be accurate to work, and as much as Bex hated to admit it, it *was* working. Between the tunnel's oppressively giant scale and the hopeless imagery, their whole group was quiet and downcast by the time Iggs and Kirok managed to push open the giant doors at the end.

Bex's hand went instinctively for her weapon as the path opened, but there was nothing to grab. Slaves didn't get weapons, so she'd moved the explosive short sword into her backpack. This left her with nothing to hold on to, so she focused on moving forward instead, walking practically on Lys's heels as she stepped through the door into the most impressive cavern she'd ever seen.

Bex stopped short, her no-longer-glowing eyes going wide. From the little Lys had told her about their time in the Hells, she'd always imagined it as a big cave full of fire. That was technically what was in front of her right now, but she'd never realized it would be so *big*.

They were standing on a ledge at the top of the outer wall of a circular cavern the size of a city. Not a small city, either. This thing was as big as downtown Seattle. Bex couldn't even see the other side thanks to the haze of smoke from the giant fires that lit the place. They burned everywhere—in metal braziers that hung from the cavern's arched stone ceiling, in troughs that ran along the walls, in big torch stands she could see burning like stars through the haze on the floor far below—*everywhere*. All that dancing orange light made it look like the entire cavern was on fire, but the air was cold, damp, and acrid with smoke, so much so that her entire crew started coughing the moment they opened the door.

Even Bex, who was used to fire, nearly hacked a lung out. She was still wiping the tears out of her eyes when she finally got enough usable air into her lungs to push past Iggs and look for her people. Given how many demons were supposed to live in the Hells, she'd thought they'd be everywhere, but Bex didn't see anything but smoke-blackened rocks. As she looked harder, though, she slowly realized that the sooty, hunchbacked shapes below them weren't stones. They were her people.

The sight made her stumble back. Bex had seen plenty of demons in rough shape before, but the ones she'd freed on Earth had been mostly house slaves and guards. It wasn't uncommon for them to be beaten and malnourished, but they'd still always been recognizable. The figures moving below her now, though, looked more like dirty little shadows than Children of Ishtar. Bex couldn't even tell what type of demons she was looking at, but there were *tons* of them.

When she'd first stepped into the firelit cavern, Bex had assumed the walls here were stone like the ones she'd seen outside. As she stared down at the wretched demons, though, she realized all the cracks and crevices she'd thought were natural formations were actually buildings. The circular walls of the giant cavern were honeycombed with thousands of tiny caves. They were stacked on top of each other like termite holes with no pipes or ventilation or safeties of any sort. The only paths connecting them were climbing routes made by cutting handholds into the stone, some of which went upside down in places. It was a basically vertical slave shantytown, and Bex wasn't the only one who hated it.

"Is that where they made demons live?" Iggs asked in a deadly voice. "Those *holes?*"

"The lucky ones live in holes," Lys replied in a tight, hard voice that didn't match the sneering face of the warlock they were impersonating. "I'll have you know that a spot on the wall is premium property. The less fortunate sleep five to a bunk in the slave barracks on the ground level."

"You're kidding," Iggs said.

"I wish I was," Lys replied with a mirthless smile. "Welcome to the Middle Hells."

"Middle Hells?" Bex repeated, confused. "I thought this was the Hell of Lust. Shouldn't that be where you were banished to?"

"This is the Hell of Lust," Lys said, waving the warlock's arm at the giant space in front of them. "Or at least it used to be. This cavern was originally five separate caves. As the demon population grew, though, Gilgamesh decided that maintaining five individual Hells for the most commonly requested demon slaves after War was inefficient, so he combined our prisons into one giant cave and dubbed it the Middle Hells."

"That sounds even less efficient," Iggs argued. "Wasn't he worried about rebellion?"

"No," Lys said bitterly, "because the demons down here don't rebel. We can't when all our necks are bound with slave bands *and* sin-iron collars *and* we're forced to work sixteen hours a day on just enough food to keep us from actually dying." They crossed the warlock's arms over their chest. "There's a reason so many demons volunteer to be slaves on Earth."

Bex could see it. Again, she'd seen plenty of abused slaves, but even the worst warlock slave quarters hadn't been this bleak. She could barely see the demons climbing over the walls below them through the grime, but the ones she could make out looked like skeletons with horns.

"How many demons are here?" she asked.

"Who knows?" Lys replied with a shrug. "It's not like Gilgamesh posts his census data, but it's a lot. The Middle Hells combined the Hells of Lust, Fear, Sorrow, Hate, Envy, and Greed. Hate's not terribly popular for obvious reasons, but the rest are all considered useful slaves, so the warlocks make sure to keep our populations high."

They frowned, tapping the blunt chin of their stolen face. "I'd estimate there's around five hundred thousand demons in the Middle Hells at any given time. That number can dip if there's been a famine or a plague recently, but it looks pretty full right now."

It looked *horrible*. Bex still hadn't caught a glimpse of the cavern's floor through the haze of choking smoke, but she wasn't holding out hope that it'd be better than the walls. Nothing about this place was acceptable, and the longer she looked at it, the more she wanted to burn it down.

"Let's get going," she growled. "Before I do something that blows the mission."

Lys didn't look like they'd mind that, but they followed their queen's command, leading Bex by the collar as befit the slave she was pretending to be, with Kirok and Iggs, their two "guards," following close behind. Nemini was probably close as well. As usual, though, Bex couldn't spot her. She couldn't see Boston or Bran either, which felt like a good sign. If half their party was so good at hiding that they didn't even need disguises, maybe they could pull this off after all.

She'd thought they'd have to climb down one of the terrifying handhold paths the slaves had cut to access their vertical housing, but Lys led them to a switchback staircase a few feet down the ridge patch that Bex hadn't noticed in the gloom. She supposed it made sense that the warlocks would have their own way down, but it still pissed her off that they'd carved this for themselves while forcing the slaves to climb slick handholds up a sheer cliff with no rope just to go to bed. She was still growling about the completely unnecessary cruelty of it all when they finally got low enough to see the floor through the smoke.

That stopped her short. She'd seen the torches glittering on the giant floor through the smoke, so she'd already guessed it was big, open, and flat, but this was the first time Bex realized it was flooded. The entire bottom of the city-sized cavern was covered in a foot of dark, sluggishly-flowing water with demons kneeling in it. They were chained together in long rows, doing something with their hands in the water while warlocks flanked by war-demon guards observed them from dry, elevated metal walkways. Bex was squinting through the smoke to try to see more when Iggs saved her the effort by just asking.

"What are they doing?"

"Making sin iron," Lys replied without taking their eyes off the treacherously steep stairs. "It's the only thing we do down here."

Bex blinked in surprise. She'd always known sin iron was in the Hells, but she'd never thought about how. Now that she was seeing the process with her own eyes, it looked remarkably like what Ishtar's demons had always been made to do. That dark water must be from the Rivers of Death she'd seen flowing into the Hells' base, and the kneeling slaves were cleaning the sin out of it.

Back in the Riverlands, they would've drunk the water and removed the sins out that way. Here, though, they did it with their hands, waving their fingers through the dirty flow until their palms were coated in black sin residue. When their hands were full, they then turned and scraped the black gunk into a metal bucket shared by multiple slaves in the same area. These buckets were then collected by yet another slave, who ran it through the water toward the cavern's center.

The smoke was too thick for Bex to see where they were taking it yet, but she could guess. The sin-collecting slaves were a mixed bag of Lust, Fear, Greed, Sorrow, Envy, and Hate demons, but they all dumped their sins into the same buckets. That fit the definition of sin iron—which was famously the amalgamation of all humanity's evils—to a T. The buckets were almost certainly being taken to a kiln where their contents would be fired and pressed into actual sin-iron ingots. That would also help explain the thick smoke in this place. When she asked Lys about it, though, Kirok was the one who answered.

"There is no forging on this floor," he explained authoritatively. "Sin collected from the Middle and Lower Hells is sent to the Upper Hells for processing. War demons are the only ones trusted enough to handle such work and hearty enough to survive it. The fumes from the processing of sin iron are quite toxic. Softer demons like Lust would perish if they attempted to forge it."

"Soft, huh?" Lys growled, but Bex cut them off.

"What else do the war demons make?"

"Everything," Kirok replied. "We forge all the metals used in Heaven and the materials that make the Anchors."

"They also make the chains that hold us down and the war constructs that guard us," Lys added bitterly. "And war demons wonder why the rest of us hate them."

"We do not wonder," Kirok said angrily. "We know exactly why we are despised, but what other demons fail to understand is that we are victims of this just as much as you are. Do you think we *like* choking on toxic fumes in Gilgamesh's factories and being forced to hurt our fellow demons?"

"Some of you seem to," Lys said as they squared their warlock's shoulders. "But we can argue about how I'm right later. We're about to hit the slave floor, so shut up and get in character."

Kirok growled deep in his chest, but thankfully for their mission—and his life expectancy given the obedience poison Adrian's mother had painted on his skin—he did as he was told. Bex got into her role as well, trailing behind Lys's warlock with her fake horns lowered as far as they would go. This made it much harder to walk down the final flight of neck-breakingly-steep stairs, but the rubber was about to hit the road on their disguises, and Bex was determined not to be the one who screwed up and got them killed.

At least it was good and dark. As expected of a path made for warlocks, the switchback stairs let out right onto one of the elevated walkways that allowed the overseers to patrol the flooded floor without getting their feet wet. This meant the way forward was teeming with warlocks, but between the constant haze of smoke and the terrible light from the torches reflecting off the dirty water, no one gave their ragtag group a second glance. Anyone who did get in their way quickly got back out of it once Lys gave them the stink eye.

Bex didn't know if that was because they were impersonating someone important or if her lust demon was just that scary, but being able to move forward without being stopped was an enormous relief. There were more guards than she'd expected after the complete nonresponse to their murderous entrance earlier, but nowhere near the number that would actually be needed to police so many demons.

Clearly, Gilgamesh had gotten comfortable with the idea that the Hells slaves wouldn't rebel. That was a weakness Bex would absolutely be exploiting the moment she got her sword and fire back. First, though, they had to get out of here.

She wasn't entirely sure how that was happening, to be honest. Lys was striding down the boardwalk like they owned it, but that was just how warlocks walked. Bex couldn't see any actual destination, just more torches and demons kneeling miserably in filthy water. There were no buildings, no brightly lit areas, nothing that looked like an office or an elevator or anything that might get them closer to Heaven. She was starting to get really worried when a giant shape suddenly emerged from the pervasive wall of smoke.

It was a tower. A shining white, cylindrical tower the size of a skyscraper. Its golden doors were even with the metal walkways, but its base was set flush against the cavern's floor, and its top went all the way to the ceiling. It looked like a white rod someone had driven straight through the middle of the Middle Hells, and inside of its smooth, completely soot-free white walls was an entire office building's worth of warlocks. Bex could see them moving through the tower's glass windows, and Lys sucked in a breath.

"There's our exit," they murmured, letting go of Bex's collar to dig the white paper out of their pocket. "Everyone play it cool. I'll do the talking."

That was always the plan, but Iggs suddenly looked like a bug had crawled into his fake armor. "*Can you do the talking?*" he whispered frantically. "I just realized, you killed your guy before he could get a word out. Do you even know what his voice sounds like?"

"Yes, because all warlocks sound like assholes," Lys hissed back. "Now *shut up*. Demon guards don't talk. Just look at Kirok."

Kirok was being the ideal of a silent war demon servant. His face looked so detached that Bex hardly recognized it, and his walk was the stiff gait of someone just going through the motions. It was a spectacular performance that Iggs couldn't possibly copy, but he still tried his best. Bex leaned hard into her role as well, hunching her shoulders to make herself look as small and beaten down as possible— something that was depressingly easy now that her horns were gone—as she scrambled after Lys's warlock toward the tower's entrance.

As they got closer, Bex finally saw where all the sin was going. She hadn't noticed them in the dark, but there were actually several black pipes running up the side of the blindingly white tower. Most of them seemed to be for river water, but the biggest, squarest one opened into a giant bin where all the runners she'd seen earlier were dumping their buckets of sin.

There was already a huge pile of black muddy-looking sin sitting at the bottom along with four tall demons with shovels who were mucking it out like a stable full of manure. They shoveled the sin into big metal troughs that were constantly being lifted on a conveyor into the pipe above, presumably for delivery to the forges in the Hell of War.

It was a simple system, but the amount they were moving was pretty incredible. The sin scrapings Bex had seen the demons wiping off their palms into the buckets had been tiny, but put it all together and the combined output was staggering. No wonder Heaven used sin iron for everything it did. They were making it quite literally by the bucketload.

Yet again, the idea of her people being worked to death and their sacred duty abused so Gilgamesh could have his toxic infrastructure was enough to make Bex see red, but what got her hardest were the demons who carried the sin in. She'd noticed them darting around collecting the buckets earlier, but now that she was closer, Bex saw that almost all of them were children. Skeletally thin, hollow-eyed children being forced to dump what were essentially buckets of food into a bin to be smelted down.

That pile of black mud might look unappetizing to Bex, but to demons who weren't queens fueled by the fires of life, sin *was* food. This place was full of food, and the demons weren't allowed to touch a crumb of it. She could see the hunger in the children's eyes as they emptied their buckets, but even though the food was right there, right in reach without a single warlock in sight to guard it, not a single one of the runners tried to swipe a handful.

Bex couldn't imagine fear strong enough to keep a starving child from reaching for food, but she hated it. She hated this whole ugly place where her people—

Ishtar's precious creations—were treated like sin-making machines. They slaved in silence, starved in fear, and worked until they died in an ugly, dark cavern that smelled of smoke and death.

And she *hated* it.

"I know," Lys whispered, reaching back to stop the growl Bex hadn't realized she was making. "I feel the same, but we have to keep it together. We're almost in."

As always, Lys was right. They were on the final elevated boardwalk that led to the tower's golden doors, which were properly lit for once with bright, sorcerous lanterns instead of smoky torches. That didn't bode well for their costumes, but Lys didn't hesitate. They just strode straight ahead, marching right up to the pair of war demons guarding the door like they meant to walk straight through them.

"You two," they announced in a sharp, annoyed voice that, even if it wasn't how the dead warlock actually sounded, matched Lys's stolen body perfectly. "Out of the way."

That probably would've worked on the kids they'd faced before, but these were mature soldiers with four arms and an apparently unflappable demeanor. Their faces stayed as still as actual bronze statues behind their golden visors, though Bex still swore she heard the taller one sigh.

"Writs are required for access, sir."

Lys went deathly silent for a moment, then they dug into the white robes with the huff of a pompous man doing something he thought was excessively unnecessary. It was flawlessly acted, proof yet again that Lys was the best at what they did. The petty display of annoyance also kept the war demons' eyes on them instead of Bex, Iggs, and Kirok, who were all much less good at this. Fortunately, the war demons didn't even seem to suspect them. They mostly just looked bored, watching in long-suffering silence as Lys retrieved the gilt-edged, cuneiform-covered paper they'd taken from the dead warlock earlier, placed their thumb strategically over the bloodstained corner, and then shoved it at the taller war demon's face.

"There," they said impatiently. "Now open the damn door before I name you into doing it by way of a pirouette."

Bex held her breath as the war demon looked over the paper clutched in Lys's transformed hand. It must actually have been what he was looking for, though, because the guard stepped out of the way at once, opening the golden door and bowing his horns to Lys without another word.

"Finally," Lys snapped as they stomped through. Bex was about to follow when one of the war demons reached out and grabbed her by the arm.

"Sir?"

"*What?*" Lys snarled, whirling around only to go still when they saw the demon holding Bex.

"There seems to be something wrong with your slave's collar," the guard explained quickly at Lys's blistering look. "Would you like us to check her?"

"No, I would not," Lys replied, pulling their warlock to his full height, which was nowhere near tall enough to look down on a war demon but still got the point across. "I would *like* you to shut up and stop wasting my time. You're both one word away from a write-up, so if you don't want to go back to the forges, I suggest you learn your place."

A write-up sounded like a pretty mild threat to Bex, but the war demon let go of her arm the moment Lys mentioned it, snapping back to his post like a spring.

"Good," Lys growled, giving the guard a final long glare before snapping the warlock's fingers in Bex's face. "Let's go."

Bex obeyed at once, scuttling behind Lys with her face parallel to the ground both because that was what an actual terrified slave would do and because it kept the headband with her fake horns out of the guards' line of sight. Iggs and Kirok tromped in right behind her, which was scary in its own way since the gaps in their ill-fitting armor were a lot more obvious in the bright white light of the tower. They were also all carrying bags, which Bex realized belatedly wasn't something people did here.

Yet again, she *really* wished they'd had more time to put into their costumes, but there was nothing to be done about it now. They were already walking into the brightly lit tower's main floor, which was set up like an airport security checkpoint. The whole thing was one big circular room with a long table in the middle where an important-looking warlock was sitting. Behind him was the entrance to a grand spiral staircase that went up the center of the tower like a corkscrew. The spiral was open in the middle, giving Bex a view of what had to be thirty floors of white-robed warlocks working at desks, talking by windows, or managing huge racks of spare chains. The quiet murmur of conversation and shuffling papers even sounded like an office, but while it was obvious that this was the stairway to Heaven they'd been looking for, Bex didn't see any stairs going down.

That was odd. She'd heard Kirok mention the Lower Hells earlier, but while this was clearly the main stairwell, there seemed to be no way to get to the lower floors. Bex supposed that didn't really matter since they were going up, not down, but it still seemed strange. She was wondering if there was another staircase hidden somewhere else when Lys's warlock came to a sudden stop.

Bex followed suit immediately, slamming her boots into the ground six inches behind the heels of Lys's shapeshifted white boots. When Lys didn't start moving again *and* didn't say anything, Bex lifted her eyes off the floor she'd been studying—both because it was strange and because she couldn't look at anything else while pretending to be a meek, downtrodden slave—to see a man coming down the spiral stairs.

A young-looking man in golden armor with olive skin, dark curling hair, and gleaming, mirrored eyes.

"*Shit,*" Iggs whispered before Lys frantically waved him back into character.

Bex didn't see the point. That was obviously a prince, which meant they were screwed. The warlock at the security table was already leaping out of his chair to greet him. Lys took advantage of the lapse to whirl around and start marching everyone back out the way they'd come. They'd almost made it to the door when Bex glanced over her shoulder to make sure the prince hadn't spotted them and saw something that stopped her dead in her tracks.

The unknown prince was still busy talking to the security warlock, but he was close enough for Bex to see the black chain dangling from his golden gauntlet. It looked like a sin-iron dog leash, and at the end of it was an all-white woman with a black cage wrapped around her carved ivory head.

The sight sent a shiver down Bex's spine. She'd never heard of a restrained princess before. Aside from the square of blue silk that had been draped over the Princess of Sorrow's shoulders, she'd never seen one wear anything other than the clothes Gilgamesh had carved onto their bodies. But while Sorrow had seemed to treasure her blue shawl, this princess looked like a muzzled dog.

In addition to the cage over her face, there was a thick sin-iron collar around her neck where the prince's leash attached, along with manacles at her wrists and ankles that were chained together to inhibit her movement. That was why she'd lagged behind her prince on the stairs, but Bex didn't understand the point. With the exception of War, who was crazy in her own way, every princess she'd ever met had been a slavishly loyal sycophant who'd happily die for their prince. Bex didn't know what this one had done to deserve the prison treatment, but the disconnect gave her hope. If this princess *wasn't* a brainwashed Gilgamesh fangirl, maybe she would help them.

This wild optimism was still running away with her when the princess turned her caged head and met Bex's eyes. The moment their gazes locked, Bex knew that she'd been wrong. This princess hadn't been chained to keep her loyal. The restraints were there because she was insane.

Her eyes were so wide they looked like two golden balls rattling inside a carved white skull, and her face—which should have been lovely—was a flat, expressionless mask. All of Gilgamesh's princesses were doll-like, but this was the first one Bex had seen that actually felt like an inanimate object. Her blank face and jerky, hobbled movements were so deep in the Uncanny Valley that just looking at her sent shivers running all over Bex's body, but the true terror came from her eyes. They were still huge and unfocused, but the interlocking golden rings that made up her eyeballs were spinning like wheels about to come off their tracks. They were turning so fast that Bex could actually hear the high-pitched squeal of the gold grinding against itself like the world's most expensive cement saw. This went on for a full five seconds, and then, all at once, the princess's hard, emotionless face split into a jaw-unhinging grin behind her sin-iron cage.

The moment Bex saw it happen, she knew. She didn't know *how*. She was a nameless, hornless shadow with a literal void inside her. She should've been as invisible as Nemini, but the moment the princess smiled at her, Bex *knew* she'd been recognized. Maybe the princess remembered Rebexa's face from the old days, or maybe it was just a lingering echo of the instinct that allowed Bex to recognize her sisters even after they'd been reduced to severed hands.

Whatever it was, Bex didn't want to stick around for it. She grabbed the back of Lys's robes and booked it, shooting past Iggs and Kirok to kick open the tower exit so hard, she knocked both of the war-demon guards outside into the water.

"What are you doing?" Lys shrieked as Bex dragged them back onto the elevated walkway. "The prince is *right there*!"

"He's about to be right on top of us," Bex hissed, looking over her shoulder to make sure Iggs and Kirok were following. "His princess already spotted me. We have to lose them fast, or we're dead. Now *run!*"

She yelled the last word as hard as she could, but her order was still drowned out by the horrific, predatory screech as the chained princess exploded through the golden door behind them. The sudden motion must've snatched her chain right out of the prince's hand, because Bex saw him stumble in surprise before the gold door slammed shut again, trapping them outside with the mad princess.

"Oh Hells," Lys muttered, jerking out of Bex's grasp to start running on their own power. "Which one is that?"

"No idea," Bex said, running faster. "But she recognized me for sure."

"That is such *bullshit*!" Iggs cried as he darted ahead to take point. "I can't even tell what you are anymore, and you're my queen! How is some psycho-looking princess we've never met able to recognize you when I can't?"

"Forget about that," Lys snapped, looking around at the slave floor as it flew by. "Where's Nemini? She's supposed to be scouting ahead to warn us about crap like this!"

Almost as if she'd been waiting for her cue, there was a crash behind them, followed by the mad princess's hawklike scream. When Bex looked over her shoulder, the chained princess was down with Nemini on her back. That was usually a fight-ender, but Nemini's normally emotionless face looked as freaked out as Bex felt. She let go of the princess a second later, vanishing into the smoky dark only to instantly reappear on the walkway in front of Iggs.

"We have to get off the main path," the void demon ordered, grabbing a very startled Iggs by the arm and dragging him off the walkway into the water where the slaves were working. "This way. Boston's preparing a diversion."

"Good work," Bex said, following them off the edge with a gasp of relief. She'd completely forgotten about Adrian's cat and broom in the chaos, but she wasn't surprised to hear they already had something prepared. Boston was *always* prepared. Sure enough, a few seconds after Nemini mentioned his name, a mist began to boil up from the water at their feet. It rose around them like a wall of smoke, making the demon slaves—who'd been frantically trying to get out of their way—yelp in surprise.

It was the first sound Bex had heard them make, but she didn't have time to reassure them. She was already charging into the fog, following Nemini's dark shape through the water, which was only calf-deep but bitingly cold. The chill soaked through her boots and turned her feet numb in an instant, but Bex shook it off and kept running, leaping over the rows of kneeling slaves like hurdles as she, Lys, Iggs, and Kirok ran in a zigzag pattern that would hopefully get them lost in the fog.

"I can't see a damn thing," Lys said angrily as they shed their warlock disguise and returned to their true, winged form. "I'm going to fly up and check where we are."

"Don't go too high," Bex ordered.

The magical fog was so thick that she couldn't even see Lys nod, only hear the beat of their wings as they flew up into the air only to dart right back down again.

"Oh yeah, she's still following," they said in a shaky voice as they swooped in to glide beside Bex.

"Did you see where we're going, at least?" Iggs asked as he leaped over a chain of terrified envy demons.

Before Lys could reply, a shriek shot through the thick fog, making them all jump. It sounded like an angry velociraptor, and it was a *lot* closer than Bex had expected.

"Shit," Bex swore, tripping over a slave chain and almost falling on her face before she kicked herself back up. "We need a better plan."

"Running does not seem to be working," General Kirok agreed. "We should try hiding instead. The Middle Hells are a big place, and our enemy doesn't seem like the patient sort. If we force her into a long search, she might give up."

"What makes you think that?" Iggs yelled. "Do you know her or something?"

Kirok shook his head. "It's just a supposition based on observations."

"Good enough for me," Bex said as she dug her boots into the slick, slimy rock beneath the freezing water the slaves were working in. "Head back to the cliffs. We'll lose her in the houses. Which way is it, Lys?"

This was why Bex loved working with an experienced team. The moment she asked, Lys pointed the direction, and their whole group turned as one. No one argued, no one asked stupid questions, no one panicked. They simply kept running, moving through the water in a tight knot with Bex in the middle. It was impossible to see how far they still had to go through the fog, but the cliffs surrounded the cavern on all sides, so even if they went off course, they couldn't miss them. They just had to get there without getting caught. That was looking like it'd be easier said than done when they suddenly got a rare stroke of luck.

Bex hadn't had a chance to talk to or even look closely at any of the silent kneeling demons they were running past. There was no way they could've known who she was without her horns, but the fact that she was being chased by a princess must've been enough to put her on their good side, because while Bex and her team had no trouble at all running across the slave floor, the princess seemed to be having a hell of a time. The fog was still too thick for Bex to see exactly what was happening, but the princess's predatory shrieks were increasingly punctuated by the clattering, unnatural sound of an ivory body falling down repeatedly.

She was tripping over the chains, Bex realized. The slaves leaned together when Bex's team ran by to keep their bindings slack on the ground. When the princess was coming, though, they leaned the other way, pulling their chains tight so that the black water suddenly became filled with trip lines.

Bex didn't know if the slaves were doing it on purpose or if the tripping hazards were just a byproduct of them trying to get away from the screaming madwoman, but she was incredibly grateful. The multiple falls coupled with the chains hobbling her limbs were the only reason their group was able to stay ahead of the princess's superhuman speed, and while the fog never actually managed to throw her off their trail, it kept her from seeing her feet, which made her trip even more.

"Keep it up," whispered Lys, who'd been darting out of the fog every few seconds like a winged dolphin to make sure they didn't start running in circles. "We're only two hundred feet away from the—"

Their excited whisper turned into a gasp as Bex heard the familiar *twang* of a bowstring, and then Lys's falling body slammed into her back. The sudden impact almost took her off her feet, but while Lys was much larger than Bex was, lust demons were made for flight, which meant they barely weighed a thing. As soon as she caught her own balance, Bex threw her arms around Lys and kept going, tossing their body over her shoulder to keep their long limbs from banging on the ground.

"Where'd they get you?"

"Wing," Lys hissed through their gritted fangs. "Gods-damned war demons always go for the gods-damned *wing!*"

That *was* the most logical place but now wasn't a good time to say as much. Bex was far more concerned with figuring out which direction the arrow had come from, because if they had war demons coming in to surround them, that was super bad. She hadn't heard any alarm bells, but surely one of the patrols had noticed a shrieking princess chasing a cloud across the sin collection floor.

Case in point, another arrow shrieked through the air in front of her. It missed Iggs by a good six inches, but it got much closer to hitting the demon he was jumping over, almost skewering the cowering man through the temple. Bex shouted an apology as she ran past and put on a burst of speed until she was sprinting next to Iggs.

"We have to get away from the civilians," she told him. "Can you get us back onto one of the walkways?"

"Haven't seen any," he panted, his huge shape barely visible through the fog even though he was right beside her. "The ground is sloping up now, though, so we've got to be close to the edge."

The water did seem to be getting shallower, now that he mentioned it. Bex hadn't jumped over a slave since the man they'd nearly gotten shot, either. That *had* to mean they were almost there. She was peering through the fog in a desperate attempt to see something useful when she heard a crunch followed by Iggs's yelp.

"Found the wall," he reported in a pained voice. "Where do you want to hide?"

"This way," Bex said, reaching out her hand to find the cliff edge. "Run along the cliff and stay low. With so many hovels, they won't know which one we ducked into. We'll keep going until we've got a bunch of false positives, and then we'll find a place that's big enough for all of us to hide."

It'd sounded like a solid plan when she said it, but after ten seconds of running past doors, Bex understood how naive she'd been. Yes, there were a lot of dwellings carved into the rock, but every one of them was the size of a broom closet. She hadn't found a single place big enough to hide Iggs, much less all of them. Nemini was a ghost—as was Boston, apparently, since Bex still hadn't spotted him—but she, Lys, Iggs, and Kirok would be sitting ducks. She hadn't heard the princess shriek in a while, but there were more war demons than ever. Bex could hear them shouting at each other through the fog as they started to organize a search of the holes the slaves lived in.

Her heart sank lower with every word. She'd known coming to the Hells was a gamble, but she hadn't expected everything to go so wrong so quickly. Running into that princess had been pure bad luck, but there was still a chance they could salvage things and try again *if* they found a place to hide. That was looking less and less likely with every house she checked. If she let the war demons corner them, though, they were finished. Bex was confident in her team's abilities, but a fight where you couldn't retreat and the enemy had endless resources was the definition of a losing battle.

No. If they took a stand here, they were going to lose. Their only option was not to fight, but Bex couldn't find a way out. If they climbed up, they'd leave the cover of the fog. If they hid in one of the tiny hovels, they'd be instantly discovered. If they kept running, they'd just end up exhausted and caught. Every strategy she came up with felt like a dead end, but then, just when Bex was sure she'd finally made the bad call that got them killed, a hand shot out of the fog to grab her arm.

"This way!"

Bex caught her shriek just in time. Her brain was scrambling too hard to place the voice, but it sounded strangely familiar. It definitely wasn't a war demon's, though, so Bex decided to trust it, turning on a dime to carry the still-bleeding Lys into the hovel the hand that grabbed her had come out of.

Iggs crowded in right behind her, then Kirok followed by Nemini, who seemed to coalesce out of the darkness in the corner. Boston flew in last, swooping out of the fog on Bran like the two of them had simply appeared from the vapor. Bex had just pulled the hovel's curtain closed behind Bran's bristles when she realized how strange their situation was. Going by the size of the door, the hole she'd ducked into should've been no bigger than a closet, yet somehow the five of them plus a cat and a broom had been able to fit inside. Bex was wondering how that could possibly be when a *sixth* figure—one who wasn't her, Iggs, Kirok, Nemini, or Lys—nudged her gently aside to place a large wooden partition with a fake stone front made from sandy paint over a hole in the *actual* dirty stone wall.

He slotted the fake chunk of wall into place just in time as a shouting squad of war demons ripped open the hovel's curtained door. They were so close, Bex could hear them panting through the wood. They must not have been looking too hard, though, because they moved on a second later, leaving the five of them—*six* of them—standing silently in the dark behind the hovel's false back. Bex was digging into her backpack for her flashlight—*and* her explosive short sword—when she heard someone laugh in the dark beside her.

"Well, well, well," said the same voice that had hissed at her earlier. "Fancy meeting you here."

Bex jerked. She *knew* she recognized the voice this time, and she wasn't the only one. It was so dark that she could only make out people's silhouettes, but that was still enough to see Lys's head snap up like a trigger. A light flashed over them a second later as someone pulled the cloth off a small lantern, revealing a hidden hallway lined with false-backed walls just like the one they'd taken shelter behind. And standing in the middle of it with a smile so wide that Bex could see every one of his fangs was a familiar fear demon wearing a prison tunic and a big sin-iron collar around his pale, slave-marked neck.

"Hello, luv," said Desh, giving her a cocky wink. "Bet you're happy to see me."

Before Bex could even think of a reply, Lys leaped off her shoulder with a snarl to tackle Desh to the ground.

Chapter 5

ADRIAN DID END UP using the sap as glue after all.

Considering how many pieces the Queen of Pride's horns were in, he'd thought he was embarking on a massive restoration project, but they actually came together astonishingly quickly once he started working. The hardest part had been getting everything into the right order, but once Adrian started fitting the broken edges into place, the black pieces had snapped together like a precision-machined jigsaw puzzle. There was no smoothing or erosion, no gaps where the thinner bits had started to crumble. Every edge was still razor-sharp and ruler-straight like the horns had broken five minutes ago, not five thousand years.

As someone who'd worked on more than his fair share of dead bodies as part of his craft, it was the craziest thing Adrian had ever seen. He'd expected to have to replace at least some lost material like he'd done with Bex's fire, but the Queen of Pride's horns were apparently immune to time. He couldn't even tell they'd been shattered on a battlefield because every single piece was there. It looked like she'd broken her horns straight into Gilgamesh's box, but the *really* crazy part was that the pieces were still warm.

He'd noticed the odd temperature the first time he handled them, but he'd been too distracted by Gilgamesh, the loss of his forest, and the potential death of everyone he loved to consider what that meant at the time. Now that Adrian was actually doing the work, though, that gentle heat changed his entire strategy, because warmth was a quality of *living* bodies. That made this Witchcraft of the Flesh, not the Bones, and unlike the delicate work of reconstructing a crumbling skeleton, Adrian could set a broken bone in his sleep.

Once he made that connection, everything got easier. Not *easy*—the horns were still split into five hundred and fifty-two tiny pieces—but putting them back together took much less work than restoring Bex because the Queen of Pride's horns were merely broken, not empty. Their power hadn't been hollowed out by eons of constant battle and nearly two hundred reincarnations, which meant he didn't have to replace it. He just had to fit all the pieces back into their correct positions and hold them there until the pine sap he was using as glue solidified.

That would've been enough by itself if he'd been back in his own forest. Since he was in Heaven, though, with all its anti-resurrection restrictions, Adrian had had to cheat by dunking the glued horns into a giant tub filled with bright-blue deathly water and healing herbs. It was a higher-concentration version of the same bath he'd used to heal Bex after she'd fought the prince in his forest, and it was apparently the most illegal thing you could make in Heaven. From the new blood stains on her white fingers, Adrian wasn't sure he wanted to know what his princess had done to collect all the materials on his list, but it had *worked*.

Just like when he submerged Bex's body in his bathtub back home, Pride's broken horns had started knitting themselves back together the second they hit the water. After ten minutes of soaking, Adrian could no longer see the yellow lines of sap he'd used to hold the cracked pieces together. Just two smooth, glossy horns even blacker and taller than Bex's.

Twistier, too. Unlike the Queen of Wrath's horns, which were as straight as spears, Pride's crown looked like a cross between a stag's antlers and an obsidian thorn hedge. The tangle of their fully reconstructed form was so wide that Adrian almost couldn't fit it in the tank. Adrian couldn't imagine wearing something that enormous on his own head, but the daughters of Ishtar were famously strong, and if any queen was going to have an iron-stiff neck, it would be Pride.

"That's amazing," the princess said when Adrian finally hauled the finished crown out of the tank and picked all the residual leaves off to make sure every crack had healed. "I can't believe you did that so fast. Gilgamesh was unable to heal the Queen of Pride's crown for five thousand years, but you did it in fifty minutes."

"It's a matter of approach, not skill," Adrian said, refusing to be flattered by a tool of the enemy but still unable to resist explaining his cleverness. "Gilgamesh is a sorcerer. That means he works by command and force of will, but you can't boss around an enemy with nothing to lose. These horns were already in pieces, and, if Gilgamesh's story is to be believed, the Queen of Pride herself was the one who made them that way specifically to keep them out of his hands."

He pointed at the enormous crown dripping on the worktable. "The pieces had absolutely no reason to put themselves back together for him, and unless he wanted to complete Pride's work by blasting them to powder, Gilgamesh had nothing he could threaten them into obedience with. I'm pretty sure if I'd tried to use sorcery, I would've had just as little luck, but witches don't approach problems that way. Gilgamesh treated the Queen of Pride's horns as a war prize to be reclaimed. I treated them like a broken bone. Look at it that way and it's easy to see why Ishtar's gift of regeneration worked for me and not my father."

"Well, I still think it's incredible," the princess insisted, smiling at him with Bex's beaming face. "Gilgamesh was so right to bring you here. You truly were exactly what he needed to complete his great work."

Adrian had been feeling exceedingly clever, but the fawning way she said that hit him like a boot to the head. He'd gotten carried away with his work, but he couldn't let himself forget for a second that he was playing chicken with the man who'd killed the gods. That wasn't a fight Adrian could win no matter how clever he was. Fortunately, he'd already stacked the deck. The highest left antler of Pride's towering black crown was missing its point. Not because that piece hadn't been in the box, but because Adrian had slipped it into his pocket earlier when he was laying everything out.

It was still in there, stuck to the sticky belly of his fur-covered wooden cat, whose sharp nose was pointing like a compass needle at the Queen of Pride's body. The fact that he could still feel it moving even through his pocket gave Adrian enormous hope, which in turn gave him the courage to take the next step in his plan.

"Gilgamesh's great work isn't complete yet," he said, pretending to dry the horns so the always-watching princess wouldn't see how nervous he was. "There's a piece still missing here, see?"

He pointed at the gap left by the tip he'd pocketed, and the princess's face grew horrified. "How is that possible?" she asked. "Gilgamesh used sorcery to collect every shard!"

"I don't think it was ever there to begin with," Adrian lied. "Whatever blow was capable of shattering these horns in the first place probably destroyed this part completely. Normally, that would mean it's lost forever, but the reason Father chose me for this job is because I have experience replicating Ishtar's lost creations, and I think I know how to fix this."

"I hope it doesn't involve something on Earth," the princess said, biting her carved lip. "Even if it's for the Queen of Pride's horns, I can't take you back down there unless Gilgamesh gives his explicit permission."

Adrian blinked. He hadn't even considered asking to go back to Earth. It was a moot point since he would never leave Heaven without Bex, but he still felt stupid for not thinking of it.

"I don't need to go to Earth," he assured her. Truthfully, this time. "The Queen of Pride was born and killed in Paradise. That means everything I need to rebuild her should still be here. I even know how to find it. Do you remember this guy?"

He pulled the cat charm out of his pocket just long enough for the princess to see it before tucking it back in.

"He's a finding charm," Adrian explained, which, again, was not a lie. "I originally used him to find what

I needed to repair the horns, but he can also find what I need to complete them."

"Really?" the princess asked excitedly. "Whatever it is, we'll get it. What do you need?"

Adrian took a deep breath. Here it went.

"I don't know," he said, turning around so she could see the full breadth of his false disappointment. "Witchcraft is not precise like sorcery. This charm can point me to the material I need, but I won't know what it is or how to use it until I see it with my own eyes."

The princess looked suspicious. "How can you look for something if you don't know what it is?"

"That's just how witches work," he said with a helpless shrug. "It's a craft, not a science. Sometimes you just have to trust the process, but I *can* promise you that, if you take me to where my charm is pointing, I'll know the solution when I see it. Since there's such a tiny portion to be replaced, I should be able to finish the horns right then and there if you can just help me get to the last part I need."

That was the biggest throw of this entire plan. If the princess refused the bait and decided that ninety-nine percent completion was good enough to call Gilgamesh in right now, Adrian would have to break the horns again to save himself. The real Bex probably would've decided what was here was good enough, but the princess was a servant of Gilgamesh, and no Heavenly stooge Adrian had met would dare present their king with anything less than what he'd asked for. He was betting she'd rather gamble on her ability to control him than present an unfinished crown to her king, and sure enough, after just thirty seconds of grinding her golden gears or whatever it was princesses did to make decisions, she nodded.

"I'll take you to find it," she said. "Where do you need to go?"

Adrian took his cat out again and made a show of checking, but he already knew. The Queen of Pride had been moving constantly since he'd found her, but she'd always been at the same depth, and there was only one thing Adrian knew of which lay below the Holy City.

"I'm afraid it's in the Hells," he said apologetically.

"The Hells?" she repeated, shocked. "I can't take you there! Your father would never—"

"Father doesn't have to know," Adrian said, flashing her a conspiratorial smile. "We're a prince and princess of Heaven working for the glory of our king. Surely we don't need to ask permission like schoolchildren just to go down a level or two, especially since we're doing it for him. He's the one who entrusted this job to us. We can't be running to him with every little thing. You didn't go bothering him for permission for all the leaves and deathly water I needed."

"Because those things were already available in Heaven," the princess insisted, looking more nervous than ever. "The Hells are different. They're restricted and *dangerous*. You still haven't been granted permission to use me as your sword, which means you'd be undefended. Even for this, I couldn't possibly take you down there without permission."

"Then we'll get permission," Adrian said, switching tactics. "The Crown Prince manages Heaven and the Hells, right? We'll just ask him to let us go. That way we won't have to interrupt Gilgamesh's important work."

The princess still didn't look happy, but she must've feared bothering the Crown Prince a lot less than she did Gilgamesh, because she didn't say no immediately, and Adrian went for the kill.

"It would mean the world to me if you did this," he said as he reached out to brush his fingers against her cold, smooth cheek. "This is the last hurdle between us and the end of this war. Gilgamesh made it very clear when he spoke to me in my forest that these horns are the final piece he needs to complete his great vision. If we bring them to him, he'll reward us with his favor, which means we'll be the top prince and princess in Heaven."

He reached down to grab her hand. The right one that was actually Bex's with the heavy lump of Drox's ring clearly visible under the thin white glove.

"We'll be in a league of our own," he promised, lifting her gloved fingers to his lips. "I won't have any more work distracting me. It'll be just me and you basking forever in the light of Gilgamesh's glory. Isn't that what you wanted?"

That was the rankest lie Adrian had ever told. Just getting the words out made him feel like he'd taken a bite out of a rotting skunk, but the princess's face was lit up brighter than he'd seen it since she first came into his bedroom a week ago. Her joy was so sincere, and so like the real Bex's, it made him feel like a heel before she grabbed him in another of those crushing hugs.

"Oh, Adrian, yes!" she cried, almost breaking his ribs in her joy. "We'll go to the Crown Prince right now and ask. He'll be mad we didn't make an appointment, but Gilgamesh told everyone your work was top priority, so I'm sure he'll say yes!" She rose up on her toes to pepper his face with hard, cold kisses. "We'll move fast and be done before anything bad can happen, and then we'll go to the top of the tower and present the crown to Gilgamesh in person. Oh, my prince, he'll be so *happy* with us!"

It was a sign of how brainwashed she was that the princess sounded giddier about making Gilgamesh happy than about being happy herself, but Adrian wasn't complaining. He was too busy trying not to flinch as she kissed his cheeks twenty more times before tugging him toward the hallway door, which was when he realized they she meant *right now* right now.

"Wait!" he cried, pulling out of her embrace. "Let me grab the horns."

The dazzling joy fell off her face. "Why? Isn't it safer to leave them here?"

"But not faster," he said as he hefted the Queen of Pride's enormous crown off the table and started carefully wiggling it into the largest of his coat's enchanted pockets. "If I leave them here, we'll have to come all the way back up. If I keep them with me, though, there's a good chance I can replace the lost piece the moment I find what I need. That way we'll be able to go straight to Gilgamesh without wasting time."

"The Eternal King does hate waste," she agreed, breaking into a smile again. "Good thinking, my love!"

Adrian was so relieved he was getting what he wanted without a fight that he didn't even wince at the endearment. He just crammed the horns into his coat. It took a bit of doing because the horns were such an odd shape, but these were the same pockets he used to haul groceries, and eventually he fit them in. This left one side of his coat much heavier than the other, but the horns themselves were completely hidden under the enchantments, leaving his coat hanging straight to his knees like normal. When Adrian was certain they couldn't be seen from the outside, he straightened his witch hat and marched to the door, following the clack of the princess's ivory feet out of his prison workroom into the grand golden corridor beyond.

He'd never admit it out loud, but Adrian found the walk to the Crown Prince's office absolutely fascinating.

He'd been through here once before when his father had first escorted him to his room, but that was right after Bex had lost her horns and he'd given himself up to save her, so he hadn't exactly been in a state to appreciate the architecture. After a week of being confined to just two rooms, though, Adrian was chomping at the bit to see more of Gilgamesh's famous palace.

He tried to make himself be good and do recon— noting the positions of staircases, exits, potential hiding places, and so on—but his curiosity was so overloaded that he ended up looking at everything, gawking like a tourist as he followed the princess through the white-and-gold labyrinth that was the Fortress of the Highest Heaven.

Gilgamesh's palace consisted of multiple towers rising from a single base. It reminded him of the river trees that sometimes had multiple trunks sprouting from one stump, except these towers clustered instead of spreading out, and there was nothing organic about them. Every hallway they walked down had a marble floor polished to a mirror shine, walls covered in gold leaf, and an arched ceiling lined with magically-glowing crystal chandeliers.

The combined effect made Malik's art-filled mansion feel like a rustic hut in the wilderness. At least on his father's private island there'd been plants and water and wind. This place was entirely artificial from the too-smooth polished floor to the unnaturally white light that streamed through the perfectly clear crystal windows.

Even the scale felt unnatural. Every doorway they passed was oversized, every hallway palatial, and the stairs—*so* damn many stairs rising in elegant, gigantic spirals through white-stone towers that seemed to go up for miles.

It was oddly deserted as well. Adrian had seen the throngs of silent human servants who brought his food and tidied his bedroom, so he'd assumed there must be a large number of people working here, but every grand hallway and staircase they walked down was empty. Princesses were pretty scary, so maybe everyone had just cleared out ahead of them, but it really looked like the entire tower was uninhabited.

At least the view was nice. The Crown Prince's office was much higher than Adrian's workshop. To get there, the princess led them down the spiral stairs of Adrian's tower, across a delicate white connector bridge, and then up another, much larger tower that seemed to belong entirely to Gilgamesh's eldest son. There *were* other people here, mostly scribes, but they all fled the second they spotted Adrian's princess, clearing the stairs to give Adrian an unobstructed view of the White City far below.

It was the best look he'd had since standing on the balcony with his father that first night. From this high up, he could see entire circle of the capital's walls, though not what lay beyond them. He *did* see the slagged-gold carcasses of the lion cannons Bex had melted during her fight last week, which made him smug, but the rest of the city was untouched. It lay around the base of the palace like a glittering blanket of new snow cut through with perfectly straight roads that actually seemed to have people on them. They looked like ants from way up here, but the city traffic was still the most normal-looking thing Adrian had seen since coming to Heaven.

He certainly had enough time to look. The climb to the Crown Prince's office turned out to be thirty floors. That would've been a slog in any building, but like everything else in the palace, the stairs had been carved to match Gilgamesh's grand aesthetics. This meant they'd been made to fit the tower's scale rather than placed at a height suitable for use by actual human legs.

Adrian had never missed teleporting so much in his life. By the time he spotted the golden doors that marked the entrance to the Crown Prince's penthouse office, his thighs felt like they were about to fall off.

Maybe the reason he hadn't seen any servants was because they had a secret elevator, because he couldn't imagine anyone climbing this torture tower multiple times a day. He wasn't sure he'd survive the trip back down, but that was a problem for the future. Here in the present, it was go time, so Adrian wiped the exhausted look off his face, got his panting under control, and stepped through the grand golden doors his princess held open for him into the fanciest waiting room he'd ever seen.

"Waiting room" felt like a sorry label for such a dazzling place, but that was exactly what it was. Like everything else Adrian had seen in this giant mausoleum of a palace, the entry to the Crown Prince's office was ridiculously enormous. It was as long as a banquet hall with soaring white stone ceilings and thirty-foot-tall walls covered in enormous gold mosaics depicting hundreds of solemn-looking warlocks and sorcerers hard at work on all the various jobs required to maintain Gilgamesh's sprawling empire.

But while it was decorated like the throne room of an industry-minded king, the only furniture available was two rows of hard white-stone benches pushed up against the grand walls. The result reminded Adrian of a fancy bus station. There was even a table set with crystal punch bowls and golden platters that was clearly meant for refreshments, but they were all empty. The whole room was empty, actually, except for a single tall white figure standing in front of a pair of slightly smaller—but still absurdly grand—golden doors on the other side.

"Welcome, Prince of Wrath," she said in a voice that wasn't welcoming in the slightest. "I trust this is important. Your princess was most insistent, but annoyingly sparse on details."

That was news to Adrian. He'd thought this was a surprise visit, but apparently Gilgamesh's princesses had ways of communicating with each other. Or at least ways of communicating with the Crown Princess, who seemed to be their boss. It wasn't too surprising since he'd always known the princess was his watcher, but it was still creepy to see firsthand, especially when the Crown Princess turned her cold, sharp, mismatched gold-and-silver eyes on him.

"My prince is always happy to meet with any of his brothers," she informed him, looking down on Adrian from her already intimidating height that got even scarier now that he knew what was hiding beneath her white princess shell. "Unfortunately, he is very busy at the moment with issues vital to the success of Heaven's Eternal Kingdom. It would be most unfortunate if you were to waste his time." Her mismatched eyes narrowed. "I hope you're not here to complain about the teleport ban."

"It's not that," Adrian assured her. "I just need my brother's permission for something. I promise it won't take more than five minutes."

The Princess of War looked pleased by the idea of Gilgamesh's new favorite coming all the way up here to ask her prince's permission. Not pleased enough to actually smile, but she told Adrian to wait and opened the golden doors behind her, ordering him firmly not to go anywhere before she slipped inside.

"Stuck-up cow," the fake Bex muttered, her golden eyes murderous. "Don't worry, my prince. We'll put her in her place soon."

Under different circumstances, Adrian would've heartily encouraged infighting among the enemy. He needed this to work, though, so he shushed her instead and took a seat on one of the long, hard benches that lined the palatial waiting room. He sat there for a good five minutes, clutching the frantically-twitching carved cat in his coat pocket. Then, just when he was growing certain that the Crown Princess had seen straight through his ruse and summoned Gilgamesh, the giant doors clicked open again.

"My prince will see you now," the Princess of War informed him, lowering her head the barest fraction as she held the door open with her long, white arm. "Quickly, please."

Adrian was off the bench like a shot. He got to the doors so fast, the Bex princess almost couldn't keep up. She looked furious when he ducked his head to her sister, but War was the princess who controlled access to Alexander, which meant she was the one he needed to butter up. Once again, she looked gratified by his humility, pushing the gold door all the way open to make room for Adrian and the scowling princess following one step behind like a white shadow to enter the Crown Prince's office.

It was different than Adrian expected. After the trip here, he'd been braced for a ballroom with a single desk in the middle, but while the office was large and ludicrously luxurious, the gold-covered walls were actually built to human scale. This made it the first room Adrian had seen in the palace since his own bedroom that didn't look like it was designed for snooty giants. But just because it wasn't overpowering architecturally didn't mean it was comfortable.

All the elements of comfort were present. There was a large white rug to soften the stone floors, couches and chairs made from actual wood and fabric instead of marble and gold, diamond-shaped shelves filled with leather scroll cases, and plenty of lamps to soften the white light streaming through the curtained windows. Those alone should've made this the coziest room in all of Heaven, but the man sitting behind the golden desk at the room's far end was anything but pleasant.

Just like the last two times Adrian had seen Gilgamesh's eldest son, the Crown Prince was dressed like a perfect soldier. He was wearing less armor than usual—just his golden scale chest plate with no gloves or helmet, which made it easier to see the embroidered patch covering his missing eye—but he still looked like the epitome of a competent commander with his perfectly starched white shirtsleeves, excessively neat desk, and thronelike chair. The only flaw in this projection of perfection was his olive-skinned face, which was haggard and sleep-deprived when he raised it to fix Adrian with a look of supreme irritation.

"Make this quick," he ordered as he waved his calloused hand at the enormous pile of scrolls waiting in a golden basket beside his desk. "As you can see, the living world is still in a panic over the closed Anchors. Heaven's faithful servants require all of my attention, so I'm afraid I don't have time to babysit Father's newest pet."

"This won't take long," Adrian promised. "I just need your permission to enter the Hells."

His eldest brother's one remaining eye narrowed. "Why?"

Adrian swallowed. He'd never realized so much suspicion could be crammed into a single word. If he'd needed a final warning, that was it, but he'd already stuck his neck out as far as it would go, so he gave it all he had.

"I'm nearly finished with the restoration of the Queen of Pride's horns," he announced, sticking as close to the truth as possible so he wouldn't have to remember what he'd lied about later. "But there's a piece missing, one vital to the crown's completion. My finding spell tells me what I need to fix it is in the Hells, but I can't go down there without your permission, so here I am."

He'd tried to keep things as straightforward as possible, but the Crown Prince's suspicious scowl didn't let up.

"Why would the final piece needed to fix Pride's broken crown be in the Hells?"

"I have no idea," Adrian said innocently. "I only know what my spell tells me. Sometimes you just have to have faith and trust the—"

"If you already know where it is, then send your princess to retrieve it," the Crown Prince ordered. "That's what she's for."

"I'd be happy to perform any service you desire, my prince," the fake Bex volunteered immediately, but Adrian was already shaking his head.

"I have to go myself," he insisted, pulling the sticky, wooden, fur-covered cat out of his pocket so the prince could see it twitching. "I'm the only one the finding spell responds to, and I won't know what I'm looking for until I see it."

"Isn't that convenient?" the Crown Prince said in a dry voice before glancing down to shuffle through the papers on his desk. "I have a report here that you've already requested and been granted a mountain of contraband from the magical materials vault. Since you've clearly made yourself comfortable pillaging our storehouses, why not go down and look for a suitable alternative there? Aren't you the one who bragged about being 'a hell of a witch'?"

"It's because I'm an experienced witch that I already know nothing else will work," Adrian argued. "Agatha was your mother, too. Even if you paid zero attention before running off to become a prince, surely you remember there are key elements to every spell that cannot be subst—"

"Do not speak of the Blackwood to me!" Alexander snarled, his one eye flashing silver. "Those *witches* sold out every one of us to protect their precious forest. You're the only child they saw fit to fight for, but while Father seems to think that makes you a special little flower, *I* do not."

He grabbed a scroll out of the basket and slapped it on his desk. "It's my job to keep Gilgamesh's Eternal Kingdom running smoothly, not to coddle favorites," he announced as he unrolled the scroll and began to read. "I see no reason to allow access to one of the empire's most sensitive areas to a spoiled child whose loyalty is so questionable that his own princess has been ordered to keep him prisoner in his rooms."

He slammed his stamp down on the scroll he'd
just read, rocking the deep-red pad back and forth
before returning it to the spotless ink tray in front of
him.

"Your request to visit the Hells is denied," he
said as he rerolled the stamped scroll and dropped it
on the golden platter that was clearly for outgoing
mail. "If you need something specific, you may submit
a requisition form through the proper channels like
everyone else."

Adrian closed his fist around the finding charm
with a scowl. The way Alexander was acting was
frustrating but not surprising. He'd encountered this
attitude from many of his sisters who didn't think a
boy who'd put the whole coven in danger should be
allowed to become the Old Wife of the Flesh's
apprentice. It didn't matter that Adrian had worked
hard for the right to study under his mother just like
he'd worked hard for all his skills. So long as they
perceived him as having privileges they didn't, he'd
never get an inch out of any of them, so Adrian
decided to try a different tactic.

"If you care about remaining Crown Prince, you
should reconsider that denial."

"You can't threaten me," Alexander told him
with a snort. "I've been Gilgamesh's right hand for
three thousand years. There's nothing a brat like you
can say that will convince Father to—"

"This will," Adrian said, fixing his face into the
hard, cruel, supernaturally confident expression he'd
learned from watching his mother speak as the Witch
of the Present.

"You know how important my work is," he said, walking across the plush carpet until he was standing directly in front of the prince's desk. "You were there when Father explained it to me. I'm on the cusp of accomplishing a feat even Gilgamesh was never able to perform, the *only* one he needs to complete his work. You claim your years of loyal service keep you safe, but we both know Gilgamesh is a man who looks toward the future, not the past."

He leaned over his brother's desk and dropped his voice to a whisper. "If that man finds out you blocked me from completing the last step needed to get him what he wants, do you really think all those years of service will matter for spit? This is Gilgamesh the Conqueror we're talking about. Crown Prince or no, if you get between him and his ambitions, he'll cut you down as fast as he did the gods. Look at it that way, and I'm not asking you to do me a favor. I'm giving *you* the chance to save your own skin, because when Gilgamesh discovers you're the reason the Queen of Pride's horns aren't in his hands, someone's going to pay, and it's not going to be me."

The Crown Prince glowered up at him from his golden chair. "You truly are a spiteful witch."

"I learned from the best," Adrian said with a smile that didn't touch his new mirrored eyes. "But this sword cuts both ways. If you allow me to enter the Hells, and I do something I shouldn't, your hands stay clean. You were just acting to ensure that the Eternal King's interests were served. I'm the one who ran wild, which means I'll be the one who eats the punishment, not you."

"Father can always punish us both," the Crown Prince reminded him before he sighed. "But very well. I still think this is all highly suspicious, but I'd rather err on the side of Father's ambition. I'll grant you permission to enter the Hells on the condition that you submit to supervision."

"That's fine with me," Adrian said. "But it's not like I'm ever unsupervised. My princess is always with me."

He could hear the soft *click* of the Bex princess's face moving as she burst into a smile behind him. The Crown Prince, however, rolled his eye.

"A besotted princess is not fit supervision for a prince," Alexander informed him as he pulled a fresh sheet of stationery from one of his golden desk drawers and began scribbling on it with an ivory fountain pen. "You will be escorted on your search by Demetrios. He's the acting prince of the Hells now that Leander is in disgrace, and he's already proved he has a swift hand for putting down unruly demons. I'm sure his presence will be sufficient to keep you out of trouble."

He said that like he hoped Adrian was going to get into as much trouble as possible, but the witch just gave him a beatific smile.

"I would be delighted to have my brother's help," he lied. "When can I meet him?"

"Right now," the Crown Prince said, rolling up the note he'd just finished writing and turning to drop it down one of the golden tubes that lined the wall below his window. "I just sent him an order to meet you at the gate. Normally, he'd teleport straight here to pick you up, but that convenience is no longer available since Father banned all instantaneous travel on this side of the afterlife."

Adrian blinked. He hadn't realized the teleport ban extended to all the princes. Maybe Gilgamesh didn't have as much fine control over the sorcery here as he'd thought. His mind was spinning over what that could mean when he realized his brother was still scowling at him.

"Your disobedience has caused everyone a great deal of inconvenience," the Crown Prince growled. "Be grateful that you are in Father's favor, because the rest of us are already tired of having a younger brother. I suggest you do your best to stay in the king's good graces. Life here could become very unpleasant for you should you slip."

Adrian already found it unpleasant, but he forced his face to keep smiling. "I'll keep that in mind," he said with unfailing politeness. "How do I get to the Hells?"

Alexander glared at him for several more seconds before returning his attention to his work. "Your princess will guide you," he said as he reached for another scroll. "Again, that's her job."

"To walk me around?"

"To serve Heaven," Alexander snapped as he mashed the scroll he'd just pulled flat. "A prince shouldn't have to be reminded of this. Now go do whatever it is you're doing, and the next time I hear your name, it'd better be followed by a good report."

There was nothing he could say to that that wouldn't get him in trouble, so Adrian didn't bother. He just nodded to his brother and jogged for the exit, forcing the fake Bex to scramble as he burst out of the

Crown Prince's office. She'd taken the lead again by the time they reached the end of the giant waiting room, throwing open the doors to lead her prince back down the millions of steps toward what Adrian could only hope was the path to Hell.

Chapter 6

"**O**I, OI, OI! I submit! *I submit*!" Desh yelled, throwing his hands up to protect his face from Lys, who was trying to slam it into the floor.

"Lys," Bex said, though she probably should've yelled. She was used to not having to raise her voice with her demons. Now that she wasn't a queen anymore, though, her words no longer carried the same weight. Lys didn't even seem to hear her as they methodically worked Desh into a choke hold. Bex was about to step in and break it up when she heard a high-pitched screech from down the tunnel right before a small figure leaped out of the darkness and threw itself onto Lys's still-bleeding wing.

The impact wasn't enough to actually knock Lys over, but it did make them hiss. They flipped over with a snarl, claws out and ready to fight, but the little creature had already scrambled off of Lys's wing to throw itself at Desh. The newcomer wrapped their arms around the fear demon's head with a snarl, showing their little fangs as they defended Desh's body with a tiny set of dusky-pink, leathery wings.

"What in the Hells?" said Iggs, squinting his red eyes against the low light of Desh's lantern. "Is that a lust demon?"

"It's a child," Bex said.

Lys didn't say anything at all. They just darted around the new demon and went for Desh's collared throat. The baby lust demon fought back, their three-foot body flickering through multiple different human girl shapes as they threw themselves over Lys's shoulder and started trying to bite through the bigger demon's wounded wing.

"Whoa," Bex said, reaching out to grab the baby demon before they chomped something critical. "That's enough of that. You, too, Lys. Stand down."

Her voice actually got through this time. Lys stopped trying to murder Desh at once, though they threw a nasty glare at the little demon whipping around like a trapped ferret in Bex's grip. Desh, however, just looked relieved.

"Much obliged, Your Majesty," he panted as he heaved himself off the dark tunnel's rough stone floor. "Looks like I owe you my life yet again."

"I'll put it on your tab," Bex said, tilting her head toward the little demon she was holding at arm's length. "Who's this?"

Before she could finish the question, the little lust demon changed back into their true shape to start attacking Bex's arm with their wings and tail as well. They almost took off one of her five remaining fingers before Bex managed to switch her grip to the child's sin-iron collar. She was still trying to find a position that would keep everything bitable away from those small but fearsome teeth when Desh burst out laughing.

"Sorry, sorry," he said, turning around to give Bex the charming smile she remembered, though a much rougher, thinner version. "That's Streya. She's the one who had eyes on the tower and spotted your trouble. Raced right through all the patrols to come tell me to get the tunnel ready." Desh grinned wider. "Regular little weasel, that one."

Streya stopped trying to bite Bex's hand off to preen at the praise, but Lys was scowling.

"She?"

"Damn right 'she,'" the little demon snapped, thrashing even harder in Bex's grip. "I ain't ever changing into a boy! Never! They can't make me!"

"You see?" Desh said as Bex finally set the flailing child down. "She's a born rebel. The overseers were planning to send her to Earth and let one of the mortal warlocks beat it out of her when Gilgamesh locked down all the Anchors. Since they couldn't ship her off, they chained her on the work line next to me. I was minding my own business, trying to make quota, when Streya made a stone-cold play to kill the warlock watching our section. I ended up helping her do it, and the two of us went on the lam."

"Went for the kill, huh?" Lys said, looking at the young demon with new respect. "Good work. I was twice your age before I killed my first warlock."

"They're easy to kill," Streya bragged, spreading her little wings proudly. "Stupid old men never think to look down."

"That's my little murder machine," Desh said, reaching out to ruffle Streya's hair between her stubby horns. "Reminds me of the good old days."

He winked at Bex, but she could only lower her eyes. Desh was always a flirt, but seeing him wink at her like he used to just highlighted how much he'd changed. He couldn't have been in the Hells for more than two months, but Desh already looked like he'd lost half his body weight. His once lithe, muscular frame was a skeletal shadow of its former strength. His bones were clearly visible beneath the shapeless, dirty sack of his knee-length prison tunic, and his pale-blond hair was stained gray from the black grime that coated everything down here. His neck had been clean the last time Bex saw him, but just like Streya, Desh's throat now sported a slave-band tattoo beneath his sin-iron collar. A fresh, dark one that made Bex's hand close into a fist.

"What happened to you?"

Now it was Desh's turn to drop his eyes. "It's not a complicated story," he muttered as he crouched down to wipe Lys's black blood off Streya's face. "After our, um, *incident* in Seattle, I got caught up in the rush of warlocks fleeing the Anchor Market. One of 'em stopped panicking long enough to banish me back to the Hells, so here I am."

Despite having just been trying to kill him, Lys scoffed. "*One* warlock was able to banish *you?*"

"Little old raisin of a wanker, too," Desh said with a self-deprecating laugh. "I could've taken his head off with a sneeze, but I didn't see the point. I'd just betrayed everything I stood for in a misguided attempt at redemption. Seemed like the Hells were where I belonged after that."

"No one belongs here," Bex said adamantly.

"So you've always said," Desh agreed as he straightened back up. "But it's amazing how stupid a man can be when he's feeling sorry for himself. I was good and ready to wallow in some proper misery, but when I saw Streya go for that warlock, my body moved on its own. Next thing I knew, my claws were in his throat." He shrugged. "What can I say? Old habits die hard."

"Nice to know you haven't turned your back on everything," Lys said, settling their bloody wing—which had finally healed, thank Ishtar—back into place. "Is it just the two of you, or are there other escapees as well?"

"There's a fair few of us," Desh said, nodding down the dark tunnel. "There's always a couple loose demons rattling around back here, but the numbers have been skyrocketing recently." He turned back to Bex with a determined look. "That's the other reason I decided to get in on Streya's escape. It wasn't just rebellious old habits. The Hells have changed since the last time I was here."

"What are you babbling about?" Lys asked sharply. "Have you seen the sin-collection floor? 'Cause it still looks like Hell to me."

"Come off, Lyssy," Desh scoffed. "How long's it been since the last time you got banished down here?"

Lys frowned, doing the math. "Not counting today, around two hundred years."

"Exactly," Desh said. "You got no idea what's normal these days. I didn't either since I was stuck in the Lowest Hell for all of my previous incarceration, but I've done my time scraping shit out of water. I know how bleak that life is, how it gets so hopeless that licking warlock boots on Earth starts to look rosy by comparison. Hells work used to be the most kicked-down a demon could get, real curl-up-and-wait-to-die shit. When they chained me to the line this time, though, it was *different*. People were talking. They were buzzing, about *you*."

He pointed a bony finger at Bex, who scowled. "What do you mean they were talking? I haven't heard any demon but us say a word since we got here."

"Just 'cause we ain't blabbing in the open doesn't mean we don't talk," Desh insisted as his face lit up with a grin that wasn't smarmy or mocking for once. It was real, the only genuine smile Bex had ever seen from him.

"Word of your war on Heaven's gotten around," he explained. "The attack on the Anchor was still going when I got tossed down here, but by the time they finished my processing and stuck me on a chain, the whole collection floor was going mad 'bout the rebel queen who'd beaten Gilgamesh's army and stolen his Anchor Market. To hear folks down here tell it, you'd killed five princes and taken over the entire state of Washington as a new homeland for demonkind. It was obvious crazy talk, and it never would've gone anywhere if Gilgamesh hadn't locked down all the Anchors."

Desh's grin got even wider. "That was the smoking gun. The longer Gilgamesh kept his doors locked, the more folks down here started saying the Eternal King was afraid of you. They said you were Ishtar's vengeance come at last. The unkillable Queen of Wrath who'd arrive any day to destroy the Hells and set us all free! It's been all anyone could talk about for weeks, and then, like a miracle, here you are."

"But I'm not here," Bex argued, pointing at her hornless head. "I lost, and I'm *not* here to free the Hells. I'm only on this side to get my powers back."

That had been the plan from the start, but saying as much in front of Desh felt like a shameful confession. Bex was already holding her breath for the moment the hopeful smile fell off his face, but the fear demon just gave her a stubborn glare.

"You think some oversized head ornaments are the only thing that makes you a queen?" he demanded. "They're just the signposts, luv. There ain't no shame in getting shot down when you're taking on the Holy City like a one-woman army. We felt you shaking the place all the way down here! Damn warlocks were pissing themselves in fear."

He paused to savor the happy memory then turned back to Bex with his orange eyes shining brighter than ever. "Look at it like that, and the biggest shame's on Gilgamesh. He sets himself to be this infallible king, but even after he stole your horns, you're still here. You're *in his Hells* giving his warlocks the slip! *That's* the Bex I signed up to follow. That's why I scrambled to grab you just now even though I knew Lys would slit my throat for it. Because crown or no crown, you've never stopped fighting the good fight, and this time, I intend to do my part."

Bex was horrified by the time he finished, because Desh was looking at her now the way Lys did, like he actually believed. Bex didn't know how to respond to that, because she *wasn't* what he said. She'd sneaked into the Hells as a thief, not a savior, but Desh was grinning at her like she was about to strike a match and burn this whole place to the ground. Bex was still scrambling for a way to explain how impossible that was when Lys burst out laughing.

"Well, well, well," they said, rising up on the tips of their clawed feet so they could loom over Desh's smaller human form with the smuggest expression

Bex had ever seen. "Looks like someone owes me an apology. I was right, wasn't I?"

The Desh Bex remembered would've had a rude remark for that, but this Desh just nodded.

"Yes, you were," he admitted humbly. "And I owe you a lot more than an apology, but I hope you'll take one anyway."

Lys looked like they were getting ready to hold this over him forever, but then Desh bent forward in a bow, dropping his wickedly curved black horns so close to the ground that Bex was amazed he didn't fall over.

"I'm sorry, Lysanae," he said in a solemn voice. "I thought I was doing the right thing when I tried to end Bex's cycle of reincarnation, but I was a damn idiot. I thank Ishtar every day that you and that witch boy stopped me. I nearly committed the worst crime of my life, and I am so, so grateful to you for staying my hand. I thank you from the bottom of my heart, and I hope you'll accept me back at your side in the fight to come."

By the time he finished, Lys was in shock. They stood there, speechless, for almost thirty seconds, before their lips curved back into a smile.

"Grovel accepted," they said, reaching down to pat Desh's lowered head. "But you're begging forgiveness from the wrong demon. Bex is the one you tried to backstab, so get down on your knees this time and apologize properly to your queen."

"There's no need for that," Bex said quickly. "I wasn't even there when he tried to kill me."

Lys harrumphed, but Bex had already put her hand on Desh's shoulder to pull him back up. "Your apology is accepted," she told him. "And thanks again for getting us out of that mess."

"Least I could do for the Savior Queen," he replied with a grin.

Bex winced. "Is that what they're calling me?"

"They're calling you all sorts of things," Desh told her excitedly, counting off on his black-nailed fingers. "We've got Savior Queen, Vengeance of Ishtar, Gilgamesh's Executioner, Hope of the Hells, and those are just the ones I remember off the top of my head. I tried telling 'em not to get their hopes up, but when the order came down to send all the constructs upstairs 'cause you were melting the cannons off the Holy City's walls, even I had nothing to say."

Lys snorted. "You? Speechless? That I'd like to see."

"There's only so many times a man can be proven wrong before he's forced to change his tune," Desh admitted with a shrug. "I wasn't the only one, either. By the time we heard the all-mighty voice of Gilgamesh announce that he was sparing the Queen of Wrath's life as a favor to his new prince, every demon down here was already convinced it was a cover-up. Even the war demons were whispering that you must've given him the slip, and now here you are with a strike force in the very heart of the Hells! What else is there to say after that except 'All hail the conquering queen'?"

"That's too far in the other direction," Bex argued, holding up the severed stump of her right hand. "I did get away, but as you can see, I'm not going to be conquering anything any time soon."

"You're still here, though," Desh argued stubbornly. "That means the rumors can't be all wrong. I mean, just look at where we're standing!"

It looked like a dusty, forgotten maintenance tunnel to Bex, but Lys's amber eyes lit up like Desh had just pointed out a miracle.

"You're *right*!" they said, whirling around. "These are the Founders' Tunnels!"

"The what?" asked Iggs.

"The Founders' Tunnels," Desh repeated. "Buncha cracks and crawlspaces dug eons ago by the first generation of demon slaves. The stories say it happened right after the war, before Gilgamesh perfected the art of keeping us down. They were trying to dig their way to freedom. Never made it, of course, but their old tunnels still make a handy hiding place for slaves who slip the chain. That's why they're normally packed with golden constructs who kill on sight, but—"

"But there are no constructs right now," Lys finished breathlessly. "Bex melted all of them!"

"I didn't melt *all* of them," Bex insisted.

"You must've melted enough," Desh said, sweeping his arm down the dark, empty tunnel. "I don't know what's going on, but there hasn't been a patrol through here in days. The warlocks are all too scared to come in themselves, so we've had the run of the place. Couldn't ask for a better breeding ground for a rebellion."

"He's got a point," Lys said, starting to sound excited. "This place should be seething like a kicked anthill after the chase we just led them on, but I can't even hear the war demons yelling outside anymore. Listen."

They were right. The other side of the fake wooden wall was silent, and the smile on Lys's face got bigger.

"I think we're in the middle of a golden opportunity," they said. "Running into that prince was bad luck, but everything else we've seen has been just as shoestring as the war-demon kids outside said it'd be."

"They could still be bringing reinforcements down from the Upper Hells," Kirok cautioned. "But you're right. Security has been shamefully sparse. During our approach to the tower, I didn't even count the minimum number of patrols on the collection floor."

"It's been that way all week," Desh said. "That's why I had Streya keeping an eye on the tower. I figured if Heaven's going to take their eyes off the ball, then we're obligated to take advantage and get a few more of our people off the chains."

"Exactly," Lys said, spinning around to face Bex. "I know you were worried about our disguises, but what if we didn't *need* disguises? What if we were able to walk right up those stairs into Heaven because every warlock in the tower was *somewhere else*?"

"Where else would they be?" Bex asked, confused.

"Attempting to do their jobs," Lys replied with a grin. "Imagine what would've happened if we'd been inside that tower after the princess bolted. The whole office would've been in chaos! Forget bullying our way through. I bet we could've walked right up the stairs without so much as a second glance."

"You're talking about a distraction," Iggs said.

"I'm talking about the biggest distraction there is," Lys replied, pointing at Bex. "You heard Desh just now. The whole Middle Hells are buzzing about the Queen of Wrath. Now, imagine she shows up and says 'riot!' This whole place would go up like a powder keg. What's left of the security force would be completely overwhelmed, leaving no one to stop *us* from scooting up to Heaven and getting everything we came here for."

"And then we could come back down to *actually* set everyone free," Iggs finished excitedly. "That's a great idea!"

"No, it's not," Bex growled, clenching her one remaining fist. "I'm not using a bunch of starving, desperate slaves as a distraction. Even if they were willing to help, I can't ask them to fight for me when they're still chained to the floor. It'd be a massacre."

Lys's face fell, but Desh was snapping his fingers like he'd just come up with something grand.

"What if they weren't chained?" he asked as the grin returned to his face. "If it's a distraction you're after, I know where there's a bunch of demons who *aren't* collared and who'll definitely want to fight."

"Are they in the Hells?" Lys asked skeptically. "Because that sounds too good to be true."

"There's a pretty big catch," Desh admitted as his eyes flicked over the crowd to where Nemini was hanging at the back. "But I think we might have a way around. Here, follow me, and I'll show you what I mean."

Bex still wasn't sure, but Desh had already scooped Streya onto his shoulders and started jogging down the dark tunnel with his lantern. Iggs took off after him at once. After a long hesitation, Lys did as well, tapping the bottom of Bran's broom to let Boston, who'd been ignoring the demons this whole time in favor of fiddling with his tiny leaf-version of Adrian, know they were moving. Kirok stayed put, clearly waiting for Bex to start moving before he did, but Bex was staring over her shoulder at the only member of their invasion team who'd yet to offer an opinion.

"Nemini?" she called softly, reaching back toward the void demon, who still hadn't budged from the shadows where they'd entered. "You good?"

Nemini didn't reply. She'd been weirdly quiet since they'd arrived in the Hells, even for her. Bex was about to walk over and just ask what was wrong when Nemini pushed off the stone and padded after the others, her snake-headed figure slipping in and out of sight like a shadow in the flickering light of Desh's tiny lantern.

Bex hadn't seriously considered the incredible feat that was the Founders' Tunnels until she was walking down them. She'd thought it'd be a few back doors and connectors, but the tunnels went on forever.

They also went every*where*. They weren't just a ring around the outside that let demons move behind the cliffside hovels without being seen. The secret tunnels went down as well, burrowing into the stone beneath the flooded sin-collection floor. The bolts that anchored the slave chains actually stuck through the ceiling in places, and there was sin-filled river water dripping everywhere. It looked like a cave-in waiting to happen, but Desh led them around every danger like an old pro, keeping the pace and pointing out all the places that were good for making camp and hiding out.

Most of these had demons in them already. Just like Desh had said earlier, there were whole camps of escapees down here. They all waved at Desh and Streya and gawked at the newcomers, but no one seemed to recognize Bex without her horns.

Bex was fine with that. It was hard enough being crownless around demons who already knew her. Having to introduce herself to a bunch of desperate, starving slaves as the Savior Queen Who Couldn't Actually Do Anything Yet might have broken her.

Just thinking about it dragged Bex dangerously close to the empty pit left by the loss of her name. The fall Nemini had helped her climb out of was always lurking at the back of her mind, but Bex stayed out of it by stubbornly reminding herself that, even after their failure at the tower, she was still doing better than any Queen of Wrath before her. None of the other Rebexas had ever made it even close to the Hells. She just had to push a little farther, be a little cleverer, and she could snatch her stolen power back from Gilgamesh and return to being a queen who was strong enough to actually help people.

Just thinking about coming back to right all the wrongs she'd seen since they arrived was the bonfire that kept Bex moving. She was still imagining all the ways she'd smash this horrible place the second she was strong enough when Desh finally came to a halt.

"Here we are," he said, gesturing at a stretch of tunnel that—to Bex's eyes, at least—looked exactly the same as all the others they'd walked past. "This is the place, right?"

That question was for Streya, who nodded frantically and pointed at a stretch of darker rock in the middle of the wet tunnel floor. It wasn't until the little demon stuck her hand through it, though, that Bex realized the spot wasn't a natural discoloration or a puddle of the black water that was constantly dripping down from the flooded floor above. It was a hole. A crack in the floor that went down into a darkness so thick, even Bex's eyes couldn't penetrate it.

"Where does that go?" she asked, crouching down for a better look.

"The Lowest Hells," Desh answered with a shudder. "I don't know if Lys explained this already, but we've got three layers down here. There's the Upper Hells where the war demons toil like good little worker bees, the Middle Hells where the rest of us commoners slave away, and the Lowest Hells, which is the polite name for the pit where Gilgamesh throws all his troublemakers."

Bex perked up. "Troublemakers?"

"Now you see the picture," Desh said as he reached up to hang his lantern off one of the sin-iron bolts sticking through the low ceiling. "Since you've been leading rebellions against Heaven for five thousand years, there's a bunch of your old followers languishing down there in eternal torment. I was stuck down there myself before Prince Leander fished me out for his backstabbing plot. It's a horrible, soul-crushing place, but it's not the sort of prison that requires chains. Why else do you think my neck was still clean when I came back?"

"Because they wanted us to accept you without suspicion?" Lys guessed.

"Because the Lowest Hells are *so* awful, they don't even bother slapping you in irons before they throw you in," Desh corrected as he tapped his bare foot against the edge of the hole Bex was crouched beside. "If you want a distraction, there's a whole army of proven rebels with clean necks right below us. The tricky part's figuring out how to get them up here."

"Tricky part?" Lys repeated incredulously. "Try impossible. The reason Heaven doesn't bother with chains in the Lowest Hells is because they're famously inescapable. My warlock threatened to banish me there all the time back when I was a slave. He said they were a prison of the mind, a place so warped and terrible that not even the strongest demon could crawl out with their sanity intact."

"Warlocks are always saying shit like that to mess with you," Desh argued. "The mind-prison thing's legit, but the rest is bollocks. It's completely possible to come out with all your marbles. Just look at me! I got my brains back the second the prince pulled me out."

"How does that help us?" Lys demanded. "In case you haven't noticed, we don't have a prince. Until Bex gets her horns back, we're just a bunch of normal demons. If we stick our heads into that hole, we'll be just as trapped as every other poor bastard that gets tossed down there."

"We're not *all* normal demons," Desh said with a grin. "We might not have a prince, but we do have *her*."

He stabbed his finger at Nemini, who was still hanging as far back from the rest of them as she could without actually being lost in the dark. She retreated even farther when Desh pointed at her, and Bex smacked his hand down with a scowl.

"Stop that," she ordered. "What does Nemini have to do with any of this?"

"Because she's a *void* demon," Desh explained confidently. "The Lowest Hells work by dropping your mind into a pit so deep you can't make your body move to get out, but Nemini lives that way all the time! Endless voids of nothingness are literally her bread and butter, which means she should be immune to the Lowest Hells' effect. She can hop right down and grab our fallen soldiers no problem. Once she brings them back up here, their minds should return just like mine did, and we'll have an army of demons with clean necks and an axe to grind against Heaven ready to raise hell in the Hells. It's *perfect*!"

He finished with a flourish, but Bex could only sigh. Not because Desh's plan was bad—it was actually pretty great—but because she didn't even need to look at Nemini to know that she hated it. She'd already pulled all the way back into the shadows, blending into the dark until she was just two yellow eyes glinting at the other end of the tunnel.

"I figured we'd tie a rope around her waist and lower her down," Desh went on, oblivious. "That way, if I'm wrong and she can't handle it, we can just yank her out. If she *can* handle it, though, we'll have unfettered access to the vault where Gilgamesh keeps all his most dangerous enemies. You literally couldn't ask for better."

There was a lot more Bex could think to ask for, but she didn't want to stomp on Desh's excitement. It was obvious from his face that he truly thought he'd found their winning ticket, and for all Bex knew, he had. Unleashing a bunch of demons who weren't starved and chained into the Middle Hells at a time when Gilgamesh's security was at an unprecedented low could be a total game changer. Before Bex could agree to anything, though, she needed to talk to the person who'd actually be doing it.

"Excuse me a moment," she said, motioning for the others to stay put as she got to her feet and walked back down the dark tunnel to where her friend was hiding.

"Hey," she said quietly, crouching beside the patch of darker shadow she was pretty sure Nemini was hiding in. "You want to tell me what's going on?"

"Not particularly," the darkness whispered back.

Bex frowned. "Do you not like Desh's plan?"

"No," she sighed. "It's fine. It'll probably even work. It's just…"

Her voice trailed off with a tremor. Bex was squinting into the dark, trying to see if Nemini had flitted away or just gone silent when an arm reached out to grab her one remaining hand. The rest of Nemini appeared a second later, falling out of the shadows to lean against Bex's side.

"I can't do it, Bexa," Nemini whispered. "I mean, physically I can, but…" She pressed her face harder into Bex's leather coat. "I'm sorry. I know I said I'd help, but I didn't think… I didn't know we'd be…"

"Hey, it's okay," Bex said, hugging Nemini close. "If you can't do it, that's fine. We'll just find another way."

"I should do it," Nemini said, closing her eyes tight as the swarm of black snakes on her head slithered down to shield her face. "You would do it, but I'm not you. I've *never* been you, and I can't... I *can't...*"

"It's okay," Bex said again, reaching up to pet her snakes, but it was just an automatic gesture. She knew she was supposed to be focusing on her friend, but what Nemini had just said was buzzing inside Bex's skull, giving her an idea.

"I'll do it."

Nemini jerked out of her arms. "What?"

"I'll do it," Bex said again as her face split into a grin. "You just said I could, right?"

"I said you *would*," Nemini corrected. "That doesn't mean it's a good idea."

"But it would work," Bex pressed, refusing to let this go. "The whole reason Desh wanted you for this is because you're a void demon, but I've also lost my name. I've got a hole inside me, too, now. That means I should be able to go down there in your stead, right?"

"*No,*" Nemini insisted, her yellow eyes more terrified than Bex had ever seen before she dropped them.

"There's no physical reason you can't go," she went on in a more measured voice. "But you don't know what's down there, Bexa. The Upper and Middle Hells were built to satisfy Gilgamesh's need for sin iron, but what's below us is a hell in the truest sense. If you go down there, you might never return."

"I came back from the void," Bex reminded her. "Is this worse than that?"

"Yes," Nemini said without hesitation, gripping Bex's one remaining hand with both of hers. "There's peace in the void. We were alone there, just the two of us, but the Lowest Hell is different. That emptiness has hands that will drag you down. If they latch on to you, they'll suck you in just like everyone else, but unlike all the other demons Gilgamesh throws down there, you no longer have a name we can call to pull you back."

"Then I won't get caught," Bex said confidently, turning her hand around so that she was the one squeezing Nemini's fingers. "If you say there's no physical reason I can't do it, then I'm going to do it."

Nemini bit her lip. "But—"

"It's my call," Bex insisted. "I'm the one who wanted to come to the Hells in the first place, but so far I've done nothing but follow behind everyone else. I'm tired of being the weakest link in my own team. I'm tired of being helpless while my people suffer. Everything I need is at the top of that tower, so I'm going to go down there and get us the biggest distraction Heaven's ever seen. I'm going to make sure the warlocks are so busy fighting the enemy in front of them, they don't even see me coming until I stab them in the back. Even if the distraction plan doesn't work, I'll still be freeing a bunch of our old allies from eternal torment. That's exactly the sort of thing a queen should risk her life for."

"Not your life," Nemini said.

"*Yes*, my life," Bex insisted. "We're all risking our lives by being here. The difference is that, unlike every other part of this mission, this is something I can actually help with. I can't burn slave bands off demons anymore, I can't toe-to-toe it with a princess, but I *can* go down there in your stead and get us what we need to make this *work*."

Nemini lowered her head again, but Bex didn't let her escape. "Is there reason other than fear for my safety that makes you think I can't do this?"

"No," Nemini whispered, still refusing to look at her. "If anyone could, it'd be you. It's just…" Her shoulders hunched higher around her snake-covered ears. "I don't want you to see what's down there."

"Why not?" Bex asked, confused. "Have you been to the Lowest Hells before?"

"Never," Nemini said, reaching up to scrub her eyes. "But that doesn't mean I don't know or don't care." She stared grimly at the wetness on the back of her hand. "I must not be as broken as I thought."

"Oh," said Bex, still not understanding. "That's a good thing, right?"

"No," Nemini replied, tucking herself back into the shadows. "But I'm done trying to stop you. Go be the bright queen and pick up my failures like you always do. I just hope you still want me around when it's over."

"I'll never not want you around," Bex said fiercely, reaching out to grab Nemini's fading hand. "You're my oldest and dearest ally, and you will never not be welcome by my side."

"You always were good at making promises," Nemini's voice whispered as her hand disappeared from Bex's grasp. "But nothing lasts forever, not even your good intentions. We'll see if you still feel the same when you come back, *if* you come back."

"I will," Bex swore, glaring into the dark where Nemini had just been. "I *will* return, and I *will* feel exactly the same way about you as I do now. That's something that will *never* change, so wait right there for me, Nemini, because I'll be back to prove you wrong."

That probably wasn't the best way to say it. Nemini was just afraid, and orders never changed anyone's mind, but Bex was so *mad*. Mad at Nemini for doubting her, mad at herself for being so weak and useless, mad at Gilgamesh for making them go through all of this in the first place.

She was mad at everything, which was a terrible way to go into a dangerous, unknown situation, but it also made her feel more like herself than she had since she'd lost her horns. Bex swore she could feel the embers of her bonfire heating back up as she slung her backpack furiously to the ground, dug out her rope, and started tying one end around her waist.

When she had it knotted good and tight, she tossed the other end to Iggs, who caught it with a confused look.

"Hang on," he said as Bex walked past him. "Isn't Nemini the one who's supposed to—"

His innocent question turned into a horrified shout as Bex jumped into the hole, plunging feetfirst into a freezing blackness that swallowed her up like a nest of hungry worms.

Chapter 7

MAYBE SHE SHOULDN'T HAVE been so cocky.

Bex had fallen off a lot of scary places in the last few months, including out of Heaven twice and down a bottomless void inside her own soul. Each of those had been existentially terrifying in its own unique way, but nothing compared to this fall, because this time, Bex wasn't alone.

Nemini had called them hands, but they were more like whole bodies coming out of the dark to wrap around her. Bex had talked a big game about not getting caught, but she didn't even get a chance to dodge before they'd bound her up like a mummy, covering her face and locking her limbs as they dragged her faster and faster into the depths.

What made it even more terrifying was that Bex had no idea what she was being dragged *by*. It was so dark that even her normally excellent night vision was useless. All she knew was that the things swirling around her were as strong as deep ocean currents, and they were sucking her into a freezing abyss that was much more terrifying than the void she'd fallen into before. That had been just empty nothing, and she'd had Nemini to help her through it.

There was no one to help her now. Bex couldn't even open her mouth to scream as the pressure binding her body began to change, sharpening into distinct shapes that felt like arms, hands, legs, even faces. Terrified, screaming faces that bit into Bex's flesh like zombies. *Ghostly* zombies, because while she could feel every ridge and point of their sharp teeth, the bites never actually broke her skin. It was just pain and the endless feeling of being devoured. And weirdly enough, that was the feeling that kicked Bex out of her panic, because unlike everything else that had happened since she'd jumped into the Lowest Hells, being held down and chomped on was a feeling she'd experienced many times before.

All at once, Bex stopped fighting and let her body go limp. This caused the things squeezing her to pause as well, loosening the pressure over her mouth long enough for Bex to get out a word.

"*Stop*," she ordered in the same commanding tone she used on kick demons.

The writhing bodies wrapped around her didn't listen, but that was normal too. Even back when she'd had her horns and the voice of a queen, the kick demons trapped in Limbo had always been too crazed with hunger to obey. Now that she was no longer struggling to escape them, Bex could feel that the phantom bodies here were the same. If she focused, she could even feel their horns. Tall, forked, antler-like horns attached to screaming, terrified demons lost in the dark.

The moment she realized that, Bex stopped being afraid. It didn't matter that she was still being dragged down into a freezing, pitch-black pit. The hands pulling her hair and the invisible teeth biting her flesh weren't evil ghosts or sorcerous phantoms made to torment Gilgamesh's enemies. They were demons.

It was so obvious, Bex felt like an idiot for not realizing the truth sooner. The Lowest Hells were uniquely horrible, but that didn't mean they didn't serve the same purpose as all the others. They were still a prison built by Gilgamesh to contain Ishtar's children. Bex even knew *which* children because all the other demon tribes were already accounted for. War was in the Upper Hells, and Envy, Lust, Greed, Fear, Hate, and Sorrow were all lumped together in the middle. Bex would never not know her own Wrath demons, so that only left one option. These were the demons who'd been cast into the void when Gilgamesh broke their queen, the tragically lost demons of Pride.

Now that she knew what she was dealing with, Bex even recognized the freezing cold darkness she was falling through. It was the same feeling she used to get when Nemini touched her before Bex had lost her name and become a void herself. But where Nemini's emptiness had always been a calm, empty place where nothing mattered and every burden could be set down, this was a screaming nightmare.

There was no peace in this void, no solace in the emptiness, because it wasn't empty at all. The darkness here was filled with terror and loss, confusion and hunger, because unlike Nemini, these demons had never hit bottom. They'd been falling and falling and *falling* for five thousand years. No wonder they latched on to anything they came into contact with. They were terrified, which perversely made Bex feel a lot more confident, because if there was anything she'd learned during the month she'd spent rescuing her people from Limbo, it was how to handle a panicking demon.

"*Demons of Pride!*" she yelled, bellowing into the dark like she could fill the emptiness with nothing but her voice. "I am Rebexa, Queen of Wrath! Like your own queen, I was broken by Gilgamesh, but Ishtar's creations are resilient! I know you've been falling for a long time, but as a wise member of your own tribe just reminded me, nothing lasts forever. Gilgamesh has trapped you in a prison of your own fear just like he trapped my demons in starvation, but we are the people of the Riverlands! If we were truly defeated, the Traitor King wouldn't need the Hells. He wouldn't need chains or slave bands, but Gilgamesh relies on all those crutches because *he has not won*. The war isn't over, so lift your horns, soldiers of Pride! Release me so that I may do Ishtar's work, and I swear on my mother's name, *I will set you free!*"

She'd shouted it with all her might, but Bex's promise still faded into the void. There was nothing else it could've done, because hers was no longer a queen's voice. She had no name, no horns, no sword, no authority, nothing at all. Despite all she'd lost, though, Bex was still a daughter of Ishtar. For one hundred and ninety-eight lifetimes, she'd refused to accept defeat. Every death, every loss, every time Ishtar had welcomed her home, Bex had picked up her sword and marched back out into the fight. Even when Nemini had offered her the peace of the void, she'd clung stubbornly to her duty because she wasn't finished. So long as her people were slaves, Bex would *never* be finished. She might not be the Bonfire Queen of Wrath anymore, but her anger would never, *ever* go out. That fire would spark back to life again and again just like Bex herself did, and when she thrust out her hand to the screaming pride demons now, Bex was the one who flared in the dark.

It was just a faint glow at the end of her fingers, nothing like the blazing inferno she normally was, but even tiny lights shine bright when the darkness is deep enough. Bex's words had been instantly lost, but her fire gleamed through the void like a lighthouse, and everywhere its glow touched, the shattered demons' screams turned back into words.

Queen! they whispered desperately. *Save us!* **Save us!**

"I will," Bex promised, reaching her glowing fingers as far as they would go. "So long as I draw breath, I swear I'll get you out."

She had nothing to back those words up with, but that didn't seem to matter. The fact that a queen had come to speak to them at all must have been enough, because the reckless words were barely out of Bex's mouth when the frantic mass of writhing demons suddenly let her go. The teeth stopped biting, the hands stopped grabbing, and the thick sea of darkness rolled away to reveal an enormous chamber.

Just like the Middle Hells above, it was shaped like a natural cavern. Since it had been made to hold only one sort of demon, this Hell was smaller, with a much lower ceiling, but the space was still massive. It was also, Bex realized with a start, absolutely packed with demons.

They'd been laid out in rows on the floor like corpses awaiting cremation. Their skin was the same dark brown as Nemini's, but unlike Bex's void demon, all of these bodies had horns. Big, beautiful, stag-like antlers that gleamed like obsidian in the faint glow of Bex's tiny fire. It didn't look like any of them had slave bands or collars, but Bex wasn't sure if that was because Gilgamesh didn't consider them an escape risk or if demons whose names had been shattered couldn't be collared.

Chains or no chains, though, they weren't going anywhere. Bex had actually landed on top of one when the grasping hands let her go, but the man didn't even seem to notice her boot on his chest. His eyes were squeezed shut like he was sleeping, but his whole body was twitching, and his mouth was open in a silent scream. He didn't react to Bex at all, not even when she shook him with her glowing hand.

That was supremely disappointing. For a moment there, Bex really thought she'd gotten some of her power back. Sadly, it looked like a little glowing was all it was. Her lit-up fingers didn't feel any warmer than usual, and she couldn't even sense the void where the demons' names should have been.

She'd just have to come back down here after she'd retrieved her horns, Bex decided. If Nemini could survive without a queen, surely these demons could too. She'd go out and pick them all up off the riverbank if that was what it took, but she was going to keep her promise, to them and to Nemini. First, though, she had to get what she'd come for.

With that, Bex stopped staring at the demons she couldn't save yet and started looking around for the ones she could. From what Desh had said earlier, she'd expected them to be all over, but other than the void demons laid out on the floor, she didn't see anyone, mostly because she couldn't see much at all. Even with the new glow from her fingers, Bex could only see a few feet in any direction. She was taking tiny steps to start exploring the area her rope could reach when she felt something cold touch her foot.

She jumped away on instinct then sighed. It was just water. Like the Middle Hells above, the floor of the Lowest Hells was also covered in a shallow flood. It was so filthy that it barely reflected her light, which was why Bex hadn't noticed it until the freezing cold seeped into her boots. Now that she was splashing through it, though, Bex could see that the whole Hell was covered in an ankle-deep, barely moving river.

Using her glowing hand like a flashlight, Bex bent down until her nose was almost touching the water's oily surface. It was much dirtier than the flood upstairs, but the water here was definitely from a River of Death. This close, Bex could see the black residue of extracted sin building up around the pride demons' unconscious bodies. It drifted like silt in the shallow river's gentle current, flowing away from the demons and eventually falling down the grates that were placed everywhere in the Lowest Hells' stone floor. The amounts were much smaller than the grime she'd seen the other slaves scraping into their buckets upstairs, but the basic idea was the same. The pride demons had been submerged so that their bodies could keep collecting sin even while their minds were lost, and the longer Bex thought about that, the angrier she became.

"That *bastard*," she snarled, clutching her glowing fist. "He keeps using us even when we sleep." She kicked her boots through the shallow water, dislodging the thin layer of black sin that had already built up along the sole. "I swear to Ishtar, I'm going to tear down every last one of his damn—"

"Bex!"

Her head shot up. As she'd noted earlier, the ceiling in this Hell wasn't very high, but the shout still sounded like it'd come from miles away. The disconnect was so jarring, Bex didn't even realize she'd fallen straight down until she spotted a glimmer directly above her head. When she craned her neck all the way back, she saw Lys staring down at her with the metal flashlight from Bex's backpack gripped in their hand.

"Bex!" they shouted in a voice gone hoarse from panic. "Are you alive?"

"I'm here," Bex called back, though she didn't think they heard. She'd been looking straight at Lys's face when she yelled, but their amber eyes were still darting all over like they couldn't sense a thing.

The hole must still look like an impenetrable pit of darkness to them, Bex realized. The void demons had let her go because she'd proven who she was, but that mercy didn't extend to anyone else, not even themselves. She was able to stand down here without being dragged into terrified madness, but every pride demon was still twitching in the shallow water like victims of the world's worst nightmare.

It was a heartbreaking sight, but there was nothing Bex could do about it. There was nothing she could do for anyone until she got her horns back, so she got her act together and reached up to tap the button on her ear comm. It took three more taps, though, before Bex realized her radio wasn't working.

That made sense in hindsight. If comms functioned down here, Lys would've been yelling in her ear this entire time. Bex didn't know if the problem was magical or mechanical, but seeing how no outside sound or light seemed able to penetrate the Lowest Hells, her money was on magic. The rope was still tied around her waist, though. So, since she couldn't call to let them know she was alive, Bex reached up and gave the line a yank instead.

She'd just been trying to communicate to Lys that she was okay, but since she'd jumped down here without setting up a signal like an impatient idiot, her first tug triggered a frantic attempt to pull her back up. Bex was ten feet off the ground before she caught her balance and pulled back, giving the rope a series of long, calm tugs until Lys—or more likely, Iggs—got the message and stopped trying to reel her in.

Once Bex was back on the ground and, more importantly, confident she'd stay there, she let go of the rope and resumed her search for all the not-pride demons she'd come down here to find. According to Desh, there should've been a ton of them, but all Bex saw were more rows of twitching void demons. She was starting to worry this whole idea was a bust when she spotted something odd in the tiny circle of light from her still-glowing hand.

It looked like a giant pile of old clothes, but as Bex walked closer, she realized they were demons. Not void demons—the last line of those had stopped a few feet back—but every other sort imaginable. They were all lying piled on top of each other in a giant heap like they'd been dropped there from the ceiling over eons. Just like the void demons, their eyes were squeezed tight and their faces were contorted with fear, but where the void demons lying on the ground were all wearing the same prison tunics as the slaves upstairs, the piled bodies were wearing a random assortment of clothing from every era of human history. Bex was still trying to make sense of the chaos when her eyes landed on a familiar face near the top.

It was a war demon. A fully transformed one who'd recently lost all four of his arms. The twiglike replacements had been frozen before they could finish growing in, but it was his dented bronze face that Bex recognized. That was the war demon who worked for the Spider, the one who'd attacked her in the train yard, Trinaeous.

She could only shake her head after that. Of all the demons she could've found, it had to be the one who'd almost killed her. Still, even though he'd run her down and tried to drag her back to his master, Bex couldn't help feeling sorry for the loyal bastard. Lys had told her all about how the Spider had still banished him to the Lowest Hells despite Trinaeous telling him the truth about Bex's identity, which was just unfair. Even traitorous bootlickers deserved better than that. He was also on top of the pile, which made him the easiest demon to reach without straining her rope.

Since she could already feel Iggs twitching to pull her back, that turned out to be the deciding factor. Before she could change her mind, Bex wrapped her arms around Trinaeous's comatose body and gave the rope three hard tugs.

She'd just finished the third pull when Iggs yanked them both into the air. Kirok must've been helping him because Bex scarcely had time to duck her head before she and her rescued war demon were hauled through the hole in the ceiling and into Lys's arms.

"I thought you were *dead*!" they wailed, squeezing Bex so tight her ribs creaked. "Why do you always have to jump into every strange hole you see?"

That had been inconsiderate. Saying sorry would only make Lys angrier, though, so Bex kept her mouth shut and hugged them back instead, giving her faithful, traumatized demon gentle, reassuring pats while Iggs finished rolling her catch onto the floor.

"Whoa," he said when he saw who she'd brought up with her. "Why'd you grab a war demon?"

"I think it was a logical choice considering we're in the middle of a war," General Kirok replied, leaning over to get a better look at Trinaeous's dented face. "I know this one. He was one of my trainees a few decades ago before he went to work as a bodyguard for the favored warlock known as the Spider."

"Not that jerk again," Lys groaned, glaring over Bex's shoulder. "Why'd you grab him?"

"Because he was closest," Bex said as she untangled herself from Lys's stranglehold.

"Big bastard, isn't he?" Desh said, reaching out to push Iggs back. "We'll want to give him his space. Coming back from the Lowest Hells can be a shock. I know I came out punchy."

"How *did* the prince get you out?" Bex asked, suddenly curious. "Can Gilgamesh's sons walk around down there?"

"Gods no," Desh said. "I got pulled out the same way they put me in: banishment. So long as you know a demon's name, you can move them just about anywhere in the Hells. I understand it costs a lot more quintessence if the demon isn't right in front of you, but paying to call them up is still a damn sight better than going down yourself. Even princes can't set foot in the Lowest Hells without falling under its curse, or so I've been told." He gave Bex a funny look. "How'd you manage it?"

"Because she's a daughter of Ishtar, you dolt," Lys snapped.

"That did help," Bex admitted, pushing Lys and Desh apart before anything regrettable happened. "But the main reason I made it was because the pride demons let me through."

Lys and Desh stopped glaring daggers at each other to gape at her.

"Pride demons?" Lys repeated in a skeptical voice.

"I thought they all turned into void demons and died," Desh said at the same time.

"They did change," Bex said, keeping an eye on the shadows where she'd last seen Nemini. "But they didn't die. The whole tribe is locked up below us. That's why the Lowest Hell is so bad. Gilgamesh used the vortex of fear and suffering caused by the loss of the pride demons' names to create a prison no one could escape from. He's also collecting sin with their unconscious bodies because he's a greedy asshole who never met a demon he couldn't exploit. There's no bottom to his behavior, and I got so mad about that that this happened."

She raised her left hand triumphantly. When no one reacted, she explained, "It's glowing."

"Is it?" Lys asked, squinting against the light of Desh's small lantern.

"It's a lot harder to see when it's not pitch-black," Bex admitted. "But it's definitely there." She looked at her barely-glowing fingers with a grin. "You know what this means, right? My fire's not entirely gone! Even without my name, I've still got a few embers left. That's how I convinced the panicked pride demons to let me through *and* it's how we're going to get everyone else out as well."

"How?" Iggs asked nervously. "I mean, it's not exactly a bonfire."

"It's not," Bex agreed, lowering her hand. "But this light still lets me navigate the Lowest Hells without getting sucked in. So long as I can do that, we can win, because Desh was right. There *is* an army down there. Banishments to the Lowest Hell must drop everyone in the same place, because I saw a huge pile of demons. If even half of them want to fight, we should have a distraction big enough to empty Heaven itself." She turned back to Iggs. "How many guns are in that bag Felix gave you?"

"Enough to cause the guards upstairs a major issue," Iggs said proudly, patting the ancient knapsack he hadn't let out of his sight since they arrived.

"Great," Bex said. "Start unloading. Kirok, you get the rope and be ready to pull me up. How many demons do you think you can lift at once?"

"Depends on the demon," the general said, furrowing his bronze eyebrows. "I'd say no more than three Iggs-sized individuals at a time to avoid exhaustion."

"I can manage that," Bex said as she rechecked the knot around her waist. "Three tugs will be the signal to reel in. I'm going to be walking around down there, so make sure you give me plenty of—"

She cut off when Trinaeous, who'd been lying as still as a fallen statue since he came out, suddenly arched off the tunnel's wet floor like he'd been electrocuted. He rolled onto his side next, wrapping his scrawny little arms—which must not have regenerated at all during his time in the Lowest Hells—around his huge body with a sob.

"That's normal," Desh assured them before Bex could say a word. "Like I said, coming back is a shock. Also, most demons don't get the big banish under happy circumstances. Put those two together and you've got a lot of issues to work through."

He reached out to pat the war demon's shaking shoulder. "He'll be better once he's had his cry. I'll explain the situation to him when he's ready. You go back down there and get us more soldiers."

Bex nodded and walked to the edge of the hole where General Kirokaltos was standing ready with the other end of the rope. Iggs had already moved farther down the tunnel and was covering the ground in weapons from Solomon's Armory while Lys organized them into rows. It was everything Bex could've asked from her demons, but there was still one matter she hadn't addressed yet.

Motioning for Kirok to wait, Bex turned away from the hole again and walked several feet back down the tunnel to the shadow where she'd last seen Nemini. To her surprise, the void demon was visible again. She was crouched beside Boston, holding up a battery-powered camping lantern Bex remembered Adrian using a few times so that the cat could see the circle he was making out of individual fir needles on the tunnel floor.

"Hey," Bex said as she crouched beside her. "Told you I'd come back."

"I'm glad to have been proven wrong," Nemini replied in her usual monotone, and then she sighed. "I'm sorry for what I said before."

"Don't worry about it," Bex said, watching Boston as he painstakingly nudged a needle into place with the tip of his claw. "I understand now why this place freaks you out so much, though I still don't get why you thought I'd think less of you. If anything, I'm even more impressed that you managed to land on your feet while the rest of your people kept falling."

"That's nothing to be proud of," Nemini muttered. "I was saved because you found me, but nothing can save them."

"I will," Bex promised, clenching her barely-glowing fist. "I know I told everyone to stay on mission, but I can't ignore this. I don't know how to fix what Gilgamesh broke yet, but I swear to you, Nemini, I'm going to find a way to save your people before we leave the Hells."

"I know you'll try," Nemini said. "You always try. That's why I chose to stay with you." She looked down at the pile of deep-green needles Boston had made at her feet. "You're the sort of queen I always wished Pride could be."

Bex wasn't sure how to interpret that, but she didn't know how to interpret most of what Nemini said. Her void demon didn't sound upset anymore, at least, so Bex left her to it, squeezing her shoulder one last time before walking back over to rejoin the group

by the hole where Iggs was breathlessly describing
what sort of badass demon he thought Bex should
bring up next.

Chapter 8

MEANWHILE, HIGH, HIGH ABOVE in the bright light of Gilgamesh's Highest Heaven, Adrian was struggling to get the princess to walk faster.

Things had started off well enough. After getting his brother's permission to visit the Hells, they'd both gone out the door like a shot. She must've just wanted to get out of the Crown Prince's office, though, because the moment they started the long, *looooooong* climb down all those damned beautiful stairs, the Princess of Wrath's pace got slower and slower until Adrian was practically towing her behind him like a boat anchor.

"Would you *please* go faster?" he growled through clenched teeth.

"Why?" she asked, giving him a look that would've set his heart pounding if he'd seen it on the actual Bex's face. "You already got permission, and Prince Demetrios has a long journey up from the Hells. Why shouldn't we enjoy this rare chance to get out?"

Adrian found absolutely nothing enjoyable about having to wait while his jailer strolled at the pace of a geriatric grandmother. He was trying to think of a way to make her get the lead out that wouldn't start a fight when the princess suddenly moved faster than his eyes could track, vanishing from the gold-patterned window where she'd been gazing out over the Holy City to reappear right beside him.

"I know you're in a hurry to impress your father," she murmured as she slid her hand—the left one made of carved bone, not the gloved right one that had been stolen from the real Bex—into his. "That's exactly the kind of prince I want to serve, but doesn't this remind you of something?"

"How could it?" Adrian asked, yanking his hand away. "I've never been to this part of the palace before."

"I didn't mean literally," the princess said with a laugh as she snatched his fingers back. "I was talking about the day we did the stakeout. You know, when we walked up the stairs to Pike Place?"

Adrian scowled at his trapped fingers. He supposed this was vaguely similar to the time he'd taken Bex's hand and walked with her to the market from the ferry. That day was one of his most treasured memories, which was why he wasn't about to let it be spoiled by a fake white doll.

"I don't like to think about those times," he lied, using the fact that she refused to let go of his hand to drag her down the stairs at the pace *he* wanted. "I was ignorant of Gilgamesh's true intentions back then, and I did many things that I regret. That's why I'm so eager to keep moving now. I want to complete the Queen of Pride's horns and redeem myself in my father's eyes as soon as possible."

It was a sign of how much this place was getting to him that Adrian was able to parrot the typical fawning Heaven-speak without choking. The princess, however, was staring at Adrian like he'd just asked her to marry him.

"Do you mean it?" she cried, golden eyes sparkling. "Have you finally realized the wisdom of our Eternal King? Do you really want to take your place at his side as a true Prince of Heaven?"

Adrian blinked. He hadn't thought he'd said any of that, but she was finally moving at a decent speed, so he kept it up.

"Of course," he lied through his teeth as he hurried them down the stairs. "King Gilgamesh is the smartest man I've ever met. We're going to have to stay on our toes if we want to impress him, so let's get to the Hells and—"

He cut off with a yelp as the princess suddenly came to a stop. The abrupt change in momentum nearly pulled his arm off, but when he looked back to see what in the Hells was the problem, the fake Bex was staring at him with a look of awestruck delight.

"I knew it," she whispered, squeezing Adrian's fingers until he gasped in pain. "The Crown Princess said you couldn't be trusted, that I'd have to watch you every minute to make sure you didn't betray our king, but I *knew* you'd come around. No one can witness the greatness of Gilgamesh's vision without coming to love him, for he is our glorious and eternal King! The one who will end all wars and lead us to true peace, and you will be his chosen heir, first among all princes!"

She dragged him closer, forcing Adrian, who'd been trying desperately to free his hand before she crushed it, to stumble back up the stairs before she pulled him off his feet.

"This is the moment I was made for," she said, finally letting go of his hand so she could pull off her white glove. "Here!"

Adrian stopped rubbing his bruised fingers to stare at the bare hand she'd just shoved in his face, Bex's stolen hand with Drox's heavy ring gleaming like a sheet of black ice on her small, elegant finger. He'd known it was hidden under her glove, but the princess had never revealed it in his presence before. Adrian had assumed that was because she didn't want to remind him that she was a fake. Now, though, he was beginning to think he'd missed something very important, because the princess was offering him Bex's bare hand like a knife. Or a sword.

"Take it," she ordered, staring at him with an eerily perfect copy of the real Bex's resolve. "I was made to be your weapon, so take my hand and claim the Bonfire of Wrath for your king. I might not be as strong as the Armor of War, but my fire is the hottest ever created, for I was the Executioning Blade of Ishtar, the flame that burned the goddess's enemies to dust! She used me as a tool of oppression, but you can use me for good. Your sacred blood is the forge that will turn my black blade white. All you have to do is take my hand. Accept your birthright, Prince Adrian, and together we will make me the strongest Blade of Gilgamesh ever to fight in our king's sacred name!"

Her golden eyes were glowing by the end, lit from within with the same smoldering fire that used to shine from the real Bex's eyes. Adrian could even smell her familiar smoky scent. It was the closest he'd felt to the real Bex since the night they sat under his tree in the Anchor, and Adrian missed it so badly that his bruised hand almost reached out to grab hers on its own before he curled it into a fist.

"I won't," he said, which was the absolute truth. The next part, however, was a lie so brazen it made his teeth hurt.

"I'm not worthy yet," he said, reaching out to touch her hard white cheek instead. "The Crown

Princess was right. I haven't proven myself, but I will. I'm going to finish Pride's horns and present them to Gilgamesh before he even knows to expect them. Only then, when I've performed an actual service to advance Heaven's mission, will I be able to draw you without shame."

"My prince," she whispered, closing her glowing eyes as she rubbed her cheek against his hand. "You are truly a son of Heaven. I never doubted, but now that I've seen the proof with my own eyes, I will not rest until I've helped you climb to the top of Gilgamesh's favor."

"Thank you for understanding," Adrian said, giving the princess a brief hug because it was the only way to keep her from seeing him flinch. "Once I prove myself to my father, I promise I'll draw you as my sword and we'll take our place together at his right hand."

"Not even the Crown Princess will be able to doubt you then," the princess agreed, her voice bright with excitement as she seized his hand yet again and started bounding down the stairs. "Come on! I don't want to waste a second. Let's hurry to the Hells and get you what you need to finish!"

Adrian was too busy running after her to reply, but that was for the best. His stomach was still churning from what he'd just forced himself to say. If he had to betray any more of his core principles sucking up to his father's neurotic parody of the woman he respected most, he was going to be sick right there on the stairs. Fortunately for him, the fake Bex locked onto goals as hard as the real one. She was already charging ahead, forcing him to run or be dragged as they descended the Tower of Heaven.

The rest of the trip went almost too fast. Adrian hadn't cared when all they were doing was walking spiral after spiral of endless, badly spaced, white-and-gold stairs, but the lower part of the palace where the multiple towers came together was a treasure trove of opportunities he desperately wanted to explore. Right at the bottom of the Crown Prince's tower, they passed a room full of white-robed sorcerers working on stone tablets that looked a lot like the ones he'd seen in the Anchor Market's control room. Adrian would've bet his hat it was a command center for the palace's magical infrastructure, but which infrastructure, and how much command?

He dragged his feet hard in an attempt to slow down long enough to see something useful, but now that he'd tied their current mission to making her his sword, nothing could stop the princess. She blazed through the palace like a charging bull, forcing servants, sorcerers, even warlocks surrounded by their war demons, to jump aside or get run over. At one point, they passed right by another prince in full golden armor with a princess sheathed at his side. The Princess of Wrath didn't even slow down to acknowledge him, for which Adrian was extremely grateful. He'd yet to meet one of Gilgamesh's sons who wasn't a pompous, violent, pain in the ass. This one certainly looked like he wanted to take him down a peg, but Adrian's princess yanked him away before the other prince could do more than glare.

She dragged him even faster after that, which was a real shame because they were now in what was clearly the public part of Gilgamesh's palace. Adrian had only seen the occasional servant upstairs, but these floors were packed with all manner of Heavenly denizens carrying all sorts of interesting things. The princess dragged him past a treasury filled with chests packed with coins of quintessence, an enormous, brilliantly lit hall full of accountants scribbling in floating, gold-bound ledgers, and a library full of scrolls that kept magically appearing and disappearing.

So many secrets of Heaven were on display that Adrian's eyes were getting tired from being so wide. Many of the things he saw were stuff he'd never expected, like women wearing the white robes of Heaven. He hadn't realized Gilgamesh employed women since every sorcerer and warlock he'd ever met had been a man, but there were plenty of them up here. Mostly in the libraries, but he also saw them counting quintessence with the assistance of greed demons dressed in the modest white robes of favored slaves.

"Why is all the quintessence piled up here?" he asked the princess when she dragged him past yet another overflowing treasury. "Do they make it in the palace?"

"Yes," she said without missing a step. "One of the palace towers is entirely dedicated to manufacturing quintessence. They normally only move the chests down here when it's time to ship them down the chains, but things have been backing up since the Anchors closed."

Adrian's ears picked up. "Are the chains close by?"

"Very close," she said, pointing the gloved hand she wasn't using to drag him at a large arched doorway that led to a wide staircase going down. "The hall where all the chains come together is right below us. Since Anchors are the only reliable entrance to Heaven other than death, Gilgamesh built the chains directly into the foundation of his palace."

"Sounds like a good way to control access."

"He did it to keep us safe," the princess corrected, pausing her breakneck pace to shoot him a chiding look. "The chains are the most obvious invasion path. If they ended in the White City, anyone could march up and all of Heaven could be put in danger."

"I never meant to question the king's judgment," Adrian said quickly. Then he added. "Can we go see them?"

It took a champion effort to keep his voice casual. Adrian was *dying* to see the place where all the chains connected, and what they connected to. In the desert, he'd seen them physically wrapped around the Wheel of Reincarnation, but he still wasn't sure if that had been real or not. What he'd perceived as a black desert of sin-iron dust could've been a metaphorical representation to make abstract concepts like reincarnation easier to understand and manipulate. There was no question that the chains he'd seen there had been much closer together than they actually were geographically, but that didn't mean it was a total fake. For all Adrian knew, the chains passed through the palace and kept going into the desert from there.

There was simply no way to know without investigating for himself, but the princess was already shaking her head.

"I'm sorry, my prince," she said. "The chains are sealed behind the same edict that locked the Anchors. We can't even enter the arrival room without Gilgamesh or Prince Hector's permission."

Adrian frowned. "Prince Hector?"

"The Prince of Envy," she explained, turning away to pick up the pace again. "He's the prince in charge of chain maintenance."

Ah, Adrian thought as she dragged him behind her. Hector must be the dirty prince he'd seen in the Boston Anchor, the one who'd heard his teleport and sounded the alarm. Also the one who'd tried to kill him when he'd stuck his head through the sin-iron wall at the bottom of the Seattle Anchor while dressed as Yearling, the crow-pecked Anchor manager. Not someone Adrian wanted to see again in either case, but he still looked longingly at the wide stairs as the princess dragged him away.

Since the space reserved for the chains apparently took up the entirety of the palace's ground floor, they ended up leaving through a side door that let out onto a balcony overlooking the White City. It would've been the perfect place for a fountain and a formal garden in a normal castle, but this was Gilgamesh's tightly controlled land of the dead. Everything down to the paving stones was sealed tight and bone-dry without so much as a hint of greenery.

It was still a nice spot, though. Adrian hadn't realized how desperately he'd missed being outdoors until he felt the gentle breeze on his skin and saw the blue sky overhead. Both were fake, of course, but it still felt good to get out of that damned mausoleum, especially when he noticed the dome of Heaven shifting toward the bright-blue velvet color that passed for night up here.

"How far is the entrance to the Hells?" he asked as the princess dragged him down the steps and across the enormous, white-paved courtyard toward the wall that separated Gilgamesh's palace from the rest of the city.

"Not as far as the outer walls," she replied. "But it's not a short walk. The Hells are where the gods' monsters are imprisoned. The Eternal King would've put it outside the city if he could have, but the guards need to be able to get to work, and the sin iron must still be shipped in, of course."

She pointed across the courtyard at a line of stoic-looking war demons pushing several dozen carts stacked high with ingots of familiar, coal-black metal through the palace's gate, and Adrian whistled.

"That looks like a *lot* of sin iron," he said, leaning in for a closer look. "Is that normal?"

"I... I'm not sure," the princess admitted, lowering her head. "I'm as new here as you are, and the Crown Princess's training didn't include things like sin-iron production." Her golden eyes slid back to the carts. "It does seem like a large amount, though."

It was tonnage. Now that they were nearly to the gate themselves, Adrian could see that the train of war-demon-pulled carts extended all the way down the fancy white street ahead of them. There had to be two hundred of them just in this area alone, and they weren't even close to the entrance to the Hells yet. The bricks of sin iron also looked even darker than Adrian remembered, though that could've been an optical illusion caused by the unnatural brightness of Heaven.

"What's Gilgamesh doing with it all?" he asked as they passed the carts. "Building another Anchor?"

"I'm afraid I don't know, my prince," the princess answered. "But I'm sure your father will tell you all about it when you're his new Crown Prince."

Adrian didn't know about that. From what he'd seen, Gilgamesh never explained anything to anyone unless he was getting something out of it. He'd been a font of information back when he was trying to bring Adrian over to his side, but the moment his youngest son was fully under his control, he'd run off to his own projects without so much as a goodbye.

Not that Adrian minded being neglected, but he still found the insincerity annoying. At the very least, he wished someone would tell him what his father was doing. He'd thought it was odd from the beginning that Gilgamesh had made such a big deal about the Queen of Pride's horns only to completely ignore them the moment Adrian was locked in, but what was all this sin iron for? And why were the Anchors still locked? Bex's rebellion had been defeated, so why was Heaven still acting like a castle under siege? What was the point of all this chaos?

Adrian didn't know, and that made him more nervous than anything else because he hadn't been lying when he'd told the princess his father was smart. If Gilgamesh was doing something that didn't make sense, that just meant Adrian wasn't seeing the whole picture yet. If he didn't figure it out in time, Gilgamesh could blindside them again just like he'd done before, but it had been impossible to investigate from inside his locked room. This trip was his first chance to actually learn something, so Adrian kept his eyes and ears open as he followed the princess through the palace gate into Heaven's White City.

It was a lot more confusing than he'd expected. The roads had looked so straight and orderly from his window, but once Adrian got down in them, the fact that every corner and building looked exactly the same turned navigation into a frustrating memory puzzle. Everywhere he looked, Adrian saw Heavenly denizens in the same white robes sitting on nearly identical balconies or lounging in overly decorated living rooms filled with the same white furniture as every other house. Even the demons that served them were all dressed in the identical white uniforms, turning the entire city into a big white blur.

It was so different from what he'd expected. He'd thought this place would be a wonderland of dazzlingly beautiful mansions filled with five thousand years' worth of hoarded treasures just like his father's island, but every single house looked the same. Adrian knew Heaven was infamous for falling into trends, but this was ridiculous. How could a city full of immortal people with effectively infinite money end up with such boring, cookie-cutter houses?

It was so odd that eventually Adrian gave up all pretense and started peering through windows to see if the good stuff was just stashed farther in. Every room he managed to get a look into, though, had the same white walls, white furniture, and occasional gold accents. It all looked exactly like his own bedroom in the palace, but while it made sense for Gilgamesh's base of power to have a unified style, the fact that the same look continued through every single house in the city was just creepy. *So* creepy that, after ten blocks of it, Adrian felt compelled to ask.

"Why does everything look the same here?"

"Because unity is beautiful," the princess answered, waving her hand at the elegant, white, three-story townhouse next to them that looked exactly the same as every other elegant, white, three-story townhouse on the street. "The Eternal King wants his people to dwell in beauty always. Also, white is the color of purity. If corruption of the gods were ever to resurface, having a pure, blank canvas makes it easy to spot and eradicate."

Adrian rolled his eyes. He should've known it'd come back to the gods. *Everything* Gilgamesh did came back to the gods. He'd complained about the obsession himself back when he'd been pretending to be a loving father and not the world's magical tyrant, but Adrian was only now beginning to understand just how much effort the king put into it. There was probably some palace official whose job it was to go through people's houses and report any walls that weren't white enough.

Again, how *anyone* could call this place Heaven with a straight face was a mystery. This was the fancy part of town near the castle too. The buildings got even more samey as they moved on to the apartment blocks by the outer walls. The big, multi-unit structures were still well-appointed and stuffed with fancy furniture, but the fact that there were haves and have-nots even up here proved that everything Gilgamesh said about fairness and freeing humanity from the favoritism of the gods was bullshit, because he was doing the exact same thing. This wasn't Heaven. It was a company town, a place where all the cronies and bootlickers showed off how important they were by having two more rooms full of identical white furniture than the guy down the street. The competitive conformity was so oppressive, it was actually a relief when the entrance to the Hells finally came into view.

"At last," Adrian said with a smile. "I thought my brain was going to die."

The princess gave him a skeptical look, which was warranted considering what they were walking toward.

The gateway to the Hells stood at the end of the street in front of them like a black monolith. It was made entirely from sin iron and shaped like a cube. Its walls were decorated with carvings of screaming demons being tormented, but its giant doors were dominated by a three-story-tall image of Gilgamesh dressed in full regalia with the crown of Anu on his head and the sword of Ishtar held ready in his hand to strike down any demon foolish enough to defy his authority.

Aside from that, there was nothing. Adrian didn't know if it was for security reasons or if even Gilgamesh couldn't find someone willing to live next to the Hells, but the black cube was surrounded by a hundred feet of empty paving on all sides. The only structures near it were four white obelisks capped with a golden ring containing a giant golden eyeball. They looked like bigger, freestanding versions of the golden eye that used to be in the wall at the entrance to the Anchor's back end before Iggs had blown it up with grenades. The closest one actually spun around to watch Adrian and the princess, the interlocking rings of its golden pupil constricting with a metallic *click click click* as it zoomed in on them.

Other than the watching eyes, Adrian didn't see any security, but he did see a *lot* of demons. This was where the train of war demons pushing the sin-iron carts started. They were all coming out through a smaller door hidden inside the carving of Gilgamesh. When Adrian started toward it, though, the princess grabbed the sleeve of his black coat.

"You can't go in yet, my prince," she reminded him. "We have to wait for Prince Demetrios to escort us."

Adrian sighed. He'd been hoping she'd forgotten that detail in her rush to get this finished, but he should've known better. Even the real Bex was a stickler when it came to following procedure, and while Adrian probably could've convinced her to at least go through the door with him, it didn't seem wise to step out of line when the golden eyes were staring straight at him.

He looked around for a bench or something they could sit on while they waited since his legs still ached from climbing all those stairs, but there was nothing. Other than the eye-topped obelisks, the courtyard was completely empty. So, since he didn't want to lean against the white apartment buildings like a loitering teen, Adrian locked his knees and reached into his pocket to check his finding spell.

It was still twitching like mad when he touched it. The charm had had time to fully cure by this point, the sap and fur merging together until it felt like he was touching an actual tiny cat with very rigid posture. If he wrapped his hand all the way around it, Adrian could feel the line running from the cat's carved nose to his target, who was deep underground below him and several hundred feet to his left. She wasn't walking anymore, but now that he was out of the palace, Adrian swore he could feel the rise and fall of her breathing through the cat's hard ribs.

A dangerous bubble of hope swelled up inside his chest. He'd been moving so fast, he hadn't stopped to think about what finding another queen might actually mean. If she was really as alive as his charm made it feel, then she had to be in a cell of some sort. He hadn't thought Gilgamesh would be stupid enough to keep queens near their subjects, but the Hells *had* been created to imprison demons, and this queen was hornless.

Maybe Gilgamesh had dismissed her since she was broken. Adrian desperately hoped so, because Bex was also a hornless queen, and it was only logical to keep similar prisoners in the same area. If the former Queen of Pride truly was as lively as she seemed to be *and* she was locked in the Hells, then there was a good chance Bex might be imprisoned right beside her.

Adrian almost burst into a grin before he caught himself. He couldn't afford any mess-ups past this point. Pretending to be a loyal prince had gotten him this far, but eventually Adrian was going to have to play his hand, and since he was going into the Hells with an escort, he was going to have to do it with another prince and *two* princesses breathing down his neck. It was a hell of a gamble, but if he could pull it off *and* he was right about the circumstances of her imprisonment, then he wouldn't just be bringing the Queen of Pride her horns. He'd also be bringing Bex's ring and lost hand right to her.

That was a big enough prize to make Adrian very reckless indeed. He was desperately trying not to give himself away by looking too excited when the princess tugged on his sleeve again.

"There he is."

Adrian's brain had run so far ahead with his plots, it took him several seconds to remember which "he" the princess was referring to. Fortunately, or unfortunately, any questions he might have asked answered themselves when he looked up to see all the war demons that had been pushing sin iron out of the Hells abandon their carts and run back inside. A second later, the little side door closed, and the enormous pair of Gilgamesh-decorated doors started to move, the huge, sin-iron slabs grinding open under the power of a dozen demons so that a man in golden armor could stride through.

He was a very handsome prince. He had the same olive skin as Adrian, but his dark hair lay flat and shiny instead of curling, and his features were both sharper and straighter. He was *definitely* Agatha's son, but the beauty he'd inherited from their mother was spoiled by the cruel gleam of his mirrored eyes as he dragged something out of the Hells behind him.

Adrian's white blood ran cold. The prince was dragging a woman on a black chain. Her body was carved from bone and embellished with gold, but even with the prince walking in front of her, Adrian had trouble believing *that* was a princess. She lurched at the end of her chain like a barely-controlled wolf, straining against the manacles that bound her wrists, feet, and neck so hard that the metal had cut grooves into her ivory limbs. Her entire face was covered in a sin-iron cage, and her eyes were wilder than Adrian had realized hammered gold could look. She didn't stop clawing at the ground the whole time her prince was walking toward them, lunging back toward the entrance to the Hells over and over with her white teeth bared like spikes behind the black cage of her muzzle.

"*Stop that*," the prince hissed, yanking her back to his side. "Or I'll feed you to the grinders."

Adrian didn't know what the grinders were, but the feral princess must have, because she stopped throwing herself at the doors, though she didn't stop pulling. No matter where the prince tried to direct her, she went right back to the end of the leash, forcing the prince to drag her the last few feet toward Adrian.

"Ah," he said when they were finally within conversational distance. "You must be the new brother Alexander warned me about. The witch."

He said that last part like he expected Adrian to start sputtering with rage, but the witch just nodded. "Adrian Blackwood," he said proudly, clicking the heels of his curl-toed boots together and standing a little taller so that his pointed black hat cast a long, triangular shadow over the prince's glittery armor. "Fully initiated member of Blackwood coven."

The prince rolled his mirrored eyes. "I'm Demetrios," he said, leaning harder against his princess's chain, "Prince of Hate and temporary overseer of the Hells."

Adrian arched an eyebrow. "Temporary?"

"Extremely temporary," the prince assured him. "My actual position is overseeing the warlocks, and I will be returning to that duty as soon as possible. The Hells are a job for the disobedient and the disgraced. That's why Leander was there for so long. That and he didn't have a princess. The Hells are hard on them. Just look what they've done to mine."

He nodded at the feral doll straining at the end of the chain, and Adrian winced.

"The Hells did that to her?"

"Not all of it," Demetrios said, giving him a superior look. "The Princess of Hate isn't an easy weapon to control. She'd always required a firm hand, which is why Father gave her to me. I've managed her for forty years without issue, but five weeks in the Hells have rendered her almost unusable. She nearly took my arm off earlier today going after a runaway demon some idiot warlock lost control over."

"There are runaway demons in the Hells?" Adrian asked with a mix of surprise and hope.

"There are runaway demons everywhere," the prince replied with a scowl. "They're a damned menace. Father should've dumped the entire race into the void eons ago, but they're a necessary evil. As are you."

He stepped closer, yanking his princess across the white paving stones until he was standing directly in front of Adrian's face.

"Let's get one thing very clear," he said in a low voice. "I know you're part of Father's grand strategy, and I don't care. All I want is for you to do whatever it is you're here to do so Gilgamesh can finish whatever *he's* doing and finally lift the ban on teleportation.

That's the *only* reason I agreed to Alexander's insulting escort request, because until you finish your damned work, I'm stuck having to walk up a thousand flights of stairs every time I want to get out of this hell pit. If it wasn't for that, I'd leave you to rot. I have no sympathy for spoiled traitors who use their position as Mother's favorite to jump the line while those of us who've served loyally for centuries get passed over."

"I can see how that would be upsetting," Adrian replied in his most disarming voice. "But shouldn't you be taking these complaints to Gilgamesh? He's the one who made the decisions."

"Don't be an idiot," Demetrios hissed with a nervous glance at the golden eye watching them from the top of its obelisk. "Questioning Father's judgment leads to things much worse than Hells duty. Now shut up and let's get this over with. What are you here to find?"

"I'm not sure," Adrian lied. "I'm sure it's the last element I need to finish repairing the Queen of Pride's horns, but I'm afraid I won't know exactly what I'm looking for until I see it."

"Are you serious?" the prince demanded, getting a tighter grip on his princess's chain.

"Witchcraft is more art than science," Adrian replied, doing his best impression of his aunt Muriel's confidently dreamy expression, the one that always drove him insane but was also impossible to argue with.

He must've gotten it close enough because Prince Demetrios shook his head and turned around without another word, motioning impatiently for Adrian to follow him toward the giant black gates.

"Why did you make them open the big doors?" Adrian asked as he followed the prince—because he refused to call this ass his brother—past the rows of bowing war demons. "The smaller one would've been a lot less work."

"Because sons of Gilgamesh don't use servant doors," the prince replied sharply, doing his best to walk at a stately pace despite the princess pulling him forward like an overeager pit bull. "And because we normally have construct soldiers to do it."

He sneered at the line of war demons who were still standing in front of the open door with their horns down. "This forge filth isn't normally allowed to set foot in our pristine Heaven, but Father's recalled all the remaining operational constructs to the palace, so we're having to make do."

That was news to Adrian. He'd been all over the palace today, and he hadn't seen a single construct. The real question on his mind, though, was "Does this mean the Hells are short-staffed?"

"Of course not," the prince huffed. "Golems are convenient because they don't need sleep and never talk back, but we ran this place using nothing but war demons for eons."

He sneered over his shoulder at Adrian. "I know that's disappointing news for someone who used to be the Coward Queen's pet witch, but I'd advise you to stay on task and not get any funny ideas. Just because Father can bring you back from the dead doesn't mean you'll enjoy the trip."

"How *does* Gilgamesh bring his princes back?" Adrian asked, completely ignoring the threat.

"Call him 'Father'," the older prince ordered. "And he's able to bring us back because he's the greatest sorcerer who ever lived. There's nothing he can't do, but that also means there's nothing he *won't* do if you make him angry, so I advise you *stop talking* before you draw his attention."

Adrian smirked at the prince's golden back. "You're really afraid of him, aren't you?"

"Everyone's afraid of the Eternal King," Prince Demetrios replied as he motioned for the war demons to start closing the doors they'd just pushed open. "Usefulness won't save you, either, so don't think you're safe just because you're his new favorite. Just ask that suck-up Alexander how quick Father is to blast his sons to bits because he knows he can just put us back together."

The prince's normally sneering voice was legitimately grim by the end, and Adrian swallowed. He wanted to ask more—despite phrasing everything as an insult, Demetrios had given him more actual answers than anyone else since he'd arrived here—but the prince was stomping faster now, dragged forward by his mad princess as she scrambled down yet another enormous set of stairs.

Adrian had to bite back a groan when he saw them. No wonder the prince was so desperate to get teleportation back. Going by what he'd seen today, Adrian was convinced the afterlife was fifty percent stairs by volume.

At least these stairs looked different than the endless towers he'd climbed earlier. The moment they passed through the sin-iron doors, the relentless white of Heaven was replaced by a black stone tunnel going down in a spiral. The stairs themselves were wide with a groove worn in the middle by thousands of years of feet. The only light came from torches on the walls that burned with a deep, reddish-orange glow that reminded Adrian of the real Bex's eyes. Unfortunately, the light they shed was so bad he could barely see the stairs under his feet, and he couldn't tell where they were going at all. Thanks to the hallway's spiral, Adrian could no longer see the doors to Heaven behind them or anything that lay ahead. Just darkness pierced by little embers of red and the soft clomp of war-demon hooves as they carried sin iron up by the armful.

"Do they transport everything by hand?" Adrian whispered.

"How else would they do it?" Prince Demetrios replied at normal volume. "We're not going to build them a conveyor. An idle slave is a problem slave. You have to keep them working every hour of the day or else they get ideas."

The war demons walking past them definitely looked overworked. Their four-armed bodies still gleamed like polished bronze, but their eyes were dark and downtrodden. They moved surprisingly quietly, their hoofed feet falling as soft as leaves on the worn stone. The prince, by contrast, went down the stairs like a dropped metal cup, his armor clattering offensively loudly down the long, curved tunnel.

"How much longer until we reach the Hells?" Adrian asked when his ears couldn't take the noise anymore.

"We're already there," the prince replied. "This is the central stair that runs through Upper Hell where the war demons live. It's enclosed to keep the fumes from the sin-iron foundries from leaking into Heaven and poisoning our air."

Adrian blanched. "What about the war demons' air?"

"What about it?" Demetrios asked, shooting a smug glance over his shoulder as he clattered down another few steps to a black wall Adrian hadn't even noticed in the dark.

This turned out to be another sin-iron door that covered the entire width of the expansive staircase. There was a small opening on the side that the line of war demons was transporting sin iron through, but once again, Demetrios made them all stop and open the whole thing for him. It was absolutely ridiculous and a waste of everyone's time, but at least it gave Adrian a chance to gawk at what lay below.

The first half of the stairwell had been enclosed to keep out the smog, but the part below them was an open spiral going down through the middle of what appeared to be a fortified stone tower. The walls were so dark, Adrian's first thought was that the whole thing was made of sin iron. When they finally made it through the door, though, he realized the stone here was just stained from eons of black smoke.

Everything was smoky. There must have been sorcery etched into the door they'd just gone through because while the air in the tunnel had been the same as it was up in Heaven, the air on this side was a toxic miasma of ash, smog, and what smelled like burning sin iron. The walls of the tower were still enclosed, so he couldn't actually see the forges, but he could hear the bang of hammers and the sizzle of molten metal through the doors at the tower's base, which were currently propped open so the line of sin-iron-carrying demons could keep moving.

Other than that, the tower was empty, though it clearly hadn't been intended to stay that way. The outside of the spiral staircase ran along the tower wall, but inside of the spiral was an overlapping fortress of covered galleries where archers could stand and shoot down the tower's open center. This arrangement meant that anyone coming up from below wouldn't just have to do so under constant fire, they'd also have to go behind the soldiers' positions to climb the tower. The shooting galleries even had walls that could be swung out to block the staircase, turning every firing position into a potential chokepoint. It was a lot of overlapping security for a place that had supposedly never had a rebellion, and seeing it filled Adrian with hope.

"Have you ever had to use this tower?"

"Never," Demetrios replied, walking at an angle with his princess's chain wrapped around both arms to keep her from pulling him down the stairs. "Leander was a lovesick fool, but he ran a tight ship. This stairwell used to be an office like the one in the Middle Hells below, but then the Coward Queen had a particularly destructive few decades, and the slave population started getting ideas. Leander couldn't have that, so he had this tower remodeled into a fortress. Just knowing what awaited them was enough to crush any whispers of rebellion, and his record continued to be unblemished."

The prince shook his head. "It's such a damn waste. Leander was a clever strategist and the best sorcerer of us all. He could've challenged Alexander for the position of Crown Prince, but he never could get his loyalties straight, so he ended up rotting down here."

"Where is he now?" Adrian asked, trying not to sound too curious.

"Only Father knows that," Demetrios replied, then he frowned. "His princess was playing the harp at our last family dinner, though, so I doubt he's still alive." He glanced at the ivory figure thrashing at the end of his chain. "Perhaps I should put in for an upgrade."

Adrian's princess growled at that, making him jump. She'd been uncharacteristically silent since they'd entered the Hells, but she seemed to take personal offense at Demetrios's suggestion that he trade in his princess. Adrian didn't know if she was mad over the insult to her sister or the general idea that princesses were interchangeable, but she was looking very Princess of Wrath by the time they reached the fortress tower's base.

"This is the main floor of the Hell of War," Demetrios announced, tilting his head at the sooty, reinforced doors that now had a backup of war demons waiting with sin iron in their arms since no one apparently wanted to walk up the tower's narrow stairs while two princes were coming down. "*Please* say the thing you're looking for is here. I'd like to eat dinner sometime this century."

Adrian already knew it wasn't, but he made a show of checking his finding spell before he shook his head.

"Farther down, I'm afraid," he said as he returned the cat to his pocket. "One, maybe two levels?"

"You'd better hope it's one," the Hells Prince growled, snapping at a large war demon with a sash across his otherwise bare bronze chest to open the door to the stairs that connected the Hell of War's tower to the rest of the Hells below.

Adrian watched them clearing the path with polite interest, but it was just for show. All his actual attention was pinned on the charm in his pocket, the little wooden cat whose nose was now moving steadily back and forth like it was following someone's pacing.

Chapter 9

BEX HAD LOST COUNT of how many demons she'd hauled out of the Lowest Hells, but it had to be over a hundred. After the first few successful trips, she'd untied the rope from her own waist and started looping the passed-out figures together like a string of onions. It was undignified, but it worked. Between her speed and General Kirok's hauling capacity, they were a demon-lifting machine.

In no time at all, their section of the Founders' Tunnels was packed with demons of every sort. Like Trinaeous, most came out sobbing or screaming, but as Desh predicted, they got themselves back together in short order. Bex was sure there was a lot of trauma suppression going on, but any demon disobedient enough to get themselves damned to the Lowest Hell was a fighter, or at least ready to get some revenge.

Iggs was taking full advantage of that last one. He had Felix's endless arsenal set up like a grab bag right next to where Kirok dumped their rescues. The moment a demon woke up, Iggs was there asking them what kind of weapon they wanted. If their response was a blank stare, he handed them an AK-47 and shuffled them down the tunnel to make room for the next catch of demons Kirok hauled out of the dark.

At least, that was Bex's understanding of what was going on. She only came up from the Lowest Hell when she needed a breather from the crushing panic. It was never as bad as the first time, but while knowing there was at least one queen still alive and trying to help had gotten the pride demons to unclench a little, nothing was actually fixed yet. They were still falling through an endless void, and while the banked-ember glow of Bex's hand made it possible to move around, she could only stand being down there for about fifteen minutes at a time before their fear grabbed her again and she started falling with them.

Every time it happened was a brush with disaster. Bex was all too aware that she was also nameless. If she forgot her purpose even for a second, the desperately grasping pride demons could easily drag her back down the hole that still existed inside her own soul, only this time Nemini wouldn't be there to help. If she didn't keep going down, though, the demons she *could* rescue would stay trapped in the Lowest Hells forever and their plan would fall through.

That made the risk worth it in Bex's mind, but she still kept her descents limited. She'd given her phone to Kirok so he could tug the rope at fifteen-minute intervals to signal when it was time for her to come back up. By alternating short dives with breaks to eat and recover, Bex was able to fill the tunnel with rescued demons without losing her soul. She'd just gotten the signal that her fifteen minutes were up yet again when her faintly glowing fingers closed around a body that didn't have horns.

Bex stopped short. She'd been grabbing demons off the top of the pile both because they were easier to reach and because newer banishment victims were more likely to speak modern languages and understand how to use Iggs's guns. The hornless body was on that same top layer, but unlike the demons in work jeans, body armor, and mass-produced suits that Bex had been pulling out for the last hour and a half, this man's clothes were extremely old-fashioned. They reminded her of the handmade stuff Adrian wore, only in white silk instead of black-dyed linen. She was wondering if the poor demon had been in his pajamas when his warlock chopped off his horns and damned him to the bottom of the Hells when she felt the darkness start to wrap around her head again.

That was her hard limit. Without wasting another second, Bex tossed the hornless body she'd been examining under her arm and ran back to the rope dangling behind her. Three hard tugs got them both lifted into the air, and not a second too soon. By the time they made it through the hole in the ceiling, Bex could barely see Lys's flashlight through the darkness swimming across her vision.

"I've got you," Lys said as they grabbed Bex by the waist and hauled her onto the tunnel's damp stone floor. "You still with us?"

Bex nodded, too overwhelmed to speak. She *had* to stop cutting it so close. Just because she'd figured out how to skate the edge didn't mean the Lowest Hells were safe. If she screwed this up, she'd be lost and her demons would be trapped down here. It was totally unacceptable behavior from someone still claiming to be a queen. Bex was still beating herself up about it when she realized the entire tunnel had gone quiet.

"What in the Hells is that?" said Iggs, breaking the silence at last.

Bex could only blink in reply. She was still lying on the floor of the tunnel where Lys had laid her, but the figure lying beside her—the one she'd hauled up in

a hurry when she'd realized she was out of time—
wasn't a demon in human form who'd been banished in
his pajamas like she'd assumed. He was *actually*
human, and one Bex recognized. His face was even
more haggard than the last time she'd seen it, and he
was dressed in dirty white silk instead of golden
armor, but there was no mistaking him. That was the
son of Gilgamesh she'd fought on the chain when
they'd freed the Seattle Anchor, the one who'd claimed
to be in love with his sword, the Prince of Sorrow.

Bex scrambled away with a gasp. Her booted
foot hit the prince's body in the process, almost
knocking him back down the hole before Iggs grabbed
him. The save must have been pure reflex because Iggs
tossed the prince away again a second later, throwing
him back to the ground with a curse. Lys had their sin-
iron dagger out by that point and was about to slit the
unconscious man's throat when Bex said, "Wait."

Lys stopped with a confused look. Totally
understandable since this was the prince who'd
stabbed them in the heart with that exact weapon. For
once in her life, though, Bex wasn't ready to slaughter
a son of Gilgamesh outright. He might be the child of
their hated enemy, but so was Adrian, which threw a
wrench in Bex's long-held belief that all princes were
inherently evil. If a son of Gilgamesh could turn out
like her witch, then maybe this one could be reasoned
with, especially considering where she'd found him. If
any prince was going to be open to the idea of
betraying his father, it would be the one Gilgamesh
had thrown away.

That was Bex's hope at least, but she kept her
hand on the hilt of her explosive short sword as the

prince began to stir. The void left by the Queen of Pride's loss must not have had as strong a hold over human minds because he came out of it much more quickly than the demons she'd rescued. There was no screaming or sobbing, either. The prince just opened his mirrored eyes with a sharp breath, staring up in confusion at the circle of demons standing over him before his gaze finally landed on Bex.

"It's you."

The words sounded more surprised than malicious, but Lys had never been one to give the benefit of the doubt. The prince's mouth had barely finished moving before they were behind him with their sin-iron knife pressed into his neck.

"I surrender!" the prince cried, throwing up his grimy hands at once. "Please, Queen of Wrath, hear me out! I can help you!"

Bex didn't buy that for a second, but she did hold up her hand to stop Lys before they added a new window to his windpipe.

"Why should I believe you?" she asked as the lust demon grudgingly relaxed their blade. "The last time I saw you, you were trying to kill me."

"Because that was my order," the prince explained as he pushed himself up into a sitting position. "I was only doing as my brother commanded, but I bear you no personal grudge." He bowed his head low. "Please, great queen, hear me out."

Bex sighed and waved for him to go ahead.

"My name is Leander," the bowing prince said solemnly, "and I was betrayed. I only fought you because my brother promised to return my beloved to me if I won, but when I failed at the Anchor,

Gilgamesh showed no mercy. He stole my princess and cast me into the deepest Hells. He said he'd be back in a few centuries when I'd reevaluated my priorities, but I never will."

He lifted his head a fraction to look at Bex with furiously gleaming eyes. "I will *never* serve that man again. He's the one who hurt my Mara in the first—"

"*Your* Mara?" Bex snarled, baring her teeth. "*My sister* is a daughter of Ishtar that *your father* kidnapped and brainwashed!"

"I know," Prince Leander said, lowering his head again as his fingers curled into fists against the stone. "I've always known my father's crimes, but I wasn't strong enough to defy him by myself. I thought I could appease him and win her freedom that way, but Gilgamesh cares for nothing but his own power. He'll never let any of us go, but you are Mara's sister. Even when she was trapped inside a prison of bone and sorcery, you recognized her and tried to save her. That's all I've ever wanted, so please, Queen of Wrath, let me help you!"

He bowed deeper at the end, but Bex wasn't convinced. "I understand hating Gilgamesh, but what about your home? If you help us, you'll be turning against Heaven as well, because when we bring back Paradise, we're not leaving a single stone of this place intact."

"That white necropolis has never been my home," Leander insisted as he straightened back up into a sitting position. "Mara and I always planned to escape to Earth together when the war was over and Gilgamesh stopped paying such close attention to his princesses."

Bex scowled. "You mean after you helped him defeat me."

"It was the only end we knew how to reach," Leander explained apologetically. "We never wanted to hurt you. You were the only sister Mara remembered fondly, but we both knew there was no way for us to be together in peace so long as you were leading the rebellion against Heaven."

"Well, that's certainly a load off my mind," Bex grumbled, rising to her feet. "But I'm not giving you my sister. If she's the price of your help, you can go back into that pit."

"*No!*" Leander cried, lurching forward to grab her boots. "Please don't misunderstand! I'm not asking you to give me your sister like a prize. All I want is a chance to see her. The real Mara, not my father's doll."

His mirrored eyes flashed as he looked around the tunnel packed with demons. "You're here to destroy the Hells, right? I can help you! I was the prince of this place for centuries. I know everything there is to know about its security, secret passages, checkpoints, whatever you need. I'll help you break into Heaven as well, if that's your intent, and all I ask in return is that you free my Mara. Give me hope that I'll finally be able to meet her face-to-true-face, and I swear, I'll do anything you ask!"

Lys had managed to pry the prince's fingers off Bex's boots by the time this speech was over, but when they started to shove him onto his back, Bex shook her head and crouched down beside him instead.

"You would go that far?" she asked. "Betray your own family?"

"Of course," Leander replied, his gaunt face collapsing into a deep scowl. "I love your sister, and I *hate* my father. All his sons do. Even Crown Prince Alexander only serves because the alternative is so much worse. I would have betrayed him and escaped centuries ago, but we couldn't leave so long as he had control over Mara's idol."

Bex frowned. "Idol?"

"The white bodies he makes to hold the demon queen's hands," the prince explained. "Gilgamesh carved obedience into them with every tap of his chisel. Mara held onto her truth better than the rest of her sisters, but all the princesses were warped by the process in one way or another. That's why they act so terribly, but Gilgamesh's bone idols were only made to control their sword hands. The rest of their bodies are still alive, just like yours."

He looked pointedly at the stump on the end of Bex's right arm before she grabbed him by his silken collar.

"Where are they?" she growled.

"I don't know," Leander said, lowering his eyes. "Mara and I were trying to discover that when we got caught the first time. Father locked her in the Crown Prince's tower as punishment and sentenced me to be the overseer of the Hells. I did that job flawlessly for centuries in the hope of one day seeing her again. Capturing you was supposed to be my chance to prove my loyalty and earn her back, but we both know how that ended."

He sighed and looked up at Bex again. "That's why I want to help you now. Before Father cast me down here, Alexander, my eldest brother, told me that

Mara was being rebuilt and her memories destroyed. I told Gilgamesh to his face that I would never serve him again if he did that, and he replied that he didn't care. He told me he'd already found a new prince, one with the potential to be even better at sorcery than I was, which meant my obedience was no longer necessary."

Leander clenched his hands to bloodless fists. "I served that monster for centuries, and he threw me away! Gilgamesh goes on and on about how he's working for the good of all mankind, but the only good he actually cares about is his own. Even his grudge against the gods only came about because of the death of his beloved Enkidu, but I don't need to indulge his grievances anymore. I've found my own great love, and I'll do whatever it takes to return her to life. *Actual* life, not the white mockery my father made. If that means helping you destroy Heaven, then I'll carry the torch that burns it to the ground. I don't give a damn about the war or the gods or who controls death. All I want—all I've *ever* wanted—is for Mara to stop crying."

"That's a lot to ask from the Queen of Sorrow," Bex said, looking up at the dripping ceiling stabbed through with sin-iron bolts. "But we could use an inside man."

Bex could tell from Lys's scowl that they were *supremely* unhappy with that decision. There were others around, though, so they kept their mouth shut. Desh wasn't nearly so tactful.

"Are you out of your royal mind?" he shouted, shoving his way to Bex through the now very crowded tunnel. "You can't trust *him*! That's the prince who pulled me out of the Lowest Hells so I could betray you!"

"Because I knew we couldn't defeat the Bonfire Queen without trickery," Leander explained, keeping his mirrored eyes on Bex. "Unlike the rest of Heaven, I've always respected her as a dangerous and clever foe. That's why I'm so confident in offering my assistance now. If there's anyone who can defeat Gilgamesh and free my Mara, it's you."

"Stop calling her yours," Bex snapped, then she shook her head. "But we're in no position to turn down help."

"Are you sure about that?" Iggs asked nervously. "Deception is the Eternal King's favorite tactic. This whole thing could be a setup."

"It's a risk," Bex acknowledged, keeping her eyes locked on Leander. "But so's this whole mission. We all knew we'd be gambling when we came here, but we still jumped in with both feet because risk brings reward. Trusting him is just another roll of the dice, but it's a roll I feel comfortable making because if there's one thing I believe about the Prince of Sorrow, it's that he loves my sister. I saw him give up victory against me on the chain to get her help when she was wounded. I've never seen a prince do that for his princess before. I'm not saying that's enough to put him on the team, but I am willing to accept his help on two conditions."

"Name them," Prince Leander said.

Bex raised two fingers into the air. "You already offered the first one, which is to be our guide through the Hells. Fortunately, the second condition is going to make that task a lot easier." She leaned forward with a smirk. "I want you to use your teleport spell to take me directly to my missing horns. Do that, and I swear I'll help you get Mara back."

Bex would be able to get *all* her sisters back if she had a pet prince smuggling her into all of Gilgamesh's secret places. She was already picturing the sweet, sweet justice that would rain down when all of Ishtar's daughters were reunited, but Leander was shaking his head.

"I can definitely assist you with the first, but the second is impossible," he said. "Gilgamesh has shut off all teleportation within his domain. I know because I've been trying to teleport away from you since I woke up, but I keep hitting a block."

"Could that just be a you problem?" Lys asked skeptically. "You were banished for being a traitor. Maybe Gilgamesh just locked *you* out."

"That's not how the spell works," Leander replied, lifting his chin. "All sorcery functions on an individual basis. So long as I've got quintessence in my blood, there's no spell I can't cast, including teleportation. The only thing that could stop me is a block placed over the entire system by Anu's crown, which sits on Gilgamesh's head." He nodded at Bex. "The shutdown probably triggered when you entered the Hells. Since the Bonfire Queen is Gilgamesh's last true enemy, he's commanded every grain of sand in this place to reject you."

"It's not that," Bex said. "The magic here hasn't reacted to me since I lost my name. If it did, I wouldn't be able to stand here."

"Well, *something* happened," Leander insisted with a huff. "Gilgamesh wouldn't ban teleportation without extremely good reason. Do you know how many stairs are in his palace?"

"I bet it happened when the princess saw us," Lys said. "There's no way they just let us escape. We must be under some kind of lockdown."

"Why would they lock down teleportation in response to us, though?" Bex asked. "I'd think Gilgamesh would want to give his princes more freedom to chase us down, not less."

"Not when his newest prince is your boyfriend," Lys said, wiggling their eyebrows suggestively.

Bex's cheeks heated, but Lys made a good point. If princely teleportation was an option, Adrian would absolutely use it, which was probably why Gilgamesh had taken it off the table. She was still chewing on all the implications of that when Leander spoke again.

"I can't teleport you to your horns," he said apologetically, "but I *do* know where they are. Gilgamesh keeps all the trophies he stole from the gods—including the crowns of Ishtar's queens—in the vault beyond his throne room. That's most likely where your horns are being stored as well. I can take you right to it, but I've never figured out how to open the door."

"We're pretty good at cracking safes," Bex assured him with a smirk. "And I definitely like the idea of going straight to a vault over searching the entire palace."

"*If* he's telling the truth," Lys added.

"I swear I've told you all I know," Leander said, bowing his head again. "I can lead you straight to the treasury door, but getting there will be perilous. Gilgamesh's throne room is located at the pinnacle of the Highest Heaven. It's as far from this place as it's possible to get."

"We'll climb that mountain when we reach it," Bex said, looking over her shoulder at the hole in the floor. "For now, I'm going back down to get more demons. If we have to go all the way to the tippy top of Heaven, we'll need a distraction big enough to empty the entire palace, and the only way to do that is to move in numbers Heaven can't ignore."

"I've still got plenty of guns," Iggs offered. "But are you sure you don't want to take a break first? You're looking pretty tired."

Bex felt like death warmed over. She'd felt that way since she'd lost to the Queen of War, though, so she just shook her head. She was picking up the rope to get back to it when she heard the unmistakable sound of a cat clearing his throat.

Bex looked up at once to see Boston perched on the carved wooden beak of Adrian's broom, which was floating over the crowd of demons so the familiar wouldn't have to dodge legs or get his paws wet walking on the tunnel's damp floor.

"If I may interrupt," Boston said with great self-importance. "There's been some interesting developments with my finding charm."

"Did you find Adrian?" Bex asked, whirling around to give the flying cat her full attention.

"That is the spell's entire purpose," Boston replied, leaning forward so Bex could see the witch-shaped leaf effigy he'd made earlier, which was now hanging from his fluffy neck on a string. "As you can see from the way it's turning, Adrian is on the move. Has been for some time, actually, but I didn't say anything sooner since there was a chance the quintessence in his blood was throwing off my readings. At this point, however, I feel safe in saying that he's definitely moving toward us."

"*Toward* us?" Bex repeated, shocked. "You mean he's coming down to the Hells?"

Boston nodded, but Bex still couldn't believe it. "Are you sure?" she asked. "Because that makes no sense. Adrian's a known demon sympathizer. Why would Gilgamesh let him come down here?"

That seemed like an obvious disconnect to her, but Boston responded with a scoff.

"Have you forgotten whom we're talking about?" he demanded with an affronted lash of his tail. "Adrian is a fully initiated witch of the Blackwood Coven! Gilgamesh likely didn't 'let' him go anywhere. I'm sure the Eternal King tried his best to cage him in, but just like the forest he's named for, my witch cannot be contained."

He tapped the pointed-hatted leaf figurine hanging from his neck with an excited paw. "I bet he's got a finding spell looking for me just like I've got one looking for him. He probably started making his way down here the moment he saw us arrive, but he's been picking up speed over the last fifteen minutes." Boston's furry face grew worried. "I know you want to keep building up your troops, but this might be a matter of some urgency. I request that we pause our efforts here and go meet him just in case he's on the run and needs our help."

Bex had zero objections to that. She'd thought they'd have to sneak all the way into Heaven before she saw Adrian again. Rescuing him before they'd even left the Hells would be a game-changing stroke of luck. Just thinking about the possibility was making her giddy, but Lys was shaking their head with a scowl.

"How are we getting to him?" they asked, finally removing their knife from Leander's neck so they could stand up and address Boston directly. "Whether Adrian's sneaking in by himself or marching down here with Gilgamesh's blessing, there's only one way into the Hells from Heaven, and that's through the central stair."

"So what?" Bex asked, refusing to let go of her hope. "We were headed there anyway."

"Yeah, *after* we caused a distraction and cleared out security," Lys reminded her. "The whole reason we're doing this is to kick off a prison break big enough to get the Hells prince out of our way, but he's not going to take the bait if the newest prince—who's famously in love with *you*—happens to show up right when things go south."

Bex's whole face flushed again. She didn't have time to be embarrassed, though, because Lys had a point. She hated thinking of Adrian as Gilgamesh's anything, but he definitely counted as a VIP. If a rebellion kicked off while he was in the tower, the warlocks would rush him to safety first and ruin everything. If they didn't run the distraction, though, the only other possibility was attacking the tower head-on.

"Why don't we?" Iggs asked, reading the dangerous line of logic right off Bex's face. "I know you don't have your horns or sword yet, but I just spent the last hour arming a hundred of the saltiest demons I've ever met. It's not just the ones who used to run with you, either. There are demons here who stood up to Heaven all on their own and got damned for it. That's a hell of a force to fight back with, especially since we've got a prince of our own now." He looked down at Leander. "Can you still cast spells with a single word?"

"Absolutely," the prince said, rising to his feet. "Sorcery is in my blood. Even Gilgamesh can't take that away from me so long as I'm alive."

"Then we can do it," Iggs concluded, turning back to Bex. "This is the guy who punted me off the top of Pike Place Market with a flick of his finger. If we've got him *and* Adrian *and* a tunnel full of armed demons, a single prince won't be able to stand a chance against us no matter how crazy his princess is."

"Or we could get slaughtered and lose the whole mission," Lys countered, crossing their arms over their chest with a glower. "I'm all for sticking it to Gilgamesh, but we came here to get Bex's sword and horns back. Freeing every demon we can get our hands on is a nice bonus, but if we jump straight to full-scale war before we've even gotten what we came for, we'll never make it out of the Middle Hells alive."

"Who says we can't make it?" Desh demanded, shoving his thumb over his shoulder at the crowd of scowling demons behind him. "I've been talking to the blokes here, and shocker to no one, they're not exactly keen about being used as a distraction. They were still gonna do it out of respect for the queen who set them free and because it was the best option on the table, but that's not the case anymore."

He flicked his hand back over to point at Leander. "We got him now, and it sounds like we'll be picking up a witch as well. That's two heavy hitters who can't be dropped by a true name added to our roster, which gives us enough for a real assault."

It did sound plausible when he put it that way, and Bex wasn't the only one who thought so. By the time Desh finished, the whole tunnel was nodding in agreement except for Lys.

"Didn't you *just say* not to trust Leander?" they snapped at Desh.

"And aren't *you* the one who's always telling me to trust our queen?" Desh snapped back. "If Bex is ready to roll the dice on this, then so am I. 'Specially if it means I'll get to punch back at the wankers who put this collar on me."

An enormous cheer went up at that, and Leander broke into a grin. "The keys that unlock the collars are all kept inside the central tower," he told them. "They're in the big metal cabinet four floors up. If you can get your hands on them, you'll be able to uncollar and unchain every demon in the Middle Hells."

"I like the sound of that," Bex said, smiling at the tunnel full of demons, who'd gone from sullen acceptance to actual excitement. "This plan has the potential to net us way more than just creating a distraction, but Lys is still right. If we charge into a tower full of warlocks, a prince, and a princess, we're going to get hammered. That's true whether Prince Leander's on our side or not, especially since our witch's status is still unknown. I'm still for a direct assault, but we need a better way in. Something that'll let us blindside and bowl the enemy over before they even realize they're under attack."

She turned back to Leander, which, now that he was on his feet instead of the ground, meant that she had to crane her neck back to look up at him. "You said you knew all the secret passages through the Hells. Do you have anything that fits that bill?"

"As a matter of fact, I do," Leander replied, brushing the black Hells grime off his white silk shirt and trousers, which Bex suddenly realized must be what princes wore under their golden armor. "I can lead you to a path that will put you right under their noses, if you trust me enough to follow me there."

Bex glanced at Lys, who nodded their head with a sigh.

"Looks like we're in," she said, holding out her hand for the rope General Kirok had already rolled back into a neatly bound coil. "Let's go kick the hornet's nest."

Another cheer went up as she finished, making Bex feel better than she had since the bombardment. She especially liked how fast the demons sprang into action. She'd barely finished the order before everyone was on their feet with their new guns ready in their hands. Even Streya had a petite submachine gun dangling off her shoulder as she clung to Desh's back like a little winged monkey. They might not have been much of an army by the numbers, but looking at all those armed demons crammed into the tunnel made Bex feel like they could actually do this as she moved to stand with Leander at the front of the crowd.

"Which way are we going?"

"Straight ahead," Leander replied, pointing into the dark.

"That's the direction Adrian is in as well," Boston said from his perch on the broom, though his voice sounded more worried now. When Bex glanced up to ask why, the cat hopped off Bran to land on her shoulder.

"Not to pile on additional complications," he whispered, "but I'm close enough now to start picking up on Adrian's mood, and he's understandably very nervous. That could be due to the Hells themselves, but I suspect he's under guard." Boston's ears went flat against his head as he leaned even closer, his whiskers tickling Bex's ear as he whispered, "Drop the steadfast leader act for a moment and give it to me straight. Can this lot *actually* beat a prince?"

"I'd say we have a solid shot," Bex whispered back. "Though whether any of this pans out or not largely depends on him."

She nodded at Leander, who wasn't supposed to hear that. The prince's ears must have been incredible, though, because he pulled himself straight as a sword. "I wouldn't have suggested this if I thought it was a suicide mission," he informed them crisply. "Unless Alexander himself is waiting for us, I'm confident I can stand against any of my brothers, provided you can keep them from getting on top of me. I'm a damn good sorcerer, but I'm afraid my sword skills are lacking."

"What are you talking about?" Bex asked. "I fought you on the bridge. You're a fantastic swordsman."

"Not if I don't have my sword," Leander replied with a sad smile. "And before you offer, I'll never use another. My sorcery should be sufficient provided you keep the enemy at least five feet away from me at all times."

"I'll do my best," she said. "But my real worry is reinforcements. I'm confident we can take one prince, but if the Queen of War shows up, it's over."

"It shouldn't be a problem if we're quick," Leander assured her. "There are alarm bells all over the tower, but ringing one is the same as admitting you failed to keep Gilgamesh's Hells secure. No warlock or prince is going to risk that unless they have absolutely no other choice, which means we shouldn't have to worry about reinforcements until the main force is already routed."

"I'd rather not have to worry about them at all," Bex said with a sigh. "But I'll take what I can get."

"Adrian should be with us by that point," Boston offered. "He'll be able to tell us what's going on."

Hearing that brightened Bex's mood enormously. "How close is he?"

"Very," Boston said, jumping off Bex's shoulder to start running down the tunnel. "This way!"

Leander looked miffed that a cat was taking the lead, but he got over it a second later, summoning a blue ball of sorcerous fire to light the way as he followed Boston into the dark. Iggs trotted after next, shooting a curious look at Bex as he passed, but she shook her head and motioned for him to go ahead.

She did the same for every other demon, shooing the whole group ahead of her down the tunnel until, at last, she was alone with the one member of her crew who kept sitting out important discussions.

"Hey, Nemini," she said when everyone else was gone. "Are you okay with this?"

"It's a little late to ask, isn't it?" Nemini replied as she emerged from the shadows. "The decision's already been made."

"That doesn't mean you have to go along," Bex said, glancing at the snakes that were curled in tight, protective coils around Nemini's hornless head. "If you want to sit this one out, I'll understand."

"What's the point?" Nemini asked, staring listlessly down at the hole in the floor that led to the Lowest Hells. "I've already passed through the worst part. If I quit now, the pain will be the same, so I might as well keep going."

"There's my optimist," Bex joked as she put her arm around Nemini's shoulders. "Thanks for sticking it out with us, Nemini. Your help means a lot."

Nemini shrugged off the gratitude, but she didn't duck out from under Bex's arm, allowing the crownless queen to walk her down the tunnel following the noise of clomping demon feet and the ghostly blue light of Leander's sorcerous fire.

"Let me get this absolutely bleeding straight," Desh was saying when Bex and Nemini caught back up with the front of the group. "You used tunnels made by our ancestors, the ones they dug to escape the Hells, as cover so you could move your troops around where we couldn't see them? Is that what you're telling me?"

"That's exactly what I'm telling you," Leander replied, ignoring the fear demon's rant as he carefully studied what looked like a perfectly normal section of the tunnel's stone wall. "The so-called 'Founders' Tunnels' have been known to Gilgamesh since their creation. He was planning to have them filled in once he'd amassed enough spare stone, but I convinced him it'd be more efficient to use the paths as a quick-access network for our own troops instead."

Desh rolled his orange eyes. "Sounds like you were quite the little suck-up."

"I prefer to think of it as good strategy," Prince Leander said. "Gilgamesh has always favored efficiency above all other virtues. I merely used his cheapness to my own advantage. By convincing him the Founders' Tunnels were more useful open than closed, not only did I avoid having to oversee a construction project involving miles of passageways filled with violent, rebellious slaves, I also gained a secret tunnel network unknown to the rest of my family. My ultimate plan was to dig a new tunnel that Mara and I could use to escape, but I didn't get to finish it before I got the summons to destroy the Queen of Wrath."

"That's a pity," Bex said, pointedly choosing to ignore the 'destroy the Queen of Wrath' part. "We could've used an escape tunnel."

"It wouldn't have worked," Leander said morosely. "Digging the tunnel was merely a matter of labor, but I was never able to figure out a way to cross the void between life and death safely without a chain."

Adrian had, but Bex didn't think bragging to Leander about the awesome accomplishments of the brother Gilgamesh had chosen to replace him would go over well. Leander was too busy staring at the wall to listen to her anyway, though Bex wasn't sure why. This part of the tunnel didn't look any different to her, but Leander was squinting at the wall like he was trying to read a novel written in a very tiny font. This went on for two entire minutes before Leander suddenly reached out to press his fingers against a patch of stone that looked exactly like every other part of the wall and began speaking loudly in Ancient Sumerian.

"Blow away all that impedes royalty's presence, Passage of the Summer Storm."

The sorcery was still ringing in Bex's ears when the stone wall in front of Leander rolled away exactly like a summer raincloud to reveal a dark staircase as wide as a two-lane highway.

"Whoa," Bex said, backing into Nemini, who was still hovering behind her like a nervous cat. "What is that?"

"The continuation of the central stair," Leander replied, lifting his ball of blue fire to show Bex the enormous, open, corkscrew staircase that went both up and down the giant cylindrical shaft in front of them. "It used to go all the way up to Heaven, but the entrance to this part was sealed off when Gilgamesh started using the Lowest Hells as a prison."

Bex could see why. Now that he'd opened the wall, she could feel the crushing, falling terror of the void demons seeping up from the darkness below. It was just an echo of what she felt when she actually jumped in, but it was still enough to make their whole attack force stop in its tracks.

"Well," Lys said with a swallow, breaking the sudden silence. "At least this explains why the Middle Hells tower has a floor at the bottom. I always wondered how the warlocks got down to the Lowest Hells, but now I see. They didn't."

"No one comes down here," Leander agreed, tossing his glowing ball of fire up to illuminate the stone ceiling that abruptly cut through the giant black stairwell fifty feet above their current position. "The Lowest Hells have been off-limits to everyone except Gilgamesh and his princes for eons, which makes it the last place they'll be expecting an attack from." He flashed Bex a superior smile over his shoulder. "Convinced I'm on your side now?"

"It's a good start," Bex said, stepping gingerly through the hole he'd made in the wall to join Leander on the spiral staircase. "Ask me again after we've actually won something."

The prince scowled, but he let the comment lie as he started up the steps, which looked very different from the ones in the Middle Hells. Bex had only gotten a brief glimpse of the inside of the warlocks' tower before the princess spotted her, but everything she'd seen had been as white and fancy as the Holy City itself. The walls here, on the other hand, were the blackest Bex had seen since entering the Hells. She didn't know if the stone was naturally dark or if years of sin had just stained it that color, but the matte black soaked up the light and made it very difficult to see. She'd just put her hand on the wall to make sure she didn't miss a step and accidentally fall to her death when Bex felt the familiar, toxic burn of sin iron.

"What the—" She snatched her hand away, squinting at the walls in the faint light of the prince's distant fire. "Are these *pipes*?"

"Sin-iron water pipes," Leander confirmed with a nod. "They're what bring the deathly rivers up to the other Hells. How else do you think we maintain a steady stream of river water for the demons to strain sin out of?"

He reached out to rap his knuckles against the wall, which Bex only now realized wasn't made of very dark stone like she'd thought. It was sin iron. All the walls of the circular, spiral stairwell they were climbing were covered in sin-iron pipes of various sizes. She was scrambling to think how they could use that to their advantage when the prince tapped her on the shoulder.

"Don't dawdle, please," he said in a low voice. "We're in a place only Gilgamesh and his direct family are allowed to access. The security measures aren't checked often, but they do exist. If we linger long enough to get caught, our advantage will be lost, and this place could turn into a trap."

"Right," Bex muttered, turning to signal General Kirok to start moving everyone in before jogging up the long spiral to join Boston, who'd already galloped up to the wall that separated the bottom of the Middle Hells tower from the terrors below.

"I can't believe Gilgamesh just bricked it over," the familiar said, standing on his hind paws to get a better look at the white stones mortared together just above his head. "There's not even a support beam to prevent collapse. What if it broke and someone fell through?"

"I told you Gilgamesh was cheap," Leander whispered as he joined them. "Speaking of which, please lower your voices. There's only one layer of stone between us and the main security desk."

Bex could hear it. Now that she was crouching right below the floor, she could hear the warlocks walking around in the tower above them. She could even hear the murmur of their voices, though she couldn't hear what they were saying or pinpoint where exactly they were standing. She was pressing her ear to the stone to see if she could pick up something more useful when Leander pressed his palm flat against the stones beside her.

"Eyes of Curiosity."

The moment the whispered words of sorcery left his lips, a shimmering window appeared in the bricks. The unexpected burst of light made Bex jump, and then her face broke into a grin.

Thanks to Leander's spell, she now had an unobstructed view into the tower above them. The huge, white, cylindrical building looked exactly like she remembered, but there were a lot more warlocks on the stairs this time. It almost looked like they were standing in line, waiting their turn to talk to a person she couldn't see, who was standing next to the golden armored prince Bex had seen before.

"Ah," Leander whispered in a relieved voice. "That's Demetrios, Prince of Hate."

"Is he going to be a problem?" Bex whispered back.

"Not for me," the prince said smugly. "Of all the replacements Father could have chosen, Demetrios is actually the least suited to handle my sorcery. His princess will be difficult, though."

Given the chase she'd put them through last time despite her chains, Bex believed it. Even more worrisome, she didn't see the princess anywhere inside the square of the magical window. She was moving her head from side to side, trying to see into the parts of the tower the window's viewpoint didn't include, when Bex finally caught a glimpse of the person the warlocks were lining up to meet.

The sight stopped her cold. Standing on the stairs with the golden prince and all the fawning, white-robed Heavenly denizens was a man dressed entirely in black. Bex couldn't see his face from way down here, but that didn't matter. She'd know that coat and pointed hat anywhere. It was Adrian.

Just knowing he was close sent Bex's heart thudding up into her throat. She'd thought about him so much over the last week, part of her was worried that she was hallucinating him now. Then Boston made an excited sound, and Bex knew this was no dream. After weeks of loneliness followed by losing him to the enemy, Adrian was only half a tower above her head, and nothing was going to keep Bex away from him this time.

"I know that look," Boston whispered with a sharp-toothed cat grin. "Ready to get our witch back?"

Bex nodded rapidly but signaled for him to wait. Her demons were still coming through the tunnel below. They'd lose their advantage if they got excited and started blasting before everyone was in position. But when she leaned over the edge of the spiral stairs to tell the demons to get ready, something slammed into the stone floor above her head like a dropped piano.

Wham!

The sudden noise almost made Bex fall off the stairs. Thankfully, Iggs was just a few steps below and was able to grab her before she went over. Bex nodded her thanks and scrambled back to Leander's sorcerous window, but when she looked through to see what in the Hells had just hit them, the chained princess was staring right back at her with golden eyes full of hate.

She bared her white teeth next, snarling through the cage of her sin-iron muzzle as she began punching a hole through the bricked-up passage with her carved white fist.

"Forget getting into position!" Boston yowled, pawing something out of his cat pack as the stone began to crumble. "Just *go!*"

That was all the warning Bex got before the intense smell of forest mixed with the violence of a thunderstorm exploded through the ceiling above her like a magical bomb.

Chapter 10

ADRIAN'S TRIP INTO THE Hells was not going as planned.

He'd thought he was finally making progress when Prince Demetrios led him out of the war-demon-only Upper Hells into a white tower at the center of a gigantic cavern. The Hell of War had felt more like the Holy City's basement with all its loyal demons toiling away without even a warlock to oversee them. This, though, *this* was the real deal.

Adrian had noted the security bells and armed war-demon guards the moment they'd stepped out of the connecting tunnel onto the white platform of the tower's top floor observation room. The air down here was even smokier than it was upstairs, but unlike the forge-warmed Hell of War, the Middle Hells were as cold and damp as a winter well. He could see why, too, when he looked through the observation room's big glass windows. The floor of the giant Middle Hells cavern was covered in half a foot of standing water. It looked like a giant rice paddy filled with chained slaves kneeling in rows, running their hands through the dark, stagnant water like they were searching for frogs.

"What are they doing?"

"Collecting humanity's sins," Prince Demetrios answered in a disgusted voice. "Heavenly King, did they teach you nothing in the Blackwood?"

Not about this. Even the demons didn't talk about the Hells if they could avoid it, but Adrian had never been more excited to be in such a terrible place. It was obvious that they'd just entered the heart of Gilgamesh's demon exploitation machine. If the Queen of Pride—and more importantly, Bex—was imprisoned anywhere, it would be somewhere like this. The cat-shaped finding spell was going nuts in his pocket, too, which meant he had to be getting close. He just needed to ditch his escort so he could follow the signal, but before Adrian could launch into his prepared speech about how *boring* this next part was about to be and how the Prince of Hate *really* didn't need to stick around, he'd been bowled over by an eager crowd of smiling men in stuffy white robes.

He'd been trapped ever since. Apparently, princes who weren't in disgrace never came to the Hells. This meant the warlocks working down here never got the chance to suck up, and these men weren't about to let an opportunity like Adrian pass them by.

They'd been lining up to shake his hand for the last fifteen minutes. He'd thought the actual Prince of the Hells would put a stop to it since all the brown-nosing was slowing them down, but Demetrios had just leaned against the wall to enjoy the show like a bully watching a hazing. Even the princesses kept their distance. Hate was straining at the end of her chain like always, but the fake Bex was beaming with pride at the sight of Adrian finally getting the attention a son of Gilgamesh deserved.

It was hell. Every time Adrian finished shaking one batch of hands, another group of warlocks ran up the steps to accost him. He'd done his best to stay polite—not because slavers deserved politeness but because he was on a mission that was going to get even harder if he pissed off the local security—but Adrian was rapidly losing his patience. It didn't help that the finding spell was kicking him constantly in his chest, urging him to action he couldn't take. He was about to give up and play the "I'm a super-important son of Heaven, don't touch me" card when Demetrios suddenly bolted out of his slouch like he'd been stung.

A heartbeat later, Adrian saw why. Prince Demetrios had lost his grip on the chained Princess of Hate. She raced down the spiral staircase with a screech, bowling over warlocks to reach the tower's open center. The moment she had open air in front of her, she jumped, falling the final five floors down the middle of the spiral stairs to land at the bottom of the tower like a princess-shaped sack of bricks.

The crash when she hit shook the entire tower, but the chained Princess of Hate didn't even seem to notice. She just started punching the floor, kicking the elegant white security desk—along with the warlock who'd been sitting at it—out of the way so she'd have more room to work. Her prince was racing down the stairs to get her back under control when the whole bottom level of the security tower exploded in a storm of raging magic.

Extremely *familiar* magic.

It rushed over Adrian like the wind before a thunderstorm, filling his lungs with the cool, wet, woodsy smell of the forest. Warlocks were screaming all around him about the hole the explosion had just blown through the bottom of their tower, but Adrian could barely hear them through the sudden, bittersweet wave of homesickness. For one glorious second, it truly felt as if he was back in his own Blackwood with the soft loam under his boots and the rustle of leaves in his ears. The feeling was so vivid, his hands went up of their own accord to touch the branches he could almost see waving above his head. He was still reaching in vain when something real and hard slammed into his palms instead, and Adrian snapped out of his haze to see he was clutching a broomstick topped with the carved likeness of a raven.

"Bran?" he said, blinking his mirrored eyes rapidly. "Is that—"

The broom yanked him off his feet before he could finish asking such a stupid question. Also just in time to avoid the Princess of Wrath, who was leaping down the stairs to grab him from behind. Her white fingers actually brushed the hem of Adrian's coat before Bran snatched him high into the air. Much higher than was necessary, Adrian thought, until he heard a new voice shouting words through the chaos.

It sounded like Ancient Sumerian. That wasn't unusual in Gilgamesh's domain, but Adrian didn't understand enough of the language to know what was being said or who was saying it. His best guess was that one of the overseers was throwing out some magic of their own, but this turned out to be only half correct. The words *were* sorcery, but they hadn't come from Gilgamesh's people. This ringing voice was speaking from inside the hole the explosion of witchcraft had just put in the tower's foundation, which wasn't actually a foundation at all. It was the sealed-off entrance to another flight of stairs. A detail Adrian could now see clearly from his new position high in the air as the incantation reached its completion, and a giant bull made from smoke and sorcery bashed its way through what was left of the floor to trample the chained princess.

The entire tower dissolved into chaos after that. Dangling from his broom's handle, Adrian had a perfect view as all the white-robed warlocks who'd swarmed him earlier started to flee. The sorcerous bull charged after them, galloping up the spiral staircase and breaking everything in its path.

The flying pieces of desks, chairs, and filing cabinets would have gone through Adrian like shrapnel if Bran hadn't jerked him out of the way. The broom did a barrel roll next, flipping himself over so that Adrian ended up sitting in his normal position on the back of the broomstick. He was still catching his balance when Bran suddenly dove for the ground, swooping like a falcon through the clouds of dust to pick up the fluffy black cat who'd just climbed out of the broken floor.

"Boston?" Adrian said, releasing his death grip on the broom's handle to rub his eyes and make sure he wasn't dreaming. "Is that really you?"

"Who else would it be?" the cat replied smugly, puffing out his chest as he hopped into his usual position on Bran's handle. "Surely you don't think a little thing like death could prevent a familiar of the Blackwood from finding his way back to his witch?"

He sounded insufferably pleased with himself. For once, though, Adrian didn't mind at all. *I'm so happy to see you!* he cried, lurching forward to pull Boston into a hug. "But what are you doing in the Hells?"

"Looking for you," Boston said, rubbing his head against the underside of Adrian's chin. "This is a rescue! Now let's get out of the way and give our allies some room."

Adrian's hopes had never risen so far so fast. He actually felt physically dizzy as he signaled Bran to whisk them back up to the top of the security tower's spiral stairwell. They'd just made it to what Adrian considered the minimum safe distance when Iggs stepped out of the dusty chasm left by the sorcerous bull.

It really shouldn't have been a surprise. If Boston had come for him, of *course* Bex's demons would be here to save her. Knowing that didn't stop Adrian's heart from hammering below its tree, though, especially when he saw the chained Princess of Hate emerge from the pile of rubble the magical bull had left behind.

"*Iggs!*" he shouted through the dusty air. "*Watch out!* She's..."

His voice trailed off in shock as Iggs reached into the ancient-looking knapsack he was wearing on his shoulder and pulled out the biggest gun Adrian had ever seen. It looked like the sort of thing that was normally bolted onto helicopters, not carried by people, but Iggs was no ordinary person. He was a demon of Wrath, and he looked every inch the part as he planted his boots on the rubble-strewn ground and began unloading the machine gun's belt into the charging Princess of Hate

The roar of gunfire that followed was deafening. It echoed up the tower like a hail of ball bearings, drowning out every other sound except Iggs's scream of fury. The giant gun had to be kicking like an elephant, but Iggs held it rock-steady, using his enormous strength to keep the barrel leveled at the Princess of Hate's chest.

It was such an impressive display, Adrian almost didn't notice that the flying bullets weren't even chipping the alabaster folds of the princess's carved dress. But while the mundane, human-made weapon clearly wasn't enough to bring down Gilgamesh's sorcerous masterpiece, the kinetic force of all those bullets was doing an excellent job of pushing the princess back. No matter how hard she dug her carved feet into the broken ground, the Princess of Hate was unable to step forward, buying time for the rest of the demons to surge out of the hole in the floor like a tide.

There was a staggering number of them. Uncollared demons of every type, size, and shape were pouring into the guard tower from below. Aside from Iggs, Adrian had no idea who any of them were, though he swore he saw Desh at the front of the pack. The fear demon was leading the charge up the tower stairs with his black scales pulled up to his neck and an automatic weapon of some sort clutched in his clawed hands.

All of the demons had guns, actually. That struck Adrian as very strange but also highly effective, because unlike the princess, Gilgamesh's warlocks were *not* immune to bullets. There were a few who managed to throw up sorcerous shields or hide behind their bronze-armored war demons, but most were caught flat-footed by the storm of bullets, falling off the tower's spiral staircase like white silk sandbags as the demons swarmed up the floors. Adrian was watching them push the line against the warlocks who'd managed to defend themselves when Bran's broomstick suddenly dipped.

His first thought was that his loyal broom had just dodged a bullet for him. When Adrian looked back toward the broom's bushy tail, though, the truth turned out to be the opposite. While he'd been watching the fight, his princess had kept her eyes on him. Adrian didn't even know where she'd come from, but the Princess of Wrath was suddenly hanging from the back of his broom, her white hands crushing Bran's broomstick as her golden eyes locked onto Adrian's in fury.

"We have to leave," she hissed as she began hauling herself hand over hand up the broomstick toward him. "I won't let them steal you from our king. I won't let them steal you from *me*!"

Her carved hand lashed out, grabbing the ankle of Adrian's black boot before he could snatch it away.

"You're *mine*!" she screamed. "*My* prince! *My* love! I won't—"

Her voice cut off as Adrian whipped his hand down and launched a blast of sorcery into her face. It wasn't even a proper spell, just the manifestation of his wish to make her go away fueled by the power of his white blood. It never would've worked if they'd been facing off for real, but the princess was dangling from a broom that didn't like her anyway. The moment her fingers loosened in surprise, Bran flicked like a whip, slinging the shocked princess off his broomstick and straight through the window across the tower to their left.

"Nice shot!" Boston cried as her white body crashed through the glass and vanished into the smoky darkness of the Hell outside. "But what was that?"

"A problem," Adrian muttered, bending over to prod the ankle she'd grabbed. It hurt enough to make him gasp, but it didn't feel broken, so he pushed the pain away and got back to the matter at hand.

"What's the plan?"

"You're looking at it," Boston said, running down the broomstick and up Adrian's chest to take his usual position on his witch's shoulder. "I'm rescuing you, Desh and his team are going for the keys that will unlock all the demons in the Middle Hells, and Iggs and Bex are—"

"Bex?" Adrian interrupted, jerking around so fast he nearly fell off his broom. "Bex is with *you*?"

"Of course she's with us," Boston said. "Who else do you think could put all of this together?"

Adrian stared at him in shock. "But..." he said at last. "Didn't Gilgamesh defeat her? Isn't she locked up?"

"Come on," the cat said with a scathing look. "Have you ever known Bex to stop after a defeat? I'm not entirely sure of the sequence of events, but she reappeared at the Seattle Anchor shortly after Heaven stopped its bombardment and just seconds before the Old Wives arrived to evacuate everyone to the Blackwood."

"The Old Wives went to *Seattle*?" Adrian repeated, dumbfounded. "How? *Why?* The Blackwood never gets involved in outside affairs, so why did—"

"I'll explain it to you later," Boston snapped. "Right now you need to pay attention before—"

His voice cut off as the river of bullets that had been roaring nonstop since Iggs climbed out of the hole abruptly ended. A loud curse came next, and Adrian looked down to see the mad Princess of Hate standing with her carved hand wrapped around the muzzle of Iggs's gun. She must've been slowly pushing forward against the bullets this whole time because there was a mountain of flattened slugs in front of her. The princess, however, was uninjured. A fact Iggs clearly recognized all too well from the look of horror on his face as she grabbed the gun out of his hands and broke it in two, snapping the metal barrel like a twig before throwing it aside to free her hands so she could drive them into the demon's chest.

It happened with the same horrible slow motion as a car crash. Adrian was certain he was about to watch his friend die in front of him, and he didn't even have a spell to stop it. There was nothing in his pockets but cat hair, the finding charm, and the Queen of Pride's horns. He was about to try sorcery again even though he already knew it was too late when the white hand the princess had been about to stab through Iggs's ribs was suddenly knocked off course.

The chained princess herself staggered a second later, kicked nearly off her feet by someone moving faster than Adrian's eyes could track. It wasn't until the black blur stopped to help Iggs get free of his ruined gun's shoulder strap that Adrian realized he was looking at a petite woman dressed in black combat gear with long, midnight-dark hair pulled into a ponytail, pale skin, and a look of pure fury etched into her lovely, determined face.

"Bex," he whispered, lurching toward her so fast that Bran had to swerve to keep him from falling. "*Bex!*"

She didn't look up, and thank the Forest for that, because the Princess of Hate recovered from the kick immediately. If Adrian had distracted her, she would've gotten blindsided. As always, though, the Queen of Wrath didn't flinch. She ducked the princess's punch like she'd seen it coming for miles, letting the white doll's manacled arm fly over her hornless head before lunging forward to slam a short sword Adrian vaguely remembered Iggs wearing once into the Princess of Hate's muzzled face.

The explosion that followed rocked the tower and sent the princess's white body flying into the air. If her head hadn't been enclosed in a sin-iron cage, Adrian was sure that hit would've blown it off. Her jaw and neck were still blackened when she landed on the second loop of the tower's spiral stair, snarling at Bex like a rabid animal. Bex snarled back, showing the princess the full spread of her fangs as she lifted her short sword for the next attack.

Adrian's heart lifted with it. Great Forest, it was good to see her. From the moment he'd first felt Heaven's attack through his tree, not an hour had gone by that he hadn't worried about her. He'd imagined all sorts of horrible scenarios where she suffered for his stupid mistakes, but at no point had he expected to find her already free and in the Hells leading what appeared to be a full-scale demon rebellion.

Dunderheaded assumption on his part. Adrian still wasn't sure how all of this had come to be, but the more he thought about it, the more he realized he should've expected it from the beginning, because this was what Bex did. She rose from her ashes. She picked up her sword and came back swinging every single time. *Nothing*—not death nor defeat nor Gilgamesh himself—could keep her down for long, and Adrian was so proud of her that he felt like he was going to burst. He was scrambling to think of a way to help her that wouldn't get in her way when a flash of white shot through the golden doors at the tower's base and tackled Bex off her feet.

It happened so quickly, Adrian didn't recognize the white streak as his own princess until she smashed the real Bex through the wall. When he rushed Bran to the window to look, he saw the two of them lying outside the tower in a kicking tangle, rolling through the dirty water while rows of chained slaves desperately tried to get out of their way.

This was normally the point where Bex would've lit up in a blaze of fury, but no flames appeared. She actually seemed to be struggling to keep her hornless head above the water as the princess crawled on top of her, using the weight of her carved body to pin the flesh-and-blood Bex to the ground. She grabbed her by the throat next, holding the real Bex in place with her carved hand while her gloved one curled into a fist to start pounding the queen in the face, but Bex didn't give her the chance. She'd already wiggled her good arm free to slam her explosive short sword into the princess's unprotected side.

The blast that followed echoed like a cannon through the giant cavern of the Middle Hells. Both Bexes were flung apart, but while the real Bex went skipping across the flooded floor like a stone, the princess grabbed one of the sin-iron slave chains.

The metal that held the Wheel of Reincarnation was plenty strong enough to check her momentum. The princess threw herself forward next, grabbing the chain in her fist to fling herself in the same direction the real Bex had been thrown. The last thing Adrian saw was the princess's white back vanishing into the smoky dark of the Hells. He'd already started climbing through the tower window to go after them when he stopped himself short.

It took every bit of his willpower to do it. He normally wouldn't worry about Bex fighting a princess, but now that the rush of seeing her again was fading, all Adrian could think about was how different she'd looked. Even in glimpses caught from a distance, it was impossible not to notice that she was still missing her horns and right hand. Adrian already knew she didn't have her sword because Drox's ring was on the fake princess's finger, but Bex's fire was part of her, and he hadn't seen a flicker of that either.

That was a *lot* of handicaps for a solo fight against a princess of Gilgamesh. The urge to run and help was overwhelming. The only reason Adrian didn't was because he already knew Bex wouldn't thank him for it. She'd chosen to charge this tower for a reason, and Adrian wasn't egotistical enough to believe it was solely for him. She had other goals here, demons to free. Bex always put the mission first, so Adrian forced himself to stop reacting and start figuring out how to actually help them win.

It definitely wasn't looking good. For better or worse, Bex had taken the Princess of Wrath out of the fight, but that left Iggs facing off against the Princess of Hate alone with only one other human as backup. It was hard to tell from way up here, but the skinny man looked a lot like the prince Adrian had seen in the Walking Memory. The one who'd picked him up and traded his unconscious body to Bex for the crazy prince's burned carcass and her sister's hand.

Adrian couldn't imagine the sequence of events that had led to that same prince fighting alongside demons in the Hells, but he was clearly on the rebels' side now. He was barefoot and filthy with no sign of his white sword or golden armor, but he was standing on the newly-revealed staircase like a sorcerous turret, sending out smaller versions of the bull he'd used earlier to keep pushing the Princess of Hate back. He sent the bulls up the tower as well, trampling the warlocks who were trying to stop Desh's army of demons.

The lightning-fast sorcery combined with the calm determination on the prince's gaunt face made for an absolutely terrifying sight. So long as he was shooting Gilgamesh's people, though, Adrian wasn't going to worry about him. He'd already dug his hand into the front pocket of his coat for the finding spell that had been stabbing him in the chest since he'd arrived on this floor.

"What's that?" Boston asked when Adrian pulled out the little carved cat. "Wait, is that *me*?"

"None other," Adrian said proudly, holding his palm flat so the finding charm could do what he'd made it to do. "Gilgamesh sealed me off from my forest, so I used my connection to you to borrow your connection to the Blackwood so I could make a modified version of the corpse-finding spell."

Boston looked affronted. "You turned me into a *corpse sniffer*?"

"That was the original plan," Adrian said. "But when I fired you up, you found something even better. Look!"

He moved his hand to show Boston the broken piece of black horn glued to the wooden cat's belly.

"What's that?" Boston asked.

"A piece of the Queen of Pride's broken horns," Adrian replied with a grin. "I've been using it to track her body."

His familiar blinked. "Her what?"

"The Queen of Pride's body!" Adrian repeated excitedly, moving his hand up and down as he desperately tried to follow the spell's wild jumping. "Gilgamesh didn't bring me up here just because I'm his son. He wanted me because I was the one who figured out how to restore Bex's bonfire, and he brought me to Heaven so I could do the same thing to the Queen of Pride."

Boston looked even more confused. "Why would Gilgamesh want to restore a queen?"

"I'm still trying to figure that out," Adrian admitted, steering Bran back out into the middle of the tower so he could get a better reading. "All I know is he's planning something that requires the horns of all nine queens to work. Since the Queen of War tore Bex's off, Pride is the only crown he's missing. The whole reason Gilgamesh pretended to be Malik and taught me sorcery was so that I would put her shattered horns back together and complete his set."

"But you didn't, right?" his familiar said nervously. "If Gilgamesh brought you to Heaven to do a thing, common sense dictates that that's the one thing you should never, *ever* do."

When Adrian didn't answer immediately, Boston leaned over to shove his nose in his witch's face. "Tell me you *didn't do it*, Adrian!"

"I didn't complete them," Adrian hedged as he craned his neck to keep his eyes on the finding charm despite the cat in his face. "But I couldn't let this chance go by. You think I'd let Bex go off to fight by herself if I didn't have a solid plan to change the tide of this entire battle? Just look at the finding charm."

He pulled his arm back to shove the wooden cat, which was spinning like a broken compass, under Boston's nose.

"It's pointing at the Queen of Pride's body," he said fiercely. "Her *moving* body, because *she's not dead*! All the statues showing her crushed beneath Gilgamesh's foot are lies. She's still alive, and she's here in the Hells. That's why I came down here in the first place. I've got her horns right here in my pocket. All I have to do is put them back on her head, and we'll have another queen back in the fight!"

He was shaking with excitement by the time he finished, but Boston's expression looked dire.

"Are you certain?" he demanded, staring into Adrian's eyes. "Are you absolutely positive that the Queen of Pride is here?"

"Of course I'm positive," Adrian snapped. "I used a corpse-finding charm with a piece of her own horn as the fulcrum. There's nothing else it could be pointing at." He glared at the charm, which was still spinning like a top on his palm. "It was giving me a clear line before I got to this floor, but all the magic flying around must be interfering with the locator."

"It's not the locator," said Boston, who still looked unhappy but was clearly unable to resist correcting Adrian's wrong assumptions. "It's spinning like that because we're on top of the target."

"You see?" Adrian said triumphantly. "I told you I wasn't messing around." He looked down at the broken floor where Iggs and the renegade prince were still smacking the Princess of Hate. "I bet she was hidden under that false floor."

"It looks more like the charm is pointing up to me," Boston said, giving the spinning cat a sniff before he sighed and stuck out his paw. "Hand it over."

"You're helping?" Adrian asked, shocked. "Does this mean you're not mad at me?"

"I'm furious with you," Boston snarled, lashing his tail. "Gilgamesh kidnapped you out of your forest to do a task and *you did it*! That was a stupid move, Adrian. Did you not think that you might be playing straight into the enemy's hands *again*?"

"Of course I thought about it!" Adrian cried. "But I didn't have anything else to work with, and I was *trying* to escape. Fixing the Queen of Pride and letting her bash us a way out of here was the best plan I could come up with, and for your information, it's worked perfectly so far. I was able to get out of my cell in Gilgamesh's palace and all the way down to the Middle Hells. Now the Queen of Pride is practically on top of us, so do you want to keep criticizing, or do you want to help me put another queen in the fight so Bex doesn't die out there?"

Boston heaved an enormous sigh before jumping off of Adrian's shoulder to land on Bran's broom handle.

"For the record," he announced, "I am absolutely right. Repairing the last piece Gilgamesh needs to put his unknown master plan into motion was reckless in the extreme, but I also acknowledge that I wasn't there and thus can't comment upon choices you were forced to make. Either way, done is done. The horns are back together, so we might as well make use of them."

"Glad to hear it," Adrian said as he held out the still-whirling charm. "Now how do I stop this thing from spinning?"

Boston gave him one more exasperated look before getting to work.

"The problem is you, not the magic," he reported. "Going through me to reach the Blackwood was a clever move, but using cat hair as a spell component hinders as much as it helps. That charm was never going to docilely do its job because cats aren't the obeying sort. Even I can't make it fully behave with so many exciting things going on, but since you used my hair as the base component, I should have better luck than you're having."

That was precisely the sort of excellent observation witches relied on their familiars to provide. Adrian surrendered the charm at once, holding his palm flat so Boston could grab the little spinning cat in his mouth. It stopped moving the moment the familiar's sharp teeth bit down. A heartbeat later, Boston's own nose went up instead, pointing like a whiskered arrow straight at the top of the tower. Adrian kicked Bran into motion the second he saw it, shooting them straight up the open center of the tower like a cork.

It felt a bit like flying through the eye of a hurricane. The entire building was engulfed in combat by this point, but the fighting was so chaotic that Adrian couldn't tell who was winning and who was dying. He also had no idea how or when the Queen of Pride's body had moved. Adrian was certain it'd been below him when he'd entered the tower, but they were already higher than the floors where he'd been mobbed by warlocks and Boston's nose was still pointing up.

The charm must have started malfunctioning sooner than he'd realized because it looked like they were going all the way back up to the Hell of War. Now that Adrian thought about it, imprisoning a forbidden queen on a floor occupied exclusively by famously loyal demons did seem like a good idea, but Boston didn't take them that far. His nose evened out when Bran reached the observation floor at the top of the Middle Hells' white tower. The enclosed tunnel staircase that led back to the Upper Hells was right in front of them, and standing beside it like a sentry was Nemini.

Adrian wasn't surprised at all to see her. The void demon was Bex's shadow, and she was doing an excellent job of keeping the more cowardly warlocks from reaching the exit. She'd also cut all the cords that rang the alarm bells, proof yet again that she was the most levelheaded demon on Bex's crew.

Adrian didn't want to get in the way of her doing her job, so he had Bran move them to the side of the tower where they could look for the Queen of Pride without blocking Nemini's line of sight. She had to be somewhere on this level, but no matter where he moved his broom, Boston's nose stayed locked on Nemini...

Who had powers no other demon seemed to possess.

Who'd been with Bex so long that none of her other demons remembered when she'd joined.

Who was the only member of Bex's crew he'd never seen her name, *and* the only demon he'd ever met who didn't have horns.

Adrian went perfectly still on his broom as all the factors he'd never thought about before suddenly came together in his mind. Boston must have been thinking along the same lines, because he froze in shock, his mouth falling open to drop the charm on the ground where it kept spinning like a top, its carved nose pinned like an arrow on Nemini, who was too busy throwing warlocks down the stairs to notice. She'd just tossed the last one when she finally spotted them staring.

"What?" she asked.

"It's you," he whispered as his face split into a giddy smile.

Nemini looked more confused than ever, but Adrian's mind was whirling faster than his charm. Of course, of course, it all made sense! Nemini's age and rarity, the black snakes that covered her head but no one else's, her uniquely horrifying and incredible powers, the way she treated Bex like family, there was nothing she could be *but* a queen!

But while the truth was becoming more self-evident to Adrian by the second, Nemini looked like she'd seen a ghost. Her confused expression had already collapsed into a look of horror, and her normally calm eyes were stretched so wide that Adrian could see the full circle of her yellow irises. She backed away next, snakes hissing defensively. She looked like a cornered animal, but Adrian was too stupid with excitement to notice.

"I can't believe I didn't realize it sooner!" he cried as he leaped off his broom to run to her. "It all makes sense now! You're the Queen of—"

She slapped a hand over his mouth before he could finish. The cold wash of oblivion followed, leaving Adrian numb and helpless as Nemini yanked him into the tunnel stairway that connected the Middle and Upper Hells. She slammed him into the wall next, knocking the witch hat off his head and grinding the back of his skull into the stone with impossible strength. Adrian was sure she was about to crack him like an egg when Boston suddenly leaped onto Nemini's back.

"Nemini, *stop*!" he cried desperately as he clawed his way up her back. "I'm realizing that we might have just accidentally trodden upon a delicate topic, but I swear Adrian meant no harm! He had only the best of intentions when he—"

"He always has the best intentions," Nemini interrupted, clenching the hand she was still pressing over Adrian's mouth until his jawbone ached. "That's his entire problem. He lets his hopes override his common sense."

That was one way of seeing it, Adrian supposed, but actual self-reflection was impossible when Nemini's void was sucking his consciousness down like a stone. He was on the verge of blacking out when Boston made it to Nemini's shoulder and pawed her arm with a pleading look. The cat's charm must have gotten through, because the demon released her grip with a long, tired sigh.

Adrian hit the ground like a sack of bricks. When he became aware of his surroundings again, he was sitting at the bottom of the stairs between the Upper and Middle Hells with Boston curled into a shaking ball in his lap and Bran hovering nervously over his head. He was waving the broom away when Adrian realized Nemini was sitting on the stair beside him, hunched over her knees with her snake-covered head in her hands.

"How did you know?"

The question came out as a whisper, and Adrian winced.

"I didn't until just now," he said, leaning forward to match her. "And I didn't figure it out on my own. I was following that."

He pointed at the tracker Boston had dropped on the floor, though it wasn't until the void demon gave him a sideways look through her fingers that Adrian realized just how strange the wooden doll covered in cat hair must look to someone who wasn't a witch.

"It's a finding spell," he explained quickly. "I was using it to find the Queen of Pride in the hope that she'd help me escape. I never imagined it would lead me to you."

"It shouldn't have," Nemini said, raising her head to give him the bitterest look Adrian had ever seen. "The Queen of Pride is dead. She destroyed herself five thousand years ago to spite Gilgamesh."

"But she doesn't have to *stay* destroyed," Adrian said, flashing her a smile. When she failed to smile back, he held up a finger, rose to his feet, and trotted back across the room to grab the still-rattling finding spell off the ground.

"Just a moment," he said as he pried the bit of horn that served as the primary locating apparatus off the wooden cat's belly. He dug into his coat's largest enchanted pocket next to pull out the magnificent set of repaired horns he'd almost finished back in his workroom. When he had the whole crown balanced in his hands, Adrian slid the final piece into place.

He hadn't brought any sap to glue it, but none was necessary. The moment the final piece touched the others, the horns latched onto it all by themselves, healing the break with the same lightning-fast regeneration he'd seen a hundred times in Bex's body. When the very last crack was repaired, Adrian turned around to offer the completed horns to Nemini.

"These are yours," he said in a reverent voice. "Gilgamesh collected the pieces and kept them for eons until he could find someone capable of repairing them. That someone turned out to be me, but I didn't do this for him. I restored these horns for all of us, for Bex and myself and your crew and everyone else who wants to escape Gilgamesh's yoke. With these, we can put another queen who never kneeled back in the fight. We can free the demons, defeat the princes, save Bex, topple Heaven itself! Everything we thought was lost when Bex was defeated is back in our grasp. We just have to reach out and grab it, so here," He stretched his arms out farther. "Take them."

He was smiling so hard, his face hurt by the end. It'd been a rough road, but Adrian had never felt so close to victory. There was no way Nemini didn't feel it too. She was one of Bex's demons, a fellow soldier in the Queen of Wrath's endless fight *and* a daughter of Ishtar. This should've been everything she'd been waiting five thousand years to hear, but Nemini was leaning away from the horns like they were a sword pointed at her heart.

"I can't."

The smile slid off Adrian's face. "What?"

"I can't do it," Nemini repeated. "Those are the Queen of Pride's horns, and I'm not her." She curled back over her knees. "Leave me alone."

"No," Adrian said fiercely, taking one hand off the towering horns to grab the no-longer-functioning finding charm.

"My magic isn't wrong," he insisted, shaking the wooden cat at her. "These horns are part of your body. It *has* to be you!"

When she didn't look up again, Adrian shoved the charm into his pocket with a sigh.

"I understand your hesitation," he said gently, trying a different tactic. "But whatever happened in the past, the truth of the present is that we're going to lose this war if we don't have a queen. Gilgamesh knows that. It's why he came down on Bex so hard and why he kidnapped me to Heaven even though it would've been much easier to fix your horns inside my own forest. He knows he can't risk your return, which is exactly why we have to make sure it happens."

He took another step toward her. "Don't you see, Nemini?" he whispered, voice trembling with excitement. "You're *it*. You're the change we've all been waiting for, the change *Bex* has been waiting for. You're how we win back Paradise, how we turn this whole war around, and all you have to do is go back to being what you always were."

He could already see it happening. Nemini would put on her horns and take command of all the demons in the Hells. He'd seen how strong the queens could be, and Nemini's powers weren't even ground down by time. She could save Bex, save Iggs, save the slaves, save everyone! Adrian didn't see how anyone could say no to such an obvious and universal good, but even when he spelled it out for her, Nemini refused to look at him.

"You have no idea what you're asking," she whispered, curling herself into an even tighter ball on the stairs. "I already gave up my life for this war once. I'm not doing it again. For the last time, the queen you're talking about is dead. Now leave me *alone*."

The final word was no louder than the others, but the way she said it sent a shiver down Adrian's spine. It was the same shiver he felt when Bex was roaring at the peak of her power, and it made his hands curl into fists around the Crown of Pride's elegant horns.

"What does it matter if you gave your life?" he demanded, voice shaking with anger this time. "Bex has given up hers a hundred and ninety-eight times. The Queen of War ripped the horns right off her head only a week ago, but she's out there fighting right now with no fire, no sword, and only one hand. If you won't do this for her sake, what about your people? What about all the pride demons your death knocked into the void, don't you care about them?"

"Again, you have no idea what you're talking about," Nemini said in a cold, flat voice. "Bex fights because that's who she is. She's the eternally loyal sword, the ever-burning Queen of Wrath, but not all of Ishtar's daughters are the same."

"I know she cares about you," Adrian snapped. "Bex would give up her life to save yours in a heartbeat. How can you just say 'no thank you' and leave her to fight on her own?"

"Because I never wanted her to fight in the first place!" Nemini yelled, her eternal calm shattering before his eyes as she whipped her head up to face him with her snakes rising around her face like a hissing black halo.

"You think this is the life I wanted for her?" she cried. "Dying over and over? Grinding herself down to nothing for a war she'll never win?"

"But we *can* win," Adrian argued. "That's what I'm trying to—"

"You're delusional," Nemini snarled, pointing at the horns in his hands. "Even if I let you put that *thing* back on my head, do you really think one queen can defeat the man who killed the gods? Because that's what I thought. Back when I was the Queen of Pride, I thought just like you. There were nine of us when he arrived. Nine sacred queens with all the might of Paradise at our backs. I thought it was impossible for us to lose, but we *did*."

She rose to her feet, clenching her nails—which had sharpened and lengthened until they looked like claws—into her palms.

"We were wrong," she said in a shaking voice. "*I* was wrong, but that wasn't the worst part. The worst part came after my defeat when I was falling into the void. All of my towering hubris had just shattered with my name. I had nothing left, no pride to shield me from finally seeing the world as it actually was."

She leaned closer, her snakes reaching out toward Adrian with their flicking black tongues. "Do you want to know what I learned that day? The truth I saw when I faced the abyss for the first time?"

Adrian wasn't sure he did, but he was the one who'd demanded she step up, so he swallowed his fear and nodded for Nemini to continue.

She did so with great ceremony, walking slowly back up the steps one at a time until she was standing over him like the ancient, terrifying queen she claimed to no longer be.

"I saw that it was pointless," she announced in a cold, heavy voice. "I'd spent my entire life fighting for the glory of the gods. I thought their power was my power, but that was never the case. The worship I reveled in when my demons fawned at my feet, the pride I felt when I knelt before my divine mother, all of it was lies. I watched my sisters die one after another defending Paradise from the mortals we'd always been taught were inferior, but when I went out to face Gilgamesh at the final threshold, the gods I'd spent my entire life worshiping as all-powerful beings didn't lift a finger to help me. They didn't even come out of their temple."

She bared her teeth, which Adrian only now realized were sharp as a viper's fangs. "They were *afraid*," she hissed. "Afraid of the humans and the death they brought. Afraid of Gilgamesh's aggression. They'd built their entire empire on the idea that mortals were docile sheep to be tended for their worship, but when the flock rose up and proved to be wolves, *we* were the ones the gods sacrificed."

Nemini's snakes went limp as she dropped her head. "That was the part that hurt the most. It wasn't that I lost. It was that Gilgamesh was right. We were never Ishtar's daughters. We were her tools. That's why queens have so much power over our demons. It's not because of our divine blood or inherent superiority. Ishtar gave us that power so that we could manage her Riverlands while she dallied with mortals. We were made to toil on her farms and eat humanity's sins while she and the other gods played in a Paradise designed for *them*. Human souls never walked the green fields of the Riverlands, and demons didn't either. We worked there. We slaved for the gods the same way we slave for Gilgamesh. The only difference is that now demons have to bow to warlocks instead of queens."

"That's not true," Adrian insisted. "It *can't* be true. I've talked to Iggs. He lived in the Riverlands, and he said it was a Paradise."

"Of course he'd say that," Nemini replied bitterly. "He was one of Rebexa's demons. Out of all of us, the Queen of Wrath was the only one who actually believed her own propaganda. When I ruled the Riverlands, I kept my demons busy building ziggurats to my greatness. War constantly sent her people into losing battles because she couldn't stand her share of the poison Ishtar made us eat. It was easier for her to get all her demons killed than to let them do the job they'd been created for, which was why Ishtar threw her in that pit."

Nemini's jaw tightened. "I was there when she did it. We all were. Eight perfect queens smirking as we watched our mother throw our sister into eternal darkness because the labor she'd been created for had driven her mad." Her yellow eyes locked onto Adrian's. "Tell me, Mr. Witch, is that the Paradise you want us to win back?"

Adrian looked down at his boots. "If that's how you've felt all this time," he said after a long silence, "why are you still fighting?"

"For the same reason you are," Nemini replied with a sad smile. "I do it for Bex. She's always believed we were on the right side, and that if we could just keep going, we'd eventually defeat Gilgamesh and return everyone to Paradise. You know how much I disagree with that logic, but that doesn't change the fact that her steadfast faith has brought hope to countless generations of demons. It brought hope to *her*. Even though we never achieved any of our goals or made any measurable difference, fighting for her people gave Bex purpose."

Nemini's shoulders sank with a long sigh. "Who was I to tell her she was wrong? If we're doomed to be slaves no matter what, then it doesn't matter who wins the war. Why shouldn't I let her be happy in her delusions? Especially since it made me so happy to fight beside her."

Her sad smile grew brighter. "I've known more love and companionship as part of Bex's team than I received as a queen worshiped by millions. I used to think my youngest sister was an idiot, a fool too dazzled by Ishtar's power to think for herself. It was only after I was shattered that I realized the truth. Bex wasn't foolish. She was good. She truly believed that being a queen and fighting for her people was her divine purpose, and so long as I was with her, I got to believe it too. Why in the world would I give that up?"

"Because this isn't like those other times," Adrian told her desperately. "I get it. Both the gods and Gilgamesh were bad, but that doesn't mean what's happening *now* can't be worse. We're no longer in the same stalemate Bex has been fighting for five thousand years. Gilgamesh came after me because he's got a plan. I don't know what that is yet or why he needs your horns, but he wouldn't be pursuing this so recklessly if he didn't think it was going to make him even more powerful. That's why we can't just leave things the way they are, because if we don't find a way to defeat Gilgamesh now, we may lose the option entirely."

"So what?" Nemini asked, plopping back down on the stairs. "Have you ever stopped to consider that it might not be so bad to let the endless war end? If Gilgamesh wins definitively, maybe Bex will finally stop throwing herself at him."

"You know that won't happen. She'll fight him to her last breath. Her *actual* last breath because there are no more reincarnations. If she loses this time, it really will be the end."

"You say that like it's something dreadful," Nemini replied in a chillingly calm voice. "But all things end. That's the truth the gods could never accept, but they'll still become the same dust as everything else one day. Death is the only inescapable force in this world. It's pointless to fight it."

"And yet you do," Adrian said angrily, clutching the queen's horns in his hands. "If you actually believed in what you're saying, you wouldn't be here, but I've seen you save Bex more times than I can count. You *always* come to save her, and I think you'll come through this time too."

Nemini's yellow eyes narrowed, but Adrian had already bent down to place the horns he'd so carefully pieced back together on the step at her feet.

"Part of being a witch is learning to accept things as they are," he said as he straightened back up. "But despite everything you just said, I don't think nihilism is your true nature. If you truly believed that life was pointless, you wouldn't fight for Bex so hard, but you *do*. You've fought by her side for five thousand years because you were telling me the truth earlier when you said how much you loved her. That's the Nemini I believe in, so I'm going to leave these here."

"There's no point," she warned, pulling her feet up to get them farther away from the horns he'd just set down. "If I put that crown back on, my divine name will be restored. I'll be dragged out of the emptiness, dragged from my freedom and forced to be the gods' slave again. Even for Rebexa, I can't do that."

"And I can't force you," Adrian said. "I *won't* force you, but I don't think it'll matter." His lips curled into a smirk. "Bex has a habit of inspiring people to do the impossible, so I'm making the same gamble I made the first day I saw her waiting in front of the airport. I'm betting it all on her. I'm betting it all on *you*, because you're loyal, too, Nemini. If you weren't, Bex wouldn't trust you so much."

Nemini's eyes narrowed even further. "That's a lot of bets for a man who's been fighting with us less than half a year."

"And yet I'm never wrong," Adrian said with a cocky grin. "Not about Bex, anyway. She's the gamble I've always won, and I intend to keep throwing all-in with her until I die."

The tower rumbled as he finished, reminding Adrian that he'd better get a move on if he didn't want those to be his ironic last words.

"I've got to go help Bex win a fight she should never have been forced into," he said, patting his shoulder to signal Boston to climb back up. "I'm trusting you to do the right thing, Nemini."

"Right and wrong are subjective," Nemini reminded him, but Adrian had already stuck out his hand for his broom. The moment Bran's broomstick hit his palm, Adrian vaulted on, holding onto his hat and bending his body low so Bran could shoot them through the broken tower window toward the smoky darkness where he'd last seen Bex.

And behind him, alone on the stairs that were the Middle Hells' only exit, the broken remains of the Queen of Pride stared down at the crown that had once been her entire world.

Chapter 11

*"**B**EX!"*

Iggs's shout rang through empty air. The second princess had come out of nowhere. He hadn't even realized there *was* a second princess until she'd tackled Bex through a wall. Now they were rolling through the putrid water that covered the slave floor, punching each other in a tangle of perfectly matched limbs. Iggs was digging into his bag for a gun big enough to blast the princess off his queen when an iron-hard hand latched onto his arm.

"Stick to the plan!" Lys yelled.

Iggs jumped. He'd thought Lys was going for the keys with Desh, but they were suddenly right behind him wearing a massive male body that had muscles on top of muscles. Like all of Lys's shapes, though, the bulging biceps were just for show. No matter what form they took, there was a hard limit to how strong Lys's bodies could get. None of them could have moved Iggs an inch if he'd really dug his heels in, but he let Lys turn him back around to face the princess Leander was barely keeping back with his bulls.

"Stick to the plan," Lys said again as they moved up to defend Iggs's left. "Bex has been handling herself for five thousand years. She needs us to do our jobs, not get distracted worrying about her."

"Okay," Iggs said nervously, eyeing the chained princess, whose white body still wasn't cracked despite a full belt of machine-gun ammo and a whole herd of sorcerous bulls from Leander. "But how do we do that? Neither of us has ever beaten a princess without Bex before."

"You don't know everything about me," Lys replied with a stubborn lift of their perfectly square new chin. "I've fought a lot of scary stuff for my queen, and it's not as if we're doing this alone."

It sure looked like they were alone. All the badass demons Bex had pulled out of the Lowest Hells had already run upstairs. General Kirok and Nemini were up there as well, which *sucked* because they were the two Iggs would've picked first to be at his side for this. With Bex kicked through the wall, that left just him, Lys, and Leander facing off against the Hells' rabid princess.

Considering the thrashing Leander had given him using less than ten words back in Seattle, that should've been enough. This princess was proving to be way more resistant to sorcery than Iggs had been, though, and Leander was hardly in peak form. He'd always been a scrawny, sleep-deprived-looking bastard, but the prince was huffing like a shut-in who'd been forced to run a marathon, the sorcerous poetry coming out of his mouth in ragged gasps as he struggled to keep the princess under control.

"Looks like we're not winning that way," Lys muttered, switching out their bodybuilder for a smaller and nimbler, but no less intimidating, female body. "You got anything in your magical murder bag that can knock her down?"

"Maybe," Iggs said, digging into the depths of Solomon's Armory. "I tried to look through everything before we left, but there's a ton of weapons in here, and Felix's goblins didn't exactly give me an inventory list."

"Just find something that can get her on the ground," Lys ordered, pulling out their sin-iron knife. "Once she's prone, I'll take care of the—"

They cut off when Leander shouted behind them. It sounded like he'd taken a hit, but when Iggs's head whipped back, the prince was still in one piece and on his feet. He did, however, look very, *very* pissed.

"Enough of this!" he roared, whipping out his hand. "Band of a Thousand Irons! Band of a Thousand Irons! *Band of a Thousand Irons!*"

Iggs's Ancient Sumerian wasn't nearly as good as Lys's, but he remembered that one. That was the spell Leander had used to tie him up before sending him flying. It worked the same way this time, but while Iggs had gotten just a single iron band around his feet, the princess got a triple, causing her to go down hard as three iron bands the size of telephone poles appeared out of nowhere to wrap her up like a mummy.

"Nice," said Iggs as the bound princess toppled to the ground.

"There's nothing nice about any of this," Leander panted. "That was too close. Where's your queen?"

"Busy," Lys replied sharply, pointing their dagger at the bound princess wiggling on the floor. "How long will that hold her?"

"Not forever," Leander admitted, still breathless. "But she's not our primary concern in that form. The real danger comes if we let her—"

"*Return to my grasp, chalice of grudges.*"

Iggs jumped. The words were sorcery, but they hadn't come from Leander. The former prince actually looked as surprised as the rest of them when the thrashing princess went still inside the iron bindings. Lys and Leander had both already switched to the next target, but it took Iggs a solid count of five to turn and see the man who was suddenly standing at the bottom of the tower's spiral stairs. The golden-armored, mirror-eyed, superiorly sneering Prince of the Hells, who was now holding a white sword bound to his armored hand by a long black chain.

"Well, well," he said, eyeing Leander up and down. "Look who finally went full traitor."

He twirled his sword by her chain as he spoke, causing the heavy blade—which was as long as Bex's but only half as wide, with a jagged edge that looked more like a sawblade than a sword—to whistle through the air. That seemed like a pretty disrespectful way to treat a princess, but the Hells Prince actually looked like he was in control for once, holding the chain lightly against his palm as he spun his weapon faster and faster.

"No one's going to be surprised, you know," the prince went on, smiling at Leander like he'd been waiting years for this moment. "You always did have a weakness for Ishtar's devils."

"While your weaknesses are too numerous to count," Leander replied with a sneer. "You've failed to master even the most basic aspects of your position. A true prince is beloved by his princess. Yours hates you so much that you have to chain her like a dog."

"She *is* a dog," the Hells Prince spat. "They're all dogs of the gods, and the fact that you can't see that is why you *failed*!"

He lashed out with his sword arm as he finished, whipping the chained blade like a missile straight at Leander, who immediately ducked out of the way. Unfortunately, this meant the white sword was now flying straight at Iggs, the cover Leander had chosen to hide behind.

If it'd been anyone else, the betrayal would have stabbed deep, but Iggs's expectations for any son of Gilgamesh were already on the floor. He didn't even bother getting mad about it. He just shoved his hand into his knapsack.

He had no time to tell the bag what he was looking for, so the gun that leaped into his grasp was random. Despite only using it for a single day though, the Armory of Solomon had already become Iggs's favorite thing in the entire world. It proved its awesomeness yet again when he pulled his hand out to reveal a M134 Minigun. He'd only seen the thing in FPS military games before, usually mounted to the deck of a gunship, but this one had been retrofitted with a stock that let Iggs brace it against his shoulder. It also came preloaded with a full drum of bullets as long as his finger, which Iggs immediately began unloading into the sword that was flying at his face.

Just like with her princess form, the nonmagical bullets couldn't actually pierce the Blade of Gilgamesh's white surface, but there were still two thousand of them hitting her per minute. That was a *lot* of kinetic force. Too much for the sword to handle, apparently. Her serrated blade sliced right through the bullets, but the combined momentum of all those hits still pushed her off course, causing her to crash into the wall behind Iggs rather than through his skull.

"Good work!" Lys yelled from somewhere to his left. "Now do that again!"

Easy for them to say. The prince had already yanked his chained sword out of the wall and was swinging it over his head like a helicopter blade, forcing the taller Iggs to hit the deck or get decapitated. This exposed Leander, who was frantically muttering something under his breath. Iggs hoped it was a barrier spell, because the drum on his minigun was already half empty. He was working the M134's long multi-barrel around to unload what was left into the prince's arm in the hopes of making him lose his grip on the chain when the golden bastard's smug face suddenly went blank.

A wet gurgling noise came next as a gush of white blood bubbled from between the prince's lips. His flying sword jerked like a shot bird as the Prince of the Hells staggered, gasping in pain from the dagger Lys was shoving into his neck from behind.

"Got you," they snarled.

They really did. The last time Iggs had seen Lys, they'd been on the other side of the tower. They must've used their wings to close the distance, because the lust demon was back in their true form with their prehensile tail wrapped around the prince's golden helmet, which they'd lifted off his head just enough to make room for the sin-iron dagger to slide through the gap and into the nape of the prince's neck.

Iggs could actually see the blade's black point sticking out through the front of the prince's windpipe. It was a solid skewer, a killing blow, but Lys wasn't letting up. They'd already braced their legs against the prince's armored back so they could leverage their body weight to push the dagger sideways for a full beheading. Iggs could hear the *crack* of the sharp blade cutting through the prince's spinal vertebrae when the dying son of Gilgamesh clenched his fist around his princess's chain. The white sword launched itself off the ground a second later, hurtling over the gasping prince's shoulder straight into Lys.

The attack sent them both flying backward into the white staircase, which now looked more like a white gravel pile thanks to Iggs's indiscriminate storm of bullets. When the dust finally cleared, Lys was lying on their back with the prince's sword stabbed through their left shoulder, stapling them to the broken ground. The prince had just yanked the chain to pull his sword back when Iggs burst into motion.

He charged across the tower like one of Leander's bulls, running past the still-choking prince to snatch Lys's body off the ground. The moment he pulled them into his arms, Iggs knew it was bad. Lys had always been a lightweight, but it barely felt like he was holding anything at all. Iggs *really* hoped that was due to the extra strength of his adrenaline-jacked body and not because Lys had just left all their blood on the ground. There was a terrifying amount of it on the stone where they'd fallen as well as streaming down Iggs's arms, but he didn't have time to panic. He'd already run Lys back to the hole Boston's spell had blasted through the floor, racing down the spiral staircase toward the Lowest Hells. The moment the prince was out of sight, he put Lys down on a step and grabbed the emergency triage kit he kept on his belt.

"Never mind that," Lys wheezed as Iggs dug frantically for a bandage to tie up their perforated shoulder. "Did I get him?"

"I'll never 'never mind' you dying in front of me," Iggs growled, holding Lys still as he wiped the black blood off with a gauze pad so he could see the damage. "What in the Hells were you thinking? Don't you remember what happened the last time you stabbed a prince in the back?!"

"That's why I went for the jugular this time," Lys wheezed. "Heaven's suck-ups call them divine, but Gilgamesh's princes are still human, and all humans have a hard time when you give them gills. Now stop fussing and let me—"

They cut off with a gasp when Iggs touched the wound in their shoulder. Lys went quiet after that, breathing in short little pants while Iggs pressed the sterile pad over the hole and secured it in place with several hastily torn pieces of medical tape. That stemmed the flow of black blood, which normally would have meant he could leave the rest to Lys's natural regeneration, but this was an injury from a Blade of Gilgamesh. Iggs knew *exactly* how impossible those were to heal after seven years of watching his queen bleed. He needed to get Lys somewhere safe until Adrian could take a look at the wound.

Quietly as he could, Iggs rose from his crouch, peeking over the edge of the hole into the tower. The prince hadn't followed them down the stairs yet, and Iggs didn't see him waiting at the top, which was a good sign. If Lys's stabbing had bought them some breathing room or—even better—forced the prince to retreat, maybe he could...

Iggs's hopeful thoughts trailed off when he spotted a glint of gold moving on the other side of the tower. Sure enough, when he eased his head a little higher over the lip of the broken floor, the damn prince was back on his feet. He'd taken off his helmet so he could apply pressure to his still-bleeding neck, but he looked more angry than pained. Definitely not the face of someone who was dying because he'd just had his throat shish-kebabed by a poison knife.

"Is he down?" Lys asked feebly.

Iggs was still trying to think of an answer that wouldn't be crushing or an outright lie when Leander appeared out of thin air beside him.

"We need to go."

"Whoa!" Iggs cried, jerking away. Then he scowled. "What was *that*? You told Bex you couldn't teleport!"

"I can't," Leander informed him crisply. "That was Fifty Steps of the Pilgrim. Completely different spell."

"I don't care if it was Fifty Shades of Grey," Iggs snarled as he scooped Lys back into his arms. "We're not going anywhere. I know things were in chaos after Boston blew the floor early, but the queen still gave us our orders before we came up. Our job is to keep the prince off the key team. If we bail, we'll put everyone else in danger."

"I'm afraid that ship has already sailed," Leander replied, pointing up through the broken tower at the enemy.

Iggs peeked back over the ledge with a curse. He already knew the Hells prince was back on his feet, a totally unfair move for someone who'd just had a knife put through his jugular, but there was more going on with him now than just ignoring deadly damage. The prince Iggs saw when he followed Leander's pointing was noticeably larger now than he'd been when Lys attacked.

That wasn't just a trick of perception. The prince's height had visibly increased, and his chest had gotten so much wider that gaps were starting to open where the pieces of his armor came together. The overlapping golden scales that formed his breastplate started popping off as Iggs watched, revealing giant veins throbbing beneath his olive skin.

Whatever he was doing must've hurt because the prince was groaning deep in his throat, but the weird growth didn't stop. He'd already doubled in size by the time Iggs turned to Leander and asked, "What in the Hells is going on?"

"It's got nothing to do with the Hells," Leander replied, never taking his eyes off his expanding brother. "It's his weapon. The Princess of Hate is a double-edged sword. She's the most unstable of all the Blades of Gilgamesh, but she's also the most difficult to deal with, because every wound she takes makes her stronger. That same power extends to her prince, which is why the Prince of Hate is usually a forward-facing combat position. The more you hurt him, the stronger and bigger he becomes."

"That sounds pretty hateful," Iggs agreed, shoving the half-empty minigun back into his bag. "So how do we stop him?"

"I'm not sure we can anymore," Leander said, looking more nervous than Iggs had ever seen a prince get. "The Blade of Hate requires a certain level of abuse to activate, which is why I was focusing on attacks that pushed back rather than maimed. I'd hoped to neutralize the princess before that idiot got brave enough to grab her, but it seems the damage from your companion's surprise attack pushed him over the line." He pressed his already thin lips tighter. "In this state, it might not be possible to stop them without the Queen of Wrath's assistance."

"Then we'd better find a way to make it possible," Iggs said, grabbing a bandage roll from his kit to tie Lys, who'd mercifully passed out at some point during this conversation, to his back. "Bex is busy with her own problems right now, but that doesn't mean we're off the hook. Our queen gave us a duty: keep the prince busy so Desh's group can get the keys and Boston can rescue Adrian. If killing him is too hard, we'll make do with stalling. So long as we keep him off of everyone else until the tower is secure, we still win."

"That's a very loose definition," Leander said sourly. "But I don't have a better plan, so how do you propose that we advance?"

It was pretty surreal having the prince who'd kicked his ass asking him for tactical advice, but Iggs had learned to be a soldier the hard way, and he rolled with the curveball like the seasoned professional his queen expected him to be.

"Our first priority is to get him away from the others," he said as he dug into Solomon's Armory. "So let's try kiting him down the stairs."

The prince scowled in confusion. "Kiting?"

"It means baiting the enemy into chasing us without running so fast that we lose him," Iggs explained quickly. "If we do it right, we might be able to trick him into following us all the way back to that Hell where you were trapped."

Leander scowled harder. "Won't that get us trapped as well?"

"Yeah, but it's better than dying," Iggs said as he felt his way through the knapsack's expansive selection of military hardware. "If you've got a better idea, say it quick. I don't know how long it takes your ugly brother to hulk out, but he's gotta be nearly done with—"

Like he'd been listening for his cue, the Prince of Hate chose that moment to finish his gross metamorphosis. He looked more like a transformed wrath demon than a human now, but his scream rang with hatred instead of anger as he ripped the last bits of broken golden armor off his giant body and flung them at his enemy.

Iggs ducked the busted golden chest plate easily, which was how he didn't see the sword coming in behind it. The white Blade of Hate wasn't bloated like her prince, but something must've changed for her as well, because she was flying like a mad hornet. She whipped at the end of her chain like a kite in high wind, shooting up to the end of her tether only to immediately slam back down like a wrecking ball. Each hit left a crater the size of Iggs, but, by a miracle of Ishtar, he managed to dodge every time, running down the giant spiral staircase toward the Lowest Hells with Lys's still-bleeding body lashed to his back and Leander hot on his heels.

The light got dimmer quickly as they descended. By the time they passed the tunnel where they'd come in, Iggs could barely see two steps ahead. The sword was still destroying everything she hit, but the crashes seemed to be getting farther behind them. Iggs was starting to think they might have to slow down to keep the enemy baited when something enormous slammed into his back.

It felt like he'd been hit by a falling tree. For a breathless second, Iggs was certain he was dead and simply didn't know it yet, but no white sword exploded through the front of his chest. He didn't even see any black blood on his shirt other than what Lys had already dumped there. He was still trying to figure out what in the world had hit him when he heard Leander's voice yelling beside him, and then the last of the light cut out.

"That should buy us some time," Leander panted, summoning the sorcerous blue fire he'd used earlier to examine something that looked like, but couldn't actually be, a giant steel umbrella. It covered their heads like a pavilion, but the strangest thing was that its edges connected to walls. Big stone ones that muffled the sound of the Sword of Hate bashing against the outside. Together with the steel umbrella, the walls formed a pillbox that completely surrounded the stairs where Iggs and Leander were standing, sealing them off from attack.

"Don't look so worried," Leander chided, patting Iggs on the shoulder. "We're inside the protection of my Seven Walled City. Even the Coward Queen going at full burn took a while to chew through these walls. Did I get the Emphatics of Steel Skin on you in time?"

"I don't know what that is," Iggs said as he pushed himself back up, "but considering I'm not dead, I'm going with 'yes.' So what's your plan now that we're in here?"

The prince's gaunt face grew grim in the eerie blue light. "I don't have one," he admitted. "Walls only delay problems, but I couldn't think of anything else. I thought we were outrunning them adequately, but then the prince threw his sword. I would have put a protection up earlier, but I didn't realize Hate's chain was long enough to go across the center of the stairwell until her blade was practically in your back." His frown deepened. "If they can attack us from so far away, I don't think the kiting plan is going to work."

"In that case," said Iggs, taking the Armory of Solomon's knapsack off his shoulder so he could dig through it properly, "it's time to move to Plan B."

"Don't say that like you actually have a Plan B," Leander snapped. "This whole mission has fallen apart! I gave us a decent chance when it was four on one against the princess, but the fully manifested Prince of Hate *and* his sword against the two of us? While carrying an injured demon?" He shook his head so hard that his hair—which had the same dark curls as Adrian's—flew. "It's impossible. There is literally no way left for us to win."

"Not with that attitude," Iggs said, struggling to picture exactly what he wanted as he shoved his hands deeper into the endless magical arsenal. "But you're on our team now, and the number one rule of running with Bex is that we don't quit. If Plan A isn't working, we move on to Plans B and C. We'll go through the whole damn alphabet as many times as we have to until we find what we need, but we don't give up while we've still got people in the field. That's how *my* queen does things."

"With respect," Leander said through gritted teeth, "your queen has been synonymous with pointless, stubborn stupidity since before I was born. Even Mara, who loved her best, called the Queen of Wrath a bullheaded fool."

"So what?" Iggs snapped, grinning as Solomon's Armory finally got the picture and coughed up four large bricks of silver-gray, plasticky-looking clay. "Fools are the ones who come up with all the brilliant solutions that sensible people who knew better can't imagine. Also, *with respect*, you Heavenly blowhards have never been much good at stopping us, so unless you've got something constructive to add, I'd thank you to kindly shut up and let me work."

Prince Leander looked mortally offended. To Iggs's great surprise, though, he did as he was told, leaning silently against the fortifications he'd conjured out of thin air while Iggs cut the gray clay into pieces with his combat knife. When all four blocks were diced, Iggs worked the moldable pieces into putty before sticking them on the wall of the pillbox, covering the curved stone from top to bottom until the inside of the bunker looked like a gray version of a mud dauber's nest.

"What is that?" Leander asked when his curiosity finally overpowered his stuck-up prince-ness. "Some kind of witchcraft?"

"Nope," Iggs replied, doing his best to ignore the constant *bang bang bang* of the princess's sword, which now sounded like it was only a few inches from his head. "These are plastic explosives. They're weapons created by good old human destructiveness, and they aren't magical in the slightest unless you count the magic of excessive kinetic force."

"Explosives?" the prince repeated in a horrified voice. "Do you intend to martyr us?"

"Not if you can do that teleporty thing again," Iggs replied as he reached back into Solomon's Armory for the wires and trigger button, which came out already connected, praise Ishtar.

Leander scowled. "Are you referring to 'Fifty Steps of the Pilgrim'?"

"If that'll do the job," Iggs said, shoving the colorful wires into the shaped blobs of C-4 putty as fast as his hands could go. "I'm not picky about the specifics. I just need you to cast something that will move us away from this position without opening the walls."

"Then Fifty Steps is the spell you want," Leander said authoritatively. "But what are you hoping to accomplish? As you saw earlier, mundane weaponry has no effect on the divine implements of Heaven. An explosion might throw them off the stairs, but without a fatal blow to finish the job, they'll quickly recover. When that happens, we'll be right back in the same doomed scenario we were in earlier except I won't be able to save us again because I can't cast Seven Walled City more than once per hour. Our enemy will be more fearsome as well since, as I already explained, any damage the Blade of Hate receives only makes her and her prince stronger."

"We'll jump through those hoops when we get to them," Iggs said as he finished prepping the wires and slung his beloved knapsack back over the shoulder that Lys wasn't tied to. "If nothing else, punching the enemy in the face with explosives is a much more satisfying way to die than hiding in a box."

The prince didn't have a quippy comeback to that, so Iggs took the chance to get himself rearranged, shifting the explosive trigger to the side he was holding Lys on so his right arm would be free to pull the ace he'd positioned at the top of his endless armaments bag if he saw a good opportunity.

"I think that's everything," he said as he stepped over to join Leander on the side of their tiny shelter that was farthest away from the plastic-explosive-covered wall the Sword of Hate had just started cutting into. "Get ready to teleport us as far away as you can on my signal."

"For the last time, it's not a teleport," Leander snapped, but he still wrapped his arm around Iggs's waist. "Ready."

The wall behind the explosives was starting to crack by this point, but Iggs still waited until he saw the actual sword break through before he yelled, *"Go!"*

Leander was reciting his poetry before the command left Iggs's throat. The moment he felt the magical movement grab them, Iggs mashed his thumb on the trigger. He actually saw the plastic explosives start to expand before the sorcery finished, and then he was suddenly outside again, standing on the opposite side of dark stairs four spirals below where they'd originally started. He actually had a perfect view of the seven enormous circular stone walls Leander had conjured to protect them. The Prince and Princess of Hate had been smashing their way straight through the layers like a brainless bulldozer, but the moment they broke into the final ring, the entire staircase filled with blinding white light.

The explosive shockwave hit the stair Iggs was standing on a fraction of a second later. Leander must not have been as durable without his golden armor, because he went down like a leaf. Iggs, however, was a wrath demon. A strong one who'd ditched the stupid slippery golden boots he'd had to put on for their disguises ages ago. He was back in his favorite combat boots now, and between their thick treads and his own heavy weight, Iggs managed to stay on his feet, watching in awe from behind the shelter of his arms as the explosion filled the dark stairway all the way down to the Lowest Hells.

Despite being the one who managed their weapons back on the RV, Iggs had never actually set off real C-4 before. The only reason he knew how to wire it was because he occasionally had to supplement his gamer rage diet with angry gun nut content. Their wrath was toxic but plentiful, plus he'd picked up a lot of useful skills, like how to use plastic explosives. But watching a redneck blow up watermelons through a screen was a totally different experience from seeing fifteen pounds of C-4 explode in real life. Nothing could've prepared him for the deafening sound of it, or the way the blast's concussion made it feel like every cell in his body was being punched simultaneously. All his instincts were screaming at him to duck and cover, but Iggs forced himself to stay on his feet, squinting through the blinding light for the moment the explosion failed.

It happened even sooner than he expected. Leander had told him flat-out that blowing the prince up wouldn't work, but the flare had barely faded before the Prince of Hate's white sword shot out of the smoke to dig its serrated teeth into the stairs on the opposite side of the spiral. The giant prince appeared a second later, using his sword's chain like a rope to swing away from the gaping hole the C-4's explosion had left in the staircase.

That was a surprise. Iggs hadn't realized the hulked-out prince still had the presence of mind to do something smart like swing to safety. He'd thought for sure they'd come right at him, but the fact that the prince had chosen to stay high actually made Iggs's next plan even better. It was actually the same idea he'd had before but without the safety of kiting. It was pretty damn unsafe, to be honest, but Iggs didn't have time to be a coward. He'd never get another shot this clear again, so, before he could chicken out, he ripped off the bandage tying Lys to his back and jumped.

He'd never be able to match Bex for distance, but the moment Iggs's feet left the ground, he knew he'd just made the best high jump of his life. By the time Lys's unconscious body landed on the stairs behind him, Iggs was flying through the center of the spiral staircase like a cannonball, shooting up through the dust and debris that was still falling from the explosion to wrap his arms around the Prince of Hate's giant, unarmored legs.

Iggs changed the second he made contact, casting off his human disguise to reveal his true self. By the time the startled prince looked down, he was already grappled by a ten-foot tall, red-skinned, red-eyed demon of Wrath.

For one glorious second, Iggs saw true fear shining in the prince's mirrored eyes. Then his giant face distorted with hate as he started trying to kick Iggs off only to discover he couldn't. Now that Iggs was back in his true form, the two of them were the same size, and flying through the air like they were, the prince had no leverage. All he could do was punch at

Iggs's horned head with his free hand, which hurt like hell, but not enough to stop a wrath demon going full throttle. The fury was burning hot and fast in Iggs's blood now, allowing him to ignore pain and forget danger as he climbed up the prince's body to grab the wrist the princess's chain was tied to with both hands.

The prince *really* started fighting then. He thrashed like a cornered animal, biting and punching with all his might. Every blow broke something important—a nose, a rib, a tooth—but Iggs had been a kick demon, and he'd lived through worse. He certainly wasn't going to let a little pain stop him as he squeezed the prince's forearm between his giant red fists. He couldn't break the sin-iron chain itself— nothing could do that except a queen's sword—but he *could* destroy the hand the prince was using to hold onto it.

Iggs did so with great pleasure, crushing his red palms together like a vise until he felt every one of the prince's overgrown bones snap. The son of Gilgamesh howled in pain, but the real prize was when his destroyed hand fell open, releasing its grip on the princess's chain.

Since they were still swinging through the air, this also released the only thing holding them up. The residual momentum would've carried them to safety anyway, but Iggs was already prepared for that. As soon as the spiral staircase came into range, he kicked off it with both legs, reversing their flight and sending them both hurtling down the empty center of the spiral stairs into the dark below.

"*You idiot!*" the prince roared, his pulverized hand hanging limply beside him while he pummeled Iggs's face with the other. "Now we're both going to crash!"

"That's the plan, asshole," Iggs growled, hugging the prince even tighter. "I'm taking you to hell."

The prince screamed again, his voice cracking with fear as he beat his fist against every part of Iggs that he could reach. Iggs let him do it, ignoring the blows to focus on leaning his weight in the right direction to flip them over. By the time the prince realized what Iggs was doing, he was already on the bottom, his terrified mirrored eyes shining with the reflected light of the tower above them. That was all Iggs had time to see before the impact slammed through him like a speeding train, and the whole world went dark.

The blackness almost felt like a trophy. Iggs had always taken pride in being the toughest demon in the crew aside from Bex herself, but that was a hell of a fall and a Hell to fall into, which, of course, was the entire point. Leander had been right when he'd accused Iggs of making it up as he went, but the one idea he'd had from the start—and the one he was really proud of—was dropping the prince into the Lowest Hells. If he could do that, then it wouldn't matter what happened after the fall. Whether he lived or not, the prince would still be trapped down here, which was the same thing as a win. Even better, Bex knew how to enter and exit the Lowest Hells without getting stuck, which meant she could pull Iggs out while leaving the prince to rot. Assuming Iggs survived, of course.

Aside from that one minor detail, though, it was a great plan. Even Lys wouldn't have been able to find something to criticize about it, which was why Iggs was so pissed when he came to with a groan.

That wasn't right. He'd never been in the Lowest Hells before, but Iggs was pretty sure he should be plummeting through eternal darkness right now, not waking up with a headache. He cracked his eyes open next, squinting in the dim, dusty light filtering down from the hole above to see he was lying at the bottom of what looked like a giant well.

The stairs, he realized blearily. He was lying at the bottom of the giant spiral staircase. The last step was actually right in front of him, close enough to see the thick layer of grimy dust on top of it. He also saw a door in the wall beside it. A giant black one carved with the same towering image of Gilgamesh that he'd seen on the entrance to the Middle Hells, which explained why his plan had failed. The stairs didn't go to the pit Bex had jumped into. They went to the Lowest Hells' front door, because of course they did. Why would Gilgamesh have a staircase that went into a Hell no one could get out of? Stupid, stupid, *stupid.*

But it was too late to regret his choices now. Iggs just hoped the fall had done some damage, because his Hells trap looked like a bust. His own body had already mostly put itself back together thanks to Ishtar's gift of regeneration, but other than Greed's healing sword, most princes didn't have the ability to recover damage in the field. It was probably too much to hope that the Prince of Hate had splatted on impact, but if Iggs had managed to break something big, this could still be an easy win. He was pushing up on his elbows to look around and see if he'd gotten lucky when a hand the size of a trashcan lid closed around his left leg.

"You little *shit*."

The voice was warped and twisted, but Iggs still recognized it as the Prince of Hate yanked his body—Iggs's fully transformed, ten-foot tall wrath demon body—off the ground like a piece of trash to dangle Iggs upside down in front of him. Leander had warned him the Prince of Hate would get stronger as he took damage, but this was ridiculous. Iggs didn't know how long he'd blacked out for, but the prince was now twice the size he'd been when they fell down here. The only reason Iggs didn't give himself up for dead right then and there was because wrath demons didn't give up, and because the Prince of Hate looked *terrible*.

He was clearly teetering on the edge of what his body could take. His olive skin was stretched so thin over his bulging muscles that every blood vessel was visible. He hadn't escaped the fall entirely unscathed.

His right hand was still curled into a useless fist from where Iggs had crushed it earlier, and he was standing with all his weight on one leg like it hurt to use the other. But while Iggs was stoked to see that his efforts had made some kind of impact, the giant prince was definitely still in killing form as he swung Iggs over his head like a club.

"This is why I hate working in the Hells!" he roared as he slammed Iggs's body into the dusty stone floor. "You demons are all *animals* constantly biting the hand that feeds you! Even when you're beaten, you never know when to *quit*!"

He smashed Iggs into the stone two more times before hurling his body across the bottom of the stairwell into the pipe-covered wall on the other side. If the pipes hadn't been made of sin iron, Iggs would have torn right through them. Instead, he bounced off like a pinball, flying halfway back toward the prince before landing on his face in the crater they'd made when they came down.

"I'm going to work you for all eternity," the prince promised as he hobbled forward on his broken foot to grab Iggs again. "I won't let you die, I won't let you rest. You will know nothing but slavery for the rest of your miserable existence. You'll never have a second of mercy, not even if you beg for it on your knees!"

"That last one I actually agree with," Iggs said, tucking a broken tooth back into place with his tongue as his body pulled itself back together. "Because wrath demons don't kneel."

The prince stopped to give him a sneer, and Iggs took his chance, shoving his still-healing arm into his knapsack for the ace he'd readied earlier. He had to add his other hand a second later, moving his arms hand over hand as he pulled and pulled and pulled out the nine-foot-long barrel of a 30mm rotary cannon, the biggest gun that would fit inside of Solomon's Armory.

It was an unwieldy beast of a weapon, and Iggs hadn't even attached the separate ammo cart yet. It was probably still in the bag somewhere, but Iggs didn't bother looking for it because he had no intention of shooting. He'd already learned that bullets did nothing against Heaven's monsters, but even without its hydraulic-fed loading mechanism, the rotary cannon was still six hundred and seventy pounds of titanium-and-steel construction. That basically made it a nine-foot-long metal bat, and Iggs used it accordingly, lunging to his feet the moment his broken legs were healed to slam the multi-barrel chassis straight into the overgrown prince's knee.

It was an easy hit to see coming. If the prince had been in better condition, he almost certainly would have dodged it, but he wasn't in better condition. His giant body was insanely powerful, but it'd been clear to Iggs from the start that he didn't know how to use it. That was why he'd smashed through all seven walls of Leander's Seven Walled City instead of just going over the top, and why he couldn't get out of the way now. His lumbering body had barely even started to move when Iggs crashed the butt of his beautifully engineered and probably insanely expensive gun into the prince's kneecap, shattering the joint with a delightfully satisfying *crunch*.

The prince roared with pain as he staggered, but he didn't go down. Both of his legs were injured now, but he was still on his feet, glaring at Iggs with all the hate he was named for.

"You'll pay for that," he promised, thrusting his not-shattered hand into the air. "Princess of Hate! Return to your master!"

The words rang out like crashing bells in the dark, but nothing answered. There was no clatter of chains, no *whoosh* as the white sword flew back to her master. Just a deep silence that grew even quieter as a worried expression stole over the prince's distorted face.

"Princess of Hate," he said again. "I command you! Come back to—"

The command turned into a scream as Iggs bashed him in the knee again. The prince did go down that time, crashing to the floor like a toppled statue.

"Princess!" he bellowed as Iggs hit him again. "*Inora*, I command you by your name! Come to—"

His voice cut off for the last time as Iggs smashed the giant cannon into his face. The first hit shattered the prince's jaw. The next cracked his skull.

The third caved in his cheek below the eye, but it wasn't until the fourth that the hulking monster of a man finally stopped moving, his giant body falling still in a rapidly spreading pool of his unnatural white blood.

Iggs slumped against the gun he was using as a club, his own body heaving with the force of his ragged breaths as he braced for whatever was coming next, but his enemy didn't move again. He was still breathing, though. Iggs was working up the strength to swing his weapon one more time and finish the job when he heard the unmistakable, blood-chilling *click* of carved bone feet landing on the stone behind him.

He whirled around with a stagger, struggling to lift the enormously heavy gun to face the new enemy, but the princess, who'd just landed at the bottom of the stairs, wasn't even looking at him. Her golden eyes were locked on the distorted body of her downed prince as she moved toward him, dragging her black chain on the floor behind her as she walked right past Iggs to kneel beside the prince's still-breathing body.

For ten long heartbeats, she hovered over him like a kneeling statue, her golden eyes staring at the spreading pool of his white blood from behind the cage of her sin-iron muzzle. This went on for so long that Iggs was seriously considering just leaving her like that and going back upstairs to find Lys and Leander when the princess suddenly raised both her fists with a scream before bringing them down on what was left of the prince's battered face.

What happened next was so brutal even Iggs had to look away. The Princess of Hate tore her prince's body apart with her bare hands. Her shrieks got louder with every piece she ripped off, rising higher and higher before they suddenly stopped, leaving only a wet silence. When Iggs finally peeked out from behind the pole of his gun, the princess was standing in a white splatter that went all the way to the walls of the stairwell. There was no sign of the prince's body left, but his princess finally looked at peace.

"I hated him most of all," she whispered, gazing at the white blood that coated her chained hands before she slung it away. She looked at Iggs next, and her lovely face split into a thankful smile behind the cage of her muzzle.

"You made this possible, demon," she said in a croaking voice that sounded like it hadn't been used in centuries. "In return for that great gift, I will kill you quickly."

"Or you could not kill me," Iggs suggested, backing away.

The princess shook her head. "You have to die. Everyone here must. It's the only way to escape this hated place. I'm sure you understand."

"I really don't," Iggs said, stalling hard as he scrambled to think of a way out of this, because he didn't think beating a princess with a giant metal bat was going to work as well as it had on a prince who was already mangled. "Why don't you explain it to me so I can—"

The rest of his bullshitting was drowned out by a high-pitched whistle. It sounded like the sound effect movies used for a charging plasma cannon, but when Iggs jerked his head up, he saw it was Leander. The former prince was standing on the spiral above them with one arm braced against the other and what appeared to be a miniature black hole floating in front of his palm. His mouth was moving like he was speaking very quickly, but Iggs couldn't hear a word. Whatever it was must have taken all Leander's concentration because the prince was sweating buckets. When he finally said something loud enough for Iggs to hear, though, his voice was steady and strong as steel.

"Royal Verse Fifteen," he said as he aimed the crackling black ball at the princess. "Heavenly King's Eternal Banishment."

The whistling sound grew louder with every word, but when Leander's spell finished, it ended with a *pop*. The black hole vanished at the same time, flickering out from in front of the prince's palms like a snuffed candle. Iggs was still wondering what all of that was supposed to do when he realized the princess was gone. Not crushed, not blasted into bits. She was simply gone the same way the orb was, and in the place where she'd been standing lay a woman's severed hand.

"Holy Ishtar," Iggs muttered, staggering away from the empty place where the princess had been. "What in the Hells was *that*? And why didn't you do it *before*?"

"The answer to both of those is the same," Leander replied in an exhausted voice as he bent down to pick up Lys's body, which he'd laid carefully on the stairs behind him. "Unless you're inside one of Gilgamesh's private spaces, Royal Verses aren't something that can be just tossed out on the fly. I needed time to build it up, and to get down here."

He frowned at the white splatter that had been the prince. "I saw the whole fight on my way down, and I'll admit, I'm shocked you survived. I thought for sure it was over when he named his princess, but I should have known she'd be able to resist. Otherwise, why would he need so many chains?"

"That does make sense," Iggs agreed. "But why did she turn on him like that? I thought even the crazy princesses loved their princes."

Leander shook his head as he carried Lys's body down the stairs. "Hate is different. Hers was the last emotion Ishtar felt before she died. Not even Gilgamesh's sorcery can overcome that level of ire, which is why her princes never last very long."

"He did seem extremely hateable," Iggs agreed, holding out his arms to take Lys from Leander. "But *you* were awesome! That black-hole spell was clutch. You even evaporated her chains!" He grinned down at Leander. "Looks like you really are on our side now."

"Destroying Demetrios is a pleasure I would have relished no matter what side I was on," the ex-prince assured him. "But yes, I am most definitely not going back to Gilgamesh. Even if he offered to forgive me, my father doesn't tolerate sons who think for themselves, and I can't tolerate him."

"Welcome to the rebellion," Iggs said, giving the prince a wink before looking down to check Lys.

That killed his victorious mood real quick.

"This is bad," Iggs muttered, pressing his big red fingers against the delicate column of Lys's throat. "Pulse is barely detectible, and they're still bleeding like a faucet." He examined the black-soaked bandage taped to Lys's shoulder before shaking his head. "We need to find Adrian."

"What's he going to do?" Leander asked, strolling over to retrieve the Princess of Hate's severed hand from the white pool of her prince's blood. "Your comrade was struck by a Blade of Gilgamesh. There's no witchcraft in the world capable of healing a wound like that."

"Adrian's can," Iggs said stubbornly, changing back to his normal size so he could wrap a fresh bandage around Lys's shoulder without having to worry about accidentally crushing them. "He's done it before."

"Oh, he has, has he?" Leander replied with unexpected bitterness. "Sounds like he's quite the golden child. I look forward to officially meeting him and finally finding out what makes him so damn special that both Father and Mother bent over backward to fit him into their plots. Must be nice to be so loved. The Old Wives of the Blackwood never fought for me."

There was a whole wide world of family drama in that statement that Iggs wasn't touching with a nine-foot gun. And speaking of nine-foot guns, the 30mm cannon was still lying on the ground where he'd dropped it when he'd realized the fight was over. Lys was in a bad way, but even though the barrel was so dented it would probably never fire again, Iggs couldn't stand the thought of abandoning the weapon that had just saved his life. He'd just put Lys down on a clean spot of floor that wasn't covered in prince blood so he could shove the battered cannon back into his knapsack when Iggs heard a strange noise.

It sounded like shouting. Iggs didn't remember hearing anything like it during the fight, but he might have just been too preoccupied with not dying to notice. There were *definitely* voices coming from the giant door on the other side of the stairwell now, though, which was where Iggs got his second shock because he'd thought the only door down here was the one to the Lowest Hell behind him.

A quick look around proved that was incorrect. They looked identical with their towering height and giant images of Gilgamesh carved into their black faces, but there were definitely two different pairs of giant doors built into the circular bottom of the stairwell. The one behind him was dusty and silent, but the one in front of him was shaking like a crowd was banging on it from the other side. A large, strong crowd yelling for help in the ancient language of the Riverlands.

"I hear you!" Iggs yelled back in the same tongue as he ran over. "What's happened? Who's in there?"

The voices cried back in a frantic chorus, pleading with Iggs in the language of his homeland. The door was too thick to make out the exact words, but Iggs didn't need to. He already knew what he'd found. Or, rather, *who* he'd found.

"What are you doing?" Leander asked as Iggs changed back into his big red form.

Iggs didn't waste his breath explaining something that was about to be obvious. He just dug his feet in and charged, slamming his now-giant shoulder into the prison door that separated him from the panicked, familiar voices on the other side.

Chapter 12

Bex was in trouble.

The second princess had completely blindsided her. Bex didn't know how she could've overlooked a murderous woman made of bone, but the white figure had tackled her through the wall before she'd even thought to duck.

She'd still managed to get a solid hit in with her explosive short sword, but the backblast had sent her skipping across the flooded slave floor like a stone. She'd landed hard several hundred feet from where she'd started, but before Bex's regeneration could even start repairing the damage, the princess had tackled her again. Now she was on her back in the water with a damn white statue crushing her rib cage and punches flying like gunshots at her head.

"You *cheater*!" the princess screamed as she clawed Bex's face with her needle-sharp, bone-white nails. "You *fraud*! I'll *kill you*!"

She was going for the throat when Bex finally got a grip on the slimy stone beneath them with her good hand and shoved up with all her strength to knock the princess off. She started feeling through the water for her weapon next, but it was no use. The exploding short sword had gotten knocked out of her hand when she'd gone flying, and unlike Drox, Bex couldn't call it back. Her combat knife was still strapped to her hip, though, so she pulled that instead, flipping the six-inch steel blade into a knife-fighter's grip as she whirled around to see which brainwashed doll of Gilgamesh she'd pulled this time…

And nearly dropped her weapon again.

It was like looking into a cursed mirror. That was definitely a princess, but the features carved into its white face were Bex's. That was *her* mouth twisted into a hateful snarl. *Her* eyes replaced with gold and narrowed in fury. They were the same height, same size—even the way the princess had braced her sandaled feet on the slippery ground was a perfect copy of Bex's current stance.

The only things missing were color and her horns, but Bex had always been paper-pale, and she didn't have her horns right now either. If her hair had been white instead of black and she'd been wearing some kind of stupid toga wrap dress instead of combat fatigues, they would have been an identical set. Those were all the details Bex's eyes managed to pick up before the red of her rage filled her vision.

If it'd been Drox in her hand, this was where he would have counseled caution. They didn't know the extent of the enemy's capabilities, and Bex's own fighting strength was severely crippled. The wisest choice would've been to run back to the tower and get help, but Drox wasn't here to remind her of that. He was on that abomination's finger. Bex could see the lump of his ring under the white glove that covered the princess's right hand.

Her *stolen* hand.

"*Give it back!*" she screamed, leaping on the princess with her knife raised over her head like the villain in a slasher flick.

Despite her blind rage, or maybe because of it, it was a good swing. Bex hit the white statue square in the chest, but unlike the original, this Rebexa was made of carved bone, not flesh and blood. Even when she stabbed with all her might, all Bex managed was to break the tip off her steel knife. The golden-eyed princess didn't flinch. She just grabbed Bex's knife hand with her carved one and peeled her fingers back, forcing the actual Queen of Wrath to drop her broken weapon in the murky water between their feet.

Bex didn't care. "Give me back my sword, you fake!" she screamed in the princess's face. "Drox is *my* weapon! You have *no right!*"

"I have every right," the princess snarled back, twisting Bex's arm until she cried out in pain. "*I'm* Rebexa now, loyal servant of the true king and beloved consort to Prince Adrian!"

"You're a puppet!" Bex yelled, thrashing like an eel in a desperate attempt to free her arm, which the princess was about to twist out of its socket. "Gilgamesh only made you so he could steal my Blade of Wrath, but Drox will *never* be yours, and Adrian doesn't give a shit about you!"

"Don't speak of things you know nothing about," the princess ordered as she hooked her other arm around Bex's neck to stop her thrashing. "Rebexa the Bonfire is the property of Heaven now. Everything that gave you worth—your name, your crown, your sword, your prince—belongs to Gilgamesh, and he gave them all to me. That makes *me* the Queen of Wrath, but I didn't want that prison sentence. Who'd choose to live their life chained to a bunch of dirty, helpless slaves if they had any other option?"

She tightened the arm she'd wrapped around Bex's throat, lifting the actual queen off her feet and turning her around to face the closest knot of terrified demons huddling at the end of their chain.

"Look how they cower," the princess sneered. "And to think these were once Ishtar's creations, the famous army of the Riverlands. Now they're just a bunch of dirty, sniveling *beasts*." She kicked her carved foot, slinging a grimy wave of freezing black water across the hunkered demons.

"Is this what you died all those times for?" she shouted, kicking again. "These *cowards*? This *trash*? They're not even real living creatures! They're pond scum, bottom-feeders bred to eat the sin out of Ishtar's precious rivers. You only fought for them because the gods gave you no other choice, but Gilgamesh set *me* free."

She stopped twisting Bex's arm and whirled her around, using her sorcerous body's superior strength to grab the flesh-and-blood version by the throat and hoist her up until Bex's combat boots were kicking an inch above the black water.

"My blessed king removed the burden of Ishtar's endless labor from my shoulders," the princess said in a grateful voice. "He's done more for me in one week than your 'divine' mother has for you in a hundred and ninety-eight lifetimes! Thanks to the benevolence of Gilgamesh, I have no more shackles, no more endless duty. I'm free to live as *I* choose. Free to serve the brilliant Prince Adrian, whom Gilgamesh honors above all his other sons! Free to live my days in peace and splendor! I'm the happy ending the ever-loyal

Rebexa *deserved*, while you're just the scraps of meat she left behind."

The princess flashed a twisted version of Bex's own smile. "That's why you can't stand the sight of me," she said, pulling Bex closer. "I'm the incarnation of everything you always secretly wanted to be: unburdened, responsible for nothing, free to put the desires of my own heart first. I live in an eternal Heaven and answer to only two men, while you're forced to belly-crawl through the Hells in the doomed service of thousands. You have always and will always be a tragedy, Ashes of Rebexa, but I'm not you. I'm *better*, yet another work of the gods perfected by Gilgamesh's brilliance." Her smile grew sweeter. "You should praise him for his benevolence."

"I'll *never* praise him!" Bex snarled, digging her five remaining fingers into the hand the princess was using to hold her throat, but not to pry it off. The whole time the princess had been spewing her pompous propaganda, Bex had been going for the lump of Drox's ring under the princess's glove. She could feel the familiar smoothness of his black metal band like a promise under the silk, but no matter how hard Bex called out to him in her mind, she got only silence. His ring wasn't even warm under the fabric because the princess had no body heat. She was just an ivory statue, a literal mouthpiece carved by Gilgamesh to spout his self-serving *bullshit*. Bex was dead certain about that last part, too, because there was no other way something containing a piece of her would ever spew such *crap*.

Realizing that made Bex feel a lot better about the other princesses she'd destroyed, but it did nothing to help her current situation. She'd been counting on her sword to even the power imbalance, but whatever Gilgamesh had done to make Drox sit quietly on the princess's stolen finger made him deaf to Bex's calls. He probably couldn't even see her since divine weapons only recognized demons by their names, and Bex didn't have one of those right now. That made her as invisible to Drox as Nemini had always been, but what was she going to do? The princess might be a carved doll in a stupid dress, but she was still stronger, faster, tougher, heavier, and in possession of two working hands.

That put her miles above Bex's present state, but what else was new? Up until this last summer, Bex had always been the underdog, and she still knew how to fight like one. She'd been focusing on getting Drox, but he wasn't responding and she was almost out of air, so Bex switched tactics and hooked her boot behind the princess's knees instead. She swung her body weight back at the same time, using her foot like a lever to force the princess off-balance and drop them both back into the water.

They landed with Bex on the bottom yet again, but she was ready for it this time. The moment they splashed into the freezing river, Bex's hand dropped to the floor to start searching for a chain.

There had to be one. The sin production floor had been a grid of demons chained together into work gangs when she'd walked through earlier. The slaves the princess had just been disparaging were still cowering only a few feet away, so the chain that tied them to the ground had to be—

Yes!

A rush of victory shot through Bex's body as her fingers closed around something heavy and metal and fixed to the ground. It was hard to feel the actual links through all the slimy, built-up sin grime, but it *had* to be a chain.

Sure enough, when Bex yanked her arm out of the murky water, a black chain was clutched in her fist. It was just a piece of the larger tether that locked the closest line of slaves in position, but there was still enough slack for Bex to reach her arms around the princess like she was giving her a hug. She slammed the stump of her right arm into the back of the statue's head, throwing Gilgamesh's weapon off-balance while her still-working left hand looped the slimy black chain around the princess's neck.

The moment the noose was in place, Bex yanked it tight. The princess pulled back with a shriek, lifting Bex off the ground with her as she tried to rip the chain off, but Bex didn't let go. She just planted her boots against the princess's stomach and pulled, using her whole body to keep the chain too tight for the princess to dig her fingers under.

That worked for a solid five seconds before the princess realized what was going on and stopped tugging on the chain to slam her fist into Bex instead. She hit the true queen hard in the stomach, knocking her out of her brace. She stomped on her arm next, grinding her carved white foot with its gold-embossed sandal into Bex's wrist to force her hand open and make her let go. The slimy black chain was still looped around the princess's neck, but its hold was getting looser and looser as Bex's grip began to slip. She was about to lose it altogether when the chain suddenly pulled tight again.

It wasn't Bex's doing. She'd been working with the part of the chain that was attached to the floor, which was now falling limp as her broken fingers finally lost their grip. The pressure keeping the princess in a choke hold came from the other side of the line where the slaves who had been shivering in the dark were now on their feet, pulling at the chain that bound them together with all their might.

Like all the slaves Bex had seen down here, they were thin and exhausted-looking, but there were a lot of them. When they pulled on the chain together, their combined force was enough to lift the kicking princess off the ground. She was thrashing her feet in the water as she grabbed at her noose, but the chain was slick with sin from so many years under the river. No matter which way her fingers bent, she couldn't seem to get a grip on the slippery links, and Bex saw her chance.

"Keep going!" she yelled, grabbing her end of the chain again with her still-healing hand. *"Pull!"*

The demons were already on it. The moment Bex shouted, they moved as one, using the combined weight of their bodies to yank the slimy chain until the princess was dragged off her feet. This meant Bex couldn't keep pulling without risking a kick to the head, but it was fine. The end of the chain that wasn't attached to the slaves was locked into the Hells' stone floor by a sin-iron bolt tough enough to hold down a whole string of raging demons. Even a princess wasn't strong enough to pull it out, especially when her smooth-carved ivory feet kept slipping in the muck that covered the bottom of the slave floor. No matter how hard she thrashed, so long as the slaves kept the line pulled tight, the princess couldn't get enough leverage to stand back up, and that gave Bex an idea.

"Keep it up!" she yelled as she dropped to her knees, scraping her fingers through the muck at the bottom of the flooded floor for something she could use. Eventually, her hand came up with a foot-long bar of metal scrap. It looked like a piece of the warlocks' elevated walkways that had fallen off centuries ago, but it could've been Excalibur from the way Bex whooped. Clutching her new weapon like a spear, she ran back around to the side of the princess the slaves were pulling on and shoved the scrap metal through the spot where the chain noose crossed over itself. When it was good and tangled in the links, Bex turned the black bar like a crank, using the improved grip it gave to twist the chain loop around the princess's neck even tighter.

The fake Bex screamed as the slimy black metal dug even harder into her carved throat. They couldn't actually choke her out since carved idols didn't need to breathe, but every material had a breaking point. Since the slaves' chains were made from the same sin iron Gilgamesh used to bind the Wheel of Reincarnation, Bex was betting the princess would snap first, and sure enough, her throat was already starting to splinter.

By the time Bex turned her scrap metal bar five times, everything from the bottom of the princess's white chin to the tops of her graceful shoulders was covered in spidering, hair-thin cracks. She was screaming loud enough to make Bex's ears bleed, a real trick for somebody who had no lungs, but no matter how hard she thrashed, she couldn't escape. Every time she got a hand on Bex, the queen kicked it away and cranked her improvised winch again, twisting the sin-iron chain noose tighter and tighter, smaller and smaller until, with the gunshot sound of breaking porcelain, the princess's white neck shattered.

"Don't let your guard down!" Bex yelled as the chained demons started to cheer. "Princesses aren't like us! She's not—"

The rest of her warning was lost in a wave of screams as the princess's white body—headless, but still just as fast as ever—shot to its feet. Its movements were jerky and uncoordinated, and it didn't seem to be able to see them now that its carved head was rolling across the flooded floor, but a princess in any state was a deadly foe. Her blind, wild swings still whistled through the air. Bex dodged the first two by inches, but then the princess launched into a blind charge, flying right past Bex to plunge her fist into the chest of one of the still-chained demons standing behind her.

The punch hit the poor old woman like a cannonball. The force snapped her bones with an audible *crunch* and ripped her body right off the chain, sending it flying off into the dark like a rag doll. Bex screamed in fury as she saw it happen, dropping the now-useless chains for the scrap metal bar instead. It was an even sorrier weapon than her combat knife had been, but she'd stabbed through war-demon armor with worse. She was running forward to plunge the sharp end into the headless princess's back when one of the chained demons sprinted away, dragging the rest of the work gang after him as he ran for the old woman the princess had sent flying with a scream that sounded different.

His howled words were nearly unintelligible, but Bex still caught the gist. The slave woman the princess had punched was his mother. The other demons gave him as much slack as they could so he could get to her, but it was already too late. The princess's hit had crushed her rib cage and shattered her spine.

In the living world, under normal circumstances, those injuries would have been recoverable through Ishtar's gift of regeneration. It would have hurt and likely taken several days to heal for someone who wasn't a queen, but it shouldn't have been fatal. Down here, though, things were different. These weren't the free demons Bex was used to or even warlock servants. These were hard-labor slaves who'd spent their entire lives being kept just above starvation in the Hells. Ishtar's gift never even got a chance to trigger. The woman was dead before her son reached her, and his scream when he realized that hit Bex like an electric jolt.

The feeling made her stop. She felt this once before the night they'd liberated the Anchor, when the war demon she'd freed turned on his warlock master. The circumstances were wildly different, but the sensation was exactly the same. The crying man was wailing too hard for Bex to make out his words anymore, but she still understood him because his wails weren't wails of sorrow.

They were screams of rage. The demon was furious, screaming at the headless princess, at the Hells themselves in a storm of raw, wounded wrath.

The sound of it rang through Bex like nothing else had since she'd lost her horns, and something inside her stirred in response. It was the same stirring she'd felt when her hand had started to glow in the Hell of Pride, but much, much bigger, because this wasn't a bunch of terrified demons pleading for any queen who would listen. This was a primal scream for justice, a war cry of pure, unadulterated rage.

The thing she'd been born to burn.

The moment Bex felt it, she reached out with all she was. Reached out with every cell of the hollowed husk the loss of her name had left behind, because she knew that feeling. It was fire, *her* fire. Now that it was sparking again, Bex didn't know how she'd ever let it die, because unlike her horns and her name and her sword, the bonfire wasn't something that could be taken away. She'd been a queen the first time her fire almost died out, but it wasn't her horns or Drox that had brought the flames back. It was Adrian's magic and her own decision to trade away all her reincarnations for one last fight, one last shot at victory.

That determination didn't belong to Ishtar or Gilgamesh. The Blackwood had poured its fire into *her*. Filled *her* with its rage at what Gilgamesh had done to its beloved witches. It was just like Drox had said. The Bonfire of Wrath had *always* been fueled by the anger of her people, and that same anger hit her now like sparks to dry kindling.

The rush caught her completely by surprise, though it really shouldn't have. As the familiar flames spread over her body, all Bex could think was what a fool she'd been, what an idiot. She'd been so devastated by the magnitude of everything she'd lost, she'd completely missed the things she hadn't. Even when a tiny bit of it had come back in the Lowest Hells, she'd assumed it was just a forgotten ember, a scrap that her defeat had left behind.

What a stupid thing to think. One ember was all it took to start a forest fire, and wasn't that what she was? How many times had Drox told her that the flames weren't something that she called? They were what she *was*. Bex *was* the Bonfire, and unlike her sword and horns and all the other powers Ishtar had given her, that could never be taken away. It could only be lost, but Bex was done losing. The wrath of her people—the wrath of *all* the demons whose lives had been stolen in the Hells—was pouring over her like gasoline, and the moment Bex embraced it, she lit up like the sun.

The explosion of her restored fire shook the Hells to their foundations. The chained slaves jumped when the roaring pillar of her fire enveloped them, but the Bonfire of Wrath only burned what she raged at, and Bex's anger wasn't for them. Her heat melted the sin-iron chains and boiled away the stagnant river, but it didn't touch a hair on her peoples' heads. The princess, on the other hand, received no such mercy.

If Bex had still had doubts that Gilgamesh's ivory dolls weren't really her sisters, the sight of that headless body flailing blindingly for an enemy would have put them to rest. It didn't even look like a princess anymore. It was just another abomination, another crime to lay at Gilgamesh's feet, and the Bonfire of Wrath was happy to burn it.

She didn't even have to stretch to engulf the headless figure in flames. There was more wrath here than Bex had ever felt. It was caked onto the walls of the Hells like soot, five thousand years of anger left behind by all the demons who'd lived and died in this darkness.

With so much fuel at her fingertips, Bex's bonfire leaped high enough to light the entire cavern of the Middle Hells. Her flames were so hot, the princess's headless body was incinerated in seconds. Not even blackened scraps were left, just a fine white ash that blew away in the howling, superheated wind coming off the tornado of fire Bex had become.

That should've made her happy, but the fire raging through her head was making it hard to think. She couldn't even see the demons who'd sparked her anymore. Maybe they'd run away when she'd melted their chains, or maybe she just couldn't see anything through the glare of her flames. Either way, the Bonfire of Wrath's fury had already moved on to the next target, engulfing one of the elevated metal platforms the overseers used to keep their feet dry while they watched Ishtar's children slave.

She'd burn it all, the Bonfire decided. Burn this entire cursed place to ash so that no demon could ever be sent here again. She'd burn until the whole rotten system collapsed under its own weight. Burn until Gilgamesh himself came down to stop her, and then she'd burn him too. She'd burn and burn and *burn* until all their anger—the fury of generations—was avenged. Burn until she burned out as well, her duty finally finished.

These were the Bonfire's thoughts, if a fire could even be said to have thoughts. Her flickering attention had already jumped from the melted overseer tower to the stockpile of slave chains beside it. The Bonfire was gleefully watching the cursed black metal melt into bubbling tar when she heard a familiar voice.

"Bex!" it shouted. "*Bex!*"

Deep in the roar of the bonfire, the tiny spark that still remembered that name lifted her head. The next memory that flickered through was Drox. Her steadfast sword was always the one who called her back when she got like this. That must be his voice, the tongue of flame that had once been called Bex reasoned, but wasn't Drox gone? Wasn't that part of why she was so angry?

The fire wasn't sure. There were so many reasons to rage that it was hard to keep track, but they'd all be burned soon. The Bonfire was about to return to that important work when the voice yelled again.

"*Bex!*" it screamed. "*Come back!*"

The Bonfire of Wrath seethed. No one gave her orders. But when she looked down to see what soon-to-be-ash fool would dare, it wasn't her sword or a demon or even one of her fellow daughters of Ishtar.

It was a human. A handsome, mirror-eyed man with curling black hair and a witch's broad-brimmed hat flapping in the wind that roared off her inferno. He was standing dangerously close to the bonfire's base, holding something up in his hands like an offering. The object was pale and small and even more familiar than the man's voice. It wasn't until he lifted it over his head, though, that the flicker of fire that had once been Bex realized it was a hand.

A queen's severed hand with Drox's black ring still gleaming on its pale finger.

"Bex!" Adrian yelled, using the arm that wasn't holding up her hand to shield his face from her raging flames. "It's over! You won! You can come back now!"

The Bonfire scoffed. This was nowhere near over. The was still so much left to burn, so many left to punish. She'd stop when the endless anger of her people was sated. But when the raging Bonfire lifted one of its thousand tendrils to destroy the mortal who presumed to give orders to the Wrath of Ishtar, Bex yanked it back down.

"*No!*" she shouted, shoving back against the flames. "We burn our enemies. We do *not* burn Adrian!"

But he wanted them to stop, and they were still so *angry*.

"And how is this helping?" Bex demanded, pointing at the random piles of chains they'd just been so righteously melting into slag. "The Wrath of Ishtar shouldn't be wasted on useless temper tantrums. I nccd this fire for burning Gilgamesh, not trashing the Hells while my people are still trapped inside! The witch is right. It's over. Now give me back my body!"

The Bonfire roared and tried to pull away, but Bex didn't let it. Just as Drox had taught her in Limbo, she wrestled the flames into submission. Her own magic fought her for every inch, but Bex had already learned this lesson. She knew that wrath was not rage. Rage was the inferno that destroyed everything, but wrath was directed. Wrath had purpose. *She* had purpose. The same dedication that had allowed her to walk out of the void of her lost name strengthened her hands now, giving Bex the edge as she wrestled the Bonfire lower and lower, smaller and smaller until it was just her again, one body burning like a candle in the black cavern of Gilgamesh's Hells.

She snuffed the last lick of fire herself, closing her one remaining good hand over it in a fist to save the flames for later, because there *would* be a later. The Bonfire of Wrath was hers again. Always had been, really, but Bex was no longer too deep in her own misery to feel it. She might not have her horns back yet, but Bex's fire was once again hers to call whenever she needed it. That felt like a miracle, but it was one she understood. The miracle in front of her, however, was almost more than Bex could process.

He was already running up to meet her. She'd known that Adrian was in the Hells, but it still felt impossible that he could just be... just be *here*, smiling in front of her. She'd expected to have to pry him free of Gilgamesh with her teeth, but he didn't seem to have any chains or slave marks, not even a chaperone. Other than his new mirrored eyes—which were creepy, but still close enough to his usual blue-gray that Bex could square the difference in her mind—Adrian looked just like he had the morning she'd picked him up from the airport. He was really here, whole and safe and alive right in front of her, and she... she...

"Adrian," Bex whispered, stumbling forward. "*Adrian!*"

She fell into him with a sob. She didn't know when she'd started crying, but her face was suddenly soaked with ashy tears, which was ridiculous because she wasn't sad. She was happy. So, *so* damn happy that after everything they'd been through, everything they'd lost, he was finally here with her. Even Lys hadn't made it over yet, but Adrian must've run straight to her, and that made Bex so happy she could burst. She knew they were still in enemy territory and she needed to get a grip, but she couldn't make her arms let go. It just felt so right to finally be next to him again, which was why it felt so wrong when Adrian took her by her shoulders and shoved her away.

Adrian's hands shook as he pushed Bex away from him. The shaking got even worse when she stared up at him with her lovely eyes—the real Bex's beautiful, fiery eyes—full of hurt and confusion. She was looking at him like he'd just pulled the plug on a miracle, which was a hundred percent accurate. This *was* a miracle—them being here together, the fire that had defeated the princess, the fact that any of this was happening at all—but Adrian couldn't let her run to him like that. Not until he told her...

"I'm sorry."

"Sorry for what?" Bex demanded, glaring at him like this was a joke in very poor taste. "Adrian, you were *kidnapped*. Boston told us what happened. You've got nothing to apologize for."

"Yes, I do," he insisted, determined to tell her the truth and be the person she thought he was. "Gilgamesh didn't kidnap me out of nowhere. I went to him."

"He tricked you," Bex argued, glancing around his shoulder at Boston, who was still crouching on

Bran's broom handle where Adrian had jumped off a good fifty feet away, staying the hell out of this. "Like I said, Boston told us—"

"Boston doesn't know everything," Adrian said. "He's my familiar and my friend. It's his job to think the best of me, but I'm the idiot who let himself get tricked. I allowed my desperation and ego to override the common sense that is the core of witchcraft. I was taught to see things as they are, not as I want them to be, but I was so desperate to get out of the trap I'd put us in that I ate up everything Gilgamesh fed me. I took the easy power, took the quintessence. I thought I was better than the average person, that I could handle it, but I ended up under Heaven's boot just like every other idiot sorcerer before me. My ego put us all in danger. I put *you* in danger. If I'd stayed at the Anchor and helped you instead of trying to outsmart the rules, everything would've been different. I'm the reason we're in this situation, and I'm sorry." He squeezed his fist around the severed hand he was still clutching. "I am so, *so* sorry, Bex."

He didn't dare look at her after that, but she was still close enough for Adrian to feel her long sigh.

"Maybe it would've been different," she admitted. "But you're not the only one who got tricked. Heaven played me too, so if we're apologizing, I'm also sorry that I piled so much on you. It wasn't your responsibility to fix the locked Anchor problem all by yourself, but I got caught up in my own stuff and left you in the lurch. You turned to Gilgamesh because you were desperate, but I'm the one who left you alone with your back against the wall."

"Only because I volunteered," Adrian reminded her angrily. "Attacking the Anchors was my idea, if you'll recall. I told you I could handle it, and then, when it turned out I couldn't, I panicked and jumped right into Gilgamesh's trap. This whole disaster could've been avoided if I'd just owned my mistakes and told you I was wrong, but I didn't want to admit I couldn't do it. I was a cocky, impatient fool who made the wrong choice at every turn. If I'd been thinking even a little, I never would have—"

"I don't care," Bex snapped, reaching up to rub the ash off her face, which was even paler than he remembered. She looked absolutely exhausted, but before Adrian could work himself into a fresh frenzy of guilt over that, Bex continued.

"I don't care if you could've done it better," she said, her voice heating with the passionate, loving anger he'd never heard in the princess's voice. "There's no such thing as a perfect fight. Everyone goes to war with the army they've got. We all have to make field decisions based on imperfect information, but no matter how much you think you've messed up, there's still nobody I'd rather have at my side. So if you're done telling me how much you suck, I'd really like a hug. It's been a *very* hard week, and you would not believe how much I've missed you."

"I think I might," he said, wrapping his arms around her. "Because I missed you just as much."

He felt her smile through his shirt, and Adrian pressed his face against the top of her hornless head. Great Forest, he really was bad at this boyfriend thing. Here he was shoveling his guilt onto her when all Bex wanted was comfort. She deserved better, and Adrian was determined to *be* better. He'd be a true partner to her from this moment forward, starting with the healing he should have done as soon as he ran over.

"Here," he said, pulling away just enough to offer Bex her hand. "Let's get this back where it belongs."

"I don't know if it'll make a difference," she told him tiredly. "I already tried calling Drox, but he's not answering. I don't think he'll be able to hear me until I get my name back."

"You still want your hand, though, right?" Adrian asked, arching an eyebrow. "Hundred-foot pillars of fire notwithstanding, having two hands is pretty useful."

"Of course I want it back," Bex said, her cheeks coloring beautifully before she went pale again. "I just don't know if it'll return. That's the hand Gilgamesh used to make his princess. What if it's as unresponsive as Drox?"

"There's nothing Gilgamesh can do that I can't undo," Adrian told her with the same cockiness that had gotten him into this mess in the first place. The risk was worth it this time, though, because Bex looked so upset.

"I can do this," he promised, looking straight into her bright eyes. "Trust me."

"I do," she said in a tiny voice. "How could I not at this point? You've healed the unhealable twice now, it's just... that's my sword hand."

She finished with a pointed look, but Adrian didn't understand. "So?"

"*So*, if I go back with two hands and Drox's ring on my finger, people are going to expect me to be the full Queen of Wrath again," Bex explained. "Fire is a good start, but a divine blade is proof of Ishtar's blessing. It was one thing when Gilgamesh had it, but if I've got Drox and still can't use him, what does that say about me? What if people stop believing I'm Rebexa?"

"Bex," Adrian said, biting back a smile. "You just lit up this entire cavern with a gigantic pillar of fire. I'm pretty sure people are going to believe you're the Bonfire of Wrath, and I *know* Drox would be much happier sleeping on your finger than he would be in my pocket."

She still looked unconvinced, so Adrian played his final card.

"Think of it as insurance," he said gently. "If your hand's back on your wrist where it belongs, it'll be a lot harder for Gilgamesh to turn it into a princess again. Do it for my sake, if nothing else. If I ever have to see that creepy fake Bex again, I won't be held responsible for my actions."

That got a smile out of her. "Glad you weren't fooled into thinking it was actually me in there."

"Not for a second," Adrian promised as he reached down to gently touch the stump at the end of her right arm. "May I?"

He waited until she nodded, and then Adrian slowly pressed the severed hand against Bex's cut wrist. Considering the massive injuries he'd seen her recover from without so much as a scar, he fully expected her body to snatch the hand out of his grasp, but that didn't happen. Nothing did. The hand just sat limply against her stump like it belonged to someone else, and Adrian felt Bex start to shake.

Oh no. He wasn't letting her go there, not while he still had a say. Other than the cut in her side from the Blade of Gilgamesh, Bex's body had always repaired any wound dealt to it, but he'd never seen her reattach a completely severed limb. The problem could be that—since the stump was healed—her body thought its work was already finished.

If that was the case, then Adrian just had to get her natural healing going again. Solution in sight, he slid his hands up to cover the gap where her wrist and hand connected. When the wound was completely encircled by his fingers, Adrian closed his eyes and reached out with his magic. Not with his father's quintessence, but with the witchcraft he'd loved from the moment he'd realized what it was.

Healing was the first magic his mother had taught him, and it was still the part of their craft he enjoyed the most. Doing the impossible and fixing the unfixable were what made witchcraft feel like true magic, and Adrian poured himself into both of those now. He even had help, because while the forest in his heart was still blocked by the lion Gilgamesh had placed inside his chest when he became a prince, Bex's fire came straight from the Blackwood. Adrian himself had been the funnel that had poured it into her, which made him intimately familiar with every aspect of it.

He used that connection now. Since he couldn't reach his forest with his own heart, he reached through Bex instead, sliding down the channel the Great Blackwood had created when it'd poured through them both to pinch back a bit of the fire they'd put into her last summer.

The flames leaped to meet him the second he got close, raging into his hands like the forest fires they'd been originally. If he hadn't been so familiar with every bit of Bex's magic, they would've burned him to a crisp. Fortunately for him, this was a dance Adrian had done before. The raging fire barely had time to flash in his mind before he passed it on, pressing the all-consuming fire of life he'd plucked from Bex's body into the cold flesh of her lifeless hand.

That should've been all there was to it. The fire of life was defined by its all-powerful drive to spread and grow. It should have raged into her hand like a grass fire entering a fresh dry field, but something was pushing it back. When Adrian gave the thing a poke, he realized it was quintessence.

Thick, concentrated quintessence had been pumped into every one of the hand's blood vessels and left to solidify there like cement. Adrian probably should've expected something like that in hindsight, but the extent of the intrusion was still a shock. His father's magic had invaded every cell, conquering the hand the same way he'd conquered Paradise. Pulling it all out again would require more sorcerous skill than Adrian possessed, but he hadn't come to this as a sorcerer. He was here as a witch of the Great Forest, and the Blackwood knew better than any that the best way to rejuvenate a rotten forest was to burn it.

The moment he realized what he had to do, Adrian reached back down the connection to Bex's fire, but not to grab another pinch. This time, he let the whole thing go, turning himself once again into a conduit for her flames. They seared through him just like they had on the day he'd put her in the bonfire his forest had built, but this time Adrian knew what to expect. *This* time, he was ready, grabbing the flames as fast as they came in and shoving them down his arms into the hand he was clutching between his fists.

The result was just as dramatic now as it had been the first time. The moment he sent the fire into it, Bex's severed hand burst into flames. The flare was so bright that even Bex looked away, but as the quintessence saturating its flesh began to char and boil away, the hand itself lost its dead, passive limpness and began to twitch.

Bex gasped at the same time. Her eyes—which were glowing like torches again, thanks to her rekindled fire—grew huge as her flaming hand ripped out of Adrian's grasp and shoved itself back onto her wrist of its own accord. The wound closed up a second later, the scar burning off her wrist like a piece of string in a furnace.

When the flames finally died back down, there was no sign that she'd ever been injured in the first place. Her hand looked just like it always had, beautiful and strong as Bex clenched it into a fist.

"Thank you," she whispered, clutching her restored fingers to her chest with a ragged breath. *"Thank you."*

"You're welcome," Adrian whispered back, pulling her against him with zero guilt this time. Not that healing her hand made up for letting Gilgamesh play him, but it was so nice to be part of a team again. Finally, *finally*, Adrian felt like he was back on the right track, which was almost as amazing as the feeling of Bex's warm body resting against his chest.

He really hadn't paid enough attention to that. A critical lapse for a Witch of the Present, and one Adrian was overjoyed to remedy. He'd just given himself over to the sheer pleasure that was the smell of Bex's hair in his nose and the feeling of her fire-warmed body seeping through his clothing when he heard something beep.

"Sorry," Bex said, breaking away from him slowly, but still much faster than Adrian preferred, to press a finger against the familiar-looking device wedged into her left ear.

"I'm here."

The reply was too quiet for Adrian to hear who it was, but the fact that Bex could still talk to anyone was incredible. He'd been the first to point out that the Bonfire of Wrath only burned things she was mad at, but it still seemed unbelievable that the comm's black plastic hadn't melted from all the heat earlier. Same for Bex's clothes, which also looked completely untouched by the raging inferno. She was even wearing her signature leather jacket, a beautifully nostalgic touch that almost made him choke up. Adrian was still getting the feeling under control when Bex's face lit up in an excited smile.

"Are you sure?"

Adrian still couldn't hear the other person's reply, but it must have been good because Bex's smile widened into a beaming grin.

"That's fantastic! Stay right there. We're on our way."

"Who was that?" he asked when she let go of the comm button.

"Iggs," Bex replied as she whirled and started running for the stairs. "He's found our wrath demons!"

Adrian hadn't known they were missing, but he didn't waste Bex's time with questions. He just ran after her toward the distant column of the warlocks' white security tower. He was struggling to move his feet through the calf-deep water when Bex suddenly turned back around. Adrian thought there must have been something she'd forgotten to tell him, but then he realized Bex wasn't looking at him. Her glowing eyes were fixed on the silent crowd standing all around them.

Adrian went still. He'd been so focused on Bex, he'd completely forgotten they were surrounded by an audience of chained demons. In his defense, it was so dark and smoky down here that he could scarcely see. The demons were just shadows crouching in the filthy water that covered the floor of this place, watching in eerie, nervous silence.

Not watching *him*. Even after Boston caught up to Adrian on Bran's broomstick, the three of them might as well not have existed. Every eye in the Hells was locked on Bex. Then, like a signal he couldn't hear had just been given, every single one of the demons bowed. The wave of lowering heads spread through the giant cavern like a ripple. Even for an outsider like Adrian, it was a silent, profound gesture, but the one who got hit hardest was Bex.

"I know," she told them in a shaking voice that sounded so much smaller than the queenly voice he remembered. "I know what he did to you, but I'm here now, and I promise it's almost over. My demons are in the tower getting the keys to unlock your shackles as we speak. Just wait a little longer, and I swear on Ishtar's sacred name, you will be free."

Adrian smiled, waiting for the cheers of joy, but no one in the cavern said a word. He didn't know if that was because they didn't believe her or if the demons here were simply too beaten down to know what hope was anymore, but all Bex got back were silent stares. She met them dead-on, holding her hornless head high.

"You *will* be free," she said again in a voice that shook with fury. "Ishtar's Bonfire of Wrath is going to burn everything Gilgamesh has built to the ground. This fire was just the start. There's a lot more coming, so hold tight. My people will be coming with the keys soon."

Again, there was no answer, but Bex didn't seem to mind this time. She just dipped her head to the silent crowd and started marching back toward the central tower again as fast as her legs would carry her. She was so fast that Adrian was forced to get on his broom to keep pace, waving for Boston to make room as he hauled himself onto Bran's back and flew after her.

"Are we really doing that?" he asked quietly when he caught up. "Are you actually here to free everyone and burn Heaven to the ground?"

"That wasn't the original plan," she admitted, her face set in a determined scowl as she sprinted across the flooded floor filled with silently watching demons. "In hindsight, though, it was probably inevitable. I should've known there'd be no way I could enter the Hells and *not* feel the need to tear it all down, so yeah. We're doing this."

"I'm glad," Adrian told her with a smile. "What's our strategy?"

"I have no idea," Bex confessed. "I'm kind of winging it at the moment, but I do have something for you." She dug her newly-reattached right hand into the inside pocket of her bomber jacket. "Your aunt asked me to give this to you when I found you."

Adrian's stomach dropped several inches. "Which aunt?"

"The one who looks like a teenager."

That was a very small relief. Considering how long his Aunt Lydia held grudges, anything she sent would probably come with sharp teeth and a taste for Adrian's bones. Aunt Muriel's witchcraft was more abstract, though that didn't make it any less lethal. As Adrian had just been freshly reminded with the Morrigan incident, the Witch of the Future's plots were only good if you could survive them. The object in Bex's hand didn't look dangerous, though. It didn't even feel magical when he picked it up, causing Adrian's healthy paranoia to collapse into befuddlement.

"I don't understand," he said, holding up what appeared to be a completely normal acorn. "What's this for?"

"I was hoping you could tell me," Bex replied, resuming her breakneck pace toward the tower. "Your aunt was kind of light on details."

"She always is," Adrian muttered, turning the acorn over in his fingers. "Considering how much is at stake, you'd think she'd be a little clearer, but I guess I'll figure it out when the time comes."

"That is the way of the Witch of the Future," Boston agreed as he climbed up the back of Adrian's coat to resume his favorite perch on his witch's shoulder. "Perhaps you're supposed to perform a divination to determine its use?"

Adrian winced. "I think I'd rather be surprised. Divination takes time and materials we don't have, and my readings always turn out wrong anyway." He tucked the acorn into his coat's quick-draw chest pocket. "Let's just play things as they come."

"Spoken like a true Witch of the Present," Boston said, patting Adrian on the cheek with his paw as Bran flew them swiftly over the water, following close behind Bex as she ran for the hole the princess's tackle had knocked through the side of the warlocks' white tower.

Chapter 13

"**I** CAN'T BELIEVE HE made a princess out of me while I was still alive," Bex growled as she raced toward the tower, curling both of her hands into fists because she could do that now. "Seriously, did Gilgamesh think you'd roll over and become his prince for real just because he kidnapped you?"

She looked at Adrian, who was hovering beside her on his broom, but he was too busy staring at the tower ahead to answer. In his defense, it did look *really* different. The whole place had been a raging battle when the princess tackled Bex through the wall just a few minutes ago. Now, Desh and his team of Lowest Hells escapees had taken it over top to bottom.

They'd already torn open the central security cabinet and were frantically handing out keys, which made Bex feel a lot better about the reckless promises she'd just made to the slaves on the floor. Lys was supposed to be helping with that, but Bex didn't see them anywhere. She did see Kirok, though. The former general was on the bottom floor, addressing all the war-demon guards who'd suddenly found themselves on the wrong side of a revolution. He nodded to Bex when she and Adrian rushed by but didn't try to stop her, proving yet again that he was an invaluable addition to the team.

Bex was going to have to thank him properly when she got a moment. For now, though, she focused on running down the spiral stairs as fast as possible.

She'd already cleared two full rotations when Adrian hovered down the open center beside her.

"Would you like a lift?"

Bex grinned and grabbed his offered hand, leaping onto the broom in front of him.

"Thanks."

"You're welcome," Adrian said, sounding extremely pleased with himself as he wrapped his arms around her and signaled Bran to start the descent, which the broom did like a falling elevator.

"He didn't bring me here to be a prince."

"What?" Bex asked, clinging to the broom as it dropped into the dark.

"Your question earlier," he clarified, completely unfazed by their rapid descent. "You asked what Gilgamesh was thinking. I won't pretend to know his actual logic, but I'm certain he didn't bring me to Heaven because he wanted to add another son to the family business. I was more like one of those captured scientists who worked on the atom bomb. Even the princess he made out of your hand was only there to make sure I stayed in my cell and on schedule."

"On schedule for what?" Bex asked nervously. "Because 'atom bomb' doesn't sound good."

Adrian opened his mouth to answer, but they were almost at the floor by this point, and whatever he'd been about to say was drowned out by Iggs.

"*Bex!*" he shouted, waving his giant red arms. "*Adrian!* Over here!"

Bex jumped off the broom the moment Adrian touched them down, running across the dusty, blood-splattered bottom of the stairs, the seemingly last level of Hell.

"What's going on?" she demanded as she ran to join Iggs at the edge of the circular floor. "Where are the..."

Her voice trailed off as her brain finally caught up with what her eyes were seeing. Iggs was fully transformed and standing in front of a pair of giant doors carved with a terrifying image of Gilgamesh. It looked just like the doors they'd passed through to enter the Middle Hells, except this pair had an Iggs-shaped dent in the middle.

He'd clearly been throwing himself at them for a while, but a door strong enough to keep Iggs out wasn't the most alarming thing down here. That honor went to the giant splatter of white blood that covered the entire back half of the stairwell's circular floor. It looked like a prince had exploded, but before Bex could congratulate Iggs on what had obviously been a massive win, she spotted Leander sitting on the only remaining clean spot with a very bloody-looking Lys laid out beside him.

"*Lys!*" Bex shouted, sprinting over. "What happened?"

"They took a hit from a Blade of Gilgamesh," Leander replied calmly, waving his hand at the wad of black-drenched bandages wrapped around Lys's shoulder. "It wasn't a fatal wound, but the bleeding has yet to stop."

It would never stop. Bex knew that firsthand, but it didn't stop her from dropping to her knees beside Lys's body to check for herself.

"How long have they been unconscious?"

That question came from Adrian, who was suddenly right beside her, gently pushing Bex's shaking hands away so he could examine Lys's wound.

Leander shot the witch a cold look and said nothing. Fortunately, Iggs was on it.

"They've been out since we jumped down here," he reported. "So maybe ten minutes?"

Adrian nodded and reached back toward Boston, who was already dumping a cornucopia of witchy-looking items out of his cat pack.

"I can't heal a Blade of Gilgamesh wound down here," he said in the clipped, stern tone Bex thought of as his doctor voice. "But I can stem the bleeding and help them regain consciousness."

"Are you sure?" Bex whispered, hands shaking.

"Nothing is sure when it comes to living bodies," Adrian warned her, then he smiled. "But I've treated Lys before. They don't give up easily, and blood loss is much easier to deal with than sin-iron poisoning." He gave her a nudge with his shoulder. "I'll take care of them. You go help Iggs."

Bex didn't want to leave. This was too close to what had happened the last time Lys faced a prince. They'd survived that, but Bex was still shaking from the idea that Lys could have died down here and she wouldn't even have known.

"They're not dead yet," Adrian said, reading the fear right off her face. "And they're not going to be. I'm fighting with them now, so you go do what only you can do and leave me to do what I do best, okay?"

"Okay," Bex whispered, giving Lys's too-cold hand a final squeeze before she forced herself to get up and go to Iggs, who was bouncing nervously on the balls of his giant feet.

"Are they going to be okay?" he asked.

"Absolutely," Bex said, forcing herself to sound confident. "Adrian's on it, and you know how good he is. Lys isn't going anywhere."

She clenched her fists as she finished, squeezing her fingers hard like she could squeeze the words into being true, and Iggs's red eyes widened.

"Hey, you got your hand back!" he cried, ducking his giant horned head to get a better look. "And your ring, too! When did that happen?"

"When I ripped the head off the doll Gilgamesh stuck them to," Bex replied, lifting her restored fist. "The princess that tackled me out of nowhere was the one Gilgamesh made for Adrian out of my stolen hand."

"Adrian got a *princess*?" Iggs said, his eyes going even wider. "So does that mean Drox is a gross white Blade of Gilgamesh now?"

"No," Bex said quickly, looking down at the band on her right ring finger. "Or, at least, I don't think so. I still don't have a name, so I haven't been able to draw him yet, but he doesn't feel like a tool of Heaven."

"That's good to hear," Iggs said, but he still looked disappointed. "Gotta admit, when I heard Desh and the others cheering upstairs, I was *really* hoping you'd made a comeback."

"Who says I haven't?" Bex replied as she called her flames to surround her body.

Iggs staggered away, his shocked face lit up by her blazing light. Instead of jumping for joy like she'd hoped, though, her demon collapsed on the ground.

"Whoa, Iggs!" Bex cried, snuffing her fire as she rushed to grab him. "What's wrong?"

"Nothing's wrong," Iggs said, his voice thick with emotion as he bowed his horns to the floor. "I'm just happy you've returned, my queen."

"I never left," Bex reminded him, but she stopped trying to pull him out of his bow. She still hated when Iggs got like this, but she'd learned long ago that he needed to do this stuff sometimes. It was like she'd told Adrian in front of the boba shop months ago: Iggs bowed for his own reasons. All Bex could do was stand there and take it until he decided to get back up.

"Sorry," he whispered, scrubbing his face as he lifted his head at last. "Got something in my eye."

"You have nothing to be sorry for," Bex promised as she reached up to dry his cheek. "You held the line and saved us all. I don't know if I could've taken a prince by myself even with my fire back, but you made it so I didn't have to." She gave him a huge, proud smile. "You've served me very well, Iggerux. I couldn't have done any of this without you, and I am very grateful."

She ducked her head, lowering the place where her horns used to be. Naturally, this sent Iggs into a panic. Before he could go too far off the deep end, though, Bex lifted her head with a smile.

"Come on," she said. "Let's go save our people. Where are they?"

It took Iggs a few seconds to snap out of the daze of everything that had just happened. When he did, though, he was all business.

"Over here," he said, striding across the white-blood-soaked room toward a large set of black doors with a fresh, Iggs-shaped dent in the middle. "I heard them yelling after the Prince of Hate died, which was some scary shit, by the way. I dropped him down here to get him away from the others, but it was his princess who actually dealt the killing blow."

"I was wondering what happened to throw his blood ten feet up the walls," Bex said. "But where's the princess? Did she get away?"

Iggs shook his head. "Leander evaporated her. He's not half bad now that he's on our team. I was going to ask him to blast the door open for me, but I didn't want any of our people getting hurt."

"Are you sure they're in there?" Bex asked, cupping a hand to her ear. "I don't hear anything."

"They were yelling their heads off earlier," Iggs insisted. "I thought this whole place was like the black cavern you fell into. That's why I dropped the prince down here. I was hoping to get him stuck in the void demons' black hole, but it turns out there's *two* Lowest Hells."

He pointed at the dented doors in front of them before swinging his arm across the room to point at a second pair of giant black doors by the stairs that Bex hadn't noticed yet. That set also had an image of Gilgamesh at his most intimidating carved into them, but they were sealed with a giant dusty clay tablet covered in humming cuneiform.

"Makes sense in hindsight," Iggs continued as they crossed the final distance to the dented doors he'd been leading her toward, which seemed to be locked only with a floor bolt. A gigantic sin-iron floor bolt, but still just a physical barrier. "Heaven's propaganda always said there were Nine Hells. I thought they were counting Limbo as ours, but it looks like Gilgamesh prepared a place for Wrath in his kingdom after all."

"Guess he figured I'd take one of his thousand surrender offers eventually," Bex said as she got down on the floor to get a better look at the lock. "Happy I proved him wrong. Can you make me some room?"

Iggs flashed her a delighted grin and grabbed the warped edge of the doors he'd clearly been slamming his shoulder into earlier. He braced his legs against the bloody floor and heaved with all his might until the bottom of the giant door lifted off the floor. It was just a hair-thin gap, but it was still enough for Bex to get eyes on the bolt that held them closed. Target in sight, Bex called her fire and pressed her burning fingers against the gap.

"Watch your hands," she warned as she fanned herself brighter. "This might get hot."

Iggs nodded and tightened his grip, pulling the tiny gap a little wider as Bex blasted her fire through. The geyser of flame she produced wasn't nearly as precise as the glowing wire Drox had used to cut Havok's armor in half, but it got the job done. It took her only thirty seconds to get the bolt hot enough to bend. The moment he felt it start to give, Iggs smashed his shoulder into the doors like a battering ram, snapping the weakened bolt in half and opening the right-hand door wide enough for Bex to squeeze through.

She did so in a blaze of fire. Part of that was because she simply hadn't put herself out yet, but the rest was a deliberate show of power. If her demons really were in here, then her Bonfire would be the surest way for them to recognize her, especially since Bex still didn't have her horns back. She did tamp her flames down to her skin to make sure she didn't accidentally engulf anyone, but it still should've been an impressive sight. When Bex actually made it to the other side, though, what she found was not what she'd hoped.

"What's wrong?" asked Iggs, shifting back to human size so he could squeeze through the cracked door as well. "What do you see?"

Bex still wasn't sure. The Hell of Wrath looked a lot like the Hell of Pride's low-ceilinged cavern, complete with the countless bodies lying in the black water that covered the floor. But where the former Pride demons were trapped in their own eternal torment, these demons looked passed out. There was a whole pile of them next to the door that had gotten pushed over when Iggs slammed it open. They weren't chained up, thank Ishtar, nor were their bodies covered in unnatural gray like they'd been in Limbo. They were actually all in human form with normal-colored skin and black horns that ranged in shape from Iggs's wide bull horns to Bex's former pointed spears.

Under any other circumstances, that would've made her sob in relief. But while Bex was happy to see her people back to their natural color and not trying to eat her in a starvation-fueled frenzy, something was still wrong. Not only were her demons not moving, they looked even worse than the slaves upstairs. Their bodies were so thin beneath their rough-woven slave tunics that Bex could see every ridge of the bones under their sagging skin. Their closed eyes were sunken into their skulls, and their arms were stained black to the elbows with what looked like a toxic amount of sin.

"What in the Hells?" Iggs cried, falling to his knees beside the collapsed demon closest to the doors, a young woman so thin she looked like she'd crack if he touched her. "I heard them all yelling earlier. What happened?"

"I don't know," Bex said, pushing up her flames to illuminate the cavern full of emaciated bodies. "They look pretty weak, though. Maybe making a commotion to get your attention took all the strength they had left."

"If that's the case, we have to get them out as fast as possible," Iggs said, looking around the room in growing panic. "But I still don't understand how they got this bad. We're all thin when we come out of Limbo, but not like this. What in the Hells did this place do to them?"

Bex was wondering the same thing. There was no way to know until someone told them, though, so she reached down to touch the shoulder of the woman lying closest to the door. She wasn't holding out hope for much, but the wrath demon opened her eyes the moment Bex's burning fingers touched her skin.

"My queen," she whispered in Riverlander, her unfocused eyes following Bex's light like a baby's.

"Don't move," Bex ordered in the same language when the woman started trying to push herself into a bow. "Tell me what happened here. What did Gilgamesh do to you?"

The woman's sunken eyes filled with tears. "He worked us," she whispered. "I don't... I don't recall how it started. I remember being hungry and lost in a gray haze for a long time. Then, suddenly, I was in this place, and the traitor, the killer of the gods... He was *here*, my queen! He walked among us."

"What did he do?" Bex asked, reaching down to clutch the woman's terrifyingly thin hand.

"He ordered us to collect sin," she whispered, her dilated pupils finally focusing on Bex's glowing face. "We told him we would not, that Wrath would never kneel, but he held your crown in his hands. He spoke with your voice, and we could not disobey. He worked us for days without food or rest, making us scrape sin out of this strange, stagnant river."

She turned her head to look at the Hell's flooded floor, and her eyes filled with tears. "So many died," she whispered. "We were still thin and weak from the gray hell, but the Traitor King had no mercy. He didn't even let us stop long enough to move the bodies. He just ordered us to keep working."

"Where is Gilgamesh now?" Bex asked in a flat, deadly voice.

"I don't know," the woman said, closing her eyes again. "I'm sorry, my queen. It's all a blur. He would appear and disappear in a clash of bells. Every time he left, he took all the sin we'd collected with him, but I don't know where. Even when he wasn't here, though, the order to keep working remained. It didn't break until a few minutes ago, which was when we all collapsed."

"I bet it was when you got your fire back," Iggs said, speaking in English so that only Bex would understand.

"I don't know if that's it," Bex replied in the same language. "If my fire and name were linked, Drox would be able to hear me. It could just be a coincidence. Whatever happened, though, we need to get them out of here."

"No argument there," Iggs said, getting back to his feet. "But how? This cavern is full of skeletons. Even if you had your horns back and could order them to move, they look like they'd fall apart."

"We'll figure it out," Bex growled, clutching the woman's hand as she switched back to Riverlander.

"Gilgamesh will not return," she promised. "I have to go see about your treatment, but my loyal servant Iggerux will watch over you until I return. I'll be back in a minute. Wait for me."

"We have always waited for you," the woman whispered, bowing her head as much as she was able. "You are the sacred Bonfire of Ishtar, the light of our people. We *always* knew that you would come for us. Even when the other tribes said you were dead, we felt you. We knew you were still alive and fighting for us."

"She's the only queen who never kneeled," Iggs agreed proudly. "And neither have we. Wrath has *never* stopped fighting, and we won't be beaten by this, either. Our queen has finally arrived. Just hold on a little longer, and she'll take us all home to Paradise."

The woman started sobbing in earnest then, her skeletal body curling around Iggs's boots as she cried and cried. Bex felt a bit like crying herself because she had no idea how she was going to keep all the promises they'd just made. She wasn't going to *not* tell her people she'd save them, though, so she sucked it up and stepped back through the cracked door to figure out how in the world she was going to get thousands of worked-almost-to-death wrath demons back on their feet.

"You found all your people?" Adrian said without looking up from the bright-green, foul-smelling goop he was meticulously smearing all over Lys's injured shoulder. "That's fantastic! I'm sorry to hear they're in such a bad state, but I'm sure they'll be on their feet again in no time. Demon regeneration is a force to be reckoned with. Just look at Lys."

Bex *was* looking, and it didn't look good. "How're they doing?"

"Peachy, thanks," croaked a blessedly familiar voice.

Bex jumped, snapping her attention back to Lys's face just in time to see the lust demon's amber eyes crack open.

"Sorry I didn't say something earlier. Your witch was very bossy about me not moving."

"I'm just glad you're alive," Bex replied in a watery voice, leaning as close to Lys as she could get without actually touching their body or getting in Adrian's way.

"Don't hover over me like I'm a corpse," Lys scolded. "I told you, I'm only lying like this because Adrian said he'd turn me into a newt if I didn't. It doesn't even hurt that much anymore. I'm mostly just pissed that I let that giant ugly bastard get a hit on me."

They rolled their amber eyes. "I must be getting sloppy in my old age."

"Never," Bex insisted, fighting the urge to hug Lys until Adrian turned them both into amphibians. "You fought a prince and lived to brag about it. I'd say that's pretty good."

"Save your compliments for Iggs," Lys said with a wide smile. Too wide, apparently, because Adrian immediately reached up to mold their face back into a neutral expression.

"As I was saying," Lys grumbled when the witch let them go. "I landed some good shots, but Iggs is the one who carried through and won." Their eyes grew soft. "I wish you could've seen him. Our little rescue has grown into a proper demon."

"Iggs has always been tough," Bex replied with a grin of her own. "He fought to defend his village from Gilgamesh's armies during the invasion of the Riverlands when he was only a teenager, don't forget."

"I haven't," Lys said. "He saved my bacon for real this time. He even got Leander to help, which is the real shocker. I thought for sure that prince was going to stab us in the back."

Bex secretly felt the same. Leander had been a solid team player since she'd pulled him out of the Lowest Hell, though, so she didn't say a word.

"Where is he?" she asked instead.

"Over by the doors to the void demons' room," Lys replied. "He's been staring at them since Adrian woke me up. Kind of creepy, to be honest."

Leander did look very intent when Bex glanced over her shoulder. He didn't seem to be doing anything dangerous, though, so she just shrugged and got back to what was important: namely Lys not being dead.

"Why is he here again?" Adrian whispered as he slathered more green, piney-smelling glop over the hole in Lys's shoulder. "Isn't that the prince who tried to kill you on the Anchor chain back in Seattle?"

"That's him," Bex said. "But that fight is also the reason we were able to recruit him. After he lost to me, Gilgamesh memory-wiped his princess and banished him to the Lowest Hells. Surprise, surprise, Leander wasn't feeling too loyal toward his dad after that, so he switched sides. He's actually the one who got us into position to surprise-attack the tower, so he's cool in my book."

"If you say so," Adrian muttered.

"We'll keep an eye on him," Lys promised, flicking their eyes back to Bex. "I'm much more concerned about what Gilgamesh was up to with the wrath demons."

Bex scowled. "What do you mean 'up to'? I already said he was working them to death gathering sin, or were you still passed out for that part?"

"No, I heard it," Lys assured her. "I just don't believe it. Gilgamesh has been after your horns so that he can control the wrath demons for five thousand years. After all that effort, you'd think he'd be a little more careful, but it sounds like he forced them to go on a seven-day sin-collection bender the moment he got his hands on the goods."

They shook their head as much as Adrian's treatment would allow. "Gilgamesh isn't exactly known for caring about demon welfare, but that's crazy. Other than the demons you pulled out of Limbo during the month we held the Seattle Anchor, the folks in that cavern are the only wrath demons in existence right now. Gilgamesh can't just breed up some more if he works this batch to death, so why's he doing it?"

"Maybe he really needs sin iron?" Bex guessed.

"He's got eight other Hells for that," Lys reminded her. "Gilgamesh has sin iron coming out of his ears. That's why this doesn't make any sense. Why's he risking the demons he worked so hard to get to make more of something he's already got mountains of?"

Bex had no idea. She'd been so caught up in the disasters in front of her, she hadn't had time yet to think about what it all meant. Fortunately, it seemed Adrian had.

"I don't think it's a matter of getting more raw materials," he said in a thoughtful voice as he started wrapping a clean bandage around Lys's gunk-covered shoulder. "I think he's after a specific combination."

"A specific combination of what?" Bex asked.

"Sins," the witch replied, taking his eyes off of Lys for a second to give Bex a worried look. "You told me once that every demon pulls a different kind of sin out of the river. That's why there are nine different tribes instead of one united demonkind. Ishtar made each of you for a specific purpose, and while I don't have any proof yet, I suspect that Gilgamesh is still working within the same system. He told me when he kidnapped me that his final goal required all nine demon queens to work. At the time, I thought he was just trying to destroy the last remaining opposition. Now that I've seen the Hells with my own eyes, though, I have to wonder if sins aren't what he was really after this entire time."

"That would explain a few things," Boston said from his perch on Lys's feet. "I always wondered why Gilgamesh bothered keeping so many demons in the Hells. If slaves were all he was after, it would've been easier to keep only a minimum breeding population, and there would've been no reason to keep Bex's demons alive at all. If Wrath was the final component he needed for a spell, though, that would explain why he went on a sin-collecting rampage the moment he got them under his control."

Bex scowled. "Yeah, well, that monster *rampaged* through my entire tribe!"

"I just wish I knew what he was gathering it all for," Adrian said in a distracted voice. "Sorcerers don't use components for their spells, so why does he need Wrath specifically? What does it do that the other sins don't?"

The room fell silent as he finished tying up Lys's arm. When he had all the bandage tails neatly trimmed, he let the demon go with a flourish.

"There," he said, "You can move now."

"Thank the gods," Lys groaned, shoving themselves up like they couldn't wait to get off the floor.

"How do you feel?" Bex asked nervously.

"Not great," Lys admitted as they rolled their bandaged shoulder. "Everything hurts, and my arm itches like crazy, but I'll live. Taking wounds is part of being a soldier. I'm way more interested in how Adrian knows so much about Gilgamesh's goals. Did the

Eternal King make you watch a video about his evil plans during your prince orientation or something?"

Adrian laughed. "Nothing that informative. He fed me a lot of lines about the greater good and being the savior of humanity but never gave any specific details. Everything I just said is my own conjecture. I don't even know why he had me working on what I was working on."

"What *were* you working on?" Bex asked.

It was the obvious question, but for some reason, Adrian dropped his mirrored eyes.

"Nothing we have time to dig into at the moment," he said quickly as he packed the remaining medical supplies into his coat. "We're still in the middle of a battle. I'm pretty sure the only reason we haven't already been assaulted by every prince in Heaven is because of the teleport ban, but they have to be coming. There's no way Gilgamesh missed the death of a prince and *two* princesses."

"Way to dodge the question," Lys said, giving Adrian a pointed look before they sighed. "You're not wrong, though. I told Nemini to guard the door to the Upper Hells, so I doubt any warlocks made it out alive, but I'd bet my horns there's a war demon army mustering to crush us as we speak."

"Probably," Bex agreed, but her eyes were still on Adrian. She'd put her fire out when she'd come over, so maybe it was a trick of the intense shadows caused by Boston's LED camping lantern, but Bex swore she'd seen him flinch when Lys said Nemini's name. That wasn't too weird by itself—Nemini made a lot of people uncomfortable—but Adrian had always seemed to get along with her. Add in his uncharacteristic refusal to answer her question earlier and Bex didn't like where this was going. She was about to pull him aside and just ask him what was going on when the worst noise she'd ever heard came screaming down the stairwell.

"What in the Hells is that?" Boston yelled over the racket, which sounded like the piercing beep of a fire alarm combined with an entire dumpster full of aluminum going through a shredder.

"Alarm," Lys said, covering their ears with their still-bloody hands. "I've never heard this one, though, so I don't know what set it off."

"Pretty sure I can guess," Bex said, glancing pointedly at the white prince blood that was still dripping off the walls as she rose to her feet.

"Break time's over," she announced, fighting the urge to clutch her aching ears. "I'm going upstairs to see what we're in for. The rest of you, stay down here and help Iggs get my demons back on their—"

Her voice cut off as the ground began to shake. It wasn't a violent, earthquake sort of shaking. Nothing was breaking or falling apart. This felt more like some kind of giant machinery had just started turning deep within the mountain. Bex was still trying to figure out what that meant and who she had to punch to make it stop when the horrible alarm suddenly ceased. For a split second, there was blessed silence, and then a new horror began as a chorus of voices tore through the air like the claws of a divine beast.

"Tools of the Gods."

Bex gasped. She'd taken a lot of blows in her life, but each of those words hit her harder than the Queen of War's sword. She managed to stay on her feet, barely. Adrian, Boston, and Leander didn't seem to feel it at all, but Lys went down like someone had dropped a lead piano on their head. Going by all the curses coming out of the Hell of Wrath, Iggs was having a similar problem. Bex needed to do something about that, but she was having a hard time concentrating. No matter how hard she tried to focus, her attention kept being dragged back to the voices that were still echoing down the spiral stairwell.

Eight divinely empowered female voices braided together, one of which was her own.

"*Demons of Ishtar,*" the queens' combined voices said from every direction at once. "*Your disobedience has been witnessed, and it shall not be tolerated. By the authority of Ishtar spoken through her divine daughters, we, your queens, command you as one: kneel before your conquerors, and present your necks to be chained.*"

The actual order was short, but the voices spoke so slowly that it seemed to go on forever. By the time they finally stopped speaking, Lys was rolling in agony on the floor, bending themselves nearly in half as they frantically tried to offer up their neck. Without her divine name to shield her, Bex's knees were bending toward the floor as well. She could make them straighten back out if she focused, but that was all she could do. Even when she called her Bonfire, the raging flames did nothing to stop the intense pressure to bow, to submit, to prostrate herself utterly before the queens' divine will.

She couldn't remember ever feeling anything like it before in her life. Even when she'd kneeled in the river before Ishtar herself, it hadn't been like this. She swore she could feel the queens' hands inside her brain, shoving her head toward the ground. Bex fought the sensation as hard as she could, but even with her fire roaring and Adrian's frantic voice in her ear telling her to fight, her hornless forehead kept creeping closer and closer to the ground. She was just about to drop to one knee when a new voice boomed through every corner of the Hells.

Bex's first thought was it must be Gilgamesh himself. There was no one else egotistical enough to follow a chorus of queens, except that wasn't his voice. It sounded like a woman, and it was oddly familiar. Bex knew she'd heard that beautiful, commanding voice before, but she couldn't remember where. She could only listen in awe as the lovely sound became lovely words that shook through the obedient silence that had fallen over the Hells like thunder on a silent night.

"Children of Paradise," the new voice said, "the ghosts of empty crowns do not control you. Death is *our* realm, so rise, People of the Riverlands. Rise and heed the words of Ishtar's true daughters. Formed from her body, crowned by her hand, named by her lips, we alone speak in the goddess' name. I am her firstborn, Queen of Pride, Ishtar's Crown, and by that divine authority, I command you: *be free*."

The pressure inside Bex's head lessened with every word. By the time the new command finished, the eight hands that had been forcing her head to the ground vanished like mist in the morning sun, leaving only one behind. One living voice whose divine command still surged through Bex's body like electricity, forcing her to rise so fast, she ended up standing on the tips of her toes. The queen's divine authority held her there like a ballerina on a string for one long heartbeat, and then the overwhelming presence disappeared completely, leaving Bex blinking in the sudden, deafening silence.

"Again, what in the Hells was that?"

The question came from Boston, who was curled into a spooked-looking ball in Adrian's arms. His witch didn't look much better, staring at Bex with a panicked expression that broke her heart to see, because what had just happened was anything but scary. Lys had already leaped off the ground with a shout so joyful it bordered on mania. Even Iggs, who'd never been a slave, was shoving the doors to the Hell of Wrath open with a roar of victory.

They were *all* roaring. Every demon in the Hells was bellowing at the top of their lungs, shattering the quiet horror that had always hung over this place. Even her exhausted wrath demons were cheering, their voices as thin as worn threads but still audible through the doors Iggs had torn open.

The sound was enough to make Bex's heart pound in her chest. She wanted to run over and celebrate with them, but now that the shock and holy awe of the Queen of Pride's miraculous—and *extremely* well-timed—reappearance was fading, Bex was starting to realize why the queen's voice sounded so familiar. It wasn't some dredged-up memory from her past in Ishtar's Paradise. The words had been warped with power and uncharacteristically emotional, but the voice that spoke them was one she'd heard every day of her current life. She'd heard it only half an hour ago in the tunnel after Boston told them Adrian was here.

That was Nemini's voice.

The connection was still crystallizing when Bex called her fire and blasted herself up the middle of the spiral stair like a rocket.

Chapter 14

BACK AT THE BOTTOM of the Hells, Adrian was in a panic.

He'd seen the exact moment Bex realized who the Queen of Pride was. It'd flashed across her face like lightning right before fire engulfed her body and she'd launched herself toward the top of the tower where he'd left Nemini staring at her horns.

He was scrambling for his broom before her boots left the ground. Great Forest, how many more ways could this go wrong? All he'd wanted was to bring back a queen who was *supposed* to be five-thousand-years dead. It should've been a miracle, but nothing was ever simple when it came to the daughters of Ishtar. Now he had to get upstairs and explain the situation before everyone involved jumped to the wrong conclusion. He was throwing his leg over Bran for the takeoff when a bandaged hand shot up to stop him.

"Not without me, you don't," Lys snarled as they hauled their bloody body onto the broomstick.

Adrian was scrambling to make them get off before they reopened the wound he'd just glued back together when Bran dipped nearly to the floor. When he looked up to see why, Iggs was sitting on the broom's bristles with a stubborn expression across his once again human-looking face.

"No, no, no," Adrian said as he struggled to keep his seat on the now furiously bobbing broom. "We can't *all* go. Someone has to stay down here and keep an eye on Leander and the wrath demons. Also, there's not enough room for—*ow!*"

He snatched his hands up with a hiss, glaring at the raven-carved broomstick that had just pecked him for implying that a broom made by the Old Wife of the Bones wasn't capable of carrying a crowd.

"I wasn't trying to malign you," Adrian told it quickly, but he was too late. Bran's honor had been impugned. The broom was already changing beneath him, transforming into its broomgrass raven form, which had plenty of room for everyone.

"Fantastic," Lys said as they plopped down on the raven broom's back. "Let's go."

"Bran doesn't take orders from you," Boston snapped from his perch on Adrian's shoulder. "We'll leave when our witch is ready."

Everyone turned to look at Adrian, who sighed.

"Hang on," he said, reaching down to tap Bran's now six-foot-wide back with his fingers.

His broom must've been waiting for a chance to show off. The second Adrian gave the signal, Bran popped off the floor like a cork, shooting up the center of the spiral stairs so fast that his passengers were crushed against his stiff, bristly wings. Adrian didn't even get an opportunity to gawk at the enormous crowd of unchained demons that had gathered around the base of the tower in the Middle Hells before they were whisked past them to the top.

The broom stopped on a pin the moment it reached the tower's highest floor. The huge spiral staircase kept going, but the tunnel to the Upper Hells where Adrian had had his disastrous confrontation with Nemini was now blocked by a sin-iron security door that looked as thick as the slab he'd beaten his head against beneath the Seattle Anchor.

Adrian wasn't sure when the barricade had come down, but he was relieved to see it. That lump of sin iron might be blocking their exit, but it was also shielding them from the army of war demons that was almost certainly marshalling on the other side. It was a small mercy, but a comforting one, because the rest of the situation wasn't looking good.

Other than the stairs leading to the blocked entrance to the Upper Hells, the entire top of the white tower was shrouded in darkness. The sorcerous sconces on the walls that usually filled the tower with blindingly white light now looked as dim as fireflies, their glare crushed by the haze of shadows that emanated from the horned figure huddled against the farthest wall.

No, Adrian realized when he nudged his broom closer, not shadows. Nemini's body was shrouded in gigantic, coiling black snakes. Their bodies looked no more solid than smoke, but their fangs gleamed with very real menace thanks to the brilliant flames roaring off the other queen in the room.

Bex was standing at the top of the staircase in full bonfire. The heat pouring off her was intense enough to crisp Adrian's hair, but her blazing fire barely penetrated the snake-filled shadows. It did, however, give Adrian a perfect view of the fury on Bex's face as she opened her mouth to demand to know how this had happened.

At least, that was what Adrian assumed she was going to say. It was certainly the most obvious question. When Bex actually spoke, though, the words that left her mouth weren't what he'd expected at all.

"Why didn't you tell me?"

The question came out in a small, hurt voice, and the snake-wrapped figure on the other side of the tower sighed.

"Because I thought I was free," Nemini said, finally raising her horned head to stare at Bex with yellow eyes that gleamed with more emotion than Adrian had seen her show in all the months he'd known her put together.

"I didn't want you to know," she whispered, burying her face in her knees again. "I *liked* being nobody. I was *happy* in the void. When I was a queen, my entire life belonged to other people. So long as my horns were broken, though, there was no one I had to be. I was free. Wholly and truly free for the first time in my life. I thought I'd get to live like that forever until your witch went and pulled off another miracle."

Adrian flinched at the bitter anger in her voice. Then he flinched again when Bex's flaming head snapped toward him with a look of horrified shock. He was still scrambling to come up with a version of the truth that didn't make it sound like he'd fixed Nemini's horns behind her back when Bex lost her patience.

"It doesn't matter," she snapped, fixing her glowing eyes on Nemini again. "However this happened, it's done now, but that doesn't have to be a bad thing."

Her face grew gentler as she took a step forward. "I understand how much you valued your freedom, but if the Queen of Pride was ever going to come back from the dead, I couldn't have picked a better time, better place, or better person than here, now, and you. Your countermand just saved all of us, including me. That's *incredible*, but it's also not surprising, because I've fought beside you my entire life. I already know how good your heart is, how much you care. I know this isn't what you wanted, but that doesn't mean we can't still make the most of it." A smile spread over Bex's face as she held out her blazing hand to the shadows. "Let's fight Heaven together like we always do. Let's use what we've got and *win* this thing so we can finally go home." Her smile grew even wider. "Sister."

She was shining like the sun by the time she finished, but Nemini—or at least the demon who'd once been called Nemini—just pulled deeper into the shadow of her snakes.

"I knew you wouldn't understand."

"I *do* understand," Bex insisted. "You're the one who showed me that the void isn't the end. I know how much it means to you, but—"

"You don't know," the queen snapped. "That's why you were able to walk out of it. When the loss of your name tore all responsibility from your grasp, did you consider the emptiness? Did you take even a second to think about what else you could be without the crown that weighed you down? No. You turned around and snatched your duties right back to your chest because you *like* being responsible. You *enjoy* serving your people, but I was never like you."

She lowered her yellow eyes, the only color left in the twisting nest of snakes she'd built around herself.

"I hated being queen," she whispered. "I hated how my demons were always pulling at me, needing me to do things for them. The only value I saw in them was how their worship made me special. I thought I was their chosen ruler, the one the gods entrusted with the safety of their treasured Paradise. That pride was the only thing that made queenship tolerable. It wasn't until I broke that I realized I'd never been special at all. Being queen wasn't an elevated privilege. It was a job. I was a cog in the gods' soul-processing machine just like every other demon. A slave with no agency or choice of my own."

"That's not true," Bex said fiercely. "Gilgamesh is the one who made us slaves, not the gods!"

The queen shrugged. "I fail to see the difference. Whichever side of the war you look at, demons have never lived according to our wants. Even Gilgamesh's slave bands are just adaptations of the names the gods were already using to control us. We've *always* been dogs at the end of someone else's leash. The only time I was ever free of that was when I had no name at all."

Her face grew sad. "I'd hoped you'd realize that as well when you lost your own name. We'd never gotten along before the war because I looked down on you. I thought all your loyalty and hard work was a show for Ishtar's benefit. It wasn't until you found me and picked me up off that dark riverbed that I realized you'd never been faking anything. You showed more love and compassion toward a nameless, broken demon than I'd ever gotten as the haughty Queen of Pride. The years I spent basking in the warmth of your fire were the happiest of my entire life. My only pain was that you wouldn't stop fighting."

She clenched her fists. "No matter how many times I told you the war was futile, you never stopped throwing yourself at Gilgamesh's wall. Even after you lost everything, you refused to let it go. I thought I'd accepted that as part of the inevitable truth of the universe. Even when your obnoxiously competent witch laid my repaired horns at my feet, I still thought there was nothing I could do. If Gilgamesh won back when there were nine of us, what could two queens possibly hope to accomplish? The whole concept was hopeless. I'd be sacrificing my precious freedom for nothing. I wasn't going to do it, but then I heard the queens' stolen voices ordering everyone to kneel. I realized you were about to lose, and my hands moved on their own."

She reached up to smack the forked tower of beautifully shining obsidian-black horns that now dominated her head, but Bex looked stunned.

"You put them back on for me?"

"I make all of my stupid decisions for you," the queen said in an irritated voice, but her lips were smiling. "I told you before, Bexa. You're the one I chose to keep. I hated being queen and thought the war was pointless. I knew we were all doomed to be slaves forever no matter which side won, so I didn't care if Gilgamesh caught us or not. You cared, though, and I care about you. I couldn't stand the thought of your despair when he won, so I made a rash decision based on emotion, and this is how it ended up, just like he predicted."

She flicked her yellow gaze to Adrian, who immediately started to squirm. Bex's eyes, however, stayed locked on her sister. She walked forward next, striding through the ghostly snakes like the sun passing through clouds until she was standing right in front of the new queen, whose actual name Adrian suddenly realized he didn't know. Not that he could've spoken it if he *did* know, but it still felt odd not knowing what to call the person Bex was staring at with her entire heart in her eyes.

"I won't let you regret it," she said as she fell to her knees, lowering her head not to bow, but so that she and the sitting queen could finally see each other eye to eye.

"You gave up your freedom to save me from my failures today," she whispered, clenching her hands into burning fists. "I can never undo that, but I swear it won't be forever. I know you think the war is pointless, but the whole reason we're fighting is so that demons everywhere can be free to live the lives they choose. That includes you. Even if I have to defy Ishtar herself, I swear on my lost name, I *will* find a way make you free again."

"You were always quick to swear," the Queen of Pride muttered. "You've made so many promises that you have no power to keep. It's always been your worst trait, but..." She lifted her head to give Bex a weak smile. "I still like that you try."

"Of course I try," Bex said. "What else am I supposed to do? Give up and let everyone be miserable forever?"

Her sister shrugged. "Suffering is inevitable, but the fact that you refuse to accept that is why I love you. If no one pushes back, all we'll do is sink."

"Don't make it sound like a lost cause," Bex growled. "Breaking into the Hells was supposed to be impossible, but here we are. Gilgamesh thought he had us cornered, but you came back from the dead and stopped him in his tracks. We've done a hundred impossible things in just the last two hours, so don't you dare tell me I can't keep my promises." She clenched her burning fists even tighter. "I'm going to set every single demon free, including you. I'm winning this whole damn thing, horns or no horns, so keep your eyes on me, Nemini, because I'm not going to let you down."

"You never do," the queen said as she leaned forward to hug her sister.

The cloud of shadow snakes retreated as she did, shrinking down until they were back in their usual place on Nemini's head. Adrian didn't know if that was a new feature of her restored horns or if Nemini had always been able to make her snakes enormous and this was just the first time she'd used the power in front of him, but he was very happy things seemed to have turned out all right in the end. More or less.

"So what happens now?" Bex asked, finally out snuffing her flames as she scrubbed her eyes in a way she probably thought no one would notice.

"I suppose I should go get my demons," the Queen of Pride replied unenthusiastically. "Now that I've got my name back, they're no longer falling into the void of my loss, which means I can feel them waking up." She scowled. "They're very confused. This is the first time they've been aware of their surroundings since the war, so, naturally, they're in a *state*." She rose to her feet with a huff. "It's such a bother."

"I'm starting to see why she wasn't a popular queen," Iggs whispered, scooting closer to Adrian on the broom.

Adrian nodded, but he didn't get to say a word as the queen formerly known as Nemini strode imperiously past them and started descending the spiral stairs toward the crowd of demons waiting anxiously below.

High, high above in the second-tallest tower of the Highest Heavens, Crown Prince Alexander was sitting alone in his office, frantically trying to read through the avalanche of report scrolls that wouldn't stop landing on his desk.

The scroll system was automated, and it was only supposed to go off when emergency protocols were triggered. It was the Prince of the Hells' job to deal with day-to-day problems, which was why the current flurry was so alarming. Alexander had designed the scroll system to only bother him if there was an actual threat to the integrity of Heaven's interests, but he couldn't even tell which part of the Hells was in trouble because reports were coming in from every section.

The first alarm had come in thirty minutes ago notifying him of infrastructure damage to the Middle Hells' central stair. Next came a bevy of letters from the tower wardens assuring the Crown Prince that the problem would be dealt with quickly, then nothing. He had plenty of reports from the Upper Hells about screaming and explosions below, but no one from the

Middle Hells had made contact in nineteen minutes, which was eighteen and a half minutes too long.

My prince?

"Finally," he growled, closing his eyes to focus all of his attention on the familiar voice sliding through his head like an intrusive thought. "Report."

I've ordered my war slaves to reinforce the Middle Hells as you commanded, the Crown Princess replied calmly. *But they've been unable to proceed due to the presence of the lockdown barricades.*

"Lockdown?" Alexander repeated furiously. "On whose authority?"

I'm not certain, his princess replied, her calm voice tinged with the slightest hint of anger. *The Princess of Hate isn't responding, so I've been unable to reach Prince Demetrios.*

"Then he's dead," Alexander snapped. "Whether he started this mess or merely failed to stop it, Father will kill him for his incompetence. What about the Princess of Wrath?"

Also unresponsive.

That was the worst news so far. If the lockdown had already been triggered, then the trouble in the Hells was contained, but Adrian was his father's current favorite, and Alexander was the one who'd let him out of his cage. Broken princes could always be put back together, but the process took time, and the Eternal King had made it clear he was on a strict deadline. If Gilgamesh's plans got derailed because of this, Alexander's head would be the one to roll.

"What do we need to do to lift the lockdown?"

I'd have to check the documentation, his princess replied. *We've never gone into full lockdown before, so I'm unfamiliar with the override protocol, but I believe Gilgamesh's personal intervention is required.*

"I was afraid of that," Alexander muttered, grinding the heel of his palm into his eye socket. He was already plotting what he'd need to say to his father to minimize the damage when his princess spoke again.

It gets worse, she warned. *When the lockdown went into effect, the Edict of Seven Voices—eight voices now—was automatically triggered. Unfortunately, it appears to have failed. The order to kneel was given, but my war demons reported hearing a countermand.*

It took every bit of Alexander's discipline not to curse. "Was it the Coward Queen?"

No, the Princess of War said. *This was a different voice, one I have not heard in a long, long time.* The presence in his head grew cold. *My eldest sister.*

Alexander did curse then. He'd *known* he should never have let that damn witch into the Hells. He'd only permitted it because Gilgamesh had specifically ordered him not to get in his new favorite's way. Alexander had also thought that Demetrios and *two* princesses would be enough to quell any bad behavior, but it looked like Prince Adrian had lived up to his miracle-working reputation. Now two-thirds of the Hells were no longer under Heaven's control, and as Crown Prince, Alexander was the one who was going to have to inform the king.

"Gather as many soldiers as you can and set up a defense on the stairs," he ordered. "I don't care if you have to pull every war demon you've got. We cannot allow this situation to spread any farther."

With respect, noble prince, the Princess of War said curtly, *the Upper Hells are already well defended, and the Eternal King requires the war demons' constant labor to maintain his schedule. If I move slaves away from the forges, it could set his plans back—*

"Any disruptions now will be minuscule compared to what will happen if we can't get this mess under control," Alexander insisted. "I'll take full responsibility. Just be ready to march the second I convince Father to open the doors."

Of course, my prince, she said, sweetly this time. *All shall be as you command.*

More like all would be his fault if things didn't work out, but Alexander had been doing this dance with his princess for a long, long, *long* time. The ability to shove all the planning and responsibility onto someone else was a huge part of why she'd bowed to Gilgamesh in the first place. So long as they both got credit for success, but only Alexander took the blame for failure, she'd execute his orders to the letter.

It was an arrangement that had served them both for centuries. Alexander just hoped he could survive his part of the bargain this time. He hadn't had to report a disaster of this magnitude to his father since the purges. If he'd been a younger, less established prince, this likely would've been his final audience, but Alexander's position running the minutiae of the Eternal Kingdom was what enabled his father to work on all his other projects. That made killing him extremely disruptive, and if there was one thing Gilgamesh hated even more than failure, it was inefficiency.

That was what had always saved Alexander in the past, so the Crown Prince put his faith in his father's love of uninterrupted operation and pulled on the quintessence flowing through his veins to speak the sorcery he only ever used in situations like this.

"The ringing of the golden bell sounds for a thousand miles," he whispered in his father's ancient language, his one remaining eye squeezed tight in concentration. "So shall the call of the faithful never fade to silence. Light of the Highest Heaven, give wings to my words so that even one as small as I may be heard. Bring my voice to the ears of my sacred king and let me know once again the blessing of his boundless wisdom."

The full verse was a little much. Leander could have done that spell with a single word, but Alexander was not his brother, and he didn't want to risk messing this up. He still wasn't entirely sure he hadn't. Sorcery wasn't one of his skills as a prince, but he must have gotten the incantation close enough. Only ten seconds after he finished the final word, a deep, familiar voice spoke like the King of Heaven himself was standing right behind him, whispering into his prince's ear.

"This had better be important."

"It is of greatest urgency, my king," Alexander assured him, bowing even though he knew this spell only transmitted voices. "I'm afraid we may have lost control over of the Middle and Lowest Hells."

There was a long pause, and then his father asked, "Who is 'we'?"

"As Crown Prince, the ultimate responsibility falls upon myself," Alexander acknowledged immediately. "The other princes involved were

Demetrios, whom I appointed to replace Leander in the Hells, and Prince Adrian."

He'd felt the great Gilgamesh's interest drifting as he gave his report, but the king's attention snapped back at that last one. "What was Adrian doing in the Hells?"

"He claimed it was critical for his work on the Queen of Pride's horns, sire."

Now Gilgamesh sounded amused. "That clever witch," he said with a chuckle. "He jumped to treason even faster than I expected."

"He did," Alexander agreed, clenching his fists under the avalanche of scrolls that were still falling onto his desk. "And now we have a problem. Whether he was directly involved in the incident or not, Prince Adrian was in the Hells when the emergency doors came down. Since you're the only one who can reverse a total lockdown, he's trapped down there until you choose to let him out."

"I know how my own security system works," his father said. "But I don't believe such measures are necessary at the moment."

"Not necessary?" Alexander repeated, shocked. "Sire, eight of the Nine Hells are inaccessible!"

"Which means the demons inside them are still trapped."

"For now," Alexander said. "But there's no guarantee they'll stay that way. My Crown Princess has also informed me that the Edict of Eight Voices was implemented and *failed*. The order to kneel was countermanded by the—"

"The Queen of Pride," Gilgamesh finished. "I'm aware."

Alexander fell into silent shock. When he didn't say anything for thirty seconds, his father began to laugh.

"Come now, Alexander," the king's disembodied voice said cheerily. "Surely you didn't think I was actually ignoring my youngest and most dangerous progeny? I left Adrian to his own devices precisely because I knew he'd work harder if he thought he was getting away with something. I'll admit I wasn't expecting a full resurrection, but Adrian's uncanny knack for pulling miracles out of his pointy hat is precisely why I picked him for this job in the first place."

"I see," said Alexander, even though he didn't. "In that case, how would you like me to proceed? I've ordered my princess to ready her war demons to retake the other Hells the moment you open the doors. She can also subdue and return Prince Adrian, if you so desire."

There was a long pause, like Gilgamesh was thinking it over, then the king said, "No."

"No?" the Crown Prince repeated nervously.

"I don't believe such measures will be necessary," his father clarified. "I've already gotten what I needed from Adrian. I gave him the impossible task of repairing the Queen of Pride's horns, and he pulled it off in less than a week! Next to an accomplishment like that, the fact that Pride's crown is on her head rather than in my hands is a minor complaint. We were overdue for a thinning of the demon herds anyway, so I say let it fall."

"I'm not sure I understand, sir," Alexander said with a swallow. "What am I letting fall?"

"All of it," Gilgamesh replied, his voice rich with long-awaited satisfaction. "The Hells are an evil whose necessity has finally come to an end. Prince Adrian, too, has already served his purpose. Asking more from him at this point would be greed unbecoming of a king. I've got enough to do what I need, so I think it's best for all involved if we cut our losses and proceed to Protocol Three."

The prince jolted so hard that he nearly fell out of his golden chair. "Protocol Three?" he repeated when he'd recovered. "But that will—don't you think that's a bit—"

"Alexander."

The voice in his ear was no louder than before, but the edge on it was enough to make the prince go still.

"Now is not the time to disappoint me," Gilgamesh warned. "Never forget that I didn't make you my Crown Prince merely because you're my eldest surviving son. You earned that position through your own merit when you proved that I could trust you to follow orders. I made myself quite clear just now. Do we need to discuss this further?"

"No, Father," Alexander replied, clutching his desk. "I understand you perfectly. I only hesitated because Leander is still undergoing punishment in the Lowest Hells. If I activate Protocol Three—"

"There you go, being soft on him again," the king scolded. "I told Leander before—*you* told him yourself that he wasn't getting any more chances. Your brother made his decisions knowing what the consequences would be. Anything that happens from here on is his fault, not yours."

"I understand that," Alexander whispered, clenching his hands tighter. "It's just... He's my favorite brother."

"I know," his father told him gently. "And I deeply respect that loyalty, but you can't make excuses for him forever. You're the one who thought this situation was so dire that you contacted me after I expressly stated I was not to be disturbed. Are you doubting your own judgment?"

"Of course not," Alexander said. "But—"

"Then handle the problem," Gilgamesh ordered. "Protocol Three. I'll be down to open the doors once I'm certain the treatment has been effective, and we'll go collect the Queen of Pride's repaired horns from her corpse together. Does that sound good?"

"Yes, Father," Alexander whispered.

"Excellent," Gilgamesh said. "You're my best, Alexander. I'm counting on you to see this through. We're so close to the future we've always wanted, the day we all get to finally escape our fate as the gods' eternal jailers. I'd hate to stumble here at the end because you allowed your pity for a foolish brother to get in our way."

The Crown Prince lowered his head. "I would never hinder your mission, my king," he said quietly. "It will be done."

"There's my loyal prince," his father whispered as his voice began to fade. "Well done, my son. Well done."

The praise vanished into nothing, leaving Alexander alone in his office once again. He sat in the silence for as long as he could bear, and then he pushed back his chair to open his top desk drawer.

Because fate was cruel, the first thing he saw when he pulled it open was the folded square of blue silk he'd confiscated from the broken Princess of Sorrow before he'd sent her to be reverted. The sight of it made him feel like a villain, but as his father had just reminded him, Leander had been warned many times. He'd chosen his fate with open eyes, and while Alexander would mourn him for the rest of his life, his hand didn't hesitate as he moved the folded fabric aside to grab the book-sized golden box beneath it.

Inside was a shaped velvet cushion with notches for three keys. Each was crafted from a different metal and marked with a different number. Alexander chose the last in the lineup: a heavy sin-iron skeleton key stamped with an elegant numeral 3.

When he had it in his fingers, he rose from his throne-like chair and carried the key to a small golden panel hidden in the corner of his office behind a curtain. The panel swung open the moment he touched it, revealing three keyholes. After a slight hesitation, Alexander fit the black key into the final slot and turned it, sealing his favorite brother's fate— and the fate of every other soul in the Hells—with a soft, resolute *click*.

Chapter 15

IT WAS A WEIRD trip back down to the Lowest Hell.

Bex was used to being the center of attention, but as they climbed down the white spiral through the conquered Middle Hells guard tower, every eye was locked on Nemini, which was honestly kind of fantastic. Bex had spent so long keeping her chin up and putting on a brave face that having someone else to soak up all those expectations for once felt like a vacation. The only hitch was that all those watching demons seemed to be staring at the Queen of Pride in mortal terror, which wasn't so great.

Bex wasn't even sure what they were frightened of. Other than her new giant horns, Nemini looked the same as she always did. She was no longer surrounded by shadow snakes—a move Bex had never seen her use before, but didn't know if that was because the snakes were a returned queen power or simply something Nemini had never felt the need to roll out during the twenty-four years Bex's current incarnation remembered—and her yellow eyes were barely glowing.

She'd never say so out loud, but Bex didn't even think the new Nemini looked all that queenly. She just looked like herself, which was always a little unsettling but nothing to trigger a reaction like this. You'd think she was coming down the stairs on a chariot drawn by demon-eating hydras from the way the crowd was plastering themselves against the walls.

"I don't see what everyone's so worked up about," Lys muttered from their spot on Adrian's broom, which the witch was graciously letting them use so the injured demon wouldn't have to walk. "You're much more impressive."

"It's not a competition," Bex whispered, keeping her eyes on the crowd of demons, who seriously looked like they were about to jump out the windows to get out of Nemini's way. "But this is super weird. Nemini just saved all our bacon. They were cheering for her just a few minutes ago, so why does everybody look like they think she's about to eat them?"

"Probably because she's an unknown," Lys speculated, rubbing their bandaged shoulder with a wince. "There've been stories about the Queen of Wrath coming to burn down the Hells since Gilgamesh made them, but the Queen of Pride is a new commodity, and the few legends that survive about her aren't exactly friendly."

"But she saved us," Bex insisted.

"So what?" Lys said. "You've saved tons of people, and most of them were scared of you after the fact. *I* was scared of you at first, because queens are freaking scary. You're practically gods. It's intimidating."

It *had* taken Bex a lot of work to get the demons in the Anchor to stop flinching when she walked by.

"Nemini's got it extra hard, too," Lys went on. "She's never had a warm personality, and that Medusa hairdo doesn't exactly scream 'compassionate ruler.' Let's just say I totally get why people are jumpy, though for my part, I'm pissed that she didn't tell us who she really was earlier."

"For all I know, she did," Bex said sadly. "Nemini could've told me the truth dozens of times, but I always died and forgot."

"*I* don't forget," Lys reminded her, scooting to the edge of the broom raven's straw wings. "I understand why she wouldn't tell you, but I've known Nemini since my first Bex kicked down the door and slit my warlock's throat. We raised you from a baby together *three times*. I thought we were parent trench buddies, but she never even dropped a hint!"

"Of course I didn't."

The sudden interjection made Bex jump. She hadn't realized Nemini was listening, but when she looked up, the Queen of Pride was staring over her shoulder with somber yellow eyes.

"Telling you the truth would only have led to disappointment for both of us," she told Lys quietly. "I was never the sort of queen you wanted to serve."

"You still could've said something," Lys grumbled, crossing their arms. "Though at least this explains why you only followed orders when you felt like it. And speaking of being a team player, can you get the lead out? I understand you've got to set a royal pace now or whatever, but we're still in enemy territory."

One of Nemini's snakes shot Lys a nasty look, but she did start walking faster, which was good enough.

"So what do we call you now?" Iggs asked nervously from where he was bringing up the rear with Adrian. "Do you have an official title or—"

"Nemini will continue to be fine," Nemini replied. "I have a name as all queens do, but since

Ishtar only gave it to me to force my obedience, I've never been fond of it." She looked over her shoulder again. "Rebexa named me 'Nemini' a thousand years ago. She's given me many names over the centuries since she always claims she has to call me something, but Nemini is the easiest for modern English speakers to pronounce, so let's just stick with that."

She finished with a smile that made Iggs shudder.

"I think I liked her better when she was deadpan," he whispered to Adrian. "At least then her snakes didn't smile with her."

"I'm more curious as to why she has snakes at all," Adrian whispered back. "Are they common for pride demons?"

"They're my sword," Nemini said without looking back this time. "My divine weapon was shattered at the same time as my horns, but unlike Ishtar's crown, Enki's loyal blade continued to follow me even though it was in pieces."

"Our swords are always loyal," Bex agreed, glancing at Drox's quiet ring. "And would the rest of you please knock it off? This is Nemini, not some stranger. If you've got a question, just ask. Don't whisper it behind her back."

She glared at her demons until they fell silent. When everyone looked properly chastised, Bex resumed descending the stairs with a huff.

"Thank you," Nemini said.

"Thanks nothing," Bex replied irritably. "That was ridiculous. They're acting like being a queen turned you into an alien."

Nemini shrugged. "I'm a very different queen from you."

"But not from yourself," Bex insisted. "As far as I'm concerned, you're still the same Nemini I've known since I was a baby, just with big new antlers and a bit more animated." She smiled. "Maybe you'll actually laugh at my jokes now."

"If you say something funny, I'll let you know."

Bex gave her an astonished look. "Was *that* a joke?"

Nemini answered with a silent shrug, proof that a crown didn't change everything.

They'd reached the floor of the Middle Hells by this point. General Kirok was still right where he'd been when Bex came through earlier, keeping an eye on the captured war-demon guards and struggling to impose order on the absolutely massive crowd that had gathered around the tower's base. Desh's key team must've been hard at work because everywhere Bex looked, there were unchained demons. The flooded floor around the tower was already packed, with more arriving every second. There had to be a small city's worth of people watching as Bex and Nemini descended the final step.

"How many demons do you think are down here?" she whispered to her sister.

"I don't know," Nemini replied, reaching up to touch her snakes. "My sword hasn't spoken to me since I broke it, so I can't count their names or cut their slave bands. The Hells are home to the vast majority of our kind, though, so I'd estimate several hundred thousand."

"It's higher than that," Lys said, floating over on Adrian's broom to butt into their conversation. "The Middle Hells are home to both Greed and Lust, which are the two most populous breeds of demon after War. Fear and Envy are in the middle, with Sorrow and Hate bringing up the rear. I don't know how many Pride demons there were, but Bex has been saying there were a hundred thousand Wrath demons trapped in Limbo since I met her."

"There's a lot less now, after what Gilgamesh did," Bex said angrily, clenching her fists.

"But they still survive," Lys said, giving her a hopeful smile. "Put them together with all the other demons, and the total population of the Hells is likely close to a million."

Bex whistled. A *million* demons. That wasn't much by human population standards, but it still sounded like an impossible number in more ways than one.

"How are we going to get them all out of here?"

"Who knows?" Lys said, then they smiled. "But I'm sure we'll figure it out. If we could manage an Anchor, we can do this."

Managing the Seattle Anchor had hardly gone smoothly, and twenty thousand demons was a *lot* less than a million. Bex didn't want to rain on Lys's optimism, though, so she kept her mouth shut and turned her attention to Kirok, who'd stepped forward to meet them at the place where the Middle Hells' staircase transitioned into the Lower.

"Great Queens," he said, lowering his horns once to Bex and then again to Nemini, which seemed to freak the former void demon out more than anything else so far.

"What's the situation?" Bex asked, reaching out to squeeze Nemini's hand before the crowd noticed her trembling.

"I've interviewed all the war demons who surrendered after their warlocks were killed," Kirok reported.

"And?" Bex asked.

"And it seems that the reason security in the Middle Hells is being neglected is because Gilgamesh has been running the forges in the Hell of War at full capacity for the last seven days. Apparently, the Eternal King personally rearranged the work schedule so that the stronger, more experienced demons would be on the forges while the younger, weaker demons were sent down here for guard duty."

Bex frowned. "I'm guessing that's not normal."

"It's the opposite of standard procedure," Kirok confirmed. "I thought the children we talked to when we first arrived were an anomaly, but with a few notable exceptions, all the demons working in the Middle Hells appear to be as young or younger."

Lys snorted. "So he's got child soldiers subjugating their fellow demons while the older ones slave in his forges? Sounds like typical Gilgamesh behavior to me."

"Do you know what he's using the forges to make?" Adrian asked as he pushed his way to the front.

General Kirok stiffened when he saw the witch's mirrored eyes. When Bex made a *go on* motion with her hands, though, the war demon grudgingly continued.

"According to the soldiers I just spoke to, the Eternal King commanded them to throw out all the sin iron currently in production and restart the forging process over with all new material. That was a week ago, and he's been working the entire Upper Hells around the clock ever since. He's even got war demons delivering the finished ingots to the palace by hand, which is highly unusual. Unless Gilgamesh needs it shipped to Earth for an Anchor, sin iron is typically kept within the Hells."

"I saw them carting it through the streets of the Holy City earlier," Adrian confirmed, tapping his wooden pinky finger worriedly against his chin. "I didn't see where in the palace they were taking it, but I bet if we follow the delivery line to the end, we'll find Gilgamesh. He likes to make the important things with his own hands."

Kirok's shoulders had been getting stiffer the whole time Adrian was talking, but that last sentence was apparently the final straw. "How do you know so much about the Tyrant King?"

"Because Gilgamesh forced me to work for him as well," Adrian replied matter-of-factly. "He never told me the real reason why, though, and that's a problem. If we're going to stop him, we need to know exactly what he's working on *before* he unleashes it. That's why I'm being so nosy. I need to figure out why he wanted me to repair the Queen of Pride's horns so badly and what that has to do with everything else."

Bex had just said she didn't care how Nemini got her horns back, but that confession still threw her for a loop.

"Wait," she said, whirling toward Adrian. "*Gilgamesh* is the reason Pride's crown was restored?"

"It's what he kidnapped me to do," Adrian told her with a nod. "Like I mentioned downstairs, Gilgamesh told me he needs the crowns of all nine queens to finish his great work, but I still don't know what that great work *is*. Going by other things he's said, my best guess is that he's trying to solve an infrastructure problem involved with keeping the gods in their graves. Other than using Wrath to make a better sin-iron chain, though, I don't know what that could be."

Bex scowled. "Could he be making a better chain?"

"Possibly," Adrian said. "But I don't think that's his endgame. He's lied to me about almost everything, but I still get the impression that the Eternal King isn't the sort who puts a bandage over a problem when he can solve the root cause."

"He did force my wrath demons to collect sin until they died from overwork," Bex agreed angrily. "He's clearly in a hell of a hurry for something, but what? And *why*? The gods have been dead for five thousand years. What could he possibly be in such a rush to—"

She cut off with a gasp when the floor of the Hells rumbled beneath her feet. The crowd of demons around them started screaming a second later, falling to the ground and covering their heads against whatever disaster was sure to follow, but nothing came. The ground kept rumbling, but no armies popped out to kill anyone, and eventually Bex got tired of waiting.

"Keep unlocking the people up here," she ordered Kirok, whose face was looking ashen despite his shiny bronze complexion. "We're going down to start evacuating Wrath and Pride."

When the general nodded, Bex turned around to address the enormous crowd cowering on the floor. "Don't let Heaven's rumbling scare you!" she yelled, bellowing as loudly as she could to make sure her voice reached all the way to the demons in the back. "The plan hasn't changed! We're all still getting out of here, so I want everyone who's capable of running to go out there and help the key teams. The rest of you clear the stairs so that the demons coming up from below have somewhere to go. General Kirok and Desh are in charge of this floor until the Queen of Pride and I return."

As always, yelling orders at terrified people left a bad taste in Bex's mouth, but it worked like a charm. The moment the demons had something to focus on other than their fear, they leaped into action, running off into the dark to help Desh's key team. Kirok himself took over clearing the tower so the demons who were still downstairs would have room to evacuate, yelling at the war demons—who did look really young, now that Bex was staring at them—to get off their asses and start forming a perimeter.

"All right," Bex said when everything was in motion. "Let's get moving."

"That was some fast work," Adrian noted as the five of them started going down the stairs again, this time at a jog. "How did you get everyone to listen without horns?"

"Everyone always listens to Bex," Lys said proudly, gripping Bran with both hands as the broom raven ramped up its speed. "But I think it's time you told us exactly what role you'd been playing in all of this, O Great Prince of Gilgamesh."

Adrian winced at the title. When Bex opened her mouth to tell Lys to lay off, though, he shook his head.

"They're not wrong," he said, fixing his eyes on the endless spiral of dark stairs ahead of them. "I am a prince with the white blood to prove it. I also repaired the Queen of Pride's horns at Gilgamesh's request, which I'm still not sure was the right thing to do."

He glanced at Boston as he said that last part, but while the cat looked conflicted, Bex's mind was already made up.

"Well, *I'm* sure it was right," she said stubbornly. "I know Gilgamesh is famously sneaky, but that doesn't change the fact that we'd all be on our knees waiting for warlocks to put us in chains right now if you hadn't fixed those horns and Nemini hadn't put them on her head. If something bad happens because of that, we'll deal with it, but I'll take being still alive, still together, and still in the fight over being cautious any day."

Adrian looked incredibly relieved to hear that, but Bex didn't have time to enjoy his smile. The mysterious shaking was getting stronger the deeper down they went, and there seemed to be a giant hole in the staircase ahead of them. She could jump over it, but Adrian was going to have a hard time. She was about to offer to carry him when the witch jumped onto his broom instead.

"Get on," he said as Lys scrambled to make room. "This way will be faster."

Bex could've gotten down by herself just fine, but she was loath to stop Adrian when he grabbed her hand and pulled her onto the broom next to him. Iggs hopped on as well, then Nemini, who reluctantly took a seat on the raven's wing where her giant new horns wouldn't poke anyone.

When they were all on board, Adrian put a hand on Boston to steady the cat against his shoulder and tapped his foot. The transformed broom dropped at the signal, plunging them down the center of the stairwell so fast, Bex didn't even notice they'd reached the bottom until Bran stopped hard enough to knock her off her feet. Adrian still had a firm grip on her hand, so she didn't actually go flying, but when Bex looked up to thank him, Adrian was staring ahead of them like he'd seen a ghost.

A second later, Bex saw why. The circular floor at the base of the Lowest Hells—which had been dry when they'd left a few minutes ago—was now covered in sludgy, black liquid. The surface had an oily gleam when she called her flames to light up her hand, but while it smelled strongly of the deathly rivers, it moved like no water Bex had ever seen. It looked like industrial waste, and while there was only a few inches covering the floor at the moment, Bex could see more oozing out of the seams of the sin-iron pipes that lined the walls. It looked like the whole stairwell was weeping, but the sludge was dripping fastest around the doors that led to the Lowest Hells.

All the breath left Bex's body. That black sludge was seeping into the Hell of Wrath. If the ground inside was already covered like the floor out here, then her people... her people...

"Bex, *no!*" Adrian yelled, grabbing her around the waist right before she leaped off the broom. "We don't know what it is yet!"

"But my demons are in there!" Bex howled, throwing out her flaming arms. "That sludge is covering the floor, and they *can't move!*"

Her scream was still echoing through the chamber when another frantic voice shouted back.

"Don't touch it!" yelled Prince Leander from where he'd climbed the stairs to get away from the black flood covering the floor. "That's Protocol Three!"

"What in the Hells is Protocol Three?" Bex screamed.

"It's a failsafe," the prince explained, waving frantically for Adrian to bring his broom over. "In the event of a security breach catastrophic enough to make Gilgamesh declare the Hells irrecoverable, the Crown Prince has three protocols he can use to ensure Heaven's survival. Protocol Three causes the least structural damage but is the most deadly. It triggers a backflow from the stagnation tanks, flooding the Hells from the bottom up with putrefied, concentrated sin."

"That's not sin," Bex insisted, stabbing her flaming finger at the sludgy water. "I've drunk from Ishtar's rivers all my lives, and that is *not* the water of death."

"It used to be," Leander said as he hopped onto the hovering broom with the rest of them. "After humanity's explosive population growth during the industrial revolution, the demon population of the Hells was no longer able to filter sin out of the rivers as fast as it was coming in. Gilgamesh didn't want to bother expanding, so he pumped the excess into tanks out in the Goddeath Wastes instead. They were designed to let the rivers stagnate, condensing the sins into a thick slurry that could be pumped back into the main river's flow and increase sin concentration for more efficient collection."

"That's horrible," Bex told him after a shocked pause.

"That's what you get when you have a frugal engineer for a king," Leander said, looking nervously down at the pool of thick, oily sludge. "Unfortunately, there's no way to stop it. Once Protocol Three's been activated, all the sludge tanks get dumped and the deathly rivers start flowing again at full force. That would not have been a problem a thousand years ago, but with Earth's current population, I'd say we've only got a few hours before this whole place floods."

He wasn't kidding. Bex could already see the torrents of freezing, deathly water gushing out of the bottom of every pipe like a broken fire hydrant. The disgusting foamy water on the floor had already risen a foot while they'd been talking, and the fumes coming off it were strong enough to burn the inside of Bex's nose. If it was that awful to breathe, she couldn't imagine what it must feel like on the skin, and she turned to Nemini in a rush.

"We have to get our people out of here. Can you order them to stand?"

"Of course," the other queen replied. "But are you sure you want me commanding your demons?"

"I don't care about that," Bex insisted. "They're too weak to stand on their own after what Gilgamesh did to them. If you don't use their names to force them up, they'll drown on their backs before they even get a chance to know they've been rescued."

She looked over her shoulder at the filthy water pouring through the broken doors into the Hell of Wrath, and her hand shot out to grab her sister's. "*Please*, Nemini! Make them stand up!"

Nemini clenched her jaw and stood without a word, pulling in the deep breath Bex recognized as the same one she also took before she said something big.

"*Demons of Wrath*," Nemini commanded in a queen's ringing voice. "By my own sacred name Netara, I order you to forget your exhaustion. Rise to your feet and march up the stairs to join your fellow children of Ishtar. Your queen will meet you there."

"Thank you," Bex said as the ringing command finished, giving her sister a frantic hug before she leaped off the broom into the freezing, filthy water. The concentrated sin started burning through her boots the moment her feet went in, but if her people were going to have to walk through this, then Bex was going to do it with them. She could already see the skeletal wrath demons rising to their feet inside the Hell. She was bashing her flaming shoulder against the busted doors to push them wider and make more room for the evacuation when Iggs splashed up beside her.

"You shouldn't be here!" Bex yelled at him. "The sin's still too strong! I can take it, but you—"

"If you're here, I'm here," Iggs said, transforming into his true, huge shape as he grabbed the mangled doors. "You never found my family in Limbo. That means they've got to be inside that Hell somewhere, and I'll let this toxic sludge burn off both my legs before I leave them behind."

There was nothing Bex could say to that. She just grabbed a door and started pushing with him, blasting her fire for extra power as she and Iggs forced the entrance all the way open to release the crowd of demons trapped inside.

They came out like an avalanche. Bex had had her doubts since ordering demons by their names only worked if they were physically capable of executing the command. Adrian must've been right about the power of demonic regeneration, though, because while they looked like a parade of skeletons, the demons of Wrath didn't slow down for anything. They rushed past her and Iggs without so much as a look, driven by the single-minded purpose Nemini's command had instilled in them to get up the stairs as quickly as possible.

"Thank Ishtar Gilgamesh never bothered to chain them," Bex panted as the disgusting water poured over her feet. "If we'd had to unlock everybody, the flood would've been over our heads before we made it halfway."

"I'm going to look for my family and help anyone who isn't able to stand," Iggs said as he sprinted past her into the Hell. "Tell Leander to put something over the hole we made in the stairs!"

"I will," Bex called after him, but Iggs was already gone, his huge red body disappearing into the dark hole Gilgamesh had buried their people in.

Seeing it caused Bex's fire to blaze up all over again, but she didn't have time to lose her temper. They still had another Hell full of demons to save, so the moment she was certain all the wrath demons were on their way to higher ground, Bex sloshed back through the putrid flood toward the rest of the team, who were still hovering on Adrian's broom in front of the sealed doors to the Hell of Pride.

"Did you get everyone out?" Adrian asked when she got close.

"Working on it," Bex replied, turning to face Leander, who'd also jumped into the water and was standing next to Nemini in front of the giant sealed doors.

"Hey, Leander," she said. "Got anything in your spell catalogue that will fix the hole in the stairs so my demons can get past?"

She'd said that pretty loud, but Leander didn't even turn around. Bex was about to ask him again, much less politely, when Boston suddenly leaped off Adrian's shoulder.

"I'll do it," the cat said as he landed on the last still-dry step of the spiral staircase. "I know several bridge-mending charms, and it looks like you've already got your work cut out for you."

"I'll help too," Lys said, flapping off the broom to join him.

"Are you sure you should be moving?" Bex asked nervously.

"They absolutely should not be!" Adrian yelled. "Lys, get back down here!"

"Sorry, darling, but you don't give me orders," Lys replied, blowing Adrian a kiss before holding out their arms to Boston, who jumped right in.

"Boston and I will handle the evacuation," they said, flapping steadily despite the pain Bex could see on their face. "The rest of you make sure the pride demons get out before we're all floating in the drink."

"Got it," Bex said. "Don't push yourself too far, Lys."

"I'll sit down before I fall down," they promised. "But only just. I've been lying around this whole operation. You can't expect me to stay bedridden and miss the fight I've been waiting for my entire life." They smiled at her one last time. "I'll be fine. Just make sure you follow me soon, or I'm coming back down here to get you."

"We'll make it," Bex said, waving at Lays as they carried Boston up the center of the stairwell toward the broken section near the top.

"They're going to reopen their wound," Adrian growled.

"Probably," Bex agreed. "But that's the challenge of working with Lys. You can give them all the orders you want, but they always manage to get their own way in the end. It's easier if you just learn to live with it."

Adrian was still scowling, but he didn't say anything else as he leaned down to help Bex out of the water.

She took his offered hand gladly. She'd been willing to stand in the sludge for her people's sake, but she wasn't going to hang out in it and burn all the skin off her legs if she didn't have to. She was delighted to let Adrian haul her onto his nice, dry, non-toxic broom. But when she bent over to examine the holes the caustic sludge had burned through her fatigues, Bran's wings tipped like a raft as Leander suddenly appeared beside her.

Bex lurched away with a yelp, nearly tumbling back into the water before she caught herself. "Don't do that!" she yelled at the prince, clutching her heaving chest. "Seriously, what is your problem?"

"We all have too many of those to count at the moment," Leander replied, his gaunt face deadly serious as he crouched down to look her in the eyes. "I need your help."

Bex didn't feel like doing anything for someone who'd just scared the life out of her and didn't even seem sorry about it. Leander had always been a strangely awkward man, though, and he *had* done a lot for them since she'd pulled him out of the Lowest Hells, so Bex forced herself to shove her ego and listen.

"What sort of help do you need?"

"I need it from both of you, actually," Leander said, flicking his mirrored eyes to Adrian, who was hovering at Bex's side. "I can undo the seal over the doors to the Hell of Pride, but in return, I need you to help me get someone out."

"There's no need to make it transactional," Bex grumbled. "I was already planning to get everyone out."

"I'm aware," Leander said. "But I also know you're in a hurry, and I believe these individuals will not be able to walk on their own even if the new queen orders them. They will likely be quite difficult to find as well, which is why I'm speaking to both of you."

He stood up to face Adrian. "I know the witches of the Blackwood are adept at finding spells such as the one I saw your familiar using earlier. I want you to cast that same type of spell again using this."

The prince flicked his hand like a stage magician. When his palm came back around, he was holding a woman's severed hand with a black ring gleaming on its third finger. As always, Bex recognized her sister's hand immediately, but she wasn't sure which sister's hand she was looking at until Leander spelled it out.

"This is all that remains of the Princess of Hate," he said. "I picked it up after I evaporated her with one of the Royal Verses to give myself a starting point."

"A starting point for what?" Adrian asked, confused. Bex, however, had already guessed.

"You're looking for Mara's body."

"And you're cleverer than Gilgamesh gives you credit for," Leander said as he held out the hand to Adrian. "Mara and I searched for her real body for years without success. Since we'd investigated so extensively, we knew it had to be somewhere that even a prince and princess of Heaven couldn't access. There are only two such locations in all my father's domains: the king's personal vault at the top of the Highest Heaven, and the bottom of the Lowest Hell, which is a place so horrid that even Gilgamesh himself cannot enter without becoming trapped."

Bex's eyes were huge by the time he finished. "You think the queens' bodies are in the Hell of Pride?"

"I'm certain of it," Leander said. "Father would never keep the bodies of his enemies close to where he sleeps. Also, the void left by the Queen of Pride's shattering is the only thing strong enough to keep the daughters of Ishtar from popping back up like you do."

His face softened. "My clever Mara was the one who realized those two facts first. She wanted to search this place herself, but princesses cannot enter the Hells for extended periods without risking their minds due to the excess of demon suffering causing cognitive dissonance with Gilgamesh's loyalty programming. I tried to find a safe way inside dozens of times while I was serving as Prince of the Hells, but I couldn't put so much as a foot through the holes in the ceiling without succumbing to the void demons' effects. When my bastard of a father finally threw me all the way in, I thought I might at least be able to catch a glimpse of where her body was being stored, but I remember nothing except fear and falling from the moment Gilgamesh banished me to the moment you pulled me out."

"Be that as it may," Adrian said uncomfortably. "This isn't going to work. I can cast the finding spell no problem, but if I do it using this hand, the magic will lead me to the Queen of Hate's body, not Mara's."

"That should still be close enough," Leander insisted. "Gilgamesh is too cheap to build nine separate prisons. Wherever Hate's body is hidden, the others will be as well. I'd bet my life on it."

"You're betting all our lives," Bex said, looking pointedly at the rising water. "I understand what you're feeling, Leander. They're my sisters too. But I have to prioritize the living over the dead, and we don't have much time before—"

"I know," he cut her off. "Believe me, I know. If things weren't so desperate, I would never have stooped to asking for help from a witch."

Adrian crossed his arms over his chest with a huff. "If you need me so badly, maybe you shouldn't talk about witches like we're trash."

"Forgive me if being sacrificed to Gilgamesh as a child in exchange for the safety of a few trees has left me with a poor opinion of our mother's profession,"

Leander replied, giving his youngest brother a cutting look before returning his gaze to Bex.

"Please, Queen of Wrath," he said as he lowered his head. "I'm begging you, help me save my Mara. I also need you to convince your other sister to move. I can't get to the seal while she's standing in front of it, and we're running out of time."

Now that he'd mentioned it, Nemini was being very quiet, even for her. They didn't have time to dawdle, so Bex motioned for Leander to wait and hopped off the broom again, landing with a splash in the now knee-deep water beside her sister.

"Hey," she said softly. "Are you okay?"

"No," Nemini whispered, her whole body shaking. "I can feel them again." She shook even harder as she cringed back from the sealed doors. "They *hate* me."

"They don't hate you," Bex said, reaching up to give Nemini's violently shaking shoulder a squeeze. "They've just been through a lot. I'm sure they'll calm down once—"

"You don't understand," Nemini insisted. "They hated me long before I broke them." She bit her lip. "I... was a bad queen to them."

"But you don't have to *stay* a bad queen," Bex told her with a smile. "I don't know what you were like before, but the Nemini I know is a good person who never stopped loving me even though I kept dying and forgetting her. I made you fight a war you didn't care about and never took a word of your advice, but you still looked after me. That's a person with the potential to be a great queen if she wants to be, but everything starts with letting Leander open this door, because the people of Pride aren't going to change their minds about you if you leave them locked inside a flooding room."

Nemini blinked and looked down at the black water covering her legs like she was noticing it for the first time. Her yellow eyes went huge after that, and she quickly moved out of the way.

Leander swept in the moment the way was clear. He raised his hands as he did so, hovering his fingers an inch above the giant, cuneiform-covered seal that held the doors shut, which looked a lot nastier than the simple metal bolt that had been used to lock the Hell of Wrath.

"What happens if you touch it?" Bex asked curiously.

"A whole host of excessively unpleasant things," the prince replied, closing his eyes. "Please be quiet. I need to concentrate."

Bex nodded and dutifully zipped her lips, stepping back to stand beside Nemini, who was staring at the prince with a mix of hope and dread. When nothing happened for a solid minute, Bex decided to hop back up on the broom and wait next to Adrian instead.

"*Please* tell me you're making progress," she whispered. "If I have to spend another second watching your brother do nothing while toxic water creeps up my legs, I think I might explode."

"That depends on your definition of progress," Adrian whispered back, never taking his eyes off what looked like a small wooden carving of a cat covered in pine sap and black cat hair that he was attempting to balance on the palm of the princess's severed hand.

"Finding spells are famously forgiving, but we've already used most of the supplies Boston brought from the Blackwood. I'm down to the dregs on this one, and the Queen of Hate's hand is *not* being a cooperative component."

"Shocker," Bex joked, sitting down next to him. "Can I help? I'm a queen too."

"True," he said, flashing her a warm smile. "But as lovely as it is, your body's already here, not trapped in there with the ones we're trying to find."

He tilted his head at the doors Leander was still silently working on, but Bex was too flustered by the compliment to follow.

"What are you going to do, then?" she asked, forcing herself to stay on target because this was *not* the appropriate time for blushing.

"What I always do," Adrian told her brightly. "Improvise. Here, hold this."

He shrugged out of his black witch coat and plopped the garment in her lap before Bex could react. When it was off, he rolled up his shirtsleeves, which were far more wrinkled than Bex had ever seen Adrian allow them to become. Seriously, what had they been doing to him up in Heaven? Keeping him locked in a cage for seven days? She was still imagining horrors when Adrian pulled out his pocketknife and slashed the inside of his arm just below the elbow.

"What are you doing?" she cried, but the alarm in her voice quickly turned to horror when she saw the white liquid dripping from his wound.

"What is *that*?"

"Quintessence," Adrian said, giving her a guilty look. "I told you I was a prince, white blood and all."

The expression on her face right then must have been a sight, because Adrian scrambled to explain.

"It's not entirely bad. One of the ways Gilgamesh lured me into his trap was by teaching me how to use his magic. It was the only promises he actually made good on. I can use sorcery as well as witchcraft now, which is why I'm able to do *this.*"

He tilted his arm, allowing the shimmery white blood to drip down his arm onto the carved cat and the princess's severed hand that it was standing on. The result was a mix of woodsy-smelling witchcraft combined with the sudden pulse of magic Bex had always associated with the moment right before attack sorcery hit her in the face. She didn't like the blend at all, but when Adrian reached down to close the princess's fingers around the bloody cat, the lifeless fist clenched tight as a stone. It stayed like that for a solid ten seconds, and then its index finger snapped back out as fast as a switchblade to point straight at the door Leander was still trying to open.

"Voilà!" Adrian said, looking exceedingly pleased with himself as he rubbed his hand over the cut on his arm to get the healing started. "Instant daughter-of-Ishtar compass! And it looks like Leander was correct. The queens' bodies *are* in there, or at least the Queen of Hate's is."

That was enough to get Bex's heart thumping as she handed him his coat back. Bringing her sisters back to life was the stuff of dreams, but it was hard to get really excited when she could hear her fleeing wrath demons moving slower and slower as they were forced to wade through deeper and deeper water. Iggs was doing a good job ferrying out the ones who couldn't walk just like he'd promised, but the polluted water was up to the demons' knees when Bex looked back, forcing them to strain for every step when they needed to be running.

It was a delay Bex wasn't sure they could afford, especially when they hadn't even started getting the pride demons out yet. She hadn't counted how many void demons she'd stepped over during her first trip to the Lowest Hell, but Nemini's people had been packed in like sardines, and there were still all the banished demons lying in piles that she hadn't had time to pull out. The caves down here were small compared to the massive Middle Hells upstairs, but that was a *lot* of demons left to evacuate, and the water wasn't showing any sign of slowing down. Bex was about to say screw it and tell Leander to get out of the way so she could bash the doors open, cursed lock be damned, when the prince's whole body jolted like he'd been hit by lightning.

The clay seal started to shake next, its cuneiform-covered surface folding in on itself like origami paper until it had formed a shape that resembled a man's smiling mouth.

"Welcome," it said, speaking Ancient Sumerian in a voice that sounded very much like Gilgamesh's. "I have no eyes, so you must say. Which of my sons is foolish enough to set foot in the place where none should tread?"

"Leander," Leander replied.

"Leander is in disgrace," the seal informed him. "Try again."

"Try this," the prince growled as the hand he'd been hovering over the seal began to glow. "Royal Verse number one, Command of the King."

"You are no king," the seal informed him calmly as the light grew brighter.

"If you didn't want to share your power, then you shouldn't have forced the work of your empire onto your sons," Leander replied through gritted teeth as sweat poured down his face. "Now, *open!*"

He thrust his glowing fingers wide, and the light in his hand flashed like silent lightning. When the glare faded, the transformed seal crumbled to dust. The last of it fell off the door as Bex watched, sinking into the rising water with a final disappointed sigh.

"Pompous old stick," Leander muttered, shaking his hand, which looked bright red and burnt. "Did you finish the finding spell?"

"Yes," Adrian said belatedly when he realized that question was for him. "It's already going."

"Good," Leander said as he dug his burned fingers into the crack of the unsealed—but still handleless—doors. "Then let's be off."

He yanked the heavy door as he finished, prying it open a fraction of an inch before doing the short-ranged teleport thing Bex remembered from the fight on the chain to reappear on Adrian's broom. Bex was about to ask him why he hadn't opened it all the way when the doors burst open on their own, thrown apart by a wave of filthy, black water. It crashed into the stairwell in a ten-foot black wall, covering Nemini before Bex even realized what was happening.

"*Nemini!*" she screamed, running to Bran's edge to dive into the water after her. Before she actually made it off the broom, though, her sister burst out of the wave on a pillar of hissing snakes, her yellow eyes flashing with fury as she raised her queen's voice.

"*Children of Pride!*" she shouted over the crashing water. "*Lift your heads!* The age of humiliation and defeat is over! Your queen has returned! Follow my voice, and I will lead you to safety!"

The booming words sailed into the darkness. Now that the initial wave had spilled out, Bex was able to see why there'd been such a build-up. The Hell of Pride wasn't just the Lowest Hell because it was the worst. It was literally the lowest point, with a floor that was four big steps below the level Nemini was standing on. The sealed doors had also acted like a dam, letting the flood build up inside.

The result was a water level several feet higher than the knee-deep lake Bex's wrath demons were pushing through. Now that the Hell of Pride was open, though, the water at the bottom of the stairwell was rising swiftly as the two spaces equalized. The churning current was so strong it knocked some of the weaker wrath demons over. Fortunately, Iggs was there to help them back up and keep them moving.

Nemini's demons were not so fortunate. The queen's command was still echoing through the cavern of the Lowest Hell, but Bex didn't see a single horned head popping out of the water.

"Are we too late?" she whispered, jumping down to land in the now thigh-deep water next to her sister. "I don't see—"

"Bexa," Nemini interrupted. "Can you light your bonfire?"

"What?" Bex asked, confused. "Oh, sure, I can do that, but why do you—"

"Just light it, please," Nemini said as she stepped to the side, out of sight of the door.

Bex still didn't understand what was going on, but she did as Nemini asked, covering her entire body in blazing flames. The firelight filled the dark Hell in front of her like a sunrise, and as it glittered off the black water, a wave of horned heads broke the surface in reply.

"You came!" they cried in the ancient tongue of the Riverlands, coughing vile water out of their lungs as they swam toward Bex's light. "You came just like you promised!"

Their shouts formed a joyous chorus, but Bex backed away in horror. She was opening her mouth to tell the demons they were wrong, that it had been their queen who'd come, not her, when Nemini reached out to touch her flaming shoulder.

"It's all right," she said in a voice that sounded equal parts sad and relieved. "My people never listened to me unless I made them, but they responded to your fire even when they were lost in the void. It's better that they have a new light to run to than an old queen dragging them back to a past neither of us enjoyed."

"It's *not* better," Bex snarled, smacking her hand away. "These are *your* people!"

Nemini blinked. "So? You didn't mind me giving orders to your people."

"That was different," she insisted. "You're the one who ate a wave to get to them. You should get the credit for—"

"I don't need their credit anymore," Nemini said, her yellow eyes lighting up as if those words were a surprise to her as well. "It's just like you said on the stairs. I'm still Nemini. The me I found in the void is still here, and unlike Queen Netara, she doesn't need her people's worship."

Bex shook her head wildly. "But—"

"If your light keeps the demons of Pride alive, then I'm doing a better job as their queen right now than I ever did before," Nemini said, her voice calm and matter-of-fact. "I can keep doing it, too. Here." She held out her hands with the palms cupped together. "Can you give me some of your fire?"

Bex had no idea. She'd never tried giving her fire to someone else before. Nemini was asking like it was normal, though, so she must've done it in the past. Sure enough, when Bex pressed her flaming hands into her sister's, a beach-ball-sized sphere detached from her bonfire to float like a magic torch over Nemini's cupped fingers.

"There," Nemini said, holding the new fire up like a signal flare. "Now they'll see me as you, which means you're free to go with Adrian. That's what you want, right?"

Not when she put it that way. Obviously, Bex wanted to stay with Adrian and go find her sisters. If Leander was right about Gilgamesh burying them down here, then there was a good chance the other daughters of Ishtar were waking up just like all the pride demons that were now jumping out of the water like schooling fish. If that was true, and she could get to them, then Bex would finally have the allies she needed to bring down Gilgamesh. It was literally the

stuff of her childhood dreams, but she couldn't reach
for it, not when Nemini's demons were—

"You don't have to do everything by yourself,"
Nemini said quietly. "I don't mind being a fake bonfire
if it gets my people to safety, which might just be the
most queenly thing I've ever said."

"But I just promised to set you *free* of being
queen," Bex reminded her. "I can't just turn around
and let you—"

"It's fine," Nemini insisted. "I'm not doing this as
queen. I'm doing it to help you. The fact that I'm also
being a responsible monarch is just a byproduct, so
stop arguing and go before the water gets any higher."

"But—"

"*Go,*" Nemini said again as she lifted her ball of
fire higher. "And put yourself out. You're confusing
people."

The crowd of demons following Nemini's torch
out of the water *was* starting to drift toward Bex's fire
instead. It was slowing down the evacuation, so Bex
snuffed herself out, though she didn't take her eyes off
Nemini.

"Thank you."

"What are older sisters for?" Nemini replied,
moving her ball of Bex's fire toward the stairs so the
fleeing demons—Nemini's demons, even if they didn't
know it—could find the way out.

"She's certainly more opinionated now that she's
got her horns back," Adrian said as he reached down to
help Bex climb back onto the broom.

"She is," Bex agreed as she took his hand. "But I
like it. I always knew she cared too much to actually
care about nothing."

Adrian pulled her up with a smile, but when he opened his mouth to reply, Leander cut him off.

"If you two are finished chatting," the prince said, tapping his foot irritably on the broom's beak.

"Right," Bex said, dropping into a crouch. "Let's go."

Adrian nodded and tapped his foot on Bran's back. The broom surged forward the second he gave the signal, shooting over Nemini's head like a raven-beaked arrow into the rapidly filling cavern of the darkest, lowest Hell.

Chapter 16

Since bex had put out her bonfire to avoid confusing the Pride demons desperately swimming toward Nemini, they were soon flying in the dark. Leander immediately summoned the blue flames he'd used to light their way before in the Founders' Tunnels, but his sorcery barely penetrated the deep blackness of the flooded cavern. It wasn't the all-consuming void Bex had fallen through a few hours ago, but the walls and ceiling of the cavern were still caked in eons of black, built-up sin, and the water was even darker. The flood was so filthy that it struggled to reflect light, leaving them flying over a choppy darkness that looked more like soot than liquid.

"This is dangerous," Bex muttered, squinting through the inky void. "I'm normally great in the dark, but I can't see past Bran's beak right now. How do we know we're not about to fly into a wall?"

"Because Father wouldn't hide them by a wall," Leander replied, holding his blue flames with one hand while he clutched the pointing princess hand Adrian had made for him in the other. "Turn two degrees to the right."

Bex couldn't see Adrian's face through the pitch-blackness, but she still knew he was scowling as he steered his broom in the direction Leander demanded.

"You know, it wouldn't kill you to say pleas—"

"There!" Leander cried, throwing out his blue-flame-wreathed hand. *Seven Walled City!*

A huge splash sounded through the darkness ahead of them, forcing Adrian to yank his broom to a stop before they crashed. He made it just in time, landing Bran's raven on the top of one of the giant stone rings Bex remembered from her fight with Leander on the chain. The prince had already vaulted off, his body vanishing instantly into the sucking dark.

"Light!" he yelled impatiently.

"I don't take orders from princes," Bex snapped, peering over the edge of the broom to try to get an idea of where they were. She thought it was near the back of the Hell, but they'd been flying blind through the dark, so who could really say? The bonfire she'd given Nemini was just a tiny star in the distance, though, and she didn't hear any demons splashing through the water.

Bex hoped that was because they'd all swum to safety already and not because they'd drowned. Whatever the reason, there didn't seem to be any demons who might get confused in the immediate vicinity, so Bex took a chance and lit herself up, filling the flooded cavern with warm, brilliant light.

The sight waiting for her when she could see again was both exactly and nothing like she'd expected. She'd been right—they *were* almost at the back of the cavern—but it was much farther away than she'd anticipated. The Hell of Pride actually narrowed to a point back here, meaning they really would've flown into a wall if they'd gone even slightly off course. Bex didn't see any horned bodies floating in the water, which was a huge relief, but she also didn't see what Leander had stopped them for. There were no landmarks, no monuments, no entrance to a hidden prison. It looked like the prince had cast his seven giant walls in the middle of nowhere for nothing.

"Hey," she said, looking at Leander, who was standing on top of the innermost stone circle. "Are you *sure* this is—"

"Yes," he snapped, holding up the princess's pointing hand. "Even without my brother's witchcraft, I'm close enough to feel the sorcery now." He turned to squint at Bex through the glaring firelight. "How much water can you evaporate?"

"I don't know," Bex said, hopping over the tops of the walls like stepping stones to join him. "I've never tested. I can melt sin iron, though, so probably a—"

"Do it," he ordered, moving down the circle to stand next to Adrian, who was busy talking to his wet and obviously miserable broom in a calm, soothing voice.

She shot the prince a nasty look, but now wasn't the time to harp on his attitude. The water was rising higher as she watched, so Bex shoved her personal anger to the back burner and got to work, blasting the water trapped inside of the innermost ring of the Seven Walled City with the hottest fire she could produce.

The resulting steam explosion almost blasted her into the ceiling. She managed to avoid a crash at the last second, kicking off the black stone to land back on the spell's outermost wall instead. When she was sure she wouldn't pitch over into the now very deep-looking lake on the other side, Bex hopped back across the tops of the walls to see what she'd uncovered.

The inside of Leander's final stone ring was only ten feet across. Between the heat of her flames and the force of the steam explosion, Bex had managed to remove most of the water, revealing nine dark objects arranged in a circle. It looked a bit like the ring of standing stones Adrian had set up in front of his cottage, except these weren't boulders. They were perfectly smooth, rectangular pillars with a weird hump at the top. Each one was taller than Leander and metallic-sounding when the prince jumped down to bang on one with his fist. It wasn't until he started feeling the sides, though, that Bex realized the pillars were shaped like sarcophagi. Nine black tombs standing on their ends, facing each other in a silent circle.

"Great Forest," muttered Adrian as he looked up from his broom at last. "Are those—"

"They're what we're here for," Leander said as he moved frantically from coffin to coffin. "Queen of Wrath, help me!"

Bex jumped down at once, wincing when she landed in the ankle-deep sin sludge that was left at the bottom. It felt like she was walking through acidic oil-spill mud, and that was with her boots on. Leander must've had it ten times worse with his bare feet, but the prince didn't even seem to notice. He was too busy pressing his hands against the closest coffin, speaking words of sorcery so fast that Bex's mediocre command of Sumerian couldn't possibly keep up.

Whatever he was saying, it didn't seem to be working. Now that Bex was in front of them, she could see that the coffins were made of smooth-polished sin iron. There was nothing carved into their faces, no names or inscriptions or even warnings. They also had no hinges or latches, not even a seam. If the finding spell Adrian had made out of the Princess of Hate's hand hadn't been pointing directly at one of them, Bex would've sworn they were standing in a ring of nine solid lumps.

"We know which one Hate's in, at least," Adrian observed from the wall above. "But how do they open?"

"They were never made to," Leander said, panting from all the sorcery that hadn't worked. "These were supposed to be eternal tombs, which means we'll have to break them."

"You'd better do it," Bex said, stepping back. "Without my sword, I'm not exactly a precision tool."

"I can't," Leander said, shaking his head. "Only divine creations can cut sin iron once it's been forged. It has to be you."

"Are you crazy?" Bex cried, holding up her flaming hand. "I'm a blowtorch, and those coffins don't have room for error. If I melt my way in, I'll cook them."

"If the daughters of Ishtar could be destroyed by mere flames, my father wouldn't have needed to lock them down here," the prince argued. "Have faith in your mother's work and burn. Just do it quick. We're running out of time."

Bex didn't need him to tell her that. She could hear the slosh of the waves breaking against the Seven Walls. The water outside had to be up to her neck by now. If they were going to get everyone and get out before the flood covered the door and trapped them, she needed to get a move on, but the coffins looked so *hard*.

Bex reached out to brush her burning fingers against their shiny black surface, wishing for the millionth time that Drox was awake. Her sword could've sliced the sin-iron coffins open in an instant, but his ring was still silent on her finger. That left brute force, so Bex closed her eyes and focused on getting mad.

It didn't take her long. Just thinking about the black boxes Gilgamesh had sealed her family inside had Bex's fire roaring like a jet engine in seconds, but the flood he'd sent to drown her people was what stomped her pedal to the floor. The thought of her people lying exhausted on the ground as the deadly water poured in, the thought of Nemini's people swimming for their lives after five thousand years of torment, the thought of all the demons upstairs fighting so hard for their freedom only to be locked in and drowned like rats. Every crime was a log on her fire, stoking Bex into an inferno so intense that the last of the water left inside the walls turned to steam, leaving the sludgy layer of sin mud dry as an old desert under her boots.

When she was as hot as she could get without risking tipping over the edge and burning out of control again, Bex slammed her glowing fist into the black tomb closest to her. The sin-iron sarcophagus rang like a bell when she struck it, rattling her bones and acidifying the breath in her lungs with the reek of molten sin. Within seconds, it was nearly impossible to breathe, but Bex didn't stop. She just kept pounding, slamming her fist into the sin iron over and over until, with a *snap* that echoed through the flooded Hell, the heated metal broke under her hand, and the black prison cracked open like an egg.

Bex leaped back immediately, clutching her white-hot fist to her chest so she wouldn't accidentally burn whoever was inside, but the body she'd been hoping for didn't fall out into her arms. It couldn't, because while the outside of the coffin had been as smooth as a river stone, the interior was lined with hundreds of swordlike sin-iron spikes. It looked like the inside of an Iron Maiden, and pinned on those spikes like a butcher bird's victim was a body.

A woman's hornless, handless body covered in black blood.

"Sister," Bex whispered as she stumbled forward. "*Sister!*"

She reached out desperately, but Leander beat her to it. He rushed the broken coffin, ignoring the spikes that stabbed his unprotected arms as he dug his hands under the woman's body and yanked it free. Her face was so damaged that Bex couldn't make out her features, but she still recognized her on the same instinctive level she'd recognized every daughter of Ishtar except Nemini. Unlike Nemini, though, this queen's name wasn't shattered. Bex might even be able to remember it once her sister's face was healed enough to recognize. Ishtar's gift of regeneration was already pulling her broken features back together when Leander unceremoniously dumped her body on the ground.

"*What are you doing?*" Bex roared, darting to grab the queen before she hit the filthy floor. "That's my sister!"

"It's not Mara," the prince said, looking wild-eyed at the eight other coffins. "Do the next one. Quickly!"

Bex bared her teeth and clutched her sister's body to her burning chest. She was still trying to find somewhere to put her where her wounds wouldn't touch the filthy sin on the floor when Adrian's hands came down from above.

"I'll take her," he said, lying down on the top of the wall so he could hold his arms out to Bex. "Go ahead and do the others. We're running out of time."

The urgency in his voice snapped Bex out of her protective trance. She handed her sister's body to Adrian at once, pushing her up from below while the witch hauled her to the top of the wall. The moment she was sure he wouldn't drop her, Bex let go and moved to the next sin-iron tomb that Leander was impatiently tapping his finger against.

It took less time to crack the second one now that she knew what she was doing, but not by much. Even when she was burning her hottest, the sin iron was hard, thick, and pure. It also didn't crack cleanly every time. Sometimes she had to melt her hand all the way through and pull the prison apart piece by piece, which took a while. There was also the problem that not every tomb was full. Since she, Nemini, and the Queen of War still had their original bodies, three of the caskets were empty, but it was impossible to tell which ones until she broke them open. They were all filled with spikes, though, and the more Bex thought about that, the less sense it made.

"Why do you think Gilgamesh did this?" she asked Adrian when he reached down to take the third body that wasn't Mara's from Bex's arms. "Does he just enjoy their suffering?"

"I don't think that's it," Adrian said as he carefully accepted the bloody queen. "Gilgamesh considers demons beneath him. He hates the gods, but I can't imagine him building something this expensive just to torture a bunch of already defeated queens."

He looked at the next coffin Leander was pressing his ear against. "I bet this is just the most efficient way to keep them under control. Ishtar's daughters are famously hard to kill, but being stabbed full of sin-iron spikes would immobilize anyone. Add in the void demons pulling their minds into the abyss and you have a simple and effective prison. Trademark Gilgamesh."

"You don't have to sound so impressed," Bex muttered, calling her fire back to her fists to get cracking on the next coffin.

The water started coming in again before she finished. By the time Bex's fist finally punched through to the center where the spikes were, the sin-polluted slime was pouring over the top of Leander's protective walls in sheets. That sarcophagus turned out to be empty, so Bex moved on to the next one, sloshing over to it through the now knee-deep water while Leander paced frantically beside her.

"Hurry," he begged. "*Hurry.*"

"I'm going as fast as I can," Bex growled, turning the water around her to steam as she slammed her fist into the tomb's shiny black surface.

At least she knew this would be the last. They'd already hit the three empties, and there was only one sarcophagus left. Now that the flood was coming over the walls in buckets, though, fear was starting to eat at the edges of Bex's rage. If the water was high enough to overcome Leander's Seven Walled City, it also had to be almost to the top of the doors out. They were very, *very* close to getting trapped down here, but Bex was so close to being finished. Just one more inch and—

"There!" she cried as her fist went through to the spike-filled pocket. The coffin didn't crack like the others, but she was still able to wedge her arm inside, bracing her leg against the wall to pry the black tomb open like a bear trap, revealing the bloody prize inside.

"Mara," Leander whispered, his voice cracking. "*Mara!*"

Her face was as damaged as all the others, so Bex couldn't say if she looked like the princess from the bridge or not. Leander had already eliminated all the others, though, so there was only one queen left that she could be. Sure enough, when the prince clutched her body to his chest, Bex saw a bloody strand of the long, straight, black hair she vaguely remembered falling around Mara's smiling face. It *had* to be her, and now that the job was done, they had to get out.

"Come on!" Adrian yelled from where he was floating on his broom above the now completely-flooded edge of the stone rings. "We have to go!"

Bex didn't wait to be told twice. Leander had already Fifty Steps of the Pilgrim'ed himself up with Mara's body in his arms. Bex would've blasted herself after him, but thanks to the water pouring in over the top, the cylinder of the innermost wall was now flooded up to the center of her chest. It couldn't douse her magical fire, but it was a lot harder to trigger the gas-expansion explosion she used to move herself around.

There was also the sin to consider. Bex was normally pretty resistant to sin toxin, but she'd been exposed to the polluted water for a while now, and all that burning had left her exhausted. Now that that flood was lifting her booted feet off the ground, she was quickly realizing that she didn't have enough strength left to tread water fully clothed. She tried climbing the walls, but they were smooth and coated with slippery black grime from the freezing, polluted water pouring over them. It poured into Bex's face as well, leaving her drenched and gasping. She was scrambling to find something to brace her feet against when a pair of strong hands reached down to hook her under the arms.

"Gotcha," Adrian's strained voice said as he hauled her out of the water. She landed on Bran's back next, gasping on the broomgrass like a landed fish next to the neatly arranged bodies of her unconscious sisters.

"That's everyone!" Leander's voice cried somewhere to her left. "*Go!*"

"What do you think I'm doing?" Adrian growled, hunkering low over Bex and digging his fingers into Bran's bristles as the faithful broom shot them forward.

Bex relaxed into the familiar stiff bristles as she felt them start to move. She'd been so desperate to get out of the water, she hadn't noticed her fire had gone out until she realized she couldn't see. This left her body cold and shivering, but Adrian was warm as a blanket above her. She'd thought that was why he was doing it until she heard something scrape uncomfortably close to her head.

When she managed to get the flames going again, Bex saw it was the top of the Hell. The cavern's ceiling was flying by just a few inches above Adrian's uncovered head. He had his hat off and was lying flat on top of her, giving Bran room to work as the broom frantically wove them around the rocky juts and other uneven bits that hung down from the cave's roof.

It was an incredibly dangerous way to fly, especially in the dark, but there was no other option. The rest of the cavern was already filled with choppy, foam-topped, polluted water, leaving them racing through a rapidly closing gap. Bex couldn't even see Nemini's light at the exit anymore, assuming there was still an exit at all. For all she knew, they'd already been flooded in. She couldn't do anything about it, though, except lie flat and hold on as Adrian pushed his broom faster and faster, shooting between the water and the roof like a bullet until, at last, Bex saw a glimmer of fire through a pointed gap she recognized as the top of the Hell's arched doorway.

"*Get flat!*" Adrian yelled, rolling off Bex to press himself into the broom beside her. Leander did the same, shielding Mara's head with his body as Bran hurtled toward the shrinking exit. For a heart-dropping second, Bex wasn't sure if they were going to hit the water or the wall. Somehow in the end, though, they missed both. Bran put on a burst of speed at the last second, slipping them through the final gap like a letter through a mail slot.

They burst into the bottom of the stairwell, which was much brighter than Bex remembered. She was still pushing her head up when she heard the familiar flap of wings coming down from above.

"*Bex!*"

Bex looked up just in time to see Lys land in front of her, using their wings for balance as they touched down on the tip of Bran's carved beak, the only empty space left on the extremely overloaded broom.

"I'm so glad you made it out!" they cried, reaching out to hug Bex as much as they could without overbalancing. "Cut it kind of close, didn't you?"

That second comment was directed at Adrian, who gave a dazed shrug. Bex had just reached down to help him up when Leander charged past them to teleport himself and Mara, who was still cradled in his arms, onto the stairs.

The very *full* stairs. The bottom of the spiral staircase was hidden under twenty feet of black, foamy water now, but the rest of it was lit up bright as day thanks to all the torches being carried by the crowd of demons going up. Mostly drenched and dazed-looking pride demons, but there were wrath demons in the mix as well, plus a ton of others.

Envy and hate demons were scattered all through the crowd with torches to light the way up for those who could walk. Those who couldn't were being carried up the center by a flock of winged sorrow, lust, and greed demons. The fear demons were there as well, using their ability to walk on walls to create a bucket chain of helpers that carried weakened demons straight to the stairwell's top.

It was the most beautiful display of spontaneous cooperation Bex had ever seen. The sight of so many demons helping each other made her heart swell up so big and fast that it was painful. The only reason she didn't start jumping for joy was because, while there were a lot of demons on the stairs, there still weren't nearly as many as she'd expected.

"Where is everyone?"

"That's the bad news," Lys told her with a somber expression.

"They drowned, didn't they?" Bex said in a shaking voice. "I was too slow."

The guilt was already pulling her down when Lys shook their head. "That's not what happened."

Bex stared at them in confusion, and the lust demon sighed.

"The evacuation went faster than expected because there weren't nearly as many demons down here as we thought," they explained. "We assumed Pride would be as big as Wrath with a population of around a hundred thousand, but they turned out to be a lot smaller. According to the pride demons I talked to, most of their villages were wiped out during the war, and the ones who survived were decimated by the Queen of Pride's death. By the time we got their Hell emptied, there were almost as many banished demons from other clans as actual void demons. The good news is that—between the unexpectedly low numbers and Nemini using your fire like a lighthouse—we were able to get everyone out before the cave flooded entirely."

That was good to hear, but Bex still clenched her fists. "What about my demons?" she demanded. "What about wrath?"

She knew it was going to be bad when Lys dropped their eyes. "That's the worst news," they said quietly. "What Gilgamesh did to them in there caused heavy casualties. The demons by the doors were exhausted and worked to the bone, but they were still able to move. The ones in the back, though…"

They didn't have to finish. Bex already knew. She'd seen her people when they came out of Limbo, how exhausted and starved they always were. The idea of Gilgamesh forcing those same demons to work until they collapsed made her black blood boil, but she understood exactly how it had happened.

"How many survived?"

"Hard to say," Lys replied, looking up at the spiral of figures climbing the stairs above them. "We'd need Drox to get an actual headcount, but Iggs thinks it's around forty thousand."

Bex's stomach dropped to her feet. Forty thousand. That was twice the number of demons she'd led at the Anchor, but only forty percent of the hundred thousand wrath demons Drox had always told her were in Limbo. If Iggs's number was accurate, then sixty percent of her people, the demons Ishtar had created her to protect, were gone. Worked to death by Heaven's selfish, arrogant, murdering *tyrant*.

"I'll kill him," Bex snarled, causing Lys to leap back into the air as her flames roared up like an inferno. *"I'll kill him!"*

"That's what we're counting on," Lys said as they fluttered back down. "We're all hoping you turn

Gilgamesh and his entire Heaven to a pile of ash, but we've got more immediate problems right now, so I need you to stop flaming and listen."

That was a lot to ask, but Lys never made requests like that without damn good reason. Bex was too full of rage and grief to put herself all the way out, but she managed to tone it down to a low burn, which Lys must've deemed good enough.

"Desh's key team has only unlocked about half of the demons upstairs," they told her in a quiet voice. "The Middle Hells have the opposite problem from the Lower. There's actually a lot *more* demons up there than we expected, and at the rate the water's coming in, I'm worried we're not going to get them all out of their shackles in time."

They both looked down at the flood Adrian's broom was hovering over, which had gone up several feet just during the time they'd been talking.

"How long do you think we've got?"

"I don't know," Lys said. "Volumetric rate calculations aren't exactly my strong suit, and the Middle Hells are pretty freaking big. Given how fast the water's coming up now that it's filled the Lower Hells, though, I'd say we need to hurry." They flicked their amber eyes to the naked, bloody bodies of the unconscious queens covering Bran's wings. "I don't suppose any of them would be willing to help us crack some chains."

"I'm sure they would if we can wake them up," Bex said, pulling her wet, filthy hair out of its ruined ponytail. "Keep working on unlocking as many demons as you can. I'll see if I can't get us more help."

Lys nodded and took off, their wings flapping unevenly to spare their injured shoulder. When Bex was certain they weren't going to fall out of the sky, she quickly braided her hair to keep it out of her face and dropped down next to Adrian, who was still on his knees.

"Do you think you can wake up my sisters?"

"Maybe," he replied in a distracted voice, never taking his mirrored eyes off the coat he was rubbing like a towel over his broom's back. "But I can't look at them right now. I have to get Bran dry before his grass gets too waterlogged and falls apart." He started rubbing harder. "He's been an absolute saint flying us around this entire time, but he's in real danger if I can't get the damp off him."

"Would heat help?" Bex asked.

Adrian looked at her with a beaming expression of relief. "Yes, please!" he said, bounding back to his feet. "A low burn, if you can. The water hasn't seeped down to his core yet, so if we can get his outer layers dry, we should be all right."

Bex nodded and closed her eyes, happy to have something simple to focus on as she raised her fire by fractions. Producing radiant, steady heat turned out to be a lot harder than violent flames, but she owed Adrian's broom big-time, so Bex gave it her all, gripping her anger in a tight, controlled ball until the air was so hot and dry it crackled.

"Perfect," Adrian said as he put his coat—which Bex's heat had also instantly dried—back on. His witch hat was more challenging. Being drenched had left it wrinkled and droopy. Adrian tried to reshape the point with his fingers, but it was hopeless. After a minute of fruitless fiddling, he shoved the hat into his enchanted pockets with a scowl and moved on to examining Bex's sleeping sisters.

"Their wounds are healed," he reported, wiping the dried black blood off their naked bodies with a healer's gentle indifference. "But they're not responding to reflex tests."

"What does that mean?" Bex asked, crouching several inches away so she wouldn't accidentally bake him with her new radiator mode.

"It means they're in a coma, and I don't know why," her witch answered grimly, sitting back on his heels. "Physically, they seem fine. Their severed wrists have all healed cleanly, and there's no sign of head trauma from their missing horns, but their pupils aren't contracting when exposed to light, and they're not exhibiting a pain response when I pinch them. That could mean damage to the nervous system, or it could be something magical. I simply don't know."

That wasn't good, but, "They're breathing, though, right?"

"Oh yes," Adrian assured her. "Like I said, their bodies seem perfectly healthy. There's just no one inside. Or at least no one who's responding to what I can do on the back of a broom."

Bex's shoulders slumped. Saving her sisters should have been the biggest triumph of her lives, but while she was happy they were with her and alive, this situation was rapidly starting to feel more like failure than success. Even without their crowns and swords, five queens was a force to be reckoned with, but five comatose bodies that had to be protected was a liability Bex couldn't afford at the moment.

"I'm going to go see if Leander's having more luck with Mara," she said as she rose back to her feet. "Are you good on drying?"

Adrian reached down to stick his finger into Bran's wing. "I think so," he said after much feeling around. "I'll have to rebristle him when this is over, but it doesn't seem like he's in danger of falling apart anymore."

The broom did feel steadier now, which was an enormous relief. Between the rising flood, her comatose sisters, and learning Gilgamesh had killed sixty percent of her demons before she'd even known he had them, the feeling that they were about to lose everything was hitting Bex hard. If she let herself think too long about any of it, she'd crumble, but Bex had been on the losing side for most of her life. She'd learned long ago to focus on the positives, like how Adrian's beloved broom was okay, her sisters weren't dead, and how there were still forty thousand wrath demons who *were* alive and needed her help.

So long as she stayed focused on the things she *could* do, Bex was able to push all the other tragedies to the background. It was a desperate sort of coping, but it kept her together as she leaped off the back of the broom to go find Leander.

She spotted him on the stairs halfway up to the Middle Hells, huddled in a nook between the pipes where he wouldn't get crushed by the stampede of evacuating demons. He must've teleported straight there because he was still dripping with filthy water, and his bare feet were black with sin muck. He looked more like a drowned rat than a prince of Gilgamesh, but his mirrored eyes were focused and determined when Bex touched his shoulder.

"She's still lost," he said before she could ask, turning his body slightly so Bex could see the Queen of Sorrow's sleeping face where he'd tucked it against his chest.

"Once," he whispered, "when we were on Earth where it's harder for Gilgamesh to spy, Mara told me what she remembered of losing her crown. She'd been betrayed by the Queen of War, but Gilgamesh was still perfecting the art of making princesses, so there was a gap between when War defeated her and when they took her horns."

He reached down to brush the wet hair away from Mara's closed eyes. "She used to have wings as well. Big, beautiful ones that let her soar over the Riverlands. War cut those off first to keep her grounded until they were ready to steal her crown. After that, the only thing she remembered was falling."

"That's how it was for me too," Bex said. "I had someone with me when I fell, though. She's the one who helped me come back to myself."

"Could she help Mara as well?" the prince asked desperately.

"I can ask her," Bex offered with a smile, reaching out to grab one of the passing void demons.

"Excuse me," she said in her best Riverlander. "Can you tell me where your queen is?"

The man responded with a look so scathing that Bex winced. Nemini had told her several times now that she hadn't been a beloved queen, but Bex had thought she was just being self-deprecating. Now, though, she was wondering if her sister hadn't been telling the bald truth because this man looked ready to spit on her just for asking.

"The Tyrant of Pride is upstairs," he replied sourly as he looked Bex up and down. "What are you supposed to be?"

That question was fair since she wasn't burning right now and still didn't have her horns. The void-turned-pride demons knew her only by her fire, not her face. He probably thought she was just a human with weirdly glowing eyes. Add in the part where she was standing next to a filthy, mad-looking prince clutching a seemingly dead body, and Bex wasn't offended in the slightest when the man started backing away.

"I'll find her myself, thanks," she said, nudging the demon back into the crowd before walking to the edge to wave at Adrian.

He flew his broom up to meet her at once, dodging the clouds of flapping demons to hover Bran's wing right next to the step Bex was standing on.

"What do you need?" he asked as she hopped over the gap.

"I think we all need to go up and see Nemini," Bex said as she reached back to pull the distracted Leander onto the broom with them. "She's the resident queen now, so let's go see what she can do."

Adrian looked skeptical, but he nodded and tapped his foot, sending the nine of them—seven hornless queens and two princes—up the middle of the stairwell toward the white tower.

And not far below, the flood kept rising.

Chapter 17

$\mathbf{T}$HE CITY-SIZED CAVERN of the Middle Hells was packed when they finally made it back. Demons of every sort had formed a massive crowd around the tower's base. The only reason they weren't inside the tower as well was because Kirok had organized the war demons into a perimeter so the evacuating wrath and pride demons would have room to actually get off the stairs. Iggs was standing right beside the general, as was Nemini, who was still holding the ball of Bex's fire over her head like a snake-haired Statue of Liberty. They all looked relieved when Adrian's broom popped into view, but that was the only positive expression to be had.

"I'll be with you in a second," Bex said to Kirok and Iggs as she vaulted off the broom. "Nemini, can you take a look at our sisters? They're not waking up."

The Queen of Pride nodded and handed Bex's fire back to her. Bex wasn't sure what she was supposed to do with that, but the moment she touched the flames, her body sucked them back in. When everything was back where it was supposed to be, Nemini hopped onto the broom to join Adrian and Leander while Bex jogged over to Iggs and Kirok, who were standing in a grim huddle on the first loop of the white tower's spiral stair.

"How bad is it?" she asked as soon as she got close.

"Not catastrophic yet," Kirok reported with the stoic calm of a lifelong soldier. "But we're getting close."

"I'd say it's pretty damn catastrophic," Iggs growled, turning to look at Bex with red-rimmed eyes. "Did you hear about—"

"I did," she said sadly, reaching out to touch his arm. "I'm sorry."

"You've got nothing to be sorry for," her demon muttered, wiping his nose. "That bastard king killed them before we even got here. I did find my sister, though."

Bex's face brightened. "Iggs, that's great!"

"It'd be a lot better if I'd found anyone else," he said, clenching his fists. "There were a lot of people running by, so there's a chance we just missed each other, but there's so many dead, Bex. What if my whole family's—"

"It's too early for that," Bex reminded him firmly. "Forty thousand's too many faces to search in the time we've had. Your family could still be alive, so let's focus on keeping them that way."

Iggs nodded silently, clenching his jaw tight in a desperate attempt to keep his emotions locked. Bex didn't ask him to speak again, but she didn't let go of his arm as she turned to Kirok.

"How many people are still waiting to be unchained?"

"Hard to say," Kirok replied. "I believe Lys explained this earlier, but the current Middle Hells used to be divided into five separate caverns. The walls were proclaimed inefficient and knocked down centuries ago, but the chains are still organized by the old divisions. Last I heard, Desh's team had finished unlocking the Hells of Envy, Lust, and Greed, the biggest three after War. They're currently working on Sorrow, which is medium. The chains for Hate haven't been touched yet, but they were always the smallest of the five, so I'd say we're about seventy percent done."

"That's a lot better than Lys thought," Bex said with a grin, happy to have some good news at last. "What about exits?"

"That's less promising, I'm afraid," the general said, turning to point across the smoky Hells at the lines of glimmering torches marking the stairs through the vertical slave towns on the cliffs that covered the cavern's walls. "I asked the winged demons for volunteers to fly the perimeter and check the banishment gates. They're not officially considered exits since all banished demons arrive on cliffs, so I thought the lockdown might not have included them."

"And?" Bex asked hopefully.

"And I was wrong," Kirok reported with a shake of his head. "The scouts that have come back all reported finding the banishment tunnels blocked with the same sin-iron security doors used to cut off the stairs to the Upper Hells."

"Sin-iron security doors, huh?" Bex said, tapping her boot. "How thick are we talking?"

"Thick," the general replied grimly. "The security doors are Heaven's final defense. They're designed to hold back hordes of rebelling demons. I actually used to train my war demons on them back when I was assigned to the Upper Hells. Young demons get cocky, so the warlocks considered it good practice to pit them against a wall they couldn't possibly break in order to curb their spirits."

"You mean break their spirits," Bex growled, craning her neck back to look up the spiral toward the top of the tower. "But there's no such thing as an unbreakable door. You keep things moving here. I'm going to go see what I can do."

"Yes, Great Queen," Kirok said, bowing his horns as Bex gave the still-silent Iggs a final squeeze before calling her fire and blasting herself up the broken tower.

Ten seconds later, she landed back on the platform where she'd confronted Nemini. She'd been too distracted by the miraculous revival of the Queen of Pride to notice anything else at the time. Now, though, Bex wondered how she could've missed the gigantic slab of sin iron that filled the entire ten-foot-wide entry tunnel to the Upper Hells.

The black metal was so thick, it didn't even clang when she banged her fist against it. The banishment hallways were bigger and taller, so maybe the doors blocking them weren't as ridiculously thick, but Bex didn't feel like going all the way out to the edge of the Hells to check. Even if the banishment tunnels were easier to break into, jumping off a cliff wasn't an escape. Enough of her people had died already. If she was going to do this, Bex was determined to take them on the path that led to Heaven. That was where the chains that could take them safely back to Earth were, along with everything else Bex was now determined to seize. This wasn't just about getting her horns and name back anymore. She wanted it all—her sisters' crowns, the destruction of Heaven, the rebirth of the Riverlands, and Gilgamesh's smug head on a pike.

That wasn't just her anger talking. Even if the banishment tunnels had been open and jumping off the cliffs wouldn't kill them, getting back to Earth without destroying Heaven wouldn't change anything. Even if they all made it, Gilgamesh would just rebuild the Hells and hunt them down again, and without her horns or sword, Bex wouldn't be able to stop him. There *was* a chance she could do it right now, though. The fact that the Hells were still on lockdown proved they had Heaven on the back foot. If they kept pushing, this could be their best opportunity—maybe their *only* opportunity—to topple Gilgamesh's Eternal Kingdom and set Ishtar's children free for good. Bex just had to get them up there alive. She was superheating her fist to get to work on that when she felt someone step out of her shadow.

"I didn't realize you could still do that," she said, glancing over her shoulder to see Nemini standing behind her.

"As you said, I'm still me," the Queen of Pride reminded her calmly. Then her face fell. "I wasn't able to wake them up."

"Oh," Bex said, crushingly disappointed. "Does that mean they're lost forever?"

"I don't believe so," Nemini said. "Their souls still exist, but they're in a very different situation than you were. We were together when you fell, so I was able to hold on, but our sisters were alone. They've also been falling for five thousand years. They could be anywhere in the infinite void at this point, and unlike you, none of them love me enough to answer when I call."

"Would they come back if we return their horns?" Bex asked desperately.

"I don't know," Nemini replied, which wasn't the answer Bex had been hoping for. "They'll probably respond to their Ishtar-given names, but only if we get close enough for them to hear us across the infinite void."

"Damn," Bex muttered. There went her dreams of backup. Not that she wasn't happy her sister's souls were just far away rather than lost forever, but she didn't have time for things that didn't fix problems right now, and six comatose bodies were not what she'd hoped to get out of this.

"Okay," she said, rubbing her hornless temples. "What else have we got to work with?"

Nemini tilted her head to the side. "Seven hundred and ninety-four thousand demons."

Bex stared at her in awe. "How do you know that?"

"My sword counted their names for me."

"I thought you said it was broken!" Bex cried.

"It *is* broken," her sister said. "It can't speak or tell me what those names are, which is why I can't cut their slave bands. It does still give me a nudge every time it finds a demon, though, so I counted those to get the tally."

Bex still couldn't believe it. "You personally counted seven hundred and ninety-four thousand demons?"

Nemini nodded. "I've been working on it since we arrived."

Bex whistled, stupidly impressed, but Nemini wasn't finished.

"I'm fairly certain of my accuracy within the bottom eight Hells," she went on. "But my sword hasn't given me any taps for the war demons above us."

"Probably because the Queen of War is hiding their names," Bex said, glaring up at the ceiling. "I bet she's got the whole damn Hell waiting to ambush us."

"That is what General Kirok suspects as well," Nemini agreed, staring through the broken windows at the distant walls of hovels that ringed the Middle Hells. "Maybe we *should* try jumping off the banishment platforms."

"No way," Bex growled, calling her fire back to her hands. "I didn't break everyone out of the Hells just to turn around and tell them to jump off a cliff." She nodded at the sin-iron-filled tunnel in front of them. "I've beaten war demons before. I can do it again."

She'd already raised her fist to start working on the tunnel when Nemini said, "You didn't beat the Queen of War."

Bex's body went still, and then she swung with a roar, punching the security door with all her might. The result was a bruised fist and no visible damage to the actual metal, but Bex hit it again anyway, because what the hell else was she supposed to do? They were trapped in a cave with the water rising, and it was all her fault. She was the one who'd decided to come here *and* the one who'd decided to keep going. An actual wise queen would've cut her losses and retreated as soon as the plan went off course, but Bex had kept charging ahead like her mother's famous bull, making reckless promise after reckless promise. No one could live up to the hype she'd built around herself. Was it any wonder she was failing now that the buck had come due?

She punched the door again, screaming in frustration that rapidly turned to pain as the hit drove the sharp edge of Drox's ring into her finger. Bex clutched it with a curse, squeezing her eyes tight against the throbbing that always hurt no matter how fast she healed. But as she stood there clutching her bruised hand, she could feel the cold, hard metal of Drox's ring against her skin like an admonishment from the sword himself, and suddenly, Bex felt very stupid.

She didn't have time for this. Punching doors and hurting herself was emotionally cathartic, but it didn't solve the problem. She was the one who'd promised to set these people free. Until she actually died, that made her responsible for them. This was no longer a duty she'd been born into. Bex was the one who'd insisted on staying queen even after she'd lost her horns, which meant she'd better start acting like it.

"All right," she said, lowering her fist. "Let's get everyone up here. It's time to make a plan."

"Yes, my queen," Nemini said, vanishing into the shadows again before Bex could remind her that she was a queen too.

Fifteen minutes and what felt like an eternity later, the team that had left the Blackwood to storm the Hells was all together again at the top of the tower, plus a few additions.

Iggs was there, his eyes red-rimmed but determined as he clenched his fist around the straps of Solomon's Armory. Nemini was there with her new horns held high next to Kirok, who was running his bronze fingers absently over the invisible curse the Witch of the Present had painted around his neck. Lys was right beside him, lying on the floor with their feet elevated on Bex's folded jacket while Adrian rebandaged their wound, which had started bleeding again from all the flying, just like the witch had predicted.

They really should've been resting downstairs with the other wounded, but they'd absolutely refused to sit this one out. Bex couldn't blame them, so she'd allowed it on the condition that Lys stayed flat. Boston was also keeping an eye on them from the windowsill next to Bran, who was leaning against the wall in his broom form, taking a well-deserved rest. Leander had refused to leave Mara's side for any reason, so he was still with the queens' bodies downstairs. Desh was up here, though, looking uncharacteristically somber with Streya hanging off his back like a deadly ornament.

Everyone was exhausted. It'd only been eight hours since they'd gotten themselves banished here from the Blackwood, but Bex's team looked like they'd aged ten years. She certainly felt like she'd been down here for a century as she munched on the plastic-wrapped emergency protein bar she'd stashed in her cargo pockets. One of the sandwiches she'd brought would have tasted better, but Bex couldn't remember where she'd put her backpack down during all the chaos and didn't want to take the time to go look, so she made do with this, chewing each rubbery, faux-chocolate bite slowly to buy herself time.

"Okay," she said when she couldn't stall any longer. "What's our situation?"

"We've almost got everyone unlocked," Desh reported proudly. "Damn stingy warlocks only had twenty keys in this whole bleeding place. Thankfully, one of the greed demons figured out how to make copies. Once those started getting around, our pace picked up enormously. Hate's the last one left, and I've got the winged demons flying around telling everyone to get to higher ground."

"They'll need to do so quickly," General Kirok said, looking down the tower at the filthy flood that was now gushing out of the hole in the bottom like a broken water main. "The central stair is no longer the only place the water's coming in. While we were moving the last evacuees, the pipes that transport river water to the Upper Hells burst. They're now dumping water directly into this chamber at a formidable rate. I'd say we have no more than three hours before the entire Middle Hells cavern is filled."

"And then we all drown," Desh finished, shaking his black-horned head. "Gotta give Gilgamesh points for creativity. Of all the ways I thought I'd die down here, 'drowned like mice in a bucket' wasn't even on my bingo card."

"We're not drowned yet," Bex said, turning to Iggs, who hadn't stopped clutching his knapsack since he came up here. "You mentioned you had a plan. Let's hear it."

"It's more of a harebrained scheme than a plan," her wrath demon admitted, reaching into his bag of weapons. "Remember when you were jumping down that hole to haul people out of the Lowest Hells? Well, I got to thinking, what if the floor between the Upper and Middle Hells is the same?"

"It's not," General Kirok said. "The gap between this floor and the Lowest Hells only exists because of the Founders' Tunnels. The ancient war demons never contributed to those works, so the floor of our Hell remains intact at ten feet of solid stone."

"But it's still rock," Iggs insisted. "Which is a lot easier to cut through than sin iron. Also, this rock is suspended."

He pointed through the broken tower window at the Middle Hells cavern's impossibly gigantic arched roof, and Bex's face split into a smile.

"You want to make a new exit."

"I want to make us a damn highway," Iggs replied, grinning back at her as he pulled a brick-sized block of gray clay out of Solomon's Armory. "I don't have shaped mining charges, but Felix's goblins loaded this thing up with a literal ton of plastic explosives. I already know they can destroy the rock down here because I'm the one who put that hole in the staircase when Leander and I were fighting the Prince of Hate. If we do the same thing to the ceiling, we can make ourselves a new exit. One that *isn't* blocked with stupid amounts of sin iron."

Lys opened their exhausted eyes to give Iggs a shocked look. "Do you have enough explosives to do that?"

"I should if we dig some fracture lines first," Iggs said confidently. "This place might've been made with sorcery, but it's still just a big stone ceiling at the end of the day. Blasting it to dust will take more firepower than we've got, but if we cut grooves in the stone and pack them with C-4, we can split the rock into chunks that will fall by themselves. It's the same method the Army Corps of Engineers uses to blast through mountains for roads, except we're making a highway *out* of Hell."

"I think you mean into another Hell," General Kirok said, crossing his four bronze arms over his massive chest. "You are all forgetting that the Hell of War is not an escape. It's full of warriors bound by their names to defend Gilgamesh's Heaven to the last breath. No matter where you break in, you'll be walking into a fight."

"Better than walking into a fortress," Iggs argued, pointing at the giant lump of sin iron blocking the path to the Upper Hells that Bex was leaning against. "You're the one who told us those stairs lead straight into a shooting gallery. If we have to go through the Hell of War to get out of here, I'd much rather bust through the back than come in the front door where I *know* there'll be an ambush waiting. This is also our chance to make an exit that's actually big enough for everyone to evacuate through. Even if it wasn't blocked with a giant sin-iron plug, there's no way we could get seven hundred thousand demons up those stairs before the flood caught us."

That was a damn good point. The tunnel into the Upper Hells was ten feet wide just like the rest of the spiral staircase. That was plenty of room for moving slaves a few at a time under guard but totally insufficient for their current numbers. They'd barely gotten the survivors of Pride and Wrath up the stairs ahead of the water, and that was with a lower-than-expected population and winged demons flying evacuees up the center to help with throughput. Moving the entire population of the Middle and Lower Hells through a single ten-foot-wide tunnel would be like trying to drain a swimming pool through a garden hose: possible, but definitely not fast.

"How big a hole do you think you could blast?" she asked Iggs.

"I was planning on doing a full football field," he replied. "That should be big enough to move everyone out before the water reaches us, though we'll have to figure out how to move people through an exit that's in the ceiling."

"We've got plenty of chains," Desh said, pointing at the black lake that used to be the sin-collection floor. "If we fish them out of the water and carry them up to the top of the cavern rim where the banishment tunnels let out, I bet we could weave the lengths together into a net. If we rig it at the right angle and make the holes small enough that people's feet won't go through, we should be able to walk right up it like a ramp."

"That still doesn't solve the problem of how we're going to escort a bunch of starved slaves through an entire Hell full of bootlicking bronze assholes who get their kicks from beating up their fellow demons," Lys pointed out before turning to flash a smile at General Kirok. "No offense."

"None taken," the general replied in a growling voice that sounded like offense had very much been taken. "It's a legitimate concern. I spent the majority of my years training war demons to be ready for attack from any angle. If the Princess of War has the main force positioned on the stairs as I suspect, it'll take them a while to reposition, but they will come, and they will crush us."

"Not if they're busy with something else," Bex said, looking over her shoulder at the sealed staircase to the Upper Hells. "Iggs, how long do you think it'll take to blow that hole in the roof?"

"I have no idea," Iggs said, scrubbing a hand through the dark hair between his horns. "I've never tried anything like this before. We've only got three hours before we all die, though, so let's say less than that."

"Better make it two hours," Lys said as Adrian finished knotting the final bandage around their shoulder. "We'll need at least sixty minutes to walk everyone out."

"Two it is, then," Iggs said with a nervous breath.

"You'll have plenty of eager help," Desh reminded him. "Nothing like impending death to encourage cooperative spirits, and Lys has always had a special talent for making people work. If they can get off their back long enough to organize getting that chain ramp made, I'll take a crew of wall-walking fear demons up to the ceiling and start cutting those fracture lines."

"Bex can probably do that herself now that she's got her fire back," Iggs said proudly, turning to grin at his queen. "What do you say? Think you can fly up there and make us some heat fractures?"

Bex shook her head. "There's another job I have to take care of. You all work on blasting through the ceiling. I'm going to make sure there aren't any war demons waiting for you on the other side."

The top of the tower went silent, and then Lys shoved themselves up off the ground. "What does that mean?"

"It means there's an army of the fiercest warriors in the Hells waiting for us," Bex said calmly. "You heard what Kirok said. No matter where we come up, it's just a matter of time before War's demons show up to kick us back down, so I'm going to make sure they've got something else to focus on."

"That sounds an awful lot like you're planning to fight them yourself," Adrian said quietly.

"That's exactly what I'm planning," Bex replied, reaching back to slap her restored right hand against the sin-iron brick blocking their way. "I can't clear this entire staircase in the time we've got left, but I should be able to melt a tunnel big enough for one person. I'll work on that while the rest of you focus on the ceiling. Then, just before Iggs blows the charges, I'll bust into the tower and get the war demon army's attention. I'm the Coward Queen who's been rebelling against Heaven for five thousand years. If I'm in their sights, I'm the only thing they're going to see, so I'll be the distraction while the rest of you evacuate into the Upper Hells. We outnumber the war demons by a lot. If they aren't picking us off one at a time as we come up the ramp, we should be able to hold our own."

"We can take 'em," Iggs agreed. "But that means you'll be fighting every soldier in the Hell of War by yourself. I'd never question your abilities—"

"Then don't," Bex said, scowling at the ring of worried faces. "This invasion was my idea. I warned all of you that the odds were against us, but you chose to follow me anyway, and look what we've accomplished! We're closer to freeing the Hells than anyone else in history. This is what I've fought a hundred and ninety-eight lifetimes to achieve. I'm not going to let Gilgamesh snatch that away from us when we're so close to the finish line."

"It's not a victory if you die for it!" Lys yelled, their face pale and desperate as they staggered to their feet. "I don't care how close we are. I'm not letting you fight an entire fortress full of war demons by yourself!"

Bex's eyes widened in surprise. Lys was normally careful never to question her decisions where others could hear. If they were doing so now, it must mean they really thought she was going to die, but Bex wasn't changing her mind.

"I'm the only one who can do it," she argued. "I'm the one Heaven's always been after. It's the same strategy we used when we were burning down warlock houses in California, just on a bigger scale."

"And a more lethal one," Nemini said, her yellow eyes flashing angrily despite her neutral tone. "If the war demons have been commanded to stop us, then it's likely their queen will be waiting up there as well. If you face her again with no sword—"

"I know," Bex said, clenching her fists. "I know exactly how bad this is going to be, okay? But if someone doesn't keep them occupied, the Queen of War's army is going to fall on *them*." She pointed out the tower window at the huge crowd of demons running for the cavern walls.

"The hammer's coming down one way or another," she continued in a shaky voice. "My plan makes sure that it only lands on me, which is fine. I'm used to this. I've been dying for my people for five thousand years. Unlike all those other lives, though, this time I've got a chance to make my death *matter*. Even if all I do is buy enough time to get everyone out before this place floods, I'll still have done more for demonkind than any Rebexa before me. That's a hill I'm proud to die on, but we're *all* going to die for nothing if we keep wasting time arguing. We've got a plan, so let's get to work."

That should've been the end of it, but everyone started yelling the moment she finished. The whole tower was descending into chaos when Bex cut them off.

"Am I still queen or not?"

"Of course you're our queen," Lys said angrily. "But that doesn't mean—"

"This is exactly what it means," Bex snapped, raising her hornless head. "You're the one who taught me that a queen is nothing without her people. You've *always* said that it's my sacred duty to fight for them."

"Because I knew you'd always come back!" Lys cried. "But that's not true this time. This is your *last life*! If you die playing decoy, who's going to lead us out of here?"

"She will," Bex said, pointing at Nemini. "*You* will, along with Desh and Iggs and everyone else who helped make this possible. This is the fight we *all* pledged our lives to. I'm not going to be an actual Coward Queen by letting my people march into danger when I can prevent it. This is why I'm here! Ishtar made me for a lot of reasons, but protecting her children is the duty *I* chose. It's the same thing every other Rebexa died for. It's the reason I walked into Adrian's bonfire, and it's why I'm not going to stop now, because this is the life where I finally get it *right*."

Lys opened their mouth to keep arguing, but Bex grabbed their hand instead. "I can't name you into obeying anymore," she said. "But I shouldn't have to. This has always been my duty, so let me be the hero Bex you used to tell me about. The one who kicked down your warlock's door and set you free. This is the victory you've dreamed of since we met. Let me be the one to give it to you. After all," she smiled, "haven't you always said that I'm the one who will defeat Gilgamesh and take us back to Paradise?"

"You can't do that if you're dead," Lys whispered, clutching Bex's fingers. "I don't want this. I've *never* wanted you to be in danger, but if this is what you feel you have to do..."

Their voice trailed off as they bowed their head. Just over Bex's fingers at first, then further, crouching their body all the way down to the floor until their short horns were pressed against the stone at Bex's feet.

"I honor your decision, my queen," they whispered.

"Glad to hear it," Bex said, reaching down to help Lys back up. "We've only got two hours to blast ourselves an exit, so I need everyone to get on that. I'll stay here and work on melting through the security door. Iggs, let me know when you're ready to blow the charges. I'll save the last inch for then. When you hit the trigger, I'll bust into the Upper Hells like a fireball.

With any luck, they'll blame the explosion on me and not even go looking for the rest of you until it's too late. That's the plan, so let's move out."

No one looked happy, but they did as she said, running down the tower to go do their jobs with only the occasional worried glance over their shoulders. Bex glared right back, browbeating them down the stairs until it was just her at the top of the tower with one notable exception.

"You can't order me to go," Adrian said, crossing his arms over his chest.

"Wouldn't dream of it," Bex replied, giving him a wary look. "You're not going to try to stop me, are you?"

"No," he said, leaving Boston watching nervously from the windowsill as he walked over to join her in front of the sin-iron barrier. "I actually think a distraction is a great plan. The only part I take issue with is the idea of you doing it alone. It'll be a much more convincing show if we go in together."

He finished with a smile, but Bex looked at the ground, too overcome with fear and gratitude to make a sound. "Are you sure you want to?" she managed at last. "It's kind of a one-way trip."

"Of course it's one-way," he said. "Who wants to come back to the Hells? But you're not going to be dying, if that's what you meant."

"I don't see how I'm getting out of it," she told him when she finally raised her eyes. "You're a prince, so they won't harm you, but Gilgamesh has been swatting me like clockwork since the fall of Paradise. If nothing else, the Queen of War is almost certainly going to be waiting for me. If I couldn't beat her with

Drox, there's no way I'm doing it without him." She reached out to touch Adrian's face with a sad smile. "I've seen you pull a lot of miracles out of your pointy hat, but I don't think even you can unpunch my ticket this time."

"Don't give up on me yet," he said, capturing Bex's hand against his cheek with a look so determined it stole her breath. "I realize I'm very late, but I still owe you a date. A witch of the Blackwood always keeps his word, so no one is dying until we get back to Seattle for the brunch I promised you."

It was completely inappropriate given the circumstances, but that made Bex laugh. "Can we get pancakes?"

"All you can eat," he promised, leaning in to rest his forehead against hers. "If I ever get my phone back, I've got a list of twenty breakfast places I want to take you to. Dinner places, too, and breweries and bakeries and parks and everything in between. There's a whole life I want to explore with you when we get home, so keep that in mind before you do anything stupidly heroic."

"Same goes for you," Bex said as she moved even closer. "Who was it that got himself turned into a prince trying to find a way to defeat Gilgamesh?"

"I suppose it is a bit pot-calling-kettle-black," Adrian admitted as he wrapped his arms around her. "But that's why we need to stick together. Who else is going to put up with us?"

"No one," Bex admitted, rising up on her toes to press a kiss against his lips.

Adrian grabbed her as soon as she moved, pulling her flush against his chest and slanting his lips over her until he was kissing her with the same overwhelming, mind-blanking sweetness as their first real kiss under his oak tree in the Anchor Market. This time, though, Bex was ready for it. She met him head-on, grabbing his shoulders and pulling Adrian against her like she could make up for all the futures they weren't going to get to share.

That sad thought was still drifting through her mind when Adrian's hands—those strong, clever hands she loved so much—slid up to cup her face. Something inside Bex moved with them, because when he held her like that, like she was the most important thing in his world, making up for lost time no longer seemed good enough. She didn't know how yet, but Bex was suddenly determined that she was going to live, because there was no way in all the Nine Hells that she was letting Gilgamesh take this away from her. Every version of Rebexa had died fighting him, but *this* Bex was determined to be the one who lived to see him fall. She'd break his tyrannical Heaven and move on to a glorious future where she was free to have a lazy brunch with her handsome witch any morning she wanted.

If there was a better reason to stay alive, Bex didn't know it. It wasn't time for those things yet, though. She still had a job to do, so she forced herself to pull away, trailing kisses down Adrian's chin to his neck as she dropped back to her feet.

"I have to go burn a tunnel," she told him, cheeks flushed as she jerked an uncoordinated thumb over her shoulder toward the blocked stairwell. "Can we pick this up again when we're done?"

"Any time you want," he promised, dropping one last kiss to the top of her head between where her horns used to be. "I also need to go to talk to Boston about what we're going to do for our end. You get to burning. I'll be right over here."

Bex nodded and forced herself to let go of his coat. Adrian also took his time, walking much slower than he needed to back over to the windowsill where Boston had turned around to give them privacy. She was watching him pet his cat just for the pleasure of seeing Adrian's elegant, long-fingered hands move, when Bex gave herself a shake and whirled around to get to work before she became the slowpoke who sank the entire mission.

The possibility hit her lust-dazed senses like a bucket of ice water. Bex fired up her flames at once, stoking her bonfire to a white-hot torch as she pressed her palms against the sin iron and began to push, melting millimeter by millimeter through the wall that stood between her and the future she wanted most.

Chapter 18

IT TOOK *FOREVER*. BEX thought she'd beat the demolition team with time to spare, but she was actually the last to finish. Even using her hottest fire, the sin iron was thick and refused to melt. The toxic fumes it gave off when it finally did burned Bex's lungs and sent her into coughing fits, forcing her to duck out for clean air every time she needed to breathe. By the end of the first hour, all Bex could think was thank Ishtar Iggs had come up with the ceiling plan. If they'd been counting on her to clear the stairs, they never would've made it.

The flood was only one floor below by the time she finished cutting a Bex-sized hole through the blockade's center. Adrian had had his part ready for ages. He was waiting patiently with his cat on one shoulder and Bran's broomstick resting against the other when Bex finally came out to say she'd made it to the final inch. She'd just pushed the button on her ear comm to ask Iggs if he was ready when she noticed General Kirok standing next to the door she'd just been burning through.

"What are you doing here?" she asked suspiciously. "I ordered everyone to help with the breach."

"You did," he said. "And I obeyed. Once all the charges were placed, however, your second-in-command Lys ordered me to return here and accompany you."

"That wasn't their call," Bex replied angrily. "I know Lys is worried, but they had no right to order you into such a—"

"The order was at my request," Kirok insisted, holding his flat, sandy-colored horns high. "You are marching into the lion's mouth, but it is my people who were forced to be its teeth. The war demons are slaves, the same as all the other demons here. If you're going to fight them, I wish to stand at your side, if only to show them there's another choice."

Bex looked away with a huff. It wasn't that she didn't understand how Kirok felt, but the Queen of War was almost certainly waiting just above them. Maybe not in person, but definitely close enough to ensure that her demons didn't get a chance to disobey.

That was the entire reason Kirok had asked the Witch of the Present to draw the curse of obedience on his neck. It was supposed to be a failsafe, a way for him to choose death rather than be forced to be the Queen of War's tool yet again. In Bex's mind, that meant Kirok needed to stay as far away from his queen as possible. After all, if War never gave him an order he didn't obey, the curse wouldn't kill him, and he'd get to stay alive. If he walked into the trap with her, though, Kirok was dead. Even if Bex squeaked through this somehow, there was no way the Queen of War wouldn't order him to kill her, and then the general would die.

Unless he'd been an inside man from the start.

That was a properly paranoid way to view things. If Drox had been awake, he would've been proud. Bex, however, rejected the idea the moment it entered her head. She'd seen Kirok's face when he talked about the betrayal the war demons had been forced to participate in at the Anchor and heard the hatred in his voice just now when he'd talked about the war demons being slaves. He was as angry as the rest of them. Bex could feel the righteous fury of his wrath from three feet away, and that more than anything made up her mind.

"Welcome to the distraction team," she said, holding out her still-flaming hand.

Kirok shook it without hesitation and moved aside for Adrian, who'd been waiting nervously just behind him.

"Are you sure you don't want to take a quick break first?" the witch asked Bex as he stepped up next to the war demon. "We've still got a few minutes before we hit the time limit, and you've been burning nonstop since you got here."

"I'm fine," Bex insisted, tilting her head toward the dark ceiling outside the tower's busted windows. "This whole place is caked in centuries of anger. There's even more fuel for me to burn here than there was in Limbo. Honestly, the real struggle is not flaming out of control again."

Adrian's scowl deepened. "Is that a risk?"

"Not anymore," Bex promised, turning back to the tunnel. "I'm no longer fighting desperately. I've got a goal to ground me now, and the war demons don't deserve to be burned. They're victims of Gilgamesh just like the rest of us, and I've got to make sure that they get free too." She smiled. "The Bonfire of Ishtar does not burn her own people."

That last part was spoken directly at Kirok, who lowered his horns in reply. It looked physically difficult, lowering his horns before a queen that wasn't his when his own was so close, but he persevered, holding the bow rigidly in place as Bex reached up to tap the comm in her ear.

"How's it looking?"

"We're ready when you are," Iggs's voice came back. There was a long pause, and then, "Are you *sure* you still want to—"

"Yes," Bex said, marching back into the oven-hot tunnel of melted sin iron until she was standing in front of the half-inch thin wall of metal she'd left at the very end.

There was another long pause before Iggs switched to Riverlander. "Ishtar guide your sword, my queen."

"May she guide yours as well," Bex replied in the same language, holding her fire ready as Iggs began shouting orders at the others.

"This is it!" his voice bellowed over the little speaker in her ear. "We're about to blow, so everyone stand clear of the blast area! Trigger teams, get ready to hit your buttons on my mark!"

There was a flurry of shouting, and then Iggs's voice came through again at a volume pitched for Bex's ears. "On your signal."

Bex glanced over her shoulder to make sure Adrian and Kirok were behind her. When she saw them waiting at the tunnel's entrance, she turned back around and pressed her burning hand against the final barrier.

"Do it."

"*Go!*" Iggs shouted.

Anything else he could've said was lost in a thunderous cascade of explosions. Bex felt the entire Hell shaking under her feet, but she was already blasting herself forward, stoking her fire as hot as it would go as she smashed through the final wall to burst out of the blocked stairwell into a second, totally different tower.

It looked like she'd just tunneled into the bottom of a fortress. The stairs she'd been following kept going up in a spiral, but where the Lower Hells had been just an empty stairwell and the Middle Hells had looked more like an office building, the tower of the Upper Hells was a citadel with all its fortifications pointing inward.

The staircase still spiraled up the outside, but there were metal gates that could be swung out every ten feet to block it, and the open column in the middle was ringed with galleries where archers could fire down from cover. Add in the open floor at the bottom, and the whole thing was basically a killing jar. And manning all those battlements, packed together shoulder-to-giant-shoulder like gleaming bronze sardines, was an army of enormous, sandy-horned, four-armed war demons.

The sight was intimidating enough that even Bex stepped back a pace. She'd never seen so many war demons packed into one place before. The fortress wasn't actually well lit, but the few torches there were reflected off all of their bronze bodies so brightly that the entire tower gleamed with light. It was *so* bright, *so* overwhelming, Bex didn't even notice that every one of those soldiers had an arrow aimed at her heart until she heard the creak of all their bowstrings pulling back as one.

It was the most weapons Bex had had pointed at her since her fight in the sky over the White City. Unlike Gilgamesh's golden constructs, though, these were not mindless sorcerous automatons firing on a predetermined system. They were actual soldiers, the only tribe of Ishtar's children bred for war. They were also *much* closer than the constructs had been. If they opened fire at this range, there was no way she could burn all the arrows before they hit. She was wondering why they hadn't just shot her yet when she heard the familiar *clack* of carved feet walking over stone.

Bex's head snapped up like a bobber on a string. It wasn't a surprise, exactly, but her heart still stuttered when she saw the Princess of War descending the spiral stairs. Gilgamesh must've fixed her fake body, because the corroded, four-armed queen once again looked like a fragile, two-armed ivory statue. Her face looked even lovelier now than it had been when she'd come down with her lion to destroy the Anchor Market, but there was more malice in her mismatched eyes than on all the faces of her soldiers put together as she pointed at Bex and said,

"Kill her."

There were no horns carved into the princess's lovely white hair, but that didn't seem to matter. She might have looked like a delicate porcelain doll, but the voice that spilled from her lips was a queen's. It rang with Ishtar's ancient authority, and the moment the war demons heard it, every soldier in the tower released their bows, filling the air with the scream of arrows. Bex was pushing her fire into an inferno in the hopes of at least burning a couple of them, when a tall black blur shot in front of her.

"*Stop!*" the Princess of War shouted.

That order seemed way too late, but—to Bex's shock—the whistle of the arrows cut off like a switch. The arrows themselves clattered harmlessly to the floor a second later, leaving Bex gaping before she understood. This was War's power. Just as Bex had full control over the fires of Wrath, the Princess of War—or, more specifically, the queen hiding inside her—had total dominion over her army's weapons. Not only was she able to stop arrows in mid-flight, she could even order them back into her soldiers' quivers, which was what she did next. Bex actually felt her magic tucking the spent arrows away, cleaning the battlefield until no evidence was left that a single shot had ever been fired at the youngest Prince of Gilgamesh, who was suddenly standing in front of Bex like a shield.

"*Adrian!*" Bex hissed, her heart pounding as she realized what had almost happened, how close he'd come to death. "What are you *doing*?"

"Helping you like I said," Adrian replied as he spread his arms wider. "Don't worry. She can't hurt me."

Bex wasn't sure about that. The princess had looked hateful before, but she was practically spitting with it now.

"Prince Adrian," she growled, her white feet clacking like steel shots as she stomped down the stairs. "Step aside! This is none of your concern."

Adrian lifted his chin and stayed right where he was, and the princess's mismatched eyes—one carved gold, one mirrored silver—narrowed to slits.

"I will not stay my hand again," she warned, snapping her carved white fingers at her demons to reload their bows. "Your status as a prince grants many privileges, but your illustrious father has no patience for traitorous sons who scorn his generous gifts and side with his enemies."

"If he has no patience for traitors, why does he tolerate you?" Adrian asked in a voice that echoed up the stairwell. "You're the biggest traitor in history. You sold your people into slavery and tore the horns off your own sister's head"—he gestured over his shoulder at Bex—"all to please a human who treats you like a servant." He lifted his chin higher still. "I'm no demon, but even I can see that Bex is ten times the queen you are whether she has her horns or not."

"Then you are an ignorant child who understands *nothing*," the Princess of War snarled, peeling her carved lips back to show the sharp, white teeth beneath. "You have no idea what I've suffered at the gods' hands, nor could you! No mortal except Gilgamesh himself can ever comprehend what they did to me. What *she* did to me!" She stabbed her white-gloved finger at Bex, who winced. "My *sister* has been Ishtar's dog since her very first birth. She stood by and watched while our 'sacred' mother kicked me into a pit. I am completely justified in everything I've done to her!"

"But not what you did to us," said a deep, angry voice.

Bex jumped. She'd been so scared for Adrian—also touched, but mostly terrified—she hadn't even noticed Kirok coming out of the melted tunnel until he walked past her. The war demon marched straight into the fortress like the general he was, pushing Adrian gently to the side to take the witch's place in front of Bex.

"Kirokaltos," the Princess of War said, looking down her delicate white nose with a sneer. "Step back."

Bex wasn't a war demon, but even she shuddered at the force of the command behind those words, which made it all the more impressive when Kirok said, "No."

The moment he spoke the defiant word, the invisible patterns Adrian's mother had painted onto his bronze skin began to sizzle. Bex could actually see the metal melting all over his neck, shoulders, and chest. It must have been incredibly painful, but the war demon held his ground, ignoring the witchcraft burning through his armored flesh as he stared defiantly at his queen.

"You abandoned us," he snarled, his words shaking not from pain, but from centuries of pent-up fury. "You chose a mortal king, a *human*, over your own people!"

"I never asked for people," the Princess of War told him sourly. "You were forced upon me, an unwanted burden thrust onto my back, and not even for a noble cause. Ishtar made demons to be bottom-feeders, scavengers who ate the poison off her precious humans."

"And yet you serve a human."

"*I serve my king!*" War roared, shaking the Hells with her divine voice. "I serve the great Gilgamesh, conqueror of Paradise and slayer of *gods*! We were raised to see Ishtar as our merciful mother, but the moment I complained that her practices were killing me, she cast me aside. My own creator buried me in a *pit* so she wouldn't have to listen to my screams, and my sisters helped! Not one of them showed me a crumb of mercy, but King Gilgamesh heard my cries. He alone came to find me in that wretched hole. He alone pulled me out and promised to make me whole again. He earned my loyalty that day, and I am proud to call him my king!"

"We know," Kirok growled. The poison had burned deep gouges into his flesh by this point, and his legs were starting to buckle from the pain. When Bex reached out to steady him, though, he pushed her away, staggering toward his sneering queen instead.

"All war demons know where your loyalty lies," he said as he dragged his hoofed feet across the fortress's black-stained stone. "We've passed the story of your betrayal down for generations, whispered in secret from parent to child so that we would never forget how eagerly our queen sold us into slavery. How she used her divine sisters' sympathy to sneak behind them and rip off their horns so she could deliver Ishtar's crowns to her precious mortal king. *We remember!*"

His shout echoed through the chamber, and all the war demons packed into the battlements began to nod.

"We remember," Kirok said again, stooping toward the ground so he could use his lower pair of arms to keep pushing himself forward when his legs grew too weak to carry him, but also so that he would not kneel. Even after the poison fully paralyzed his lower half, he did not allow his knees to touch the ground.

"It's true that you had no choice when Ishtar made us your subjects," he told his queen. "But every decision you've made since is on your shoulders. *You* sold us into slavery for your own benefit. *You* let our homeland burn. *You* commanded us to kill our fellow demons and stain our hands with treason so that *you* could please your new human master." He stabbed his upper right hand at her face. "You did all these things yourself, Dalanea, and I will not be subject to your grievances anymore!"

The whole tower gasped when he said the Queen of War's true name. Just forming the syllables was enough to send black blood pouring from his bronze mouth, but Kirok was past the point of pain. He locked his useless legs and forced himself upright to stand in front of her once more, and even though the princess was still physically above him on the stairs, the expression on Kirok's face made it clear that he was the one looking down.

"Ishtar made you our queen," he rasped through his torn throat, "but I say you are unworthy of that name. There is only one queen who has ever fought for the people of War, and that is the Queen of Wrath."

He jerked his arm backward, slinging an arc of his black blood across the floor at Bex's feet.

"She has done more for us in three months than you've done in five thousand years!" he roared. "She forgave our ancient treason and welcomed us to join her fight for freedom. Even after you cut off her hand and stole her crown, she got herself damned to the Hells *your king* built to be our prison. Gilgamesh calls her a coward and claims she ran away, but she is the only daughter of Ishtar who *never* turned her back on us! Her loyalty and devotion are why I am alive to stand before you now. I am proud to die defending her, but prouder still to do it defying *you*."

"If you're so proud of it," War snarled, holding out an arm that was already covered in her divine weapon's armored plates, "then go ahead and *die*!"

The sword exploded into her hand as she finished. Bex barely had time to recognize Havok's deadly black blade before the princess flung it at Kirok. It was the same move she'd used to spear Bex out of the sky a week ago, and now as then, her shot found its mark. Bex didn't even have time to shout a warning before the giant sword was buried to the hilt in Kirok's chest.

"*Kirok!*" she screamed, running to his side even though she knew it was already too late. Kirok was a war demon in his prime. If circumstances had been different, he might have been able to stand back up, but his bronze body was already crippled by the witch's curse, and his opponent was a queen. Not even Ishtar's gift of regeneration could hold him together as the Princess of War called her sword back to her hand, leaving Kirok to topple and break like an overripe fruit on the tower's already bloodstained floor.

The fortress fell utterly silent. It was so quiet, Bex could hear the soft *drip, drip, drip* of Kirok's blood falling from the Princess of War's sword as she lowered it to her side. The sound echoed in her suddenly empty head like a pounding hammer, and then her flames roared up so hot and bright that even she was blinded.

"You killed him."

"Of course," the Princess of War said, narrowing her mismatched eyes against the raging inferno Bex had become. "Such is the fate of all demons who defy their—"

"You *killed* him!" Bex roared as her flames leaped higher, reflecting off the bronze bodies of the war demons until the whole tower was lit up like the inside of a mirrored lamp. "He was your demon, your charge! Even if you didn't want him, he was *yours*, and *you killed him!*"

War opened her sneering lips to reply, but whatever sound came out was lost in Bex's enraged scream as she leaped up the tower to wrap her flaming hands—both of them—around her sister's hard white throat.

This was not how it was supposed to go.

Adrian watched Bex jump onto her sister in a panic, scrambling to figure out how everything had gotten so out of control. It'd been such a simple plan: use his status as a prince to stall the fight and force a different outcome. There was still some risk, which was why he hadn't told Bex ahead of time so she wouldn't try to stop him. Treason or no treason, though, Adrian was still the only son of Gilgamesh who could blend sorcery with witchcraft. His stingy father would never permit the destruction of such a useful tool no matter how many times Adrian turned on him, which meant the Crown Princess couldn't either.

That made Adrian the perfect shield for this situation, and he'd intended to stand his ground until

Gilgamesh himself came down to move him. At the very least, he'd hoped to confuse the situation long enough for the rest of the demons to evacuate. It was supposed to be his big play to reclaim his honor and prove once and forever that he was someone Bex could rely on, but he'd barely started his grand gesture before Kirok had shoved his way forward and everything had gone very literally to hell. Now Bex was fighting the same princess that had defeated her a week ago, only this time she was doing it barehanded.

It was the worst possible way this situation could have gone. But while Adrian was scrambling to come up with something, *anything* he could do to save her, he realized Bex was doing... not that bad, actually.

She was burning brighter than he'd ever seen. Her whole body was covered in white-hot flames so intense they hurt to look at, but it wasn't the wild, out-of-control fire he'd seen earlier. That fire had been a storm that filled the Hells. This was a cutting torch, a single focused flame of wrath so intense, even the Princess of War looked surprised before her beautiful face contorted into fury.

"Do you really think you can win against me?" she screamed, covering her carved body in white, shell-like armor as she swung the huge black blade that had killed Kirok at Bex's head. "You rage-drunk fool, you don't even have a sword!"

Bex didn't say a word. Adrian didn't know if she *could* speak. He'd seen Bex get mad plenty of times, but he'd never seen her like this. He couldn't even make out her face through the blazing white fire as she swept her leg up fast as lightning to kick the incoming blade off course. She moved again the instant the sword went crooked, using the opening she'd just made to dart inside her opponent's guard and slam her glowing fist into the Princess of War's armored stomach.

The moment her fist connected, Adrian knew the hit hadn't gotten through. The princess's white armor was simply too thick for a bare fist to crack. The hit still sent the princess flying, though, flinging her armored body clear across the tower into the stone on the other side.

The walls must've been thicker up here than in the white tower downstairs because the princess didn't go through them like Bex had when her double tackled her, but she still made a hell of a dent. She lay there stunned for a second, then the princess heaved herself out of the crater with an enraged roar, reaching up with the hand that wasn't holding her sword to clutch her carved white face, which was now as cracked as the stone she'd just slammed into.

"You *animal!*" she screamed as the white shards broke away to reveal the pitted bronze face of the monster Adrian had seen Bex fighting on the battlements a week ago. "*He just made that one for me!*"

The final word turned into a screech as the Princess of War launched herself off the cracked wall with enough force to finish breaking it. She moved so fast that Adrian's eyes could barely keep up, but the white-hot Bex was even faster, running across the battlements full of fleeing war demons to meet the princess halfway. The Princess of War swung her giant sword with a bellow of fury, but Bex darted under it like a flickering candle to slam the flat of her empty palm against the inside of her enemy's sword arm.

Once again, the princess's strike was thrown wide, but War was ready for it this time. When Bex turned to drive her fist into the princess's broken face, War slammed her knee into her stomach instead, knocking Bex off the stairs with enough force to shatter the rest of her white façade.

It was a startling transformation. The Princess of War had looked like a living ivory statue when she'd first come down the stairs. Now, though, her truth was revealed as the four-armed, corroded-bronze body of the hornless Queen of War ripped off the last of her false white shell to bare her cracked teeth at Bex.

"You want death so badly?" she bellowed as the thick plates of her heavy armor rearranged themselves to fit her new, much larger body "Come and get it, *sister!*"

She must've been holding back earlier to avoid damaging the body Gilgamesh had carved for her. Now that her beautiful shell was broken, the Queen of War was swinging hard enough that just the wind off her blade was enough to knock the legions of war demons off their feet. The whole tower fell into chaos as soldiers raced down the stairs to get out of their queen's warpath. Adrian had just scrambled back into Bex's melted tunnel so he wouldn't get trampled when he felt a familiar weight land on his shoulder.

"Great Forest, look at them go!"

"Boston!" Adrian hissed, grabbing the cat off his shoulder. "I told you to stay back. It's dangerous up here."

"Exactly," Boston said, squirming out of his grip. "What kind of familiar stays behind when his witch is in danger? And you can't possibly expect me to miss this." He scrambled back onto Adrian's shoulder, putting his paws on his witch's head so he could stand up for a better view.

"They're like gods," he whispered in an awed voice, his green eyes shining like emeralds in the white light of Bex's fury. "Is this what you saw when they fought before?"

"No," Adrian said, letting go of his cat with a defeated sigh. "This is different. Bex had her sword last time, and she wasn't so..."

He trailed off, unable to find the words to describe the blinding flash Bex had turned into. The Queen of War was attacking indiscriminately now, slicing off entire battlements that fell like boulders onto the fortifications below them. She'd done more damage to the Hell of War's tower than Bex had at this point, but no matter how hard she swung her black sword, she couldn't land a blow. Bex didn't even seem to have a body anymore. She was just a tongue of flames. A pure, blazing star of wrath that danced around every one of War's strikes, which seemed slow and ponderous by comparison.

"How is she doing that?" Boston asked in an awed voice. "I thought losing her horns made her weaker."

"I don't think this is about her horns," Adrian said, leaning against the still uncomfortably hot wall of the melted tunnel to get them both a better view. "Bex told me once that that her horns were proof of her identity as Ishtar's daughter, but she isn't using Ishtar's powers right now. She's angry in her own right."

Boston scowled. "Isn't the Queen of Wrath always angry?"

"Not like this," Adrian said. "She's *really* mad this time."

"Again, how is that different from usual?" Boston asked. "Not that she doesn't have a lot to be upset about currently, but this seems extreme. Where's she even getting all that energy from?"

Adrian didn't know. He'd felt the intense magic rolling off Bex when she'd turned into a firestorm, but this was different. It looked like all that raging fire had been condensed into a single, Bex-sized flame that felt both more controlled and much, *much* more dangerous than the raging bonfire she'd been before.

"However she got to it, that level of output doesn't look sustainable," Boston observed. "We should stop her before she hurts herself."

"I don't think we can," Adrian said. "More importantly, I don't think we *should*. Look at that."

He pointed ahead of them at the base of the tower where Bex had made her first stand. The room had been empty when they entered, a barren circle of stone designed to provide the archers above with a nice, clean kill box. Now, though, the bottom floor of the Hell of War's tower was packed with war demons. They'd squeezed their bodies into every available inch, standing shoulder to shoulder like bronze bullets packed into a magazine. The only open spot was the place where Kirok had died.

Between the princess's brutal execution and the curse that, oddly, looked like the work of Adrian's mother, there wasn't much of the former general left. What little there was, though, was surrounded by an honor guard of the biggest, meanest war demons Adrian had ever seen. They stood over Kirok's fallen body like a fortress, watching in determined silence as the two queens fought on the stairs above them.

All the war demons were like that. Adrian wasn't sure when the change had happened, but no one was panicking or scrambling for safety anymore. The entire army was just standing at the bottom of the tower like bronze statues, waiting to see who would triumph.

"I think we might be too not-demon to interfere with this," Adrian said, clutching his familiar to his shoulder as he inched them back into the shelter of the melted tunnel. "Bex can handle herself. Let's just stay here and wait for her to win."

"Are you sure she will?" Boston whispered nervously.

"No," Adrian confessed with a worried look at Bex's swordless hands. Then his eyes moved to her opponent, and he smiled. "But the Queen of War's the one who looks afraid."

"Blackwood protect us," his familiar muttered, curling into a ball on his witch's shoulder as the daughters of Paradise's most violent god crashed like comets above them.

At the same moment, on the other side of the almost-entirely-flooded Middle Hells, Lys was flying harder than they'd ever flown in their life.

They'd been skeptical of Iggs's plan the first time he described it, but the detonation had gone off without a hitch. The moment the trigger teams hit their buttons, the long lines of C-4 they'd pressed into the gouged stone had exploded with flashes of white light and a deafening crash. When Lys's overloaded senses finally recovered, the dirty ceiling that used to be the only sky they'd known when they'd lived here as a child was falling. Building-sized chunks of stone were still crashing into the black floodwater that filled the gigantic bowl of the five combined Middle Hells when Iggs's voice roared over the comm.

"Lys, you're up!" he yelled through the speaker in Lys's ear.

"On it," Lys replied, gritting their teeth against the pain in their still-bleeding shoulder as they spread their wings and flew up through the hole Iggs's explosives had just made for them.

"Ramp team!" they bellowed, waving the metal flashlight they'd taken from Bex's backpack like a guiding torch through the still-falling dust. "Grab your chains, and let's go!"

An answering cry rose from hundreds of throats as winged demons of every sort launched off the ridge path at the top of the cliffside slave towns, the only part of the Middle Hells that was still above water. Each of them was carrying a long rope of black chain. It was the same chain the warlocks had used to hold them down, but Desh's team had reworked it, weaving the black chains together into a net big enough to cover the entire hole Iggs's teams had just blasted in the ceiling. One end of the net was already bolted to the rock at the top of the cliff. The other end was in the winged demons' hands as they flew up, following the beam of Lys's flashlight into the Hell above them.

Lys would've been carrying a chain, too, if the stupid prince hadn't stuck his stupid sword through their stupid shoulder. Since their arm still couldn't bear weight, they'd had to settle for being the torchbearer. This still put them out in front, though, which was exactly where Lys wanted to be. They'd waited their entire life for this moment. Nothing short of death was going to stop them from being on the frontline as they exploded through the haze of smoke and rock dust into the firelit darkness of the Hell of War.

Lys had seen the Upper Hells several times on their way to be sold to this or that warlock, but only from the inside of the fortified tower. They'd never seen beyond the stairwell's walls into the actual Hell of War, which looked a lot shabbier than expected. Lys had always pictured the Upper Hells as a place where bootlicking war demons lived lavish lives as Heaven's pampered guard dogs, but it didn't look that different from the Hell they'd just left. It was still a big, dirty cavern with a flooded work floor covered in chains that were now dangling like ripped threads through the giant hole Iggs had just blown.

The dangling chains were all empty, thank Ishtar. Traitors or not, even Lys's bloodlust didn't extend to slaughtering other demons. Fortunately, it looked like Kirok had been right about the Upper Hells being overtaxed. There wasn't a demon to be seen on the work floor, and the slave houses—another shantytown of shallow, depressing holes carved into cliffs just like the one in the Middle Hells below—were dark and quiet.

It was *all* quiet. Lys had come up here ready to fight the bronze dogs of Gilgamesh, but everything they saw made the war demons look just as exploited and downtrodden as the slaves who lived below. They were still trying to wrap their head around that when the wave of flying demons carrying chains caught up with them.

The deep roar of hundreds of beating wings knocked Lys out of their gawking. Just like their first Bex had taught them, Lys pushed all the questions out of their head and focused on the mission, ignoring the pain shooting across their back as they pumped their own wings harder to get back to the front of the pack.

"Lock your chains to the slave lines!" they yelled when they got there, pointing at the half of the sin-collection floor that wasn't currently crumbling into the flooded Hell below. "Those bolts were made to hold war demons, so they should be strong enough for us. We've still got a big crowd to move, though, so make sure to tie your lines off at least three feet apart to spread the weight. *Go! Go! Go!*"

The horde of flying demons obeyed, darting away from Lys in a fan formation to attach their chains—and the metal net trailing behind them—to the bolts that were set deep in the Hell of War's floor. When Lys was certain everyone was doing what they were supposed to, they landed in the ankle-deep waterfall pouring over the edge of the Upper Hells' flooded slave floor and tapped their comm.

"Nemini?"

"Yes?"

The voice spoke in their ear and behind them at the same time, causing Lys to jump into the air before they realized what was happening.

"I'm starting to think you do that on purpose," they growled, whirling around to land in front of Nemini.

The former void demon met the glare with her usual blank stare. "I don't know what you're talking about."

"Yeah, right," Lys said as they reached up to adjust the bloody bandage the panicked jump had just dislodged. "Playing dumb is unbefitting of a queen, you know."

Nemini shrugged. "You wanted to talk to me?"

"You should've been talking to *me*," Lys snapped. "The wing team is tying off the net as we speak. That means Desh and Iggs's attack group will be running up here any second. You were *supposed* to be up here finding all the guards they needed to subdue before we start evacuating the noncombatants, so why haven't you called in?"

"Because I haven't found anyone who qualifies as a threat yet," Nemini replied, reaching out to point at something over Lys's shoulder.

Lys whirled around with the sin-iron dagger ready in their hand. There was nothing to stab, though, because Nemini was right. About twenty feet behind them, well away from the giant hole Iggs's explosives had just put in the floor, a large crowd of war demons was kneeling with their hands raised. There were two other figures lying in the water at their feet: a Heavenly warlock with a red stain on his white robes and a war demon wearing the ornate golden armor of a trusted guard. That last one was still kicking, squirming beneath the weight of the towering female who was holding him down. She ducked her horns when she saw Lys staring, planting both her bronze knees on the struggling guard's back so she could lift all four of her arms in surrender.

"Are you servants of the True Queen?" she asked.

"I serve the Queen of Wrath, Ishtar's Sword and last champion of Paradise," Lys replied proudly, flipping their dagger into a knife-fighter's grip to get the most leverage out of their one remaining good arm. But while those should have been the fightingest of fighting words, the war demon just nodded like Lys had answered correctly.

"What are you doing?" the guard on the ground bellowed when he saw the woman's head move. "Their queen is a traitor! We were ordered to stand guard and protect Gilgamesh's Hells! The Queen of War will kill you for this!"

"She's going to do that no matter how we act," the female war demon said, reaching down to remove the guard's helmet so she could cuff him on the head. "But I for one am tired of guarding my own prison, and I'm sick to death of taking orders from this trash." She kicked the bloody warlock with her hoofed foot. "That explosion just killed the human who's been our tormentor for a century, which means the servants of Wrath have already done more for us than our queen ever has. I'm not going to repay such kindness with the treachery our queen has made us famous for."

"Then you're a traitor as well!" the guard yelled, thrashing on the wet ground. "The queen will make you crawl on your belly like a worm!"

"So, no different than normal, then," the woman replied with a chuckle, kicking the guard in the face to shut him up before turning back to Lys and Nemini.

"Our queen has forbidden us from aiding you," she explained as she lowered her horns again. "But she didn't explicitly order us to attack, so until she comes down here to say otherwise, neither I nor any of mine will get in your way. You can rest your wounded there." She pointed at one of the metal walkways the warlocks had used to move above the flooded slave floor before Iggs had punched a hole and let all the water out. "We've got plenty of space since Gilgamesh ordered everyone but the old and weak into the forges."

"Thank you," Lys said cautiously, lowering their sin-iron knife. When the old woman didn't move and no other war demons leaped out of the shadows to take advantage of the distraction, Lys reached up to tap their comm.

"Ramp's in position," they reported, glancing at the line of winged demons standing with their arms up to signal that their chains were secured. "No hostiles, so come on up."

"Wait, no hostiles?" Iggs's astonished voice replied in their ear. "Isn't the Hell of War hostile by definition?"

"They're still children of the Riverlands," Lys said, glancing at the scowling face of the old war-demon woman with a smile. "If they don't want any, I'm not going to bring it. Bex would want us to get along, so stop stalling and get our people up here before they're forced to swim."

That wasn't entirely a joke. Thanks to the waves kicked up by the falling ceiling, the floodwaters were already sloshing over the last bit of high ground left in the Middle Hells. The top of the cliffs was narrow, too, which had forced the enormous crowd of evacuating demons to spread out into a miles-long line. Combine that with the fact that almost everyone was moving slower than normal due to sin-toxin overdose, and they were in a pretty terrible situation, but Lys was determined not to fail. Bex had sacrificed herself to buy them this chance. Lys was going to get her demons to safety even if they had to fly every single one of them up here on their own wings.

"Do you want me to go check on her?" Nemini offered.

Lys shook their head. "I haven't become such a bad soldier that I'm going to ignore a direct order from my queen," they said as they slid the sin-iron dagger back into its sheath below their wing. "You're your own queen now, so I guess you can do what you want, but I'm going to stay and do the job Bex entrusted to me."

"Are you sure?" Nemini asked, tilting her snake-covered head. "It sounds like a scary fight."

It did. Now that Nemini mentioned it, Lys could hear crashes echoing through the Upper Hells. It sounded like someone was being slammed into a wall over and over again. As always, Lys's brain went straight to Bex. Not the queen she'd grown into, but the bright-eyed little girl who used to ride on their shoulders and listen intently while Lys did their best to teach her everything a queen should know. Lys's instinct had always been to gut anyone who hurt their little firespark, but part of being in the Queen of Wrath's service was learning to let those feelings go.

"My queen gave me a job," Lys repeated as they turned away from the horrible sounds. "I already let my personal feelings get in her way once. I won't do it again. I will have faith and see my duty through. That way, when Bex survives, as I *know* she will, I'll be able to hold my head high and tell her I succeeded in my charge."

Those were old, familiar words. Lys had said different versions of that exact same speech dozens of times over Bex's last four lives, usually to Nemini. It was probably wrong to say them to her again now that she was herself a queen, but that didn't stop Lys from doing it or Nemini from nodding at the end the same way she always did.

"I'll go help Iggs with the evacuation, then," she said. "You stay here and make sure the net doesn't slip."

"Will do," Lys promised as Nemini disappeared, leaving Lys standing alone at the top of the chain ramp the demons of the Hells had woven out of their own bonds. The bottom half was already full of freed slaves sprinting toward safety with Iggs leading the charge.

Lys grinned when they saw him. They leaped into the air next, waving their flashlight and shouting at the top of their lungs for everyone to get up the ramp and move immediately to the back so they wouldn't clog the way for the people behind them.

And far in the distance, through the acrid smoke of the War Hell's ever-burning forges, the roar of the queens' fight grew louder.

Chapter 19

Bex HAD NEVER BURNED so hot in her life.

She'd burned bigger plenty of times, including just a few hours ago when she'd incinerated the princess who stole her hand. Those infernos were always terrifying, but this was different, because this time, Bex was in control. She wasn't a raging bonfire blindly consuming everything she touched. These flames burned clean, powered by a righteous fury that had sparked on behalf of someone else. They were untainted by fear, doubt, grief, or even her own anger, and they burned hot enough to ignite the air itself.

The flames were especially unkind to the Queen of War, painting her in a harsh, white light that made the pits in her corroded body look even deeper than they were. Her mismatched eyes reflected the glare like miniature suns, turning her scarred bronze face into an exaggerated mask as the queen's split lips pulled into a hateful smile.

"Still as impatient as ever, I see," she mocked, grinning at Bex over the edge of Havok's blade. "You're burning the candle at both ends now, idiot. I won't even have to swing to carry out my prince's command. You're going to kill yourself, just burn right up into a useless pile of—"

The queen's insults cut off as Bex ducked under her oversized sword, using her smaller stature and blazing speed to dip past Havok's guard and come up inside the cage of War's four arms. She barely had time to appreciate the look of shock on her sister's scarred face before she slammed her fist into the underside of War's jaw at full burn, knocking her into the air like an armored bronze croquet ball.

Bex flew after her like a rocket. With so much white-hot fire roaring through her body, she didn't even have to use her hands to blast herself off the ground like she usually did. The moment she thought about going up, the blazing flames covering her body shifted to make it happen, shooting her up like a jet through War's open guard to hit her again.

It was even more satisfying the second time. War was a heavy-armored fighter. She wasn't used to being juggled, but with so much fire at her fingertips, Bex's punches hit like concentrated avalanches. She still hadn't managed to break through Havok's white armor—at this point, Bex was starting to wonder if anything could break through that stubborn sword's defenses—but it didn't matter. The sheer force of her hits was enough to knock War higher and higher, crashing her through the empty archer galleries that lined the inside of the spiral staircase like a baseball going through window after window.

With no ground to stand on and no ability to fly of her own, War couldn't even fight back. Bex intended to keep punching her all the way up to Heaven when her sister suddenly curled her four-armed body into a ball and yelled something Bex was burning too hard to understand. It sounded like a command, but it wasn't until a sword flew out of nowhere to stab her in the side that Bex understood just *what* she was commanding.

Just as she had dominion over the flames of Wrath, her sister could control the weapons of War.

She'd already done it once tonight when she'd stopped her demons' arrows from striking Adrian. Now, War turned that power on her sister. With a single command, all the armaments carried by the war-demon soldiers watching from the bottom of the tower tore out of their wielders' hands to hurl themselves at Bex. Spears hurtled out of their cases, arrows shot out of their quivers, swords flew from their sheathes. Every weapon that Gilgamesh had made for his slave army shot up in a volley that filled the tower before honing in on Bex.

She blocked with a gasp, letting go of War to shield herself as the storm of weapons crashed into her from below. The arrows and spear hafts and everything else that wasn't made of metal was instantly turned to ash by her fire, but the metal tips, spearheads, and sword blades were another story. They'd been forged from the same sorcerous gold alloy as the war constructs, and while they melted under Bex's fire just like the golden lion cannons had, molten metal was still metal, and it was still flying at high velocity.

The result was a shotgun blast of searing hot, glowing gold that knocked Bex out of the air. The molten metal couldn't burn her—nothing could do that now—but it stuck to her limbs like tar, and it was so *heavy*. The sheer force was enough to whack her into the tower wall like a mosquito. She was still struggling to get the molten sludge off her when three huge hands appeared to rip Bex out of her crater.

"Now you will learn," the Queen of War's furious voice huffed in her ear as she wrapped her armored arms around her struggling sister. "I am still Ishtar's strongest daughter, and this time, I'm the one who'll throw *you* into the *pit*!"

She leaped off the stairs as she finished. Bex was still so covered in molten metal, she didn't even see where they were jumping until they slammed into the tower floor.

The impact shattered every bone in Bex's body. Any other time that would have been a serious problem, but Bex was burning so hot right now that she barely felt it. There was so much wrath searing through her that all her injuries were healed by the time Bex shook the molten metal off her face, clearing her eyes to see the Queen of War kneeling on top of her.

That was a much bigger issue. Just like when she'd fought Havok's armor form back in Felix's prison, the queen was too heavy to budge, leaving Bex trapped on her back. It looked like all the war demons who'd been watching down here had managed to get to the edges in time, but while Bex was happy she hadn't crushed anyone when they came down, having so many demons so close meant she couldn't blast the Queen of War off of her without risking innocents getting caught in the explosion.

The Queen of War had no such concerns. She swung her sword over her head without even looking, carelessly slicing open any demons unfortunate enough to be standing too close. When the floor was cleared to her satisfaction, she pulled her sword back into its black ring so she could pummel Bex with all four of her armored fists.

"This is what you deserve," she informed her sister calmly as she pummeled Bex into the black-stained stone only a few feet away from where she'd killed Kirok. "The Glorious Gilgamesh gave you everything. He accepted you as his princess, gave you freedom from our eternal responsibility and the love of his favorite son. If you'd been smart and died, you could have lived forever as the Princess of Wrath in the Heaven our Eternal King made for you. But you never were smart, were you, Bexa? You've always been just like our mother, too stubborn and wrathful to know when you were *beat*."

Her fists fell like anvils with every sneering word, bashing Bex's flaming body deeper and deeper into the thick layer of stone that divided the Upper and Lower Hells. If she'd landed closer to the tunnel, the sin iron would've stopped her, but War had slammed her down at the opposite side of the tower, which meant there was nothing but rock between her and the flooding Hell below.

"That's right," War said, punching even harder when she saw the realization flicker across Bex's face. "I'm going to do to you exactly what you watched Mother do to me. I'm going to cast you into that toxic flooded pit where not even your fire can burn. And while you die choking on the sins your precious Ishtar created us to eat, I'll return to Heaven in victory to kneel before my king and tell him it is done. The Coward Queen is gone forever, and the whole world is better for it."

"Would you *shut up*?" Bex roared, flaring her fire as hard as she could, but it didn't work. The Queen of War was dug in now, and even the Bonfire of Wrath couldn't blast her off. But just as Bex was starting to panic, she felt a fresh blast of rage hit her fire like a dry log. That normally didn't happen unless she got angry about something, but Bex was focusing too hard on keeping War from crushing her head to think about anything else. Her flames had actually started burning lower as her fear and frustration smothered them, but the fury that was suddenly piling into her like fresh kindling got them going white-hot again, and as the unknown anger pumped into her system like gasoline, Bex heard it.

"Keep fighting," someone whispered near her head. "Don't let her win again."

"Kill her," begged another. "Set us free!"

"Avenge us," said a man's furious voice, speaking loudest yet. "Don't let Kirok's death be in vain!"

The pleas were barely audible over the *clang* of her sister's punches, but the Queen of Wrath heard them. The crowd of war demons hadn't run away when their queen landed. They were all still here, huddling close around her despite their Queen's sword. Their dark eyes gleamed as they watched Bex take hit after hit, but not with fear or pity. Behind the stoic soldier masks they wore on their bronze faces was eons of suppressed, smoldering rage. All Bex had to do was let it in, and the anger of the war demons roared inside her like fire engulfing a drought-stricken forest.

Bex embraced it with open arms, because these were also Ishtar's children. They were not traitors. They were proud, brave demons who'd been forced to kill their own people to satisfy their queen's twisted grievance. They were victims of Gilgamesh the same as her own wrath demons, and they were begging for her help. They offered their anger up to her like a sacrifice, and Bex was happy to accept because the creature crouching over her was no longer her sister. Ishtar's poison had scarred her body and mind, but she was the one who'd made herself a monster.

She could have taken her freedom and run when Gilgamesh pulled her out of that pit, but she'd gleefully joined him and turned her sword on her own people instead. She'd killed demons who never had a prayer of standing up to her. She'd killed Kirokaltos, who'd barely been able to keep himself upright, merely for the crime of calling her out. She was a spiteful, selfish creature who chose Gilgamesh again and again with no concern for the people she dragged into slavery behind her. That made her even worse than the warlocks in Bex's eyes, and for that, she was going to die.

The moment the goal crystallized in her mind, Bex's wild flames grew steady. Her mind stilled, her heat sharpened, her breathing slowed. There was no more flailing, no more wasted movements, not even any pain. As the war demons' ancient anger filled her to the brim, Bex finally became what Drox had always told her she was: a weapon forged in fire, the Blade of Wrath.

It was the one truth that had never been tied to her crown. Bex didn't need a name or a divine sword to burn like she was made to. All she needed was fuel, and she had that in plenty, adding her own fury to the war demons' silent scream as she shot up to wrap her flaming arms around the Queen of War's armored body.

They were deep in the hole by this point. War had pounded her about halfway through the floor, but the pit she'd dug for her sister left her no room to maneuver as Bex locked them together. She filled the hole with her fire at the same time, blasting the two of them with her full heat until they molded together like two metals in a crucible.

Bex was so hot at this point that bits of her body were turning to ash faster than her regeneration could replace them, but her sister had it even worse. War had always been resistant to her heat, but everything had its limit, and from the sound of her screams, War was rapidly approaching hers. Her bronze body was bubbling like a molten river, but when she tried to rip her sister off, Bex's body was too hot to touch. She was still desperately trying when Bex heard something big go *crack*.

The sound brought a smile to her burning face. She was pressed against War's armored chest, which meant she had a front row seat for the moment the heat got too much for Havok. His black ring was still untouched, but the white armor plates he used to cover his queen were breaking apart like bones in a blast furnace. Bex could see the fractures spreading like lightning across every piece of War's armor, and the moment they got big enough, she released her sister to swing again.

The punch landed very differently this time. Even fresh off the anger of Kirok's death, the best Bex had been able to do was knock War around. Now that they'd both been fired in the rage of an entire demon tribe, though, one hit was all it took to shatter Havok's armor. His defenses broke like glass turning back to sand, the little bits burning up in flashes when they hit Bex's flames as she slammed into War again, smashing her into the air this time before following her out of the hole in a blaze of white-hot fire.

If she'd been anyone else, that would have been the end. Despite her treason, however, War was still a queen, the strongest of all Ishtar's daughters. When Bex landed back on the floor of the tower outside their hole, she was already waiting with her black sword in her hands. She was no longer covered in Havok's armor, but like every war demon, her own skin was armor enough. Her body didn't even look naked thanks to the smooth bronze of her true self, but what should have been gleaming perfection was marred by huge pits where her body had corroded.

The scars that covered her face covered the rest of her as well. Her body's regeneration was rapidly fixing all the places Bex's fire had melted, but it couldn't touch the deep gouges that covered her metal body like corroded canyons. The old wounds still looked raw and painful, but War didn't let that slow her down as she braced her exposed hooves—the same hooves all war demons had in their true forms—on the bloody ground and swung her giant sword like a bat at Bex's head.

Even with her rage-fired speed, Bex knew immediately that she wouldn't be able to dodge. War was too close, and Havok's blade was too long. Even if she jumped straight back, the sword was going to hit something, so Bex did the only thing she could think of. She held up her right hand, tilting her palm at the perfect angle to catch the edge of Havok's sword on the band of Drox's ring.

The sound of the two swords clashing rang through the tower like the great crash of Gilgamesh's bell. Bex hadn't been sure it would work, but while Havok's swing drove her back several inches, it didn't knock her over, and it didn't cut through her hand. His black blade had been totally stopped by the thick band of Drox's sleeping form, and the moment Bex saw it, she knew what to do.

Moving fast as lightning, she clamped her hand down on Havok's sword, using the width of Drox's band to keep the blade's sharp edge from actually cutting into her skin. The second she had a good grip, Bex darted forward, using War's shock to get behind her. She dragged Havok with her as she went, forcing War to choose: Would she let go of her weapon, or would she let Bex wrench her arm behind her?

It turned out not to matter in the end. War was fast, but Bex was moving faster now than she ever had. By the time the disgraced queen realized she had to make a decision, Bex had already twisted her arm behind her back, using War's grip on her own sword as leverage to snap the joint where her top right arm connected to her shoulder.

She'd only been aiming to dislocate her shoulder, but Bex must've been moving even faster than she realized because she ended up tearing the ligaments out completely. She could actually feel the moment War's arm went slack in her grip as her muscles disconnected, and then her sword clattered to the ground.

Bex was on it in an instant. She literally dove at the ground to grab Havok's hilt in her own burning grip. The sword fought back with all the violence she'd come to expect from him, but Bex was burning with the righteous fury of all the war demons who'd been forced to bow their horns to this traitor. Their rage had built her bonfire into something even the Blade of War could not overcome, and she got her way in the end, forcing the massive sword off the ground by pure burning strength until its black tip was pointed at its own queen's throat.

"*No!*" War shrieked, clutching her useless arm, which was healing much slower than Bex expected. "You're a crownless worm! A defeated *coward*! You can't possibly use my—"

Bex swung before the queen could finish. The Blade of War did his best to spoil her shot, but Bex had fought Havok enough times now to know that he didn't retreat. Where her practical, loyal Drox would've vanished back into his ring the second he realized he was up against an enemy he couldn't overwhelm, Havok stayed stubbornly on the field, forcing the Queen of War to leap out of the way before she was beheaded by her own sword.

"Enough of this!" she cried as she landed on the broken stairs one spiral up from where Bex held the tower floor. "Demons of War, attack her! *Defend your queen!*"

The command came down like a hammer. Bex couldn't feel it through the raging inferno of her wrath, but she saw the crowd of war demons watching from the tower's edges shudder as one, which was a problem. Unlike her sister, Bex would never kill her fellow demons, which meant if they rushed her, she'd be trapped. She had to defeat the Queen of War before that happened, but as she struggled to force Havok into position for another strike, something incredible happened. Something she never would've expected in all her lives put together.

The war demons didn't move.

"What are you doing?" the Queen of War shrieked, forgetting Bex for a moment as she whirled to stare in shock at her people. "I said *attack*!"

Once again, the order slammed down, but once again, the watching demons did not respond. Now that Bex had time to look, she realized there were even more of them now than there'd been at the start. Most had been forced out when the Queen of War had brought the fight to the bottom of the staircase, but Bex could see huge crowds of bronze faces watching through the large doors that opened into the rest of the Hell outside the tower. She could see the pain resisting the order was causing them, but even though some demons were clenching their fists so hard they drew their own black blood, not a single one of them moved. They stayed just as they were, standing in perfect, defiant stillness, and the longer it went on, the more furious the Queen of War became.

"Don't make me do this," she warned through clenched teeth. "I swear on Gilgamesh's name, you'll all suffer for centuries if you make me do this!"

When the silent demons still didn't respond, the queen threw up her three remaining functional arms.

"On your heads be it, then!" she roared. "By my own sacred name, I, Dalanea the Fortress, Queen of War and Shield of Ishtar, command you to strike down the Coward Queen! Do it now or slit your own throats in shame!"

Just like when Nemini had invoked her name earlier, the force of the queen's command shook the

Hells to their foundation. Even Bex was knocked sideways, losing her grip on the Blade of War, who immediately flew back to his queen. War caught her sword with a triumphant look, cradling her still-healing top right arm to her bronze chest as she waited for her people to tackle Bex to the ground, but it didn't happen. The tower was still rattling with the force of her command, but the war demons made no move to attack or to slit their own throats. They turned away from their queen instead, giving her their backs so she couldn't see whose mouth was moving when one of them said, "No."

It sounded like it had taken everything the demon had to force that one word out, but War's pitted bronze face still snapped toward the sound like a hunting snake. "Who said that?" she demanded, her mismatched eyes shining in murderous fury as they darted around the room. "What blasphemous soon-to-be-*corpse* dares defy their queen?"

"You're no queen of ours," growled a different war demon, one who sounded much closer this time.

"You have no crown," added another. "You gave up your horns to Gilgamesh!"

"We're all slaves because of you!" cried a third.

"You made us traitors!" yelled a towering demon, who actually turned around, meeting his queen face-to-furious-face as he bared his flat teeth. "All the other demons hate us, and for what? We still have to slave for the gods-dammed warlocks!"

That must have been the final straw. They'd had to force the words out at the start, but now that they were going, every demon in the tower was suddenly shouting at the top of their lungs. The Queen of War shouted back, but for the first time, her voice was not the loudest, because she was no longer their only queen. Bex was still burning like a welding torch with the power of the rage they'd offered to her, and while she had no horns to raise or name to invoke, she was still a daughter of Ishtar. One the demons of War respected far more than the traitor who'd sold them to their greatest enemy.

Bex wasn't sure which of those factors was the tipping point, but the balance of power was definitely swinging. The more openly the war demons defied her, and the longer the Queen of War was unable to make them stop, the weaker she became.

It was something that never should have happened to a queen, but like the war demons themselves had just said, she *wasn't* a queen anymore. She still had her original body and name, but there was no crown atop her wavy bronze hair. The powers she'd used in the fight came from her own innate ability as Ishtar's greatest soldier just as Bex's flames belonged to her alone, but the authority to command demons was different. *That* came only from Ishtar herself, and since she'd already given up her horns to Gilgamesh, War was forced to borrow her own sovereignty back from him.

That made her little better than a warlock, and, just like a warlock, there seemed to be a limit to how many demons she could command. One or two were easy to crush, but a whole military unit in rebellion was more than her secondhand authority could handle. Bex could actually see her bronze body shaking in fear as a squad of fearsome-looking war demons broke off from the main crowd and stomped up the stairs to grab their former queen.

Bex was happy to get out of their way. It was obvious by now that this was no longer her fight. Even her flames were settling down as the war demons reclaimed their wrath for themselves. She *was* worried when they got within range of Havok's sword—no matter how weak a daughter of Ishtar became, Enki's blades could still bite—but War didn't even take a swing. Before a single demon actually got close enough to make a grab for her, the defeated queen thrust her still-healing right hand into the air.

"Gilgamesh!" she cried in a terrified voice. *"Great King, save your loyal servant!"*

Bex jumped to stop her the second she saw what was happening, but she was already too late. Gilgamesh's teleport ban must not have extended to himself, because the moment the disgraced Queen of War yelled his name, an enormous golden bell rang out like a bomb blast.

The wave of sound knocked everyone, including Bex, to the ground. By the time she rolled back up, the Queen of War had already grabbed hold of the scarred, masculine hand that had appeared out of the empty air above her. It was the same hand Bex had seen when Gilgamesh showed up to snatch the Princess of Greed's hand out of her fingers the first time she'd fought a prince in Adrian's forest. Now as then, though, there was nothing she could do. The moment the Queen of War's bronze fingers touched Gilgamesh's, she vanished into thin air, leaving Bex leaping at nothing.

She hit the ground where War had just been with a frustrated scream, pounding her empty fists against the broken stone. She was still trying to catch her breath when another hand appeared in front of her face. A big bronze one that belonged to an even bigger bronze demon.

"Great Queen," he said, lowering his horns in reverence. "Allow me to help you up."

Bex didn't need help, but it felt rude to refuse, so she grabbed his hand and let the demon pull her back to her feet. As she went up, though, everyone else in the room went down, leaving Bex standing on a broken battlement in front of hundreds of kneeling war demons.

"Honored Queen of Wrath," said the kneeling demon who'd helped her up, whom she just now noticed had an official-looking sash draped across his bronze shoulders. "I am Roga, captain of security for the Upper Hells. The soldiers in this tower are under my command, and I now surrender them to you so that you may render judgment."

"Judgment?" Bex repeated, confused. "What would I judge you for?"

The bowing demon lifted his horns just enough to give her a nervous look. "We turned against our queen," he explained. "We have broken the oldest law of our kind. You were the one who should have dealt with her, not us."

"I was dealing with her," Bex reminded him, relaxing a little now that she understood the problem. "But I stopped when the rest of you spoke up because you deserved that victory more than I did. You say you broke the law, but the Queen of War broke faith first when she turned her sword on the people she'd been made to protect. She betrayed her goddess and behaved in a manner unworthy of her sacred name, so it is my judgment that you acted rightly."

That should've been obvious to everyone, but proper old demons like this Roga always liked for things to be spelled out formally. Sure enough, the captain looked enormously relieved when she finished. All the war demons did, though not enough to stop bowing.

"Thank you for your respect," Bex said, doing her best not to sound impatient. "But if you really want to honor me, go help my people. They're evacuating into the Hell of War through a hole we blew in the ceiling."

Roga jolted upright. "You blew a *hole* through the Hells?" he cried before he remembered himself and ducked his horns again. "How was such a thing possible?"

"It was pretty simple, actually," Bex told him with a smile. "Gilgamesh's power isn't as absolute as he likes to pretend. As you all proved just now when you defied your queen, most of his control depends on us being too scared or beaten down to challenge him. That's how men like him work, but we're not his cowards any longer. Just as you threw off your queen, we can throw all of Heaven off our backs, but we have to work together."

The big war demon nodded. "Then we shall do whatever we can. I know the word of a traitor doesn't carry much weight, but we—"

"War demons aren't traitors," Bex interrupted. "You're soldiers of the Riverlands and Children of Ishtar just like the rest of us. Kirok gave his life to prove that, and I will honor his name and sacrifice. I refuse to hold you responsible for what your queen made you do, and I humbly ask the people of War for help."

"And we are happy to offer it," Roga said, rising to his feet at last. "Where are your people?"

Bex's mouth made it all the way open before she realized she didn't actually know. She'd been so focused on burning her tunnel, she hadn't actually looked to see which part of the ceiling Iggs was blasting. She was still scrambling to come up with something useful to say when Adrian came to her rescue.

"It's on the far western edge," he said as he pushed through the crowd toward her. "Directly above the exit for the Lust banishment gate into the Middle Hells."

That sounded like a great description to Bex, but the war demon captain was glaring at Adrian even harder than he'd glared at the Queen of War.

"My queen," he whispered, reaching for one of the many swords strapped to his waist. "This man is—"

"I know," Bex said quickly. "But it's fine. Adrian's an involuntary prince who hates Gilgamesh as much as we do." She smiled at her witch, who was still elbowing his way toward her. "I couldn't have made it here without him."

Captain Roga looked deeply skeptical, but he must not have wanted to rebel against two queens in one day, because when Adrian finally made it all the way up to Bex without doing anything princely like threatening to gut them all, he eventually ducked his horns and turned to yell at his men.

"Squadrons three and four," he bellowed. "Go to where the prin... where the *queen's companion* described and offer whatever help you can. Squads one and two, go tell the forge workers they can finally rest. We're not slaving anymore!"

An enormous cheer went up at that as the war demons ran off on their assignments. Bex was starting to think this might actually all work out when the captain dropped back into a bow.

"If you would permit it, Great Queen," he said solemnly. "I must thank you one more time for my own sake. Kirok was my combat trainer when I was rising through the ranks. He was a great warrior and an honorable demon, and he deserved better than this."

They both turned to look at the bloody stain that was all that was left of Kirok's body, and Bex sighed.

"I wish he could have had a kinder ending," she said. "But I disagree that this wasn't what he deserved. Kirok died bravely fighting for what he believed in. He said what no one else was able, and without his sacrifice, we wouldn't be standing here right now." Her face split into a smile. "I think he'd be proud to see what his death accomplished, so please don't say it wasn't deserved. He's the reason I was able to stand against the Queen of War, and he deserves all the credit I can give."

The captain dropped his head again, but not in a bow this time. "Then I was wrong," he whispered in a voice that shook with real emotion. "I will remember him as you say, Great Queen."

"Thank you," Bex said, reaching out for Adrian, who'd just made it to her side. "Now if you'll excuse me for a moment, I need to sit down."

The war demon looked shocked, but he moved out of the way at once, clearing space for Bex to sink to the floor in a controlled collapse.

"Whoa," Adrian said as he went down with her. "Are you okay?"

"I'm amazing," Bex said, giving him a lopsided smile. "I mean, I can't feel my legs, and my whole body feels like it just came out of a blast furnace, but we're alive, and we *won*! The Queen of War got her butt kicked so hard she had to run home to Gilgamesh, we've got help coming for the people evacuating from the flood, *and* we freed the Hell of War." Her smile grew wider as she looked down at the war demons running to and fro across the tower. "You know what the means, right? We freed all Nine Hells!"

She threw her arms up for a whoop but stopped when it made her dizzy.

"I think you should just sit there for a minute," Adrian said as he eased her back against the wall.

"It's too bad you couldn't keep the Queen of War's sword," he said as he settled in beside her. "It was terrifying watching you fight barehanded."

"Havok would never serve me," Bex replied with a snort. "And I wouldn't take him even if he did. Drox will always be the only sword for me." She looked down at her ring with a sigh. "He's going to be sad he missed this when he wakes up. I finally managed to do all the stuff he was always yelling at me to do."

"It was very impressive," Adrian agreed, putting his arm around her shoulders. "And highly effective, thank the Forest. I had some last-ditch ideas for sorcery if things went really bad, but I'm *very* relieved I didn't have to use them. I'm not nearly as good with my father's magic as I am with my mother's."

"That's fine," Bex said as she relaxed into him. "Being bad at sorcery is a sign of good character. I just wish you didn't have to know it at all."

Adrian looked like he was still deciding how to respond to that when they were interrupted by the beep of Bex's comm.

"I'm here," she answered at once.

The speaker in her ear exploded into static from Lys's enormous sigh of relief. "Thank Ishtar," they said. "I feared the worst when I heard that giant bell. Where are you?"

"In the tower," Bex replied as her face split into a grin. "I won."

"I knew you would," Lys said, which was a blatant lie, but Bex was too happy to call them on it.

"It's not just that," she continued with an even bigger smile. "I *won* won. I beat the Queen of War so hard she turned tail and ran! All the war demons are free now. I just sent a bunch over to help you, so make sure you tell everyone not to shoot them when they show up."

There was a long, shocked pause, and then Lys's voice came over the speaker again in a whisper so full of hope it shivered.

"Does that mean it's over?"

"Yep," Bex replied proudly, craning her neck back to look up the spiral of the broken stairs. "All Nine Hells are ours now, but I don't want 'em. We're getting everyone out of here ASAP. You keep pulling our people out of the water. Adrian and I are going up to check out the situation in Heaven."

Adrian blinked like this was news to him, but the comm in Bex's ear fell into a long, terrified silence.

"You're going into the Holy City?" Lys squeaked at last. "And you're only bringing *Adrian*?"

"He's a prince," Bex reminded them. "There's no one better suited for the job. Just keep our people moving. I'll see about securing us a way back to Earth."

Lys nervously mumbled something affirmative-sounding, and Bex cut off the call before they got any more worked up.

"An exit back to Earth is going to be hard," Adrian warned as he rose to his feet. "The chains are the only sure path, and they're sealed at the base of Gilgamesh's castle."

"That's fine," Bex said as she grabbed his offered hand to haul herself back to her feet. "I was headed there anyway."

Her witch laughed at that before his face grew worried again. "*How* are we going to do it, though?" he asked nervously. "Heaven's much more heavily guarded than the Hells were, and you're carrying a lot of liabilities. Most of the demons you rescued look more like concentration camp victims than soldiers. How are we going to transport them safely through Gilgamesh's warlock city?"

"I have no idea," Bex confessed. "That's why we're going first to scope the situation. Whatever's up there, though, we're going to break it, because there's no way in the Hells—or the ruins of the Hells—that I'm leaving any of Ishtar's people behind."

"I know you wouldn't," Adrian assured her quickly. "I only brought it up because I wanted to make sure you knew what you were walking into."

"I've always known," Bex said, flashing him a smile. "But if I was the sort who quit just because something was impossible, I would've died for good a hundred lifetimes ago." She turned back to the stairs and started climbing faster. "We've bashed our way through everything else Gilgamesh has thrown. I'm sure we'll find a way to beat this too. It's that or give up and die down here, so we might as well try. Who knows? Maybe we'll catch Gilgamesh by surprise for once."

"Anything's possible," Adrian agreed, pausing to let Boston—who was racing up the stairs behind them—catch up. "He has been very distracted lately, and I'm certain he didn't expect you to win just now." His smile grew wicked. "Maybe it *will* work. Hubris is famously the downfall of kings."

"Then let's go make sure he gets his," Bex said, reaching back to offer him her hand.

Adrian grabbed her fingers with a smile that made Bex's heart skip a dangerous number of beats. She was still trying to get her breath back when he ran past her, pulling Bex up the final spiral of the broken staircase that led to the enemy's Heaven.

Thank you for reading

. . . .

Thank you for reading *Hell Hath No Fury*!

I hope you enjoyed the story and that you'll consider leaving a review. Reviews, good or bad, are vital to every author's career, and I'd be extremely grateful if you'd take a moment to write one for me.

With this book finished, we're almost to the end. The fifth and final novel in Bex's battle, *Tear Down Heaven*, is already written and will be coming out in early 2026! It's one of the most epic conclusions I've ever put together, and I can't wait for you to read it.

Want to be the first to know when new books come out? Sign up for my **new release mailing list**! (rachelaaron.net) List members get first dibs on all my books and I only email when I've got something new, so there's zero spam. Signing up is free and easy, so come join the fun!

Again, thank you so much for giving my stuff a chance! Readers like you are why independent books exist. Thank you from the bottom of my heart, and I'll see you soon for the epic conclusion of *Tear Down Heaven*!

Yours always and forever,
Rachel Aaron

WANT MORE BOOKS?

. . . .

Tear Down Heaven is only the latest addition to the Rachel Aaron library. I have plenty more books of all sorts for you to enjoy, including five finished series! Keep paging to see my top picks for new readers or visit **rachelaaron.net** for the full list, and, as always, thank you for reading!

Fortune's Pawn

(written as Rachel Bach)

A propulsive space opera perfect for fans of *Firefly* and *Killjoys*!

"Devi is hands-down one of the best sci-fi heroines I've read in a long time." - **RT Book Reviews**

Devi Morris isn't your average mercenary. She has plans. Big ones. And a ton of ambition. It's a combination that's going to get her killed one day—but not just yet.

That is, until she just gets a job on a tiny trade ship with a nasty reputation for surprises. *The Glorious Fool* isn't misnamed: it likes to get into trouble, so much so that one year of security work under its captain is equal to five years everywhere else. With odds like that, Devi knows she's found the perfect way to get the jump on the next part of her Plan. But the Fool doesn't give up its secrets without a fight, and one year on this ship might be more than even Devi can handle.

Powered armor and kissing, what more could you want?

Nice Dragons Finish Last

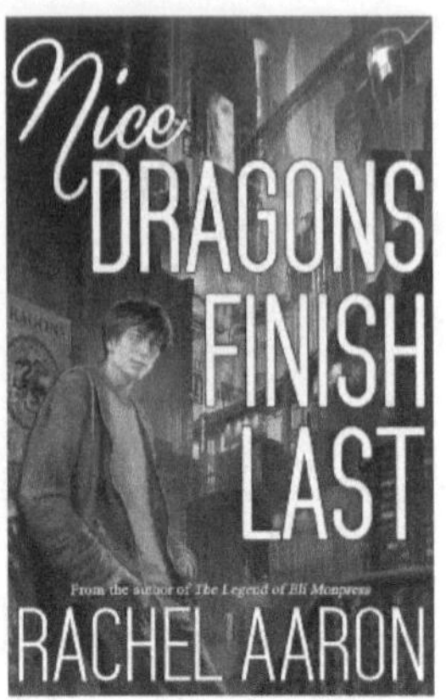

"Super fun, fast-paced urban fantasy full of heart, and plenty of magic, charm and humor to spare, this self-published gem was one of my favorite discoveries this year!" - **The Midnight Garden**

"A deliriously smart and funny beginning to a new urban fantasy series about dragons in the ruins of Detroit...inventive, uproariously clever, and completely un-put-down-able!" - **SF Signal**

As the smallest dragon in the Heartstriker clan, Julius survives by a simple code: stay quiet, don't cause trouble, and keep out of the way of bigger dragons. But this meek behavior doesn't cut it in a family of ambitious predators, and his mother, Bethesda the Heartstriker, has finally reached the end of her patience.

Now, sealed in human form and banished to the DFZ--a vertical metropolis built on the ruins of Old Detroit--Julius has one month to prove to his mother that he can be a ruthless dragon or lose his true shape forever. But in a city of modern mages and vengeful spirits where dragons are seen as monsters to be exterminated, he's going to need some serious help to survive this test.

He just hopes humans are more trustworthy than dragons.

The first and most popular DFZ series, complete at 5 books.

Minimum Wage Magic

The DFZ, the metropolis formerly known as Detroit, is the world's most magical city with a population of nine million and zero public safety laws. That's a lot of mages, cybernetically enhanced chrome heads, and mythical beasties who die, get into debt, and otherwise fail to pay their rent. When they can't pay their bills, their stuff gets sold to the highest bidder to cover the tab.

That's when they call me. My name is Opal Yong-ae, and I'm a Cleaner: a freelance mage with an art history degree who's employed by the DFZ to sort through the mountains of magical junk people leave behind. It's not a pretty job, or a safe one-- there's a reason I wear bite-proof gloves--but when you're deep in debt in a lawless city where gods are real, dragons are traffic hazards, and buildings move around on their own, you don't get to be picky about where your money comes from. You just have to make it work, even when the only thing of value in your latest repossessed apartment is the dead body of the mage who used to live there.

A fun, standalone adventure set in the always-wild DFZ, complete at 3 books.

About the Author

Rachel Aaron is the author of twenty-plus novels both self-published and through Orbit Books. When she's not holed up in her writing cave, she lives a nerdy, bookish life in Colorado with her perpetual-motion son, long-suffering husband, and mountains of books. To learn more about Rachel and read samples of all her work, visit **rachelaaron.net**!

Cover Illustration by *Luisa Preissler*
Cover Design by *Rachel Aaron*
Editing provided by *Red Adept Editing*

As ever, this book would not be as good without the amazing Linda Hall, the sharpest beta reader of all time. Thanks for all you do, Linda!